Undressed

Undressed

STEF ANN HOLM

ISBN 1-55166-730-4

UNDRESSED

Visit us at www.mirabooks.com

Printed in U.S.A.

Lanie's desire to wow her friends was suddenly overshadowed by a feeling she hadn't prepared for—feeling undressed without her uniform. It was such a part of her that she felt strange going somewhere without being in dark blue from shoulders to toes.

"What's that on your feet?" her mom asked, entering the bedroom.

"Shoes."

"Those are not shoes. They're flat sandals."

Gazing at her feet, the toes painted geranium-pink, Lanie asked, "What's wrong with them?"

"They're too casual to go with your dress." Lucille opened the closet door and handed her a shoe box. "I bought something new for you."

Lanie peeked inside. On a bed of tissue lay a pair of black evening shoes with square rhinestone buckles. They were very sexy in a strappy sort of way—and also very impractical.

"I'll break my ankles in these. I'm used to Nikes."

"They're perfect with your dress. Try them on, sweetie."

Lanie sat on the edge of the bed and fastened the buckles. Standing up, she saw she'd gained three inches of added height—just what she didn't need. But her mom had had the right instincts. The heels gave her calves a great shape.

Her mom grew sentimental, her eyes tearing. "You look so beautiful."

"Thanks, Mom."

One

A film crew from Hollywood arrived in Majestic, Colorado, in 1968 to shoot scenes for an upcoming Western starring the Duke—Mr. John Wayne. Big Panavision cameras were set up at various locations by Canyon Falls for outdoor shots of *True Grit*. Just about everyone in town stopped doing what they were doing to watch the actors work and ask for autographs.

Standing larger-than-life with a smoldering cigarette between his lips and a cowboy hat shading his face, Mr. Wayne obliged anyone who handed him a pen and paper. Nobody thought much about a signature from Robert Duvall or Dennis Hopper, but they got them just the same. Ladies swarmed around Glen Campbell, swooning over his dazzling smile and asking him if he could sing "Gentle on my Mind." Kim Darby had her share of admirers as well, mostly the young boys who lived at Laramie Ranch.

After the picture was released, *True Grit* became known as the finest Western John Wayne ever made and earned him an Oscar statuette.

The little town of Majestic had never been prouder.

The Duke was their hero—but not strictly in a Hollywood way. To this day, what happened at the Motor Inn with John Wayne and Midge Fremont is still discussed and debated, with the details becoming more and more embellished with time. But, for sure, Mr. Wayne's bravery has never been forgotten.

As the story goes, the movie studio had put up the *True Grit* actors and crew in the Motor Inn for the duration of filming. Back in those days, the motel boasted air-conditioning, five-channel reception on color televisions, a telephone in every room, and Magic Fingers on all the beds where a quarter bought a fifteen minute massage.

Midge Fremont was vacationing from Poughkeepsie, New York, along with her cousin Brenda and they thanked their lucky stars for having reservations at the Motor Inn. Both girls were head over heels infatuated with the Duke.

With their hairdos sprayed into a high-teased luster and their feminine bodies molded into nylon suits, they drank iced tea and tanned by the pool. Every day they waited anxiously for the six-foot-four-inch actor to arrive after a day on the set and, when he did, they blushed and giggled as he askcd them how the *pilgrims* were doing.

The sunset was glorious one Friday when he came back to the motel fully costumed as Marshal Rooster Cogburn. Midge and Brenda quickly reciprocated the disarming smile he offered—except this time, the craggy lift to the corner of his mouth was short-lived. The next thing they knew, he froze and ordered them not to move.

Confused by the sudden change in his affable manner, the women were puzzled. Then Midge heard the buzz of a rattlesnake directly under her chaise. Although she couldn't see it, the snake was coiled and menacing, head up and alert. Frightened, she locked her jaw tight and ceased to breathe or bat an eyelash.

With a lightning-quick draw, the Duke fisted the butt of his gun, aimed and fired. The explosion echoed off the mountainside like a cannon shot and Midge's body went limp in a dead faint. When she came to, she learned her life had just been saved by the incomparable Mr. John Wayne.

To everyone's surprise, they learned the gun in his holster was no prop. They should have known it was the real deal—earlier that week he had insisted on doing his own stunts and had jumped a four-rail fence on a horse.

News of the Duke's heroics traveled fast and there was a big to-do that night at Majestic's White Horse Saloon. The cast members came and it was one hell of a party. Over shots of tequila, it was decided the rattlesnake would be stuffed and displayed.

When the movie crew finally packed up and left town a few weeks later, a gray cloud cast itself over Majestic. The citizens were sorry to see John Wayne go. He was a true gentleman and they'd been honored to make his acquaintance, however brief.

To everyone's surprise, after the film was in the cans, the Duke sent his complete Marshal Cogburn costume—his eye patch and marshal's star, his pearl-handled revolver and a taxidermic rattlesnake. On a unanimous vote of the town council, the Majestic café was renamed Rooster's Place in Mr. Wayne's honor and the mementos were displayed behind a glass wall case.

Since that time when Hollywood had the whole town starstruck, people have come and gone, new families have started and the dearly departed have been buried in the old cemetery.

The permanent population of Majestic still stays at

seven hundred year round. Main Street is still two miles long and the only change has been the stoplights added just a few years ago. Just about everything in Majestic is the same: the houses built pre-1900 or in the early '20s, the buildings painted a palette of Victorian colors, the aged elms lining the boulevards. Kids still ride bicycles to the snow-cone shack in the summer and they continue to sled down the steep incline of Wooded Creek Road in the winter.

Majestic still has its share of lawbreakers. The police department is five officers strong—one chief and four full-time deputies. Back when the Majestic Police Department was formed, the town was ambivalent about keeping the town's Old West ambiance, but there was never a question that the police officers would be called "deputies," so they could be issued six-point tin stars instead of badges.

It was due in part to that archaic way of thinking that Lanie Prescott couldn't pack fast enough to get out of Majestic.

In Lanie Prescott's opinion, Police Chief Herb Deutsch suffered from a bad case of sexist behavior driven by misplaced testosterone in the brain—not in his briefs where it should have been.

Lanie was an intelligent woman, thirty-three years old, and she'd passed her POST exam at the police academy with high scores. Her agility was excellent, as was her strategic training. She had memorized every criminal code in the policy and procedure manual. But for all the good it did her, she might as well have memorized the phone book.

Dutch—her male counterpart's nickname for Chief

Deutsch—never saw her potential in the four years she worked for him as a deputy.

The reality of her lowly status hit hard a couple of months ago at the grand reopening of the Pay and Pack Grocery Mart. Her assignment was to enforce crowd control over dozens of coupon-carrying shoppers. Keeping a Gor-Tex boot between herself and the red ribbon, she listened as women talked produce prices. As her thoughts drifted she thought about the shoplifter Deputy Ridder had booked the prior day, and the bail-jumper Deputy Griswold had hooked at the Motor Inn.

There was no reason the two arrests couldn't have been made by her. A nab-and-cuff situation always went to someone else. The most action she saw was preparing traffic citations.

Fed up, the next day she drove to the Ludlow, Colorado, police department's open house and went before their hiring board. To her total elation, after passing several interviews and tests, she was accepted.

All she needed was to complete an eleven-week Lateral Recruit training program, and then she'd start as a patrol officer with a radio car district and a partner. No longer would she be singled out to be the school safety crossing guard, funeral procession director and meter maid.

Tomorrow night was Lanie's going-away party at Ken's Steakhouse. All week she had been on cloud nine in anticipation of starting her new job—but not without some bittersweet emotions. She was moving five hours away from the close relationship she shared with her mother. Lanie would miss their coffee conversations. Visiting home as much as possible would definitely be a priority.

Balancing boxes in her arms, Lanie loaded them into

a moving trailer parked at the curb of her Victorian-style house. On a return trip inside for another box, she found her mother in the dining room.

Lucille Prescott sat at the oval table. Bemusement marked her facial features and a soft smile tipped the corners of her mouth. Fair-skinned with blond hair, the sunlight, streaming through the window, caught her in its golden hues.

She was supposed to be taping the boxes closed. The flaps on the one marked Photos were still open. Lucille smiled at Lanie's childhood picture. "This is so cute. Look."

Lanie gazed at the snapshot of herself around age five in the bathtub. "I'm naked and pouring a cup of water on my head."

"You were so chubby and little. Now look at you."

"Yeah—what happened?"

She stood at a curvaceous five feet eleven inches. Tall genes ran in the family. Her mother was five foot ten and her father had been six three.

Lanie recalled her younger, awkward years. They had moved to Majestic when she was twelve and there was only one large school for all of grades K through twelve. Until the ninth grade, she towered over most of the boys. Being statuesque and in a C cup bra was painfully embarrassing. She had wanted to be short and petite like her best friend, Sherry Bongiorno.

"Mom, I need the photo box for the bottom row. Lighter stuff has to go on top—so seal her up."

Personal belongings would be going in the trailer with her to Ludlow. She had rented out her house for the summer fully furnished so there wasn't much left to pack, and the next two nights she'd spend at her mom's before getting an early start on Sunday morning.

A thrill sent shivers across her skin. Each time she thought about how great it would be working for the Ludlow PD, she couldn't stop smiling.

"But look." Lucille grabbed a stack of photographs and shuffled through them. "Here you are on Ranger— the pony at Ashford's Orchards. I remember you cried for Ray to take you off him."

"You don't realize how big a horse is until you're on one. I've never been a pony girl."

"Your Barbies drove the convertibles while Sherry's mother got to buy those adorable plastic horses at Coronat's Five and Dime. They came with realistic saddles and reins that clipped on."

Lanie smacked tape over the seam of a box. "Her Barbies wanted to be rodeo queens and mine wanted to be beauty queens."

A nostalgic sigh rose from Lucille. "And here's my very own beauty queen. You're so beautiful with a crown on, sweetie." She admired Lanie's prom picture with Kevin Mooney beside her, his stance uncomfortable in a black suit. They had been voted King and Queen at their senior prom.

Holding the picture, Lanie stared hard to see if she looked guilty for knowing in advance she was going to lose her virginity that night. All she saw was youthful happiness and love on her and Kevin's faces.

Thin curtains covering the dining-room windows fluttered, letting in the warm July afternoon air. The next photograph in Lucille's stack caused them both to grow reflectively quiet.

It was taken the day Deputy Ray Prescott was sworn in as Majestic's chief of police. He had earned the honored promotion at the age of fifty-five by serving the community for nine years.

The dark crispness of his uniform gave him a sharp confidence. His jaw thrust forward; his firm mouth curled as if on the edge of uncontainable laughter. He stood proudly between his wife and daughter. He said it was the best day of his life next to Lanie being born.

This November would mark the fifth anniversary of his death. He'd been killed in the line of duty chasing a robbery suspect. The funeral the department gave him was somber and patriotic. Lanie would never forget the ear-piercing discharge of rifles in salute. She couldn't think about it for long or she'd cry.

When her father died, her mom almost didn't come out of her grief. But the encouragement and love from Lanie and friends helped pull her back together, and she rebuilt her life as a widow.

Lucille carried a regal kind of beauty that had people fooled—many had pegged her as much younger than her actual fifty-seven years. She actively participated in activities held at the community center—she taught a stitchery class, enjoyed her swim aerobics and played bingo every Saturday night.

Over late-night cups of decaf, her mom confided in her about missing male companionship. Lucille had always been content as a homemaker and mother. When she found herself without a spouse it left a sad void of time on her hands—time she occupied with things that didn't mean as much as her marriage had. No longer was there a man to cook and keep house for, nor to talk to in bed while watching a shared favorite television program.

Lucille put the pictures away. With a shaky breath, she said, ''Hand me the tape and I'll get this box closed.''

''Mom—''

"The weatherman said Sunday shouldn't be too hot for your drive."

Lanie put her hand on her mom's shoulder.

Lucille whispered, "You know what I really want to say."

"Yes," she said softly.

"You want to be like your father and have the respect he had doing something you love. Everyone should have their dream fulfilled. It's just that yours is really hard for me to live with."

"I'll be careful, Mom." As she spoke the words, she knew there were no guarantees.

She hadn't planned on going into police work. Like most little girls, she wanted to be a schoolteacher. Her college courses focused on teacher education programs. In the summers, she worked as the clerk/dispatcher for the station. Each day something different happened due to the variety of calls. Tourists filled the campgrounds, the Motor Inn, and took over rental homes in town and in the mountains. The Cottonwood River ran high with frequent accidents due to irresponsible liquor consumption. Scenic Majestic provided the perfect getaway for actors and actresses.

The first time she answered the dispatch radio, a call came from the White Horse Saloon—assault on private property. She sent Deputy Delroy Ridder. He ended up booking a prominent rock star for busting out the glass on the jukebox. Tall and tattooed, his actions came from beer muscles. In his defense, someone had set the repeat button on the selection pad and someone had to put Willie Nelson's bloody twang out of its misery.

When she mentioned the famous singer Deputy Ridder had arrested to her dad, he said, "That's what cops do. We keep law and order—no matter what a person's name is.''

The more time Lanie spent at the station, the more she knew she wouldn't be satisfied teaching. So at the age of twenty-seven, she redirected her goals by enrolling in the police academy. No one's face beamed brighter than her father's when she passed the POST.

Sadly, she never got to work for him. He was killed three days later. She almost walked away from the department without a backward glance, but she remembered what he told her. *We keep law and order.* By keeping her oath—*to protect and to serve,* someone else might be prevented from being hurt and a family scarred. She would be the best officer she could be. She had tried, unsuccessfully, under Dutch's watch to be that perfect deputy but she never got a chance to prove herself.

Lanie pressed a cheek to her mom's and gave her shoulders a squeeze. Her skin was soft and smelled of Joy perfume.

"I'll miss you, Mom," Lanie said. Her good spirits fought to remain upbeat. "You're my best friend."

"Mothers aren't supposed to be best friends." She injected a teasing note in her voice, forcing her mood to noticeably lighten. "We're supposed to nag and make sure you're eating right, have clean laundry and are dating the right man."

Lanie laughed. "No worries there. I'm not dating anyone."

She hadn't had a serious relationship since dating a reserve officer at the station before getting her deputy's star. Her full schedule didn't leave a lot of free time. Actually—that wasn't quite true. An active social life was something she had failed to create. Job frustration had her not wanting to rely on romance to make her happy. She had to do that herself.

This past year she'd grown increasingly uptight. Dutch's approach to assigning duties, as much as she hated to admit it, created some self-doubt in her capabilities as a female officer.

"I sometimes wish I wasn't seeing Ken," Lucille announced after sealing the last box. "He's a very nice man, but he's just not...he just doesn't... Oh, I don't know."

A respected businessman, Ken Burnett owned Ken's Steakhouse. He and Lanie's mother had been keeping company for almost a year. They'd known each other forever. They seemed to enjoy their time together—at least when Lanie saw them. But her mom's hedging implied something else.

Lanie filled in the blank. "He doesn't make you feel passionate."

"No. Yes. I mean, I'm not talking about *bedroom company*," Lucille emphasized. "He's just so darn perfect it almost annoys me. Nothing is ever out of place on him—his hair or his clothes. He always says and does the right things. Everyone in town thinks he's great."

"Except you."

"I think he's...nice."

"Nice isn't enough, Mom."

"Nice gets me by, sweetie."

"Life's too short to just 'get by.'" Lanie stacked the last box. "Find a man who knocks your pearls off."

Lucille Prescott's love of a string of pearls around her neck—even when she was watering the lawn or cleaning the house—provided ongoing banter between them.

"I'd rather you found a man for yourself."

"I'll get on that as soon as I get settled."

For a second, she believed she might. Maybe she would look for love. But what kind of man would be attracted to a woman who scored high at the shooting range and carried a pair of handcuffs in her purse?

Paul Cabrera's sunglasses reflected the burnished landscape as a warm current of air skimmed over his Porsche convertible. Endless rolling hills and not much else swept by as he drove the desolate two-lane highway. The Eagles sang "Tequila Sunrise" from the compact disc player and a thirty-two-ouncer of iced cola rested in the console cup holder.

Every so often a ranch house and outbuildings sprang from earth that didn't look like it could support one horse much less a full corral. Occasionally he'd spot cattle grazing under the shade of a lone manzanita bush.

Soon he'd have to raise the top and switch the AC on. Brittle dry air blew through the car's interior, a reminder that he was no longer in Miami's humidity.

Stretching his neck muscles, he sipped the cola through a straw. He'd slept five hours last night and needed a dose of caffeine to reset his internal clock. Normally at this hour he was getting ready to go to bed, not waking up.

He hadn't set an alarm in years because he knew his Miami-Dade PD pager would go off before the afternoon alarm. His body didn't stay in step with daytimers and he always felt off by late noon if he didn't catch a few hours of sleep.

He was a career coffin crawler—the officer assigned the dusk-to-daybreak shift. He thrived on nocturnal hours, and since he didn't have a wife or kids he always made himself available. The more heated dispatches occurred Friday nights when paychecks bought a case of beer and an eightball of blow. Saturdays were crazy and anything could happen. Weekdays ran more routine in the Domestic Crimes Unit; heartbreaking in ways most people could never imagine.

Until relatively recently, if anyone had predicted he'd leave the beaches of Miami behind and move out West, he would have said they were full of it. But too many case files had collected on his desk, and he began to acknowledge the signs of something every officer hopes he never has to confront.

The progression of his cynicism began gradually, but eventually drained him to where he started to feel used up and smothered. His desire to return to the job day after day waned. Motivation went dry and his stress coping skills grew ineffectual. Hell, maybe he hadn't coped at all.

He knew he needed to make a change when he caught himself moving through cases and missing key elements. He'd show up on a call and exist almost as a physical presence only—a cop, a body with a badge who happened to be on duty. Writing reports grew tedious and his concentration slipped. Assignments became perfunctory.

A big warning sign. The crimes he handled should never have been categorized as routine. Two years ago, he confronted the unthinkable: He was on the road to burnout.

Burnout.

The phrase was unacceptable, even inside his head. He hated what it represented. Hated that he felt the way he did about a job that had once motivated him to do better in situations that were, at best, the worst.

Paul had weathered a lot in his thirty-seven years—things that could have worn him down long ago. He survived a rocky childhood and troubled home life. Growing up with hard knocks had toughened him. Being sent to Juvenile Hall had been the turning point. In many ways, it had set up the next phase in his life.

And now, here he was years later having been a police officer for thirteen of those years. He now realized he could no more stop crimes than he could stop breathing. Accepting that truth was what was bringing him to Colorado.

He hadn't driven this highway in a long time. He didn't remember the terrain being so dull and empty—maybe nothing was different but his recollections from years ago.

Using one hand, he punched numbers into his cell phone. It rang once and was picked up.

A man's voice came across the line. "Lieutenant Sid Cisneros."

"Sid, it's Paul."

"Hey, kid. Where are you?"

"Texas."

"See any armadillos?"

"Just grazing T-bones."

Sid laughed. "So how the hell are you doing?"

"Good. I was wondering the same about you."

"I'm up to my ass with probation officers and dispositions, and I haven't poured my second cup of coffee yet." The constant ring of telephones could be heard through the background noise.

The Miami-Dade Juvenile Division was always busy with caseloads from troubled minors and juveniles booked on various classes of felonies or misdemeanors.

Paul had firsthand experience without having ever worked a day in the department.

When he was nineteen, Paul was booked and brought in as a minor on a Class C misdemeanor charge—interfering with an officer at the scene of an arrest. Sergeant Sid Cisneros, with his black hair and needlelike piercing brown eyes, sat across from him and told him he was a stupid kid, a punk. A real piece of shit, and that if he didn't want to land in prison, he'd better take a reality check now or forget about having a real life.

Harsh words, but given it wasn't Paul's first encounter with the law he listened and waited, half-bemused by the new guy's guts and his blatant *"I will mold you into a decent man"* attitude that most of the seasoned cops had lost years ago. When Sid was finished with his heated lecture Paul told him to go screw himself. Sid laughed and said, "I'll be collecting from you for that, kid."

Paul hadn't known just how much it would cost him. His probation was four months of community service at the Everglades Project—a youth program Sid supervised. For one hundred and twenty days, Sid "collected" the debt and worked Paul so hard clearing trails and constructing campsites, he lost weight. The unbearable humidity sweated pounds away, and his six-foot-five frame turned lanky.

By summer's end Paul knew two things: Sid was the biggest prick he'd ever met, and also the best thing that ever happened to him.

Sid Cisneros was true to his word and sent him back into society on the right path. But without an education, Paul's prospects were limited. Sid arranged a scholarship at the local college. Going back to a classroom after being out of high school for two years was a difficult adjustment, but Sid's encouragement gave him the motivation. With a loan Sid co-signed and community donations, Paul was able to earn his degree. Weeks after his graduation, he entered the police academy.

Later that year he was hired by the Miami-Dade PD. No surprise for Sid, but it was for Paul. He never expected to become an officer himself. It just happened. The desire to make a difference came from his high regard for Sid, and from what the youth program had done for him, so going into police work was a natural direction.

"So, kid, have you gotten into any trouble?" Sid inquired.

The age difference between Paul and Sid was only seven years, but Sid still singled out the gap.

"Not yet," he said, passing a road sign listing how many miles to the next town.

"Seriously, Paul. How are you doing—really?"

Sid knew the reason Paul had retired prematurely from a position that most officers held on to—if for no other reason than to receive a good pension. Former partners knew everything about each other after working the DC Unit together for seven years.

"I'm hanging in," Paul replied, using the same response that Sid had spoken in the past. There had been tough moments when Sid's sobriety was tested. The pressures of a stressful job were always there. But not even Sid's divorce last year had pushed him toward the bottle again.

"So when you get to this hole in the wall, you'll have to tell me about all the women who can't resist a man in uniform. You always looked better in yours than I ever did. That's why I'm in plain clothes now," he chuckled.

"And you think you look good? You never had any style."

"What do you call my tailored suit from Guido Bros. Clothiers?"

Paul took a sip of cola, an arid breeze dancing through the car. "A three-piece pile of polyester crap."

The easy conversation was a disguise for what was really on Paul's mind, and Sid somehow sensed it. He responded in a reassuring tone, "Hey, I know you're worried about the Torres case. Don't. It's still an open file and it'll stay that way until we find her."

"I appreciate you staying on that for me, Sid."

"You got it, kid."

They talked until Sid had another call to take, then Paul tossed the disconnected cell phone onto the passenger seat. The compact disc player had changed to an Eric Clapton disc and the aging rocker's whisky-mellow voice sang out over the breeze.

Paul braced his hand on the windshield frame, his wristwatch band catching the sunlight. Listening to the music, he thought about Miami. The palmettos and palms, sparkling beaches and the bass-heavy Latin beats that drummed from stereos as convertibles crawled down Ocean Drive.

He was leaving behind his mom and stepdad, and a man who'd made him realize he could do anything he set his mind to. He was giving up a lot for a fresh start. The more miles the Porsche covered, the more distance he put between himself and the familiar. He had to believe he was doing the right thing.

Reason and hope dominated his mind. He was anxious to explore his desire to recapture what it was like *not* to contemplate his last case. What he had seen, what he had heard, what he had done—and what he should have done.

Paul was ready to relearn the basics of police work and rekindle the spark he'd felt the day he took his oath.

Maybe Clapton's song said it best—

Paul Cabrera still could change the world.

Two

The tall oval mirror stood on the floor and Lanie gazed at an eyeful of curves and legs. *Wow…*

She wore a matte jersey dress in black with bold white flowers. The flutter sleeves came to her elbows and the hem was uneven in front. A wraparound bodice fit snugly with a neckline that plunged lower than it had appeared in the picture. That's what she got for ordering from an online catalogue.

She adjusted the neckline, bringing it higher. Her party started in less than an hour and she gave herself a critical assessment.

She'd swept her straight, light brown hair in to a twist that masked its below-the-shoulder length. Since her eyes were both a little violet and a little blue, she had applied an earth-toned eyeshadow, like the magazine article suggested. A pair of her mother's vintage earrings and the matching necklace finished her look.

And it was definitely a look. Working a job where her femininity was subdued beneath a shirt and trousers, she had purposefully picked a fluid dress and hairstyle to bring out her features. Nobody in town saw her dressed up often—almost never. There had been the night she was crowned Prom Queen, and one other occasion that she kept filed in her memory bank under "Old History."

The desire to wow friends was suddenly overshadowed by a feeling she hadn't prepared for—feeling undressed without her uniform. It was such a part of her that she felt strange to go somewhere without being in dark blue from shoulder to toes.

"What's that on your feet?" her mom asked, entering the bedroom.

"Shoes."

"Those are not shoes. They're flat sandals."

Gazing at her feet, the toenails painted geranium pink, she asked, "What's wrong with them?"

"They're too casual to go with your dress." Lucille opened the closet door and handed her a shoe box. "I bought something new for you."

Lanie peeked inside. On a bed of tissue lay a pair of black evening shoes with square rhinestone buckles. They were very sexy in a strappy sort of way and also very impractical.

"I'll break my ankles in these. I'm used to Nikes."

"They're perfect for this dress. Try them on, sweetie."

She sat on the bed's edge and fastened the buckles. Standing, she gained three inches of added height—just what she didn't need. But her mom had had the right instincts. The heels gave her calves a great shape.

"You aren't wearing panty hose." Lucille plucked a corner of Lanie's dress to reveal her smooth thighs minus the knit torture.

Lanie said, "I put three runs in the legs before they were at my waist so I threw them away. Those things are inhumane. I don't know how you can stand to wear them."

"When you're my age you need a little control top to keep everything in place."

Lucille was dressed in a tailored ecru suit with a top-of-the-knee-length skirt and matching pumps. She rarely wore prints, preferring instead solids in light-colored pastels.

Her mom grew sentimental, her eyes tearing. She shook her head, as if that would keep her from crying. "You look so beautiful."

"Thanks, Mom."

"Come stand in front of the fireplace so I can take your picture. You look so beautiful," she repeated.

In the living room, numerous family photos had been taken in front of that standard prop. Not even the discomfort of Italian leather insoles and high heels could detract from Lanie's excitement.

This evening marked a new beginning for her. She was ready to plunge into her eleven-week training course, then start with the Ludlow PD. She wondered what her new partner would be like, how it would feel to make her first significant arrest, and how she would react if she had to draw her weapon.

"When is Ken picking you up?" Lanie asked, giving herself one last check in the entryway mirror.

"Seven. Promptly."

The doorbell chimed and Lucille glanced at the clock. "You could set a bank timer to this man's punctuality."

She swept the door open to a butter-blond man in a gray sport coat. The orangish tan on his face made his smile seem overly white. How his parents had known to name him after the popular plastic doll—Malibu Ken—was anyone's guess.

"You look like a million bucks, Lucille," he said in greeting, the scent of his aftershave on the tropical side. "Hi, Lanie. The cooks are grilling a bunch of tenderloins and T-bones over at the Steakhouse. Nothing but the best.''

"We'll see you there, Lanie," her mom said.

Lanie locked the front door behind them and grabbed her little nothing black purse as the phone rang. Skirting an ice chest on the kitchen floor, she snagged the cordless. "Hello," she breathed into the receiver.

"I'm looking for Lanie Prescott," a man's voice stated.

"I'm Lanie Prescott."

"Ms. Prescott, this is Sergeant Gobelman with the Ludlow PD."

"Oh, hello! I remember you. You were on the interview board."

"Yes, I was."

Warmth flowed through her, her heartbeat giddy. "I'm ready to leave first thing tomorrow and I can't wait to get there."

"That's what I'm calling about. The officer you were replacing had a civil rights geek—er, lawyer, file a writ to prevent him from losing his job on a disability case. We can't legally fire him. I'm sorry to have to tell you this—but a case such as this one is probably going to be tied up in court for a month. Or longer. In the meantime, I'm afraid we can't hire you until we get this shit—er, mess, cleaned up.''

White-hot panic blurred Lanie's vision as she pulled open the heavy door to Ken's Steakhouse. Normally the rich, onion-scented aromas wafting through the restaurant would have made her stomach growl. Now it pitched.

She had to stop the party before things got out of hand, but she was barely inside when a group of well-wishers converged on her from all sides. Between all the congratulations, cards and even a plush teddy bear shoved into her hands, she had no chance to tell anyone she wasn't going away this weekend.

A hand curled over her arm and she was steered away from the group by her friend, Sherry. "You looked like you needed rescuing," Sherry said above the music, a country and western tune. She'd brushed her dark hair away from her face and pinned it up; her beauty was subtle and classic with her high cheekbones and dark brown eyes. She was the only daughter of the only Italian family in Majestic.

"You don't know how badly I need rescuing," Lanie confessed, then telling Sherry all about the telephone call. "I was so upset on the drive over, I almost ran a red light and broadsided a convertible Porsche."

"Ooh, the last time Nicholas Cage was in town he drove a Porsche."

"I didn't recognize the driver. He went through the intersection too fast and I slammed on the brakes." Lanie sucked in a breath. "I stopped in the empty crosswalk, gripping the steering wheel—and then it hit me— I could very easily end up in a financial mess because of this delay."

"I thought you said you had a nest egg."

"I cracked into it to pay for the first and last months' rent and the security deposit on my apartment in Ludlow. I can get most of it back, but it's going to cost me in cancellation fees." Lanie pressed her fingertips to her temple. "I used almost the entire balance of my savings to repair the heating system on my house. If that hadn't happened, I'd be in better shape. As it is now, I could find myself behind in my bills in a matter of weeks unless I start earning a paycheck again."

"Doing what?"

"I love police work—it's what I want to do. I'll send my application to other departments, but getting called for an interview takes time. For the short term, I don't know. I need something right now." Lanie was at a loss. She had been a waitress at Rooster's Place during her college years and she supposed it could be an option. But going back seemed like such a step in the wrong direction.

"Ask Chief Deutsch for your old job back," Sherry said.

"Never. I'd rather have a root canal. Besides, my position's already been filled by an officer coming in from Miami."

"I read in *Inquiring Minds* that Miami has the highest cross-dressing population in the U.S. The article was on the cover next to a picture of a two-hundred-pound baby."

Lanie groaned and gazed at friends laughing and having a good time. "How am I going to tell all these people the party is over?"

Sherry may have been short in stature, but her resolve was stacked a mile high. "You don't, because it's like you said, you're still leaving, only there's been a holdup. Everyone is already gathered so you might as well enjoy the send-off. Look at it this way—you're saving them from having to throw a second party."

Lanie found some sense in that twisted explanation.

Sherry continued, "I really think you should approach the chief. It's the easiest way to wait things out."

In spite of her resistance, Lanie considered Sherry's suggestion. Since this was an emergency, she could deal with Dutch for another month. ''Even if I wanted to, there are no deputy openings.''

''Then how about proposing you ride along with the new guy and show him the ropes? This way you look like the one sacrificing, temporarily, while you're waiting for another job to surface.''

Lanie examined the idea from all angles. ''You know what—? That sounds so absurd, I buy it.''

''Good! And by the way, you look fantastic in a dress. If I had your legs, I'd never hide them.'' Sherry snatched a cheese puff off a waiter's tray as he passed by. Popping the morsel into her mouth, she smiled. ''Mmm. This is the best *not going away yet* party I've ever been to.''

Sherry went to find her husband and Lanie spotted her mother sitting with her group of bingo friends. She hated to interrupt and tell her what had happened. The news wouldn't make her mom unhappy. She'd probably be glad, but she'd never come out and say it.

''God bless America—is that you, Prescott?'' Deputy Delroy Ridder asked, his voice rising an octave.

From the way he was gawking, she had to give her neckline a quick inspection to make sure nothing was showing that wasn't supposed to.

Delroy was barely five feet seven inches, but he could take her down in a foot pursuit challenge. What he lacked in height he made up for in muscles. Short and steely was an apt description.

''It's me, Ridder,'' she replied to the top of his head.

''You look taller in a dress, Prescott.''

''It's the shoes.'' Lanie folded her arms beneath her breasts, the tiny purse swinging from her fingertips. Driven by nervous energy, she wanted to get things over with and talk to Dutch about her situation. She'd have to confess Ludlow had been shelved, but that was all right. Everyone was bound to know sooner or later.

Deputies Wylie "Coyote" Jenkins and Gordon T. Griswold stood at the bar and waved them over. Once there, the two men swept their gazes over her with approval.

Coyote was thin and gangly, but highly astute. "Good Lord, Prescott, if I'd've known you looked this good in a dress I would've worn my leisure suit."

The deputy had on a pair of faded jeans, a crisply pressed Western shirt and a bolo tie with a turquoise nugget riding at his collar.

"Ditto to that," Griswold added, his mouth stretched so wide in a grin, the corners practically touched his ears. The portly, red-mustached deputy drank a nonalcoholic beer.

"What are you drinking, Lanie?" Coyote asked.

"Ginger ale." She slid onto a bar stool and joined the men.

She was determined to straighten out the havoc wrecking her meticulous plans. Sherry's idea could happen if she presented herself just right, and Dutch was in a good mood.

"Ridder," she said, swirling a straw through her drink. "Have you met the officer taking my place?"

"No," Ridder replied. "The chief interviewed him at the academy."

Coyote added, "Dutch says Paul Cabrera's really great."

"Yeah, a regular guy with a lot of smarts," Griswold said. "I heard he carries a Schwarzenegger-sized Glock."

Great. A big-city boy coming to play Cowboys and

Glocks. She was hoping she wouldn't be here long enough to see him in action.

Sipping on her ginger ale, Lanie inquired, "Has anyone seen the chief this evening?"

"He's here somewhere, Prescott. He doesn't want to miss sending you away," Ridder said. Then quickly, "I mean he wants to give you his best wishes."

Everyone in the department was aware of the tension between her and Dutch. The deputies knew about their conflicts, and sometimes they were part of the problem. Not in ways that were degrading, but they were overprotective. They made sure she was always in a safe situation and never in harm's way. Even on an assignment as mundane as school crossing guard, one of the deputies would just *happen* to be passing by and check on her. She knew they did it because they were emotional about losing her dad as their chief and they didn't want to lose another Prescott. But it didn't help her to be a better officer. She felt weighed down.

"Lanie! Here you are. They're ready for you at the table," her mom said, gathering the stuffed bear and cards Lanie had left on the bar.

"I need to find Chief Deutsch first."

"He's over there waiting for you."

Tables had been decorated with white tablecloths and candles burned in the centerpieces. A double layer cake was ablaze on the largest table, the pink candles dripping wax onto the frosting.

Dutch dominated space at the head of the table. Even though it was dark outside, he wore sunglasses. A Colorado Rockies baseball cap sat on his precision crewcut, and a knit polo shirt stretched over his full chest.

"Make a wish and blow them out," Ken said, his face beaming.

Everyone stared at her, waiting. She suddenly knew what it was like to stand in a roomful of people completely naked. She blew an obligatory breath of air to a rousing chorus of cheers.

Lanie's nerve endings began to unravel. Asking Dutch for her job back with all these people around would be impossible. He was hardly the approachable type even when he was alone. He grunted answers when he wasn't in the mood to converse. And he got that way a lot.

Lanie would bet money he only watched action adventure movies so he could laugh at all the wimpy actors who paled in comparison to his high-octane machismo. When she drove past his house, it wasn't uncommon to find him under the hood of the department's Ford Explorer. He probably changed the spark plugs just so he could get greasy and look leathery tough like his idol, Clint Eastwood.

"I've had the honor of working with Officer Prescott for four years," Dutch began, his voice on the gravelly side, "and during that time she's shown nothing but exemplary work."

Exemplary? He must have looked that word up in the dictionary, and his use of "honor" didn't characterize his behavior toward her over the last four years.

Shoved into the spotlight, Lanie smiled weekly as Dutch proclaimed her trip to Ludlow would be safe and speedy. He ended with a toast, a lift of his beer, and uttered, "Success in the work force is not an easy thing to measure, so some people don't even try. But Deputy Prescott here is searching for her ruler and has found it in Ludlow. So good luck and farewell, I hope your efforts are as tall as you are."

Somewhere in there, Lanie was certain the metaphor

was twisted. He was, however, in a good mood—a good mood that came from getting rid of her.

Expectant faces around the table waited for her to say a few words of farewell. They were having a wonderful time. Ken had gone to such trouble with the food, and her mother's camera flashed as she took another picture. Lanie's thoughts spilled together and became muddied, and she couldn't sort through things fast enough to make a coherent response.

"I'm speechless," she managed to say. "Thank you all for coming."

Applause rose, dinner was served, the cake was cut and Lanie stared blindly into her plate. Her mother said she'd make sure the cards, balloons and gifts were brought home. Lanie nodded mutely, knowing tonight she'd confess everything to her mother when they were alone. Tomorrow she'd send her apologies to friends.

Dutch excused himself from the table and went to the bar. Lanie stayed and spent time with those who'd come to say goodbye. When the seats began to empty and the guests scattered, she stood and sought out Dutch.

As she approached him, he gruffly pointed out, "Prescott, you're in a dress."

Ridder piped up, "We covered that. She looks nice, doesn't she?"

This was the time when Lanie was supposed to have made a joke, a remark—something quick and funny— a parting commentary of silliness and happiness that would be her send-off. The last note in her farewell song. But witty words escaped her because there was no music. Just the incessant beat of her heart drowning all sound from her ears.

"Yeah, swell," Dutch remarked in the barrel-like

rumble of a grizzly bear with a broad grin. Then to the bartender, "Carl, another draft beer."

Dutch jerked his head first to the left, then to the right. Lanie heard the soft crunch of bones as he cracked his neck. She hated when he did that and would swear sometimes it was intentional.

Did she really want to work for him again?

It wasn't as if he were a negligent leader—break-ins were down under his watch. But that didn't mean he was a super guy. During roll call she observed his attitude. He stood there and every pore in his body screamed he was a force to be reckoned with. She'd swear he thought of himself as the original lethal weapon. Since his position was appointed by the town council, he could have it as long as he got enough votes. And he always did because he was a man's man who appealed to many.

He was pretty pleased about her leaving Majestic and Lanie felt insulted. At least he could have acted with a little remorse instead of being unabashedly relieved.

While the other deputies were involved with the baseball game on the television, Lanie made up her mind.

"Chief Deutsch, I just found out my Ludlow position has been put on hold, and I won't be able to start there as soon as I'd planned," she said, barely dragging in a gulp of air. "In the interim, while I wait for another offer, I'd like to rehire for a short term and ride along with Paul Cabrera. I could fill him in on all he needs to know about Majestic."

Dutch shoved his sunglasses to the top of his forehead. She could see his eyes clearly now. The black irises, anchored in pale blue puddles, looked narrow, much like his mind.

"I know this is a surprise. It was to me, too. But my rehiring with the PD would be beneficial to all those concerned."

"No, it wouldn't. You're off my watch, Prescott. We're through."

On the bar, the walkie-talkie that the officers carried with them went off. Dutch snagged the radio and activated the service button.

"This is response," he said into the receiver. "Over."

"Four-fifty-nine on east Elm Street. Attempted car stereo theft. The suspect is identified wearing a red ball cap backward; white T-shirt. He's on foot, proceeding toward Main. Copy?"

"Copy that," Dutch said into the receiver, then clicked off. "Have to run, boys," he grunted to the group, the slight cleft in his chin folding a little into his freshly shaven skin.

He retreated through the rear door. She had underestimated him. He was more of a hardnose than she gave him credit for.

The deputies went their own ways and Lanie was left alone. She sat down and ordered a cocktail to go with her cocktail dress.

"A lemon drop, Carl," she said, as the bartender set a cocktail napkin in front of her.

"Coming up."

Inside her black purse were loose bills, her driver's licence, a tube of pink lip gloss and a set of single-action handcuffs. She fingered the paper money and counted. Twenty bucks. She had better make it last.

Her mind raced like a runaway train. On one hand, she felt like she was still going forward, but on the other she was screeching to a halt. She'd have to call the apartment manager to cancel, and right now she didn't want to know how much she'd lose in that transaction. Then there was the business of her house being rented for the summer. Reversing that agreement would be complicated, if not impossible.

Carl presented her with a lemon martini. "It's on the house."

He was burly and brainy and bald as a baby's bottom. They'd been in the same sixth-grade class.

"Thanks, Carl."

The lemon drop must have had a double shot of vodka in it because she felt relaxed almost instantly. Her muscles grew languid, as if she were melting into a warm pool of wax. She should have eaten more dinner.

Johnny Cash was singing through the speakers and, for a moment, she forgot about everything. Until she felt someone's gaze on her, and she knew immediately it wasn't a martini-induced illusion.

She slowly turned her head to the right. A man stood at the end of the bar, definitely staring at her. He was clean-shaven with inky black hair cut short, neatly smoothed and tapering over his ears. The look was almost a buzz cut, but not militant in any way. It was sexy....

He had to be well over six feet tall. A dark T-shirt showed every ridge of muscle in his upper body and biceps. His arms were folded over a wide chest defined with perfect proportions. He had his back pressed into the bar, legs crossed at the ankles. Forefinger and thumb held on to a bottle of beer by the neck. Leather hiking boots were visible from the bottom of his jeans.

She had a hard time taking her eyes off him. He was incredibly good-looking. She'd never seen him before—she would have remembered. And so would the other women in town. Gossip would have sweetened jars of sun tea if he'd been in Majestic before tonight. He was probably one of the new rafting instructors, since the summer season was just getting underway.

She held her breath and faced forward when he headed in her direction.

"Looks like there's a party here tonight," he commented, taking the seat next to hers.

Her entire career was hanging in the balance and, in the middle of the chaos, this man's appearance attracted her in a purely physical manner. His height, his breadth, the way he carried himself with a hint of street smarts and not all *GQ* masculinity.

"It's a going-away party," she informed him, damning the heat of a blush on her cheeks.

His lips completely captured her attention when he asked, "So who's going away?"

"Me." There was no hesitation in her tone, yet the "M" sounded like she'd hummed it: *Mmmmmmme.* She gazed at her martini glass. Half full.

"That's too bad," he drawled, making her wonder where he was from. He had an accent she couldn't quite place. It reminded her of the South, but the sound wasn't country and western twang.

"But I'm not leaving right away," she replied, surprised she had admitted so much to a stranger.

"Then I'll be seeing you around." The thickness of lashes that framed his to-die-for chocolate-colored eyes claimed her attention.

Everything inside her zeroed in on the warmth of his gaze. "You're new in town."

"That obvious?"

"Yes…no. I mean, I would have remembered seeing you before."

"Just got here."

"And what brings you to Majestic?"

"Work."

Just as she had suspected. The hiking boots and worn jeans, the height and the muscles, his tall, lean body—he was built solid enough to paddle upriver without breaking a sweat.

"You'll like it here." A note of melancholy drifted into her voice as she thought about everything she would miss when she moved. She envied him for his arrival.

Touching the stem of her glass, she caught a bead of moisture on her fingertips. "The local pace is slow, but we have a lot of interesting people come through our Main Street. We get visitors from Los Angeles and New York—mostly actors and actresses, sometimes musicians and sports players coming to spend time in our beautiful mountains."

Close to her on the bar stool heat radiated from him and she could almost feel the rough texture of his jeans against her bare leg.

He nodded with a half smile, his teeth even and straight against firm lips. "So which celeb drives a red Trailblazer?"

Lanie's hand froze. She studied his scowling profile and her stomach felt as if it would collapse. "Uh, why?"

He popped a few salted peanuts into his mouth. "The driver almost clipped me in an intersection."

Lanie suddenly became preoccupied with dusting sugar crumbs off the bar top.

* * *

Paul watched the woman beside him move like a finely tuned violin, shoulders softly swaying, as she gave the bar an impromptu brush with her palms. Subtle cleavage at her neckline made the exposed skin all the more suggestive. Her upswept hair bared the column of her neck, wispy pieces kissing the pale, tender skin. Caught in a twist, he admired the sun streaks of blond that ran through her hair.

The dress she wore was amazing on her body. She was exceptionally tall and that's what had attracted his attention when he came into the lounge for a beer after his dinner.

He'd eaten at a café called Rooster's Place. They were real keen on John Wayne over there, just like he remembered. An entire glass case was devoted to the movie, *True Grit*.

Nothing in Majestic seemed to have changed since he'd vacationed here with an old girlfriend years ago, but a lot had changed for him. He and the girlfriend had split up, he'd married someone else and then divorced, he'd been awarded a ten-year service recognition from his PD, and he'd completed his education at the University of Miami.

Worn out from his long day, he had observed the customers coming in and out of Rooster's Place. After a short while, he concluded he had left Miami far behind.

There was no waterfront strip here. No neon lights and surreal blue ocean shoring up Ocean Drive. Absent was the rhythmic techno music booming from convertible BMWs as they drove past sidewalk bistros.

While the whole population of Majestic couldn't be defined by a small percentage, it was this group in Rooster's Café that gave Paul an impression of the town. Men wore cowboy hats, had circles from chew tins imprinted on their back pockets, and drove pickup trucks with rear windows that sported gun racks. If anyone pulled that in the metro Dade area, they'd be arrested. Feathered haircuts were still popular on both sexes. The ladies were friendly. He had two waitresses eager to refill his water glass.

For all the gaping differences, Paul reestablished a connection with the Norman Rockwell-like town. It would be good for him to be a part of the small setting.

He drank a pull of beer, wiped his lip with a knuckle and asked the woman beside him, "Why are you leaving?"

"The same reason as you. Work."

She had the most incredible eyes. A mix of violet and blue that set off the trace of shine on her lips.

Curiosity drew him. "So what do you do?"

"I'm in law enforcement."

He tilted his head and leaned back to view the full image of her in a killer dress. He'd known many female cops and she didn't seem the type to strap on a holster. She looked more like the office division. "Dispatch?"

Ridicule and incredulity flamed in her expression. Blue fire snapped in her eyes. *"Deputy."*

Paul instantly regretted his lapse in judgement. He, better than anyone, knew never to form a decision based on appearances. Even so, he couldn't keep from saying, "I don't mean any disrespect—but you don't look like a cop."

"Because I'm not stocky and wear my hair short? If you buy into that stereotype—"

"I apologize." His mind was recovering from the knowledge that, in all likelihood, she was the deputy he was replacing. He was no sexist, but the thought that he would be replacing a woman hadn't crossed his mind.

"With thinking like that, you've definitely convinced me that an officer who carries a Glock is trying to make up for a personal deficit," she said, making the last of her martini disappear. "Just take my word for it—I like men."

Paul's muscles grew taut and he wondered if she was kidding about the Glock. Maybe she knew who she was talking to and was stringing him along as a joke. "I don't see the connection between the size of a cop's gun and the size of his anatomy."

"It's a known fact that men who use exaggerated firepower are lacking in other areas. They need a powerful symbol to make them feel masculine because they're short in that department."

"Do you have any firsthand experience to back up your theory? Like seeing the proof for yourself?"

She frayed her napkin's edge, then looked up as if letting him in on a little confidence. "There's a hotshot cop coming in from Miami to take my position and I'm sure it will be only too obvious by looking at him."

He found it difficult to keep a straight face. She was something else, a woman who had definitely captured his attention. Less than an hour ago he was dead ass tired from the eight-hundred-mile drive. Now he'd forgotten he wanted to go to bed early. "Let me buy you another drink."

"No, thank you. I should be going." She stood, swayed slightly, then sat back down while holding on to the bar for balance. "Actually, I'd love a black coffee."

In a moment, a hot cup was placed in front of her and she blew the steam off the top.

"So how come you quit your deputy position?" Paul asked, more than a little curious.

The delicate arch of brows rose as if she might have been regretting her decision. "I jumped into a new position because my old one didn't fit anymore. Actually, it was never the right fit because my boss was a..." She refrained from filling in an obvious negative blank.

Paul had hit it off with Chief Deutsch on the phone and again during his Colorado Police Academy oral interview. Dutch seemed ethical, dedicated and fair as a leader. No outward pressures and not popping a roll of antacids every five minutes like his last commander, who, as it so happened, was a woman.

She drank her coffee, growing more reflective. "I'm definitely a long-range planner and going to Ludlow because I was angry wasn't really like me. I'm not saying I shouldn't have, but if I'd checked out more than one position I would have alternatives right now." On a blunt note, she confessed, "I'm not spontaneous."

"That's too bad."

"Now I have to figure out what to do. I need some time to figure out my next step, and if it weren't for this Miami guy coming in Dutch would still need me. I'll bet he wears gold chains and waxes his chest."

Paul almost choked on his beer. "Sounds like he's gay."

Stifled laughter floated up her throat. "Oh, Dutch would just about croak!"

The cocktail waitress appeared. "Okay," she said in a giggling voice, a twinkle lighting her eyes. "Do you know Oprah or Rosie O'Donnell? I read in *People* that they have seasonal homes in Miami."

Earlier, when this same waitress had asked him where he was from, she immediately wanted to know if he knew Sonny Crockett. He'd had to explain that Sonny was a fictional character played by Don Johnson.

"But I saw Donald Trump once," he offered.

"Really? I don't know why him and Ivana split up. Their daughters are so pretty. One's a model. I could have been a model myself. I got a postcard invitation to attend the Barbizon school, but I chipped my tooth the week before I was supposed to enroll."

The day had been long and hot, and talk about modeling schools and him being gay had him feeling tired again.

"Close out my tab, darlin'," he said to the waitress. "I'm ready to call it a night." He handed her his credit card.

Beside him, the sun-kissed blonde, with all her sexy appeal and long legs, grew cautious while studying his face. Something apparently clicked in her mind and he was pretty sure it was the reference to Miami. He could almost feel the adrenaline rushing through her veins as her teeth snagged her lower lip.

She breathed tightly and asked, "What did you say your name was?"

The cocktail waitress placed his bill and a pen in front of him. He slanted his signature hard enough to go through two copies. "I didn't."

There was a lapse of silence before she prodded, "What is it?"

Without a word, he flashed her his credit card and she leaned forward to make out the tiny imprint.

"Paul Cabrera," she read, then brought her fingertips to her pink mouth. A very plump, very kissable mouth. "Oh, my God," she gasped. "Excuse me. I have to go drown myself."

She fled Ken's Steakhouse faster than a palmetto bug runs for cover in the daylight.

Three

If Lanie had a bucket of water, she'd stick her head in it.

Stepping into the summer night air, she took in deep breaths. It felt surreal to have been inside, giving her uninformed opinion on a man who turned out to be the man she was talking to.

She was mortified, upset and just plain mad for going on about the gun and gold chains and mad at *Paul Cabrera himself* for not stopping her from shoving her foot deeper into her mouth. Embarrassment didn't begin to describe the way she felt right now.

Her mind worked to remember what she'd said to him about her job with Dutch, about the Ludlow fiasco. Had she outright confessed she was in limbo? She didn't think she'd been real clear. On the other hand, that vodka lemon drop had gone straight to her head.

But uncovering Paul Cabrera's identity had her mind clearly focussed now.

On her way out of the steakhouse, Lanie had caught Sherry and asked her to tell her mom she was leaving. Sherry said she'd relay the message and call her tomorrow.

Since Lanie had been late for the party, the convenient parking spaces in front of the restaurant had been taken. She'd left her Trailblazer around the corner from

Main on a side street. The residential block wasn't lit well; the ancient street lamps gave off only a marginal pale glow.

Fishing through her purse, she found her car keys. When she looked up, movement at the driver's side door of her Trailblazer slowed her steps. The window glass had been busted in and a man sat on the front seat. From his jerky motions, Lanie could tell he was yanking out her stereo.

Her mouth dropped open in disbelief.

The clothing description matched the perp Dutch had been sent out to chase: Red ball cap on backward and white T-shirt.

Keys slipped from her fingers and she traded them for her handcuffs. The metal rings were cool and solid; she felt a sure confidence erupt to life. She picked up her pace, trying to walk quietly in her evening shoes and not tip him off. But the heels made an unfamiliar *click-click* noise she couldn't muffle.

He cocked his head her way and saw her coming. Flinging the door open wider, he jumped out and took off with her Bose in his sticky hands.

"Hey, you!" she shouted hoarsely. "Stop right there!"

He pounded the street with slick speed.

She gave chase in hot pursuit, but running in heels proved to be an unwieldy challenge. She couldn't get the same traction as athletic shoes.

"Stop! Police!" she called. While the latter was a stretch of the truth, the ink on her resignation was still fresh enough that she was closer to being a deputy than an ex-deputy.

But her reasoning didn't matter. Her command was ignored.

The thief hurdled a row of bushes and sprinted to the next block. It was hard to keep him in sight. He was fast. With the disadvantage of high heels, Lanie stuck to the sidewalk with only a thin sole to cushion the balls of her feet from the concrete.

He cut across a lawn and headed for the alley behind a house. Lanie had no choice but to follow and took flight over the grass. But within short seconds, her right heel sank and she was down.

Her outstretched arms prevented her from falling face first and the leg beneath her took the brunt of the impact. Buckled forward, she lay partially on a walkway and partially on the grass. In a stunned daze, she managed to sit up. Examining her palms under the starlight, she could see that the skin was scraped from the rough cement. When she tried to move her leg, the pain was brutal. It shot through her shin and exploded near her kneecap. Electrical shocks set her calf muscles on fire.

Something was not right.

Lanie leaned back on her elbows, legs beneath her and the hem of her dress hiked to her thighs. Pins had fallen out of her up-do and pieces of hair hung down, framing her face. She fought to regain her breath, closed her eyes and swore.

No, this was not good.

She uttered softly to the dark blanket of sky, ''I knew I shouldn't have worn these shoes.''

As soon as the words were out of her mouth she heard the bubbling sound of pop-up heads come to the lawn's surface and then the timed sprinklers erupted in a fountain of water.

Paul turned at the corner, deciding to take the residential streets back to the Motor Inn. As he drove past gingerbread-style houses, a lone woman caught his attention. She was on the lawn, and even though she sat under the shadows created by a tree, he easily identified her as the woman from Ken's Steakhouse.

He downshifted and pulled to the curb with a sharp screech. The grass was wet and so was she from the look of her long hair. Clinging to her body, the black dress stuck to her skin. He thought she'd been assaulted, then reconsidered when her face came into his view more clearly. It was apparent she was disturbed and not distressed.

"It would have to be you," she said, lowering her chin and her voice breaking with pain. He'd expected the next time he saw her she'd be in a bit of agony because of what happened at the bar, but her weak tone sounded like pain of another kind.

Crouching, he placed a hand on her shoulder. "Talk to me."

Water dripped from her hair and spiked her eyelashes. "I've been calling for help, then realized I'm at the O'Neil house. Nobody's home. They're on vacation and the sprinklers go off at midnight. Ten minutes each station. I tried to get up...."

"What happened, darlin'?"

She shoved the hair from her face and yanked her dress down, then winced from the quick motion. Her hands trembled, and it took a visible effort for her to gain composure. "My car stereo just got stolen and I was chasing the suspect."

The contents of her purse were scattered, notably a pair of handcuffs. Not an everyday item for a woman to carry—except she wasn't ordinary. A former deputy who was, or wasn't, on a force at the moment—he hadn't been able to follow that.

With a cursory scan of their surroundings, Paul asked, "Was he armed?"

"Only with my Bose."

Fighting the urge to laugh, he gathered the spilled personal items and returned them to her purse.

"He wouldn't stop when I ordered him to and nobody can run in these shoes." She covered her face with her hands and talked through her fingers, as if unable to look at him while admitting, "My heel sunk into the grass and I fell."

"How badly are you hurt?"

"I don't know."

He examined her outstretched leg with a soft glide of his hand. She started; the lightest contact from his fingertips caused her to muffle a cry. Her shin was swollen and darkened with bruises. No compound fracture, but she'd done something fairly damaging.

"What's your name?" He took her hand. Her fingers were cool and soft, and she gripped his as if she needed an anchor to rely on.

Hesitation delayed her reply as if she were questioning whether or not he already knew—and maybe even more than just her name. "Lanie Prescott."

"Lanie," he said, his thumb brushing over her knuckles with a reassurance she was going to need, "you broke your leg. It's bad, but I've seen worse."

"I'm sure I just twisted something. It's painful, but not too bad."

"It hurts like hell, I can hear it in your voice."

"I can't have a broken leg," she protested. "Help me up. I just need a little support to get me going."

He stood, taking her slowly with him. Her fingernails dug into his forearms, cutting his skin. She trembled as her left leg bore all her weight and her hands gripped his arms like talons. For long seconds the battle to attempt to place pressure on her right leg was a struggle.

"I can't..." she murmured. "I can't have a broken leg."

She slumped into him and all the breath left her lungs as he scooped her into his arms.

He kept his stride soft but each step he took, each shift of his weight, her moist breath fanned across his neck. She fisted the cotton covering his shoulder and heat flexed through his body.

He forced the rawness out of his voice. "I'm going to lower you into the front seat."

"It does hurt like hell," she lamented reluctantly. "It's like electrical shocks. Little needles. I've never broken anything before. I can't believe I did this."

"Put your hand behind my neck and don't let go until you're sitting."

His biceps strained with controlled strength while manipulating her as gently as possible. A shaky cry ripped from her throat when she touched the seat and slowly rested her foot on the floorboard. Her fingers uncurled from around his neck and she leaned her head on the headrest.

The night was warm, but she was wet. He had a sports coat tossed on the backseat. He covered her with the coat, tucking the sleeves behind her shoulders.

Paul slipped behind the wheel. "Where's the hospital?"

"We don't have one. There's the Clinic, but it's closed. The closest E.R. is in Montrose—thirty minutes away."

"I'll make it in fifteen. Direct me." He turned over the ignition.

"Wait—I can't leave my Blazer here with a broken

window. And the guy who stole my stereo is still out there. We have to notify the department. Do you have a cell phone handy?''

"Always." He called the dispatch number, relayed the information on the last location of the suspect, and requested the SUV be taken to impound for the evening.

"I'm parked right here." She pointed several cars away. "We should wait until a unit comes."

"The chief said he'd send an officer out. You don't have anything to worry about—it's handled." Paul drove past the red SUV, the pavement beneath the driver's door glittering with glass pieces. "No wonder you had no answer for me. It was you who almost ran me down earlier this evening."

She didn't acknowledge almost running the red light and taking him out in the intersection. Her thoughts had apparently drifted elsewhere. "It would be best if you drive me home. I think a bag of ice will help."

"Ice isn't going to fix anything. You need X rays and a doc to take a look."

"Fine. My mom can take me. She's supposed to be at the party I just left but I couldn't find her."

"Call her cell phone."

"She doesn't have one. I'll call the house." Lanie did and ended up leaving a message on the machine. "I don't know where she is. Probably with Ken…he doesn't have a cell phone, either."

"Everyone has a cell phone."

"Not in Majestic. Half the population still has rotary dial telephones. If you haven't noticed, we aren't a very modernized town. But it's part of our appeal."

The boundaries of Majestic just got smaller to him. Cell phones were the heart of Miami. Everyone had one—or two. Good guys, bad guys, kids, seniors. It was a way of life.

Paul pulled onto Main Street. "Left or right?"

"Left. But wait—considering our history, brief as it was, I don't think it's a good idea for us to go together."

He was already headed east. "I don't have an opinion about you one way or the other, Lanie." He tested the sound of her name in his voice and liked it. "You stated what you thought. I can't change your mind about an opinion you have. To you, a guy with a Glock is a guy without assets."

Slumped against the door frame, her eyes half closed. "Don't remind me I said that. Take Highway 550 all the way there."

Wind licked through her messy hair, teasing it into the dark breeze.

He shifted through the car's gears, eating up the road out of town.

This was a hell of a first night in Majestic and it wasn't over yet.

The diagnosis: Right fibula, incomplete fracture. Three weeks in a fiberglass cast, then the cast would be removed and her leg X-rayed again. Cast likely back on for another three to four weeks. After that, a walking boot for three to four weeks.

Worst-case scenario: fourteen weeks of hell.

Best-case scenario, and for extreme optimists only: six weeks, then physical therapy.

The doctor told her she was lucky. No rods.

The examing room smelled like plastic and medicine, the curtain drawn to make a cubicle. Paul sat in a chair closest to the wall, his large frame an attention getter.

A nurse had come in and out on several pretexts, sorting a tray of bandages and taking an inventory of tongue depressors.

The gurney Lanie lay on was engaged in the up position. A soft pillow cushioned her head and a splint immobilized her right leg. An IV drip gave her fluids and something else to take the edge off her pain. She wore a wrinkled hospital gown, her underwear on beneath.

Earlier, the attending nurse asked Lanie if "her boyfriend" wanted to help her get out of her wet dress. She declined, adamantly stating that they didn't know each other that well. In fact, not at all.

The two strangers who had met barely two hours ago, waited for the orthopedist to come in and apply her cast.

Lanie gave Paul stolen glances, trying to read his expression. He had been extremely good-looking in a darkened lounge, and with unforgiving light from an E.R. cubicle, he was even more so.

Unbidden, her hand rose to her cheek to disguise imperfections. She hated to think about her disheveled appearance. Vanity had never been one of her traits, but it suddenly had her preoccupied.

A wedge of silence pushed between them.

She was withdrawn and worried. All her hopes, her dreams and the future she'd chosen for herself had caved in. Light at the end of the tunnel was nonexistent with a broken leg. The very thought upset her stomach.

Accepting her fate wasn't easy, nor did she want to try. She'd much rather the nurse turn up the drip going in her arm so she could fade into a temporary delirium.

But the Miami cop prevented her from succumbing to a self-serve pity party. If he wasn't here, she would let go and have a full meltdown.

The rich timbre of his voice filled the enclosed area. "So why do you need my job? I figure you're the deputy I'm replacing."

She eyed him with suspicion. "It's complicated."

"I've already figured out you're complicated and that I'm part of your complication. I have to tell you—I worked for the Miami-Dade PD thirteen years and nobody ever called me a hotshot carrying a weapon too big for my pants."

If she were able, she would have hugged her knees and put her head down. Of all the comments to keep coming back to haunt her. She vowed never to drink a lemon martini again. "I shouldn't have said what I said at the bar."

His smile was simple. "We've got time—give me the complicated answer."

"The police job I was offered in Ludlow has been rescinded due to a civil rights suit. I'm in limbo for the duration. It'll take a month or so while they duke it out in court."

"Sounds like you got a tough break."

"Incomplete fracture," she replied.

"That's not what I meant."

"I know," she said humorlessly.

He sat in a relaxed manner, leaning forward with his arms resting on his knees. His virility was unquestionable. Larger than life and city smart, even in a hospital his presence was compelling.

Something clicked in her mind: The delicate straps of her black shoes dangled intimately between his fingers. He appeared at ease holding a pair of ladies' evening shoes. His strong hand made her size nines look tiny, and she forgot her train of thought.

"You really do look more like a rafting instructor," she commented at length.

Dark eyebrows arched. "Why would you say that?"

"Because that's who I thought you were when I first saw you."

"What gave you that idea?"

"You're very built, Cabrera," she stated, then frowned for speaking her thought aloud. The medicine flowing through her IV had a sedating effect and had loosened her tongue.

Using his last name sounded out of place to Lanie, but she couldn't bring herself to call him Paul. It felt too familiar in this unfamiliar set of circumstances.

"I don't follow you," he remarked, baiting her for an explanation.

She snapped somewhat, "You know what I mean. You're muscular."

When he kept grinning without another word, she gestured with her hands and brought them apart to emphasize his size and shoulder breadth. "Your height attracts attention."

"I'm six foot five and use it to my advantage in ugly arrest situations. When I'm off duty, women ask me how tall I am and what I do for a living." The underlying sensuality in his words captivated her. "They rarely guess right."

"I wonder how many people will guess what happened to me today?" she mused. "I'm going to have a lot of explaining to do about why I won't be leaving. When did Chief Deutsch hire you, if I can ask—since I already know how tall you are."

"Over a month ago."

"He must have called you the same day I told him I was quitting."

A page sounded over the E.R. intercom system, and the siren from an ambulance wailed announcing its arrival.

"Maybe. Couldn't tell you for sure."

She closed her eyes for a moment, rubbing her lids in exhaustion. Black mascara smudged her fingertips. She disregarded her makeup disaster and said contemplatively, "I don't see why you would choose to relocate in Majestic. We don't have badges, Cabrera. Just a little tin star."

"I don't need a big badge to make me feel like a big man."

The orthopedic doctor returned. Age-wise, he didn't look a day over sixteen. He showed her a tray of colorful fiberglass wraps and asked her to pick one. She chose basic white. The same ogling nurse was paged, and she spent more time looking at Paul than paying attention to her tasks.

The leg splint had to be removed, and that caused her to grit her teeth. Squeezing her eyes closed, she breathed in and out, forcing tranquility to block the pain.

Unexpected warmth and strong comfort encircled her fingers. Paul had slid the chair toward her and held on to her hand. His compassion and quiet understanding calmed her pulse.

The plaster began to heat; a strange sensation she'd never felt before and hoped she would never have to feel again.

Lanie sighed. "You look like you've done this before—wait in an E.R. room with a woman."

"It's almost a given in Domestic Crimes."

She searched his face. He was an ever-changing mystery. "I assumed you were homicide or vice."

"Domestic violence, child exploitation and abuse of the elderly. All handled under the DC Unit. Most of my caseload was domestic."

"You're a cop?" The nurse was evidently impressed.

Paul supplied easily, "We both are."

Inexplicably, his answer gave her a small pleasure. She wondered if he had intended to do that.

When the cast was finished, her lower leg was swathed in white. Her leg burned and steamed as the hardening agents set up into a shell. The doctor gave her two prescriptions: one for pain and the other an antibiotic. And a pair of crutches. She was instructed as to what her limits would be, none of which would give her any freedom for the next couple of weeks.

Before long, a wheelchair arrived in the room and Lanie was aided into it. The cast on her leg felt like a ten-ton weight. Blood drained from her face, leaving her clammy and cold. The slightest movement was excruciating. Paul covered her shoulders with a blanket.

The candy-striper rolled Lanie down the sterile hallway, Paul beside her with her little black purse and strappy shoes.

At the vending machines, she insisted they stop. She bought several bags of M&M candies and a bottled water. As they neared the parking lot, she held them tight as if they were the only links to normalcy on this crazy night.

On the drive home, she fell asleep and he had to wake her up when they reached town.

"I don't know where you live," he said, his voice intruding into her dreamless state.

She directed him to a street lined with aged trees. Punchy from her medicine, she almost didn't recognize her surroundings until the moving trailer in front of her mom's reminded her she wasn't moving tomorrow.

Paul stuck to her like chewing gum as she slowly progressed up the walkway, metal crutches tucked into her armpits. The porch light was on, winged bugs bouncing off the bulb.

"You must be tired," she said, fatigue engulfing her senses. "You said you'd driven all day."

She'd noticed at the hospital that stubble had begun to darken his jaw.

He shrugged as if tonight were no big deal. "I can get by on a couple hours sleep."

An awkward span of time stretched between them.

"Well…thanks again for everything."

"Not a problem."

Her mom opened the door dressed in her housecoat. She'd waited up after Lanie had phoned from the hospital and told her not to.

Paul was given a quick introduction to Lucille Prescott, then he was back in his Porsche driving to the Motor Inn.

Much later he was still awake, a late movie blinking at him from the television screen.

Four

Bright sunshine slanted through the window blinds of Rooster's Place Café. The smell of fresh brewed coffee hung in the air, blending with the aroma of frying bacon. Paul's coffee cup steamed next to the dessert menu featuring mud pie. Chief Deutsch and the deputies sitting at the table with him didn't need the breakfast menu. They had the selections memorized.

He'd been introduced to Deputy Gordon T. Griswold and Deputy Delroy Ridder. Deputy Wylie "Coyote" Jenkins was the assigned Duty Officer who had clocked off at three in the morning so he wasn't here. He took a ham radio home with him and calls were rerouted there until his responsibility ended when the six o'clock shift came on.

Dutch invited Paul to their morning meeting at Rooster's as a way for him to get to know his fellow officers in a relaxed setting.

The trio wore uniforms, walkie-talkies lying on the tabletop with cowboy hats hooked on the combo coat/hat rack mounted on the booth's vinyl arm.

They seemed like an easygoing group.

The pectorals of Ridder's chest leveled just slightly above the table's edge as he sat tall and alert after his fourth cup of coffee. Spilling artificial sweetener into his cup, he asked, "How was the drive from Florida?"

"Not too bad."

"That stretch of highway across Texas gets hot enough to fry eggs on this time of year."

Griswold motioned to pass one of the individual creamers. "How are you doing in the altitude?"

Paul shook his head with chagrin. "It's killing me."

"It takes some time to get used to. Be sure to drink lots of water." A shard of white sunlight caught on Dutch's silverware. "Twist those blinds the other way, would you, Griswold?"

The waitress came and Paul read off his order. The rest of them took their turns in placing their requests. Dutch's bowl of oatmeal got some razzing from Griswold. When the waitress was gone, the menus tucked beneath her arm, Dutch spelled out the department's routine.

There would be new penal codes to memorize, a new schedule to fall into and new people to get to know. Lanie Prescott came to mind.

He wondered how she was doing. He'd thought about stopping by to see her. Maybe later today he would.

Tucking his newspaper on the seat, Dutch said, "We like to think of ourselves as the modern-day Wyatt Earps."

"You meet any movie stars over in Miami, Paul?" Ridder asked.

"I ran across a few."

"I hate to mention it—doubt it would be an issue for you, Cabrera," Dutch said, "but any officer found seeking an autograph while on duty will be put on suspension."

Paul ran his fingers beneath his jaw, feeling fine stubble from a short night of sleep and a long drive yesterday. "I've been getting the impression the town is real interested in celebrities."

"We have our share of them visiting here. It makes life less ordinary when you see them up close." Dutch's face was work-hardened, but a smile overtook his features. "You know that big actor in those commando movies? His private wedding ceremony at an 'undisclosed location' was here. Reporters fell over themselves trying to track it down, but we kept the whole thing tight-lipped. He was a helluva nice guy."

Ridder chimed in. "He thanked each of us with a bottle of Chivas Regal and Cuban cigars."

"We have a chopper in case we need to aid the mountain rescue," Dutch said. "The department doesn't own it—John Bob Nedermeyer does and he lets us use it whenever we have an emergency that needs aerial help."

"Ever watch *Magnum P.I.*, Cabrera?" Griswold asked.

"A time or two."

"Nedermeyer bought the helicopter off the set when the series got the ax. It's the Island Hopper and it's still painted with red, yellow and black stripes. What's that guy's name again who owned it on the show?"

"T.C.," Dutch and Ridder replied in unison.

A grin widened Griswold's mouth beneath the fringe of his mustache. "This is going to be a change for you, Cabrera."

"I'm ready for it."

"Hell, it won't be that different from Miami," Dutch remarked with a shake of his head. "We've got crime. Did you boys read the log I left last night? Another robbery strike at a Montrose jewelry store. They're calling him a serial thief now and neighboring counties are to be on alert. The glass display case doesn't stop him from getting what he wants. He's a slam and grab son of a bitch."

"Did you catch that car stereo runner last night?" Paul asked, taking a drink of coffee.

"Got him behind the bowling alley. I entered Prescott's Bose stereo into the evidence room. She can come and get it. Same goes for her Blazer. Unless she's having Earl at the auto shop put a new window in it first." He slumped lower into his seat, the vinyl creaking. "I wanted her out of here first thing this morning. Dammit if that job of hers didn't fall through. Now she's stuck in Majestic."

"I didn't know that," Ridder mused aloud. "When did that happen?"

Dutch's eyes sharpened. "Yesterday sometime."

"Geez, she seemed fine at the party last night."

Griswold folded his arms. "I thought she was looking might-t-fine."

"Never seen her in a dress before," Ridder commented with his lips together. "Well, hell—this is unfortunate for her…and for us, if you get my drift. You aren't going to hire her back, are you, Dutch?"

"Not a chance."

Paul opted not to mention Lanic's broken leg. It was her business and she'd handle it her own way. However, he did find it odd that the deputies seemed to be brushing her off so quickly. And the chief's unflinching adamance about not rehiring was puzzling. She had gone on about not getting along with Dutch. There was more to the story, but he wasn't going to ask.

Dutch continued his verbal tour of the Majestic PD. Its history was as colorful as the mountains. In the sixties, Chief Jeb E. Scanlon hung himself in a jail cell over lady trouble. And 1979 marked the year the former mayor was charged with two misdemeanors for accepting Super Bowl tickets from a company that did business with the city. Arresting somebody they'd voted for had been tough for those officers. But their reservations disappeared when they discovered he'd been growing some serious marijuana in his basement. Most residents changed from being Democrats to Republicans because of the scandal that year.

"How long have you been with the department?" Paul asked Dutch.

"About five years now. I took over for Chief Ray Prescott."

Paul's interest was pulled. "Prescott?"

Ridder's voice lowered to a respectful tone. "Lanie Prescott's father was our chief until he was killed when a robbery went sour. During a foot pursuit the suspect shot him rather than surrender his weapon. There were a lot of dark clouds hanging over the PD and the Prescott family. Lanie didn't do so well for a long time afterward."

Rarely did something knock Paul off guard. This news did. Why exactly, he couldn't pinpoint. The worst thing to happen in a department was losing one of their officers in the line of duty. The officers were like family and morale was a difficult thing to repair.

"I hate to be the one to say it," Gordon Griswold professed, tilting his head and slanting a look at everyone sitting around the table, "but it's going to be a big relief not having Lanie working for us." Nods went around the table. "We had to watch her back every time she was on call."

Deputy Ridder added, "You won't understand this, Cabrera, but we shadowed her because she was part of our family. None of us could forgive ourselves if something happened to Ray's daughter."

Quietly Paul asked, "Did they get the guy who shot Prescott?"

"Oh, yeah," Griswold said, his reply gritty. "Ridder got the son of a bitch."

Staring into the oily black depths of his coffee, the cords in Delroy Ridder's neck muscles grew taut as a stressed rope. "Damn right...damn right. Yeah, it was a bad time."

Even Dutch seemed to soften. "Nobody likes to hand over a flag. It tears your heart out. Glad I never had to do it and I don't want to start here with any of you bastards. Watch your backs. Watch your fronts. Don't let the three Bs get you into trouble. Booze, broads and bookies."

A lightness came back into Deputy Ridder's eyes. "Did you have the three Bs in Miami, Cabrera?"

Paul momentarily lost himself in his own reveries, then pulled out of them. "We had the three Ms."

Dutch questioned, "The Scotch tape company?"

"Models, moguls and movie stars."

Ridder tested the top of the salt shaker, twisting to make sure it was on tight. "Hey, did you know Don Johnson?"

"*Miami Vice* was canceled when I got hired." Paul rested his arm on the padded back of the booth. "But I encountered wise guys making more a week than I made in a year."

"I hope you got your rental lined up like I suggested, Cabrera," Dutch said. "This town floods with tourists in the summer and vacancies are scarce."

Paul had left his furniture and most of his belongings in a Miami storage facility. He didn't need much because the house he had rented here came fully furnished. "I'm good." Paul slid his silverware and napkin out of the way when the waitress came to the table balancing four plates on her arm. "I'm headed over there after we eat."

The group then fell quiet as catsup bottles were smacked, salt and pepper was shaken out and toast was jellied.

While Colorado might not feel like home yet, its western setting inspired Paul to eat steak and eggs for breakfast instead of an energy bar.

After all, he was a lawman of the Wild West now.

Lanie reclined on her mother's sofa, leg propped on a bed of pillows. The television remote was within reaching distance along with her last bag of M&M's. A bowl of soda crackers and a can of lemon-lime with a straw sat on the coffee table.

She didn't know which was worse. The pain or the upset stomach she got from taking the pain pills.

At seven o'clock this morning she had called the local property rental offices and reached their recording. The realty manager wasn't in on Sunday, but an agent was there giving out keys and location maps. Lanie left a message to say she had to speak with someone who could get hold of her renter right away—she needed her house back to recover from an injury. But after taking one of her pills, Lanie had fallen back to sleep and soon it was after eleven.

So much for getting a jump on the day.

She dialed again and was put on hold as soon as the line connected.

This was the first time Lanie had ever arranged to rent out her property. Historic Majestic advertised seasonal lodgings in magazines and an agency handled the transactions, running credit checks and collecting payments. Many of the locals had second homes elsewhere and the rental arrangements were a lucrative business practice for seniors who preferred to winter in the warm climate of Arizona.

Lanie felt badly for her renter, but she'd be laid up for months and she needed her house back to recuperate. Surely alternate accommodations could be found for them.

The agent came on and listened to Lanie's story. While she was very sympathetic, she told her she was sorry but she'd given out the key already. There were no available rentals for June—the town was booked. But she'd see what she could do and get back to her. So, in other words, the tenants would be taking possession today as planned.

On that bleak note, Lanie called the Ludlow apartment manager and was met with more of the same discouraging news. She was looking at eight weeks before a drastically reduced refund check would arrive in the mailbox.

The truth was, she couldn't afford to reimburse her renter even if she could get them to cancel. The sizable deposit had gone toward her deposit on the Ludlow apartment—which was now on hold.

Lanie closed her eyes and reconciled herself to the inevitable. Her life had no butter to stick to her bread. In spite of her attempts to get ahead, she'd only succeeded in being jobless, homeless and stuck in a leg cast.

Her mom came into the living room.

"Are you sure you'll be all right alone?" she asked, her purse looped in the crook of her arm.

"I'll be fine. You should enjoy your Sunday."

It was her mom's Sunday ritual to attend church, then hit every yard sale within a five-mile radius. She'd forgone those plans today in order to take care of Lanie and run to the store.

"I'll enjoy next Sunday. There's a bazaar planned at the community center."

If there was something that could be handmade rather than purchased, Lucille Prescott made it. Curtains, doilies and throw rugs. Stenciled or stamped greeting cards and one-of-a-kind objects she revamped from tag sales—such as the vase with the beads glue-gunned onto it. She was a therapeutic crafter. Constructing things with her hands had been what got her through her grief when Dad died. Fruit fragrance votives and Victorian-theme welcome plaques, detailed silk embroidery work on her eyeglasses case and the crocheted hearth and home mantel scarf—these homespun items decorated each room in her house.

"How are you feeling, sweetie?"

"Lousy."

Lanie relayed the news she'd just received from her two phone calls.

Her mom leaned closer, makeup beautifully applied and her clothes a perfect shade of milky plum. "Things can only can get better from lousy."

Lucille offered her the candy bag. Lanie took it. Chocolate was as good a consolation as anything.

"I'm so sorry about everything." Her mom smiled softly. "The job delay and the leg. For selfish reasons I wanted you to stay here, but you had to follow your dreams. Oh, Lanie, when you told me about the phone call, my heart broke for you."

"I know it did."

"I'm going to talk to Haskell Ehrlich at the next swim class. He's a lawyer. Let's see if we can sue that police department for false promises." Her mom poked a finger into one of the many violet plants shelved on the baker's rack. Positioned by the front window, the flowers thrived. Vases filled with flowers from the party were on the top shelf. "Things might have you feeling down right now, but you've got me and you can stay here as long as you need."

Lanie tore the brown bag open and poured a handful of candy-coated chocolates into her hand. "Later today can you help me figure out how to notify everyone about my change in plans?"

"You won't have to do that. I talked with Cookie Baumgarten this morning and told her everything. By now the whole town knows. She said for you to keep the pen she gave you. She wants you to have it as a get-well pick-me-up. Myrtle Sanders called three minutes later—I told you Cookie works fast—and said the same thing about her teddy bear."

"That was nice of them."

Lucille headed for the front door. "While I'm at the Pay and Pack, is there anything else you need beside the orange, cherry and grape Popsicles and the nausea relief prescription?"

"Grab this week's television guide and every tabloid at the checkout stand."

"Lanie, why do you want that trash?"

"Because reading about a housewife who finds an alien's mummified head in her husband's bowling bag might make me laugh."

"All right. I'll buy the silly things. Do you have to use the bathroom before I leave?"

Cringing, Lanie replied, "No."

Being thirty-three years old and requiring assistance getting into the bathroom was something she couldn't avoid. Tackling the stairs and lugging the cast with her was bad enough.

Checking her grocery list, her mom said, "I shouldn't be long unless I'm tempted by a sign that says a yard sale is around the corner. I would only drive by, I promise. I won't get out of the car. And I'm only leaving you because you said Sherry is coming over. In case you need something, have me paged at the store."

"I'm not going anywhere," Lanie stated grimly.

Alone in the house, she nibbled on crackers and watched a soap opera re-run she hadn't caught since college. The lead vixen heroine looked exactly the same; she hadn't aged.

Dozing off into a light sleep, Lanie woke when she heard a noise coming from next door.

Lanie and her mother lived in a double residence. The five-thousand-square-foot Queen Anne had been built at the turn of the century. An unbroken common wall joined the interiors. Intricate exterior architecture created the look of a single house. There were two separate verandas and front doors, and each house had the same three-story floor plan.

The first floor came with a kitchen, dining room and a parlor used as a living room. Beneath the kitchen was a concrete floor cellar and basement laundry. The second floor held one larger bedroom and three smaller. Only one bathroom, the fixtures original, located off the main bedroom, serviced the entire house. On the third floor was an attic for storage.

Not long after Lanie moved in, she had urged her mom to buy the other half of the double residence when it came on the market. The house Lucille had shared with Ray Prescott had too many memories in it that Mom couldn't face without Dad at her side. Ending up being here and starting a home business had been her saving grace. She jarred blackberry jellies and sold them to the curio shop in artist's alley on East Filbert Street.

The sound came again. Sherry was supposed to drop by, but the kids might have had something planned that she had to go to first. Besides, if it were Sherry outside, she'd have come in by now.

Then the wall muffled a soft reverberation of pipes, as if someone was in her kitchen turning on the faucets.

It had to be her renters.

Lanie listened, wondering what else they were doing. This was too strange to be lying here when somebody was in her house, sitting on her sofa and testing her bed. Thoughts like that hadn't crossed her mind until this minute. She'd been too busy thinking about her furnished apartment and making it her home to worry about what would be going on in hers.

Getting up to greet them was out of the question. She couldn't move her leg off the sofa without help. Each step with her crutches was like fiery shards exploding in her leg. The doctor had said if she kept her leg elevated for the first forty-eight hours to keep the swelling down, she'd heal faster. She planned on following his advice to the letter.

But that didn't prevent her curiosity from besting her intentions. The bay windows in the dining room were open to let in a cross breeze and if she turned her head far enough she could see out of them. The span of veranda was empty.

Her front door closed and she heard a key turning in

the lock. Good, whoever it was had the presence of mind to secure the house before leaving.

As she twisted her upper body to angle for a better view, the bottom of her blanket knocked the empty soft drink can off the coffee table. Distracted, her gaze strayed from the window as the can rolled over the hardwood floor with a tinny sound.

It grew quiet outside. The renters must have walked past and down the veranda steps. She never saw them. Somewhere down the block, a lawn mower started. Then children rode by on bicycles, their laughter abandoned and animated.

Lanie sensed someone had approached her mom's door, but no knock followed.

Gooseflesh rose on Lanie's skin. She was a sitting duck for a lurker if they decided to peek in the windows and...

...and what?

She fumbled for the cordless, thumb on the 9 button just in case.

A knock came and Lanie all but jumped off the sofa.

"Hello?" she said. "Who's there?"

"Paul Cabrera."

Cabrera.

He'd been beside her like a shadow last night, touching, holding and helping. When he carried her to his car, he smelled too good to describe. She had been weak and clung to the strength he offered as if to suck his energy into her broken spirit. The man had an amazing gentleness.

"Come in," she said, then remembered she'd barely managed to brush her teeth and wash her face this morning because she couldn't tolerate being upright very long. Sleeping flat on the sofa gave her bed-head.

Uneven pieces of hair stuck out of her scrunch even though she'd smoothed them into a lumpy ponytail.

Paul stood over her and smiled—a smile that was too good-looking to be staring down at her when she was at her worst. Brown eyes gazed at her and she felt as though she was drowning from too much chocolate.

Last night she'd been too busy organizing her own agenda to dwell on his chiseled features or the way he held her shoes looped through two fingers.

Well, maybe once or twice she'd thought about him.

Sunglasses hung from his shirt pocket, faded jeans molded his legs and he wore leather flip-flops. His feet were nice with a smooth, tan appearance.

"Mornin'," he said, his voice smooth and Southern. She knew now it came from Florida.

"Good morning."

"How's the leg?"

"What do you think?" Being sarcastic wasn't like her and she hated its bitterness in her mouth; but biting humor seemed to be the only way she could handle herself without crying—something she rarely did.

"I think somebody needs a nap," Paul replied in response. He picked up her pop can and set it back on the coffee table. "When I saw you on the grass last night, I thought I might have had a two-eighteen."

"Did I look like a corpse code?"

"Not in the bar—you looked real good."

The roots of her hair tingled from the flattery and she flushed.

Staving off the heat, she asked, "Did you see somebody at my house just now?"

"Yeah."

"Who was it? A couple?"

"No. A single person."

"Male or female?"

"Male."

"A guy rented it..." She caught her lower lip with her teeth. "Did he look normal?"

"Normal?" His dark eyebrow lifted. "I don't know."

"I wish I could have seen him. It's my house he's renting. This is a double residence."

"I figured that out. So who lives here?"

"My mom."

The expression on his face changed—like he knew something she didn't—and wouldn't want to know anyway. Not a good sign after their conversation at the steakhouse. After he'd figured out that he was her replacement, he neglected to mention it while she had been busy putting gold chains on him.

Paul Cabrera may have come to her aid when she was down, but he was the same man who assumed she was a dispatch operator because she said she was in law enforcement. His conclusion that she was more suited to answering 911 calls bothered her.

"I've been wondering about something, Lieutenant." That much she knew about him from Dutch when he announced he'd snagged a Miami-Dade lieutenant with a thirteen-year exemplary record for her deputy spot. "Just why would you take a demotion to come to Colorado?"

Among the fine-handcrafted Victorian furniture in her mom's living room, his exaggerated masculine form was out of place. He exuded more sex appeal than an underwear commercial.

"What makes you think I took a demotion?"

"Because you're a lieutenant stepping down to a deputy."

Without being patronizing, he said, "Lanie, I was hired on as a chief-deputy."

A hitch stopped her pulse from beating, only for a second, before she recovered. "There is no chief-deputy position."

"There is now."

He wasn't joking. This was real. Cabrera had received a promotion. All she'd been allowed to do was ticket parked cars and he was elevated in stature for doing nothing. She realized she didn't have the experience like he did, but who was to say she was less qualified?

The embarrassment of breaking her leg was the blatant answer.

How many years working for Dutch had she waited for an apprehend situation to fall into her lap so she could prove herself? Then when it did, heeled shoes had defeated her efforts. She'd never let herself live the failure down.

It wasn't Cabrera's fault he was being rewarded while she was laid up without prospects. But accepting his promotion didn't ease the sting of salt in the wound. The information was yet another reason to think even less of Chief Herb Deutsch and his narrow-minded, flat-skulled justification. If ever Hollywood opted to remake *King Kong,* Dutch would be the perfect gorilla.

She stoically gazed at Paul, her mouth flat. "I think I will take a nap."

He went toward the door, but paused before leaving. "You should be aware of something before I go."

She didn't know if she could take knowing anything else that would make her feel bad. "What?"

Had his back not been to her, she would have seen the irony curving his smile. "I'm your renter."

Five

Herb Deutsch's childhood and most of his adult life, for all intents and purposes, had been uneventful. He grew up in the midwest, a farm-bred son of a police officer in the town of Mill, Illinois. After he was born, his parents were unable to conceive a second child. Doted upon felt like a good way to describe how he was treated as a boy. He was the apple of his parents' eyes.

His mother never worked outside the home a day in her life. She got pleasure from taking care of his father and him. Nightly hot meals were dished up on plates and brought to the table awaiting their praises. Dirty clothes were washed and ironed without them ever noticing they'd been missing from the closet. No dust marred the furniture and the floors gleamed with fresh wax. Groceries were bought and stored with neat precision. Never once did Minerva Deutsch complain about her household duties.

In return, Herb's father provided them with a middle-class lifestyle in a modest two-bedroom, one bath home with a single car garage kept in good order—no carport for the Deutsches. He always filled the gas tank on the Buick so his mother wouldn't have to soil her hands at the filling station. Any time something needed fixing, his father knew how to make the repairs whether it was a kitchen mixer or the transistor radio.

Ralph Deutsch handled the yard work except for the flowerbeds which he felt required a woman's touch. Every year to commemorate their wedding anniversary and his wife's birthday, he brought Minerva a dozen roses and a box of chocolates.

His father didn't much talk about the job on his off time. Ralph pulled the car into the garage and left the daily hardships of being a police officer with the paint cans, carburetor cleaner and other compounds that smelled metallic and pungent. It was almost as if the door's threshold marking the inside of the house and the outside world were an invisible line.

In short, he didn't bring garbage into the house.

To Dutch's way of thinking, the strong values he inherited from his German family were the ideal way to mold his own life.

When he graduated from high school, he didn't question what his path would be. After a run in the Navy and Coast Guard he settled down with his sweetheart, June. Police work was what the Deutsches did. His grandfather had been a police officer, and before that, his great-grandfather served as a Chief Constable with the Munich Police.

Dutch's marriage ended after seventeen years. Simply: His wife left him. While he didn't discuss his divorce with people, the failure did bristle. And hurt. But he dealt with it.

He'd been single for twelve years and had managed on his own. From his mother, he'd observed enough domestic skills to survive. He didn't care for laundry so he sent it out for washing and ironing. His uniform was taken to the dry cleaners for precise pressing. Since he wasn't too keen on picking up after himself, he had a woman come by once a week to clean the house.

One aspect of the bachelor's life where he did shine was probably the most unexpected.

Dutch enjoyed cooking.

His foray into culinary expertise happened out of necessity. His physician told him all the fatty breakfasts he was packing away at Rooster's Place, not to mention the donuts at the station, were going to give him a heart attack faster than a speeding cholesterol bullet. Scared about jeopardizing his health, he went to the Pay and Pack Grocery Mart and bought every variety of lean frozen meals and stocked his freezer with them.

His first sampling of chicken enchiladas gave him bad heartburn. He realized after the first bite, that to make up for the lack of abundant cheese and meat in the little microwaveable tray, the manufacturer had pumped in the spices—especially those with some fiery kick. His next few meals met with the same result as the enchiladas—a trip down the garbage disposal.

One day after work he couldn't face another convenience supper, so out of desperation he opened a can of soup and sat down to eat it in front of the television. Bowl of soup on the television tray, he waited for the steaming vegetables to cool off while surfing through the channels. An act of fate must have intervened for he stumbled upon Betty Porter's *Cooking For Life* show and watched it instead of the football game.

As he ate, he watched her fix a well-rounded meal. A roasted herb chicken, light-whipped mashed potatoes, caramelized carrots and baked apples for dessert. Instantly, his mouth watered at the beautiful presentation of food. He grew even more interested when she added the calories and nutrients of the entire meal and saw they were where he needed to be.

For the first time in his life, he saw that if a willing person took their time in the kitchen and had a plan, a nice meal could be the result. The next day he came home and tuned in Betty Porter again. As she began cooking he was ready with a pad and paper. He wrote down the recipes for the day's menu and drove to a grocery in Montrose to buy the ingredients and stock up on foods. He didn't need anyone in Majestic asking questions about what he needed Italian parsley for.

The life-changing decision to cook for himself had happened nearly six months ago.

He had all of Betty's cookbooks—ordered online to keep the transaction private from the town's only bookstore where gossip could fly off the shelves faster than new releases. He didn't want to be known as the chef rather than the chief—so he preferred to keep a low profile when it came to his culinary skills.

He still watched Betty's show when he had the opportunity and he could now cook any recipe he set his mind to. All the bachelors out there who said cooking was for pussies just couldn't cut the mustard in the kitchen.

Dutch sat down in his recliner and flipped on the set to watch Betty Porter—the only woman on the tube to divert his attention from his collection of John Wayne movies.

Betty came on clearly and her voice was smooth as bourbon. He liked her hair. He liked her skin. He liked her humor. Much like another woman in town who— hell, he wouldn't go there right now. Betty was whipping up a three-bean salad.

Several cars passed by his window as he watched the program.

Dutch lived on East Filbert Street, a part of town that was residential with a mix of commercial. Some turn-of-the-century homes were converted into small businesses. There was the Calico Corner that sold ladies' bric-a-brac—all that homespun craft decor that irritated him. Give him plain and simple, sensible and sturdiness when it came to home decorating. The Music Store sold instruments and tutored in the playing of them. On a warm night it was a little torturous when the windows were thrown open and Tommy Baxter's trumpet playing drifted over. Then there was Cookie Cutter's beauty parlor which was directly across from his front lawn. Sometimes he had to give the ladies warnings not to block his driveway with their automobiles.

Recently he'd taken more than a passing interest in their activities. He had a front-row view of who came and went. He wasn't getting any younger and he thought about remarrying. For a time, he'd seen a woman over in Montrose to grease the wheel, but they'd broken things off last winter.

One of Majestic's Explorers drove by going through town—Lanie Prescott's old unit with Paul Cabrera behind the wheel. That Paul was one kick-butt cop with an impressive record, and Dutch was damn glad to have him on board. Not saying that Prescott was an inferior officer. She had served her time well as the meter maid and in other assorted positions that she was better equipped to handle than his men.

He'd never been able to make her see his reason— men are physically stronger than women. Women were, by all accounts, the weaker sex and Prescott should have been thankful he kept her from situations where she may have needed to draw her weapon and could possibly have been hurt.

As the Explorer disappeared, he further ruminated that Prescott thought he was a prick. She focused too much on how he didn't behave toward her than how he did. He'd bet his service revolver she never realized he'd always held a door open for her, pulled out a chair when she needed one, and paid her portion of the breakfast bill at Rooster's Place when she left the rest of their group in a hurry to go ticket a car with an expired meter.

Her being out of commission stayed on his mind more than it ought to. He felt badly for her situation, but there was nothing he could do.

Movement outside caught his attention while Betty Porter chirped about mixing olive oil into beans. An instinctive awareness flared inside Dutch and he switched the TV to mute. He shot to his feet, the recliner thumping into the wall as he stuck his fingers into the blinds, separating them to get an unobstructed view.

Parallel parking in front of Cookie Cutter's a white Eldorado gleamed like strands of fine cultured pearls. The pearl who drove the Caddy stepped out wearing ivory slacks and a matching color blouse, her hair styled in a crown of golden curls. With a black handbag strap riding on her shoulder she walked inside and his heart didn't quit pumping in a code nineteen pulse for seconds after she'd disappeared.

His right eye ticked with a sudden case of anxiousness while his whole being focused on the beauty parlor hoping for another glimpse of the pearl. He caught a tease of warm blond hair as she moved past the window. Then she was gone.

Dutch's mouth went dry.

Lucille Prescott was getting her hair done.

Six

In the week since starting with the Majestic PD, Paul had learned that the gas station had two pumps and both were full service. The police weren't required to pay; arrangements were made for their bills to be sent on a monthly basis to the station. Lloyd's Dry Cleaners cleaned their uniforms at twenty-five percent off, and if he wanted a good donut and a decent cup of joe, Sissy's was the place to go.

Riding in a marked street unit was like starting over with the basics and the Ford Explorer gave him solid ground. He knew what he had to do and he slid into his new job in a seamless manner.

Paul learned the department had several repeat callers, but none more regular than Ben Hermann who had a ranch off Milepost Forty-Four. Every day he called in a coyote alert at two in the morning. There had never been one found in the culvert; he was just lonely for company. He always asked the responding officer to bring a can of tuna for his cat. Fancy albacore and not the bargain brand. Miami and Majestic truly were worlds apart.

By choice, he'd been working mostly graveyards, but Dutch had him on the day shift today.

Lights flashing, but without the wail of the siren, Paul was en route to a minor traffic accident on the corner of Grove Street and Lazy River Road. Arriving at the scene he noted the two vehicles involved: a compact coupe and a midsize SUV were both were pulled over at the curb. Two women waited for him on the sidewalk.

He lowered the volume on his radio as he walked in their direction. After plainclothes duty, being back in full uniform with a heavily equipped holster took some getting used to. Just like the markedly different elevation that was still affecting him. He felt as if he was constantly fighting for breath. When he ran or climbed stairs, his chest constricted as if a cinder block crushed the air from his lungs.

"Ladies, what happened this afternoon?"

"I'm Sherry. She rear-ended me." The woman was petite and dark-haired. She had two children with her, a son and daughter with a noticeable gap in their ages. The little girl was wary about his appearance, as if her mommy were in trouble with the police.

"It's my fault, Officer," the other woman confessed; her green eyes brightened appreciatively as she swept her gaze over him. "All my fault." Her voice was low and purposefully seductive and her long auburn hair looked to be natural. She dressed in contemporary uptown clothes, the kind of styles displayed in Ocean Boulevard boutiques. "Honestly, Officer, I only looked away for a second when I was dialing on my cell phone."

The SUV hadn't sustained any rear bumper damage, but the coupe's grill looked as if it would require some serious bucks for cosmetic repairs.

"I need your drivers' licenses and insurance information."

As the women dug through purses, he smiled at the

little girl. "Hey, darlin', are you hurt? Tummy? Your head?"

She shook her head. Her big brown eyes were fringed with extra-long lashes. Baby-fine brown hair was swept up into two pigtails, and she wore a polka-dotted pink-and-white dress with white sandals.

Crouching, he gave her a smile. "What's your name?"

"Hailey."

"How old are you?"

"Thwee. My brother is twelve."

"Is that your brother?"

"Yes."

"What's his name?"

"Poop-head."

Paul grinned. "What does Mommy call him?"

"Mawk-you're-in-twubble-again." She wrinkled her nose, lips pouty. "Are you gonna take my mommy to jail?"

"No. Hey, Mark," he called to the boy who was jumping off the curb retainers imitating a snowboard maneuver. The answer seemed obvious, but Paul had to ask, "Are you hurt anywhere?"

"Are we almost done?" The boy's light brown hair was on the shaggy side and both his forearms were marked with scabs—probably from encounters with the pavement. "I wanna ride my skateboard."

"It won't take too long." Paul wrote up an on-site report, taking down the ladies' names and an account of the accident.

The sophisticated redhead, Raine Ithaca, gave him a flirtatious smile that said she'd love to have a drink—and something more—with him. "Do you like modern art?"

"It depends on what I'm looking at."

"I have more than enough for you to look at. I own a gallery that has wonderful one-of-a-kind-pieces." With nicely manicured fingers, she shoved her card into his hand. He tucked it into his shirt pocket without reading the inscription. "It would be my *pleasure* to show you around personally."

"I'll keep that in mind."

Sherry shot Raine a disapproving glare, and Paul had a hunch it had more to do with warning the other woman to back off rather than agitation due to the accident.

"So how will this work since it was her fault and not mine?" Sherry inquired. "I don't want to have to pay for her mistake. My husband would kill me."

Hearing that phrase out of a woman's mouth, no matter how flippantly innocent, never ceased to disturb Paul. He'd seen the prediction come true before and had testified in trials on behalf of deceased wives.

"You won't have to," Paul clarified, "since my report shows Ms.—"

"*Miss*," Raine jumped in to correct.

"—Miss Ithaca is admitting blame."

"I always own up for everything I do." She lowered her voice to a husky purr. "Good, bad *and* naughty."

Sherry rolled her eyes, then told her son to quit fooling around or he'd crack his skull. Hailey clung to her mom's leg and continued to stare at Paul with skepticism.

Raine's cell phone rang and she fielded the call. While talking, she gestured questioningly toward Paul to ask if she was free to go. He gave her the affirmative, and before she got back into her car, she sent him a wink and pointed to his pocket where her card was hidden inside.

When Raine Ithaca drove away, Paul turned to Hailey.

"I have something for you," he said, then went to the backseat of his unit and picked out one of the stuffed animals from a box. Early on in the DC Unit he'd started this practice. A scared child who just had a dad taken away in handcuffs while Mom's injuries were being assessed by the EMTs needed something friendly to cling to.

He picked a pink bunny with soft fur and satin feet. Presenting it to Hailey, he suggested, "This one needs a good home and a name. What do you think?"

Cradling the bunny, she peeked shyly at him through the ears. "I like Bawbie."

"Barbie the Bunny. That sounds good."

She beamed and extended her arms to show Sherry.

"What do you say, Hailey?"

"Thank you."

Mark hopped off the curb, bounced over the pavement in a three-hundred-and-sixty-degree body spin, landing on the other side of the street, all the while commentating on his technique. "He rotates, he's got the degree of difficulty, and he nails the lip trick!"

"Mark, get out of the street and back into the car. We're leaving."

"Yes!" he cheered with a fist. "I'm riding my skateboard as soon as we get there."

"That's fine." Sherry strapped Hailey into a toddler seat, then closed the door. Resting her hand on the window she said, with a friendly curve to her lips, "You live next door to my friend, Lanie Prescott. Actually, you're living in her house. How are you liking Majestic?''

"I like it."

"Have you been seeing much of anything…or anyone…since you got to town?''

"I've been pretty busy."

"All work and no play," she said with a transparent hint.

Paul took her advice with a smile. "I'll remember that."

Sherry held on to her car keys, visibly hedging, then questioned, "Are you interested in contemporary art?"

Holding back the amused rumble that caught in his throat, he replied, "I don't have any room on my walls right now to hang anything."

She responded quickly. "Then you won't be visiting the gallery?"

"I don't have any plans to."

"How about any other…galleries or homes…in town?''

He returned her licence and insurance card. "Drive safely, ma'am."

"I always do." And with that Sherry took off in her SUV.

As Paul watched her drive away he realized he could have nailed her for speeding.

"Raine Ithaca rear-ended me just so she could check out your hunky replacement and throw herself—and her phone number—at him! It wasn't too smart on her part since she drives a small import. I'll bet she's looking at five hundred to fix the damage. My SUV doesn't have a scratch on it."

Sherry's observation was spoken as she came

through Lucille's front door with Hailey, while the clacking of Mark's skateboard could be heard rolling over sidewalk cracks out front.

"Are you and the kids all right?" Lanie asked.

"We're fine."

"I gots this." Hailey showed her a pink bunny.

"Very cute."

Lanie sat on the sofa with her leg propped up on the coffee table. Cardboard boxes labeled with various identifying words for her personal belongings were arranged against the walls. The moving trailer had been unloaded on Monday by the deputies and her things were stacked throughout her mom's house.

Seven days of rest had helped improve her navigational skills on the crutches, and her discomfort was more controlled, but an unfamiliar bed in her mom's guest room hadn't given her a good night's sleep. Oftentimes at home she slept on her couch. She missed the ivory brocade, and its coziness that was too inviting to leave. After unsealing her "favorites" box, she found her mocha throw and used that to keep her toes warm.

An unplanned thought rushed through her mind: Is Cabrera sleeping on my sofa and laying his head on my pillow?

Giving Sherry a cursory glance, Lanie said, "So you met my neighbor."

"I thought when I saw him I'd be snippy to him for getting your job—with a promotion to boot. God help me, I couldn't do it. He's gorgeous. One look into those eyes of his and you forget your own name, never mind being pissed off over the injustice."

Lanie half smiled. "I'm glad you didn't let him go to your head."

"He's not in my head, but Raine Ithaca practically threw her bra at him. It was disgusting. I think you should strike while you've got exclusive territory on the veranda and he's only ten feet away," she hastened to add.

"You've got to be kidding."

Hailey stuffed her bunny beneath her dress, then popped it out with a swish of her hand. "Mommy, how do babies get in your tummy?"

"The timing is perfect while you're laid up," Sherry reasoned, leaving her daughter without an answer. "I think we should sit outside and wait for him to come home. I'll make lemonade and we'll offer him an ice-cold glass. The man needs some Southern comforting so he's not homesick, and lemonade is just the thing."

"Mommy, how do babies get in your tummy?" The bunny hid again, then "presto," was born once more.

"I think the lemonade is a bad idea," Lanie said as if she were serious. "Mint juleps are better. See if my mom has any Kentucky bourbon hiding in the pantry."

"I didn't know your mom drank hard liquor."

"She doesn't. Sherry, *I'm kidding.*"

Sherry's mouth opened and she heaved a sigh. "I'm not. I manipulated the conversation and found out he's not seeing anyone. But you need to act fast because he won't be single for long."

"Is this my oldest and best friend talking? Are you crazy? You want me to hook up with the guy?"

"Absolutely. He's delicious. It's about time you found a man and let your hair out of that ponytail."

Tugging on Sherry's blouse hem, Hailey said, "*Mom-eee!* How does a baby get into your tummy?"

"It usually happens when Mommy has her guard

down from Daddy,'' Sherry hastily explained with a wry hook to her lips.

Hailey giggled. "Mommy, you're silly."

Lanie motioned to her mom's craft cabinet. "Hailey, on the bottom shelf there are some crayons and paper. Do you want to draw me a picture?"

"Uh-huh."

"I'm not letting you off the hook," Sherry said, flopping into one of the chairs. "What do you *really* think of him?"

"I don't have an opinion."

"Liar."

Lanie laughed. "Okay, fine. If he'd been a rafting instructor I would like him a whole lot better. And, yes, I know that the women in this town are after him. I sit here all day and I've counted at least a dozen cars driving by with gawking faces looking at my house in the hopes he'll step outside. Ridder said the station's been flooded with pies, cakes and cookies for him. And three days ago, dispatch answered the non-emergency line and sent him to Cookie Cutter's beauty salon to settle a dispute over which one of their stylists got to set and tease a Dolly Parton wig. It was all a sham—they just wanted to shampoo his hair."

Sherry's eyes widened with humor and she covered her mouth with her hand. "Oh my God, you're kidding me!"

"I wish I was. It's pathetic. Just as pathetic as I am." Lanie blew her bangs off her forehead. "I have hit rock bottom. At the age of thirty-three, I am once again living at home with my mother."

"At least she's a nice mother." Sherry nibbled on popcorn that sat in a bowl on the coffee table. Chewing thoughtfully, she said, "On the bright side—the only way you can go from here is up."

"That's exactly right. I'm not going to take this lying down. Literally or figuratively. I sent three applications to three other departments. I have to mend well enough to enroll in Lateral Recruit training, but I need to get things moving now."

"That's good." Sherry's answer was positive, but her smile was regretful. "I wish you could get back on with the Majestic PD."

"It's not going to happen."

"Lan-*eee*, can I dwaw a pixture on your leg?"

"Sure, sweetie."

Hailey colored streaks of blue and purple near Ridder, Griswold and Coyote's signatures on her cast. They'd signed it before taking the moving trailer back to the rental yard.

Lucille came into the house through the kitchen door. She'd been at the nursery and carried a new pair of gardening gloves and hand trowel. Setting them on the counter, she said, "Hi, Sherry."

Hailey ran up to her, arms wide.

"Sweetpea!" Lucille scooped her up and planted a kiss on her cheek.

Giggling, she asked, "LuLu, how do babies get in your tummy?"

Lucille's finely shaped brows arched. "Ask your mommy."

Hailey wiggled free and continued coloring on Lanie's leg.

Entering the living room, her mom said, "I saw Herb Deutsch at the nursery just now."

Lanie replied blandly, "I'm sorry."

"He was buying a new dogwood tree." Lucille straightened the classified ads Lanie had spread out on the couch. "It seems like whenever I leave the beauty parlor he's always in his front yard overwatering his dogwood tree. It finally yellowed and died. He says hello, by the way."

"Excuse me?"

"He says hello and he hopes you're recovering nicely."

Lanie found that difficult to believe.

"I told him you were doing fine, but could use some work. I said if he hears of anything to let us know."

"You didn't!"

"I've mentioned all over town that you're available for light jobs that can be done from the house." Her mom placed hands on her hips and addressed the glower Lanie sent. "I never would have said anything if you hadn't insisted you wanted to earn your own keep while you're recuperating."

"You're right, Mom. I'm sorry." She truly was, because she couldn't lie here and stay idle. It was making her crazy. "It's just that asking Dutch is like getting an apple in my trick-or-treat bag—I'd need to X-ray it and see if there's a razor inside before I take a bite."

"I thought he was very pleasant and he really meant it. In fact, he was bending over backward to be solicitous like he was..." A faraway look came into her eyes, similar to the look she had when she watched a William Holden movie. With a few blinks, her mom's expression cleared. "I'm going to be in the backyard if you need me. I bought a flat of pansies."

Sherry and the kids left soon after and the breeze filtering in from the window screen was so heavenly, Lanie had to sit outside and enjoy it.

She slipped out the front door and held the wood-framed screen open with her crutch. Stepping onto the sunny porch, she reveled in the change of scenery. The day was glorious. Painted with swaths of blue, the sky was vast and the air warm, but not uncomfortable. Jet sprinklers watered a lawn across the street. Cardinals fought in the big tree, then flew off.

She positioned herself on the wicker lawn set, a pillow already on the tiny table so she could hoist her leg onto the cushion.

It felt out of place sitting on this side knowing the other side of the veranda was off-limits because she didn't reside there at the moment. She supposed she could have gone over if she really wanted to.

She briefly wondered if Paul had returned home and she hadn't heard him. Since she didn't sleep soundly, she knew his work schedule for the week, waking when he moved around in her bedroom on the other side of her mother's guest room. She couldn't help noticing the sound of running water or the deep inflection of his voice when he spoke on the phone. Most of the time, she got up when she heard him in the kitchen making coffee at different hours. The chief had Cabrera on rotational shifts. Right now he was working days.

As far as tenants went, she couldn't have asked for a better one.

Why then was she wishing he wasn't in her house? Maybe because she was tempted to "gawk" at him herself.

His blue sports car pulled into her driveway. He killed the whisper-smooth engine. Nobody in Majestic who worked on the city's ticket could afford a Porsche. Pay in Miami must have been pretty good.

She thought about Sherry's suggestion of luring him with lemonade. The idea was ridiculous. She hoped he wouldn't think she was waiting for him. But as she thought about it, she began to wonder about her appearance. So what if she didn't have a speck of make-up on?

Agitated with herself for doing so, she corrected the lopsidedness of her ponytail—but definitely *not* taking it out—smoothing the wisps above her ears.

She wore an aqua drawstring tank and jeans shorts. The toenail polish on both her feet was beginning to show wear. *Tacky,* she shuddered.

Paul walked to the house wearing mirrored sunglasses; the standard-issue cowboy hat was nowhere to be seen. Broad shoulders and lean legs filled out his police uniform. The black leather of his gun belt was buffed to a sheen, and in it, all that she desired—gun, ammo and handcuffs. He really did pack a Model 22 Glock.

The sight of him clad in official dress shouldn't have bothered her but it did—seeing him outfitted in something she coveted. She shoved away a sigh as he walked onto the veranda that wrapped around the entire double residence.

"How's the leg today?" he asked, slipping the temple of his sunglasses into his breast pocket where the six-point badge flashed like a diamond.

"Getting better."

To her dismay, he sat down on one of the chairs.

Please don't let him think I planned this little rendezvous.

She forced herself to be decent about everything even though it killed her to ask, "How are you getting along in the job?"

She wanted to say *my job* and ask *how are you liking my metal desk, the one with the wobbly leg and the matchbook I stuck under it to keep the desktop from*

*rocking—or did you get a better one because of your
elevated status?* But she didn't. She was bigger than
the curve Dutch had thrown at her.

Paul stretched his long legs out in front of him and
locked his hands behind his head. The end-of-the-day
relaxed position said it all; today had been a long one.
"I'm trying to figure out Karen's filing system."

"That can be a challenge."

Karen McGinty was the dispatch operator/file clerk/
coffeemaker at the station. She was also very pregnant
at the moment, awaiting the arrival of her fifth child.
Even with normal hormones she could be absentminded. Sometimes she started a fresh pot of coffee
while the old one still brewed. It wasn't out of the ordinary to find watermark stains on documents she'd laid
on the counter when the coffeemaker overflowed.

Paul wore a lazy smile that conveyed his frustration,
but not scorn. "I'm missing files and when I ask her
where they are she has a hard time finding them."

"It's because she's dyslexic. The glasses don't help.
She files last names under first name letters or vice
versa. You never know which way until you have to
track something down."

"Then next time I'll look in the opposite place from
where I think it will be," he said smoothly.

Lanie was strangely drawn to the easy quality of his
voice. She found herself asking him another question
just so she could hear him talking. "Did you notice the
turn signal column on the Explorer sometimes sticks?"

"I fixed it."

The local repair shop hadn't been able to get it right
in a couple trips to the service bay. "You know about
auto mechanics?"

"Enough to get by. Every once in a while, a guy needs to get greasy."

For reasons she couldn't explain, a shiver of awareness ran through her body. Before she could stop herself, she had visualized him in a tank shirt with grease-smudged biceps and a crescent wrench in his hand.

"What do you like to do?"

Since her thoughts were elsewhere, she heard a different meaning in his question. "For what?"

"To relieve job stress?"

"Oh—that." She came back to her senses. "I shoot at tin cans."

An irresistible grin caught on his mouth. "I would not have guessed that."

"What did you have in mind? Crocheting? Needlepoint? I'm not a girlie girl."

"Movies. I took you for the escapism type."

She gave him credit where it was due. "I like to do that, too."

The leisureliness of their conversation felt like that of longtime friends, but Lanie knew better than to get comfortable. She didn't know him aside from the basic facts Dutch had read off Paul's application—not enough for her to form a personal opinion. What kind of man was Paul? What had driven him out of Miami to live in a town where thirty percent of the population swore they'd sighted Elvis and Bigfoot in the woods near Canyon Falls?

Lanie had had a lot of time to speculate about him. "Why did you leave Miami-Dade? You're too young to make a retirement move. It's not common to leave a position where you've got lots of seniority to start at the bottom again."

His face showed no emotion and nothing in his eyes

gave any clue to his thoughts. "Sometimes you need a different sunrise to look at."

She was about to say something further when Sissy Lanford's boatlike 1995 Grand Marquis drove slowly in front of the house. Lanie had seen the huge car cruise by twice yesterday—strange, since Sissy lived on the other side of town.

As soon as Sissy saw Paul, the electric window came buzzing down. She waved, a smile on her face the size of Texas. "Well, hello there! I set aside a box of vanilla cruellers for you, Paul. You come in tomorrow and pick them up free of charge. I have to spoil the town's finest."

That's funny, Lanie thought. She and the deputies always had to buy their own. Sissy was just as infatuated with Paul Cabrera as the rest of the women in Majestic—they were all after more than a traffic cop. But Sissy was a little different—she was in her mid-seventies. Lanie supposed a lovesick woman knew no age boundaries.

"That's nice of you, but I'll pay."

"Good heavens, no. I wouldn't dream of it. See you soon, Paul."

The big V8 engine rumbled with precision as she drove off.

Lanie slanted a glance at Paul.

He warned, "Don't say anything."

"I wasn't," she replied, although a comment had been on the tip of her tongue.

A quiet lapse fell between them and each grew occupied by their own thoughts. It was Paul who broke into the sounds of the summer afternoon.

"I miss watching the sun reflecting off the Atlantic ocean. Right now I'd like to be sitting at my favorite table in Salty's Sea Bucket, watching the waves roll in, eating some shrimp and drinking a dollar mug of beer.''

The white of his teeth contrasted next to the five o'clock shadow dusting his jaw. ''On my way home I'd stop by Sid's for a while. We'd talk shop, maybe watch some sports on the tube.'' He fell silent, his chiseled facial expression distant.

She sensed he'd gone to a place where he needed her to listen and to allow him to continue at his own pace.

He went on, ''I knew leaving would be difficult, but I didn't think it would be like this. I worry about my former partner and good friend. He loves what he does, but all around him is depression and an endless caseload.''

Paul massaged his brows with one hand, closing his eyes. When he opened them, their brown color cleared of nostalgia, and gone was the brief moment of insight into his character.

She realized that while she thought of him as invading her territory, he was leaving some of his own behind. She hadn't seen past the superficial until now. He had friends and a life with a foundation elsewhere. It hit home that she'd be doing the same thing, maybe talking to a stranger herself and missing all that was familiar to her. Lunches with Sherry, nights with her mom, Rooster's Place omelets and the way the wind whispered through the trees outside her bedroom window.

As she swallowed the unwanted lump of melancholy caught in her throat, an itch crept over her ankle just out of reach. She wiggled her toes and winced at the tingles of pain. How could her leg hurt when it was in a hard impenetrable shell?

''You're taking the cast pretty good,'' Paul said.

"Not really."

"Men don't make good patients. We think everything should be fixed by cartoon physics."

"What's that?"

"Cartoons. The physics of being hit in the head with a shovel and the 'toon character shaking off the shovel's impression from his face. A man's mind works on animation physics. He expects to be one hundred percent by the next commercial."

"I have to be honest with you and say that's the stupidest thing I've ever heard."

His laughter coaxed a smile out of her.

"What's that right there?" Paul referred to Hailey's coloring artwork scribbles on the cast.

"It's a flower."

He withdrew a black pen from his shirt pocket and drew an outline of a stick flower over the crayon colors. Then he signed his name over a free spot. His masculine penmanship was bold and slanted on the cast's rough surface.

She followed the motion of his hand when he returned the pen to his pocket, her heartbeat trying to recover from something that had felt sensual in a way she hadn't expected. An unexplainable foolishness surfaced in her and she couldn't take her eyes off him.

She focused on the strength he commanded, and on his utility belt where power rode on his hips. His weapon, extra rounds and a Streamlite flashlight next to his cuffs.

Just looking at him gave her heart a lurch of excitement. She was totally entranced.

Dryness scorched her throat. She couldn't believe that simply sitting next to him could muck up her intelligence level. So it was no wonder she said, "Do you want to have dinner with me and my mom?"

Seven

A few days later, Lanie opened the front door to find Chief Deutsch standing on the veranda holding a large portable filing box. The lid was jammed on top and beneath the brown cover paperwork threatened to spill out. His chin was tucked against a bound manual that was balanced precariously on the tall pile.

He hadn't crossed her mind for three days—not since her mother ran into him in the nursery and brought up his name. And last they'd spoken at her going-away party, he told her he wasn't going to deal with her anymore. His showing up at her mom's house unannounced, and with a mystery box, gave her cause for suspicion.

"Prescott, do you still have a working laptop?"

He'd recently had his hair cut. The flattop was clipped as precisely as a freshly mown golf green.

She silently wondered why he wanted to know. "Yes."

"I need these files updated."

His unprompted visit and request put her thoughts on high alert. She leaned into her crutches and asked, "What files?"

"These files. The department has the budget to pay

you an hourly rate to update the Policy and Procedure manual.''

She had firsthand experience with the current Policy and Procedure manual. Some pages were outdated and current addendums were loosely shoved in and unbound. Incorporating new articles, updating information and typing it into the correct computer program would be tedious and time-consuming. But after thirteen days of the same routine and oodles of time, the prospect of doing something—as well as earning money—interested her.

However, that didn't make her less suspicious about his motives since he had never been concerned about fixing up the P&P before. ''Why?''

''Why what?''

''Why do you want me to do it?''

''Because your mother said you needed the income.'' His chin lifted, his posture straightened and he looked behind her shoulder. She swore he was wearing spicy cologne. To her knowledge, he'd never worn it before. ''Is Lucille here?''

''Tonight's her bingo night.''

She watched a play of emotions across his face. She didn't want to speculate what they meant. Whatever his feelings were, she doubted they ran real deep.

''You were always good at filling out paperwork when you had to,'' he commented. ''I know I made you do a lot of it, but that's the way it went.''

If he was trying to get on her good side with his thin acknowledgment of her skills…it just wasn't going to… Well, seeing him somewhat humble—it was working. But she wasn't going to plunge into anything major without viewing his offer from all angles.

With cool reserve, she said, "I appreciate you thinking of me."

"Do you want to do it or not?"

The way he shifted his feet in that annoyed and impatient way said she had five more seconds to make up her mind before the entire deal was off.

"I'll do it." She stepped away from the door. "Put everything on the coffee table."

Dutch entered her mother's house, his gaze traveling from one homey object to the other. A tick played at the corner of his left eye, a sort of mild twitch. She'd never noticed him doing that before.

He wore a bowling shirt and had fixed himself up for something. Or someone. She concluded he definitely wore Brut. The aftershave's distinct smell filled the air. She wasn't aware they still made that brand.

Unceremoniously, he dropped the filing box on the table. "You get a police position yet, Prescott?"

"My applications are being considered at several departments."

"That's good."

"Good for who?"

"You," he barked as if she were dim-witted; then he cracked his neck and followed with his knuckles.

Whenever he did that, her skin chilled listening to the popping of his joints.

"I guess you can take your time since you've got time, but we could use a good copy as soon as you can get one done. Make contact with Karen every Wednesday and have her get you onto payroll for a Friday check."

"Okay."

"Okay," he concurred, then showed himself out with the screen door slapping closed behind him.

For a long moment afterward, Lanie wasn't quite sure what to make of his visit.

"*N-42!* That's *N-42!*" the bingo announcer called.

Fluorescent-colored bingo daubers hovered over rows of game cards. Some players were lucky enough to ink out N-42, while others waited in hope of better luck next time.

Lucille Prescott was one of the fortunate. She had N-42. She always played five cards at the same time and had an uncanny ability to keep all the numbers straight. The speed and skill and agility required to keep up a five-card game wasn't something just anyone could do.

She had bingo in her blood.

For Lucille, her knack for playing bingo was like second sight, or something one of those eight-hundred-number Jamaican fortune-tellers would call a clairvoyant tendency—not that she'd ever telephoned Miss Sally. Well, there had been that time she'd picked up the phone, but she caught herself before she did something stupid. She was too smart to fall for a scam.

Her Ray had been the world's biggest skeptic, him being a police officer and knowing firsthand the kinds of cons this world had to offer—Majestic being no different than any other place. There had been that pyramid scheme going on in the Econo Gas-and-Lube on the outskirts of town that Ray had shut down. He'd been given a commendation for his cunning and savvy in handling the sting.

Lucille lost her concentration when the memories of

her husband surfaced. Although he'd been gone from her life for nearly five years, she still missed him. Their love wasn't the kind that came around every day.

"*I-23!*" the announcer said into the microphone. "*I-23!*"

"I think I have that one," Ken said. He sat beside her and looked as if he was playing the game, but he wasn't a very good dabber. He'd comment when he had a number, but he never got around to coloring it off so he never won anything.

His one flaw was being an imperfect bingo player.

Lucille would much prefer he sporadically run late to take her out or mismatch his socks than be sloppy at bingo.

Bingo night had become less and less fun. Instead of having him pick her up tonight, she met Cookie for dinner, then drove herself here.

Motion over by the double doors caught Lucille's attention. Herb Deutsch entered the community center and walked the rows of tables to take a spot several chairs down from her and Ken.

She sent him an nondescript gaze over the rims of her reading glasses.

He wore beige slacks with a loose-fitting black, short-sleeved shirt; it was quite distinct and unlike anything the other men wore. Embroidered with red thread on the breast pocket was his name. Across the back of his shirt were the words *Clydesdale Bowling League* with an image of a stocky horse, bowling pins and ball that went from shoulder to shoulder.

The chief of police had never attended a Saturday night bingo game before. He paid the card girl for several cards, studying the squares with a fixed gaze. Since this round had already begun, he couldn't play.

She bit her lip, contemplating his presence. Seeing him here brought a queer fluttering in her stomach, a winged brush against her ribs.

Glancing her way, he shot her a smile. She returned one of her own, a tentative soft curve to her mouth.

"B-8!" the announcer added to his list of called numbers. "B-8!"

Ken had the square, but instead of marking it off, he sagely offered the perspective, "Did you know that GR8 on a personalized licence plate means 'great'?"

In a polite tone, she replied, "I didn't know that, Ken."

A winner was declared, the card verified and the game was officially closed, then a new one began. She snuck another glance at Herb who stared at his card, the marker in his hand held in an awkward grip.

Lucille didn't know him well aside from what Lanie had told her. They bumped into each other around town, at the grocery or filling station—more so lately—or so it seemed; and last year at the Founder's Day picnic in September they'd exchanged pleasantries.

Their association was guarded on her part. There was too much sad history between herself and the department that she didn't want to relive so she chose not to put herself in a position to discuss the past or spend prolonged amounts of time with any of the officers.

She would have liked to settle on one man, one new heart to take hold of and fill with her love. But it just hadn't happened. Not with Ken and she had tried. God knew she had. She really had no complaints with his character or his appearance other than he just didn't excite her in the way a man should. Sparks were missing. The fire wasn't there. Lukewarm wasn't keeping her happy. She'd been debating breaking things off with him. It wasn't fair to occupy his time and not want to occupy his life for the long run. She kept hoping her feelings would change, hoped she would get past seeing him as lackluster, see him as more of a gem.

Refocusing on her game cards, she needed one more combination on the diagonal for a bingo on her first card. But her concentration was pulled and she glanced down the table once more and caught the chief staring.

Her face warmed. It was the same feeling she'd had in the nursery. It was perplexing, fascinating...and objectionable.

"Lucille." Ken leaned closer, his shoulder touching the delicate knit of her short-sleeved cardigan. "When this is over, we'll go to the restaurant and have a bite to eat."

She wasn't hungry and didn't answer his invitation. She turned her head toward Herb. He looked her way, then back at his card but she could tell his mind wasn't on the game. It was on her.

Heat spread down her neck and across her collarbone.

Letter-number combinations called for this round swirled in her head. The telltale signs of a headache developed, the kind she got when she spent way too much time browsing a tag sale underneath the beating heat of the summer sun.

"There's a good movie playing at the theater," Ken said. "We could cut out early here and go take it in."

Another number on his card was called—another number he ignored.

"It starts at nine-twenty so we should think about leaving soon or the next round will start and we'll get stuck staying."

"I'm fighting a headache," she fibbed.

"A cup of coffee and an aspirin could help," he suggested, his bingo card still empty of color. "It's early and I like spending time with you, Lucille." His hand cupped her knee and he gave it a squeeze. "You're an amazingly wonderful woman and I'm lucky to have you." Lowering his tone, he went on, "I've been thinking—it's time we became a permanent couple. Like us getting mm—"

"I don't have O-62!" she said and shifted her leg so his hand fell off her kneecap. "But you do!"

In the throes of distress, but with the dabber poised in her grasp, she got a jolt of energy and did what he should have been doing.

Stamp! Stamp! Stamp! Stamp! Stamp!

"Bingo! Ken Burnett has bingo," she declared to the announcer while pushing back her chair and standing.

Ken's voice rose an octave. "I've got bingo?"

"Yes, you do." Clutching her handbag, she said, "Ken, I really don't feel well. I'm going home. You stay and collect your winnings."

Then she made a fast departure from the building, very thankful she'd driven herself tonight.

The night air cooled her lungs as she drank it in. She hadn't realized how stuffy the atmosphere had grown inside.

Walking to her Eldorado, she lifted her open purse up to the streetlight for a better view and, to her horror, realized her keys weren't in her purse like they should be. A sinking feeling gripped her. She looked through the driver's window and saw the ring of keys hanging in the ignition.

How could she have done such a scatterbrained thing? This was the second time in a week she'd been forgetful—the first leaving the hose turned on all day to deep water her blue spruce. A flood had spread through her backyard.

Perhaps declining her doctor's recommendation to take estrogen hadn't been prudent. On the other hand, Mother Nature had made her body clock quit at forty-nine and she didn't want to artificially restart it with a manmade pill. Men never designed anything right unless they had to use it.

Slumping next to the Cadillac, Lucille muttered, "Wonderful."

"Is there a problem, Mrs. Prescott?"

She swung around to face Herb, surprised he'd followed her out here. Or maybe she wasn't surprised at all. "I've locked my keys in my car."

He took a look for himself. "I've got a Slim Jim down at the station and can have them out for you in a jiffy."

"I don't want to trouble you."

"It's no trouble."

Her mind raced. Should she go back inside and ask Ken for help? But he was no expert with cars. Herb Deutsch could have them out for her in no time. Indecision caused her to bite the inside of her lip. "I really should—"

"—let me help you," he concluded.

She let out a sigh. "I hate to trouble you," she repeated.

"You aren't."

The community center's door opened and she couldn't see who'd come out. If it were Ken coming after her, she...the thought brought with it an urgent need to run in the opposite direction.

"Let's go," she blurted out, intent on finding Herb's car.

"It's a nice night. We'll walk over." His voice was rough, but oddly soothing. "It's only five minutes away."

"All right." Anxious to be off, she walked briskly, thinking that this was an interesting turn of events. One minute she'd been inside with Ken Burnett, and the next she was outside walking beside the town's chief of police.

Quite certainly, she'd lost her mind.

Dutch had his own thoughts, his pulse racing like a squad car in hot pursuit. He might not have scored a bingo win, but he'd hit some kind of jackpot to be walking beside Lucille Prescott.

She was the only reason he'd come tonight.

For months now he'd kept his distance, thinking her and Burnett had a romantic thing going. He wasn't the kind of man who butted into another man's territory. But from the way he saw things, Burnett had no territory to defend.

Dutch was a people reader—he had to be in his line of work—and he saw a passiveness in Lucille that spoke volumes. She was not in love with Burnett. Herb knew this for sure last month when he'd gone to Dirty Harry's Car Wash on a suspicious person call and observed the couple together.

Body language said a lot. And Lucille's was closed off. During the liquid wax cycle, she wandered to the postcard rack while Ken plastered his mug to the observation glass and watched his car run through the rinse. A real man would have done the job himself in his front yard.

And a real man didn't play bingo, that was for damn sure.

He had wanted to catch Lucille at home when he dropped off those boxes to Prescott. Doing a good turn for the daughter would hopefully place him in good favor with the mother, but it was more than that. He knew Prescott was in a bad way and, what the hell, that P&P manual was a mess.

Having to come to the community center wasn't what he'd planned on. Jealousy had flared when Ken leaned in close and whispered words to Lucille. But who wouldn't want to whisper to her?

Lucille's sunny beauty reminded him of a TV commercial actress who plugged household products that smelled lemony. She never wore prints; just solid pastels. He'd noticed, not because of any fashion consciousness, but rather as an officer of the law who logged that sort of data. At the grocery she brought her coupon holder, and she always allowed a bag boy to help her to her car with her bags. He liked that she wasn't a feminist type who insisted on doing it herself.

He had access to city records and had felt justified in looking through her small business permit to see if it was up-to-date. She made blackberry jams out of her house and sold them to the public through several of the town businesses.

While he was nosing around, he took a look at her driver's licence stats. She was an organ donor. Her hair and eye color were respectively filled in as blond and blue. All right—so he wasn't looking her up for a legitimate reason, but he'd had enough principle not to read her weight. He'd closed one eye and squinted the other to blur the three-digit figure and moved on to her date of birth and what she'd turn this year.

She was fifty-seven to his fifty-six—a year older than him.

She was five feet ten and a half inches—an inch taller than his five feet nine and a half inches.

And damned if those two things *hadn't* bothered him.

She'd never committed a traffic violation—moving or otherwise. Her driving record was impeccable, just like the outfit she had on. Her reading glasses were suspended on a gold chain around her slender neck, graceful as a swan's. Her sweater was a buttery yellow. He was sure it felt as soft as it looked.

Dutch searched his mind for something to compliment her on without being too obvious.

After a moment, he ventured, "I bought some of your jam." He neglected to tell her that he'd given Karen, the police department's dispatch operator, the money to go to the Calico Corner and buy a few jars for him. That frilly stuff displayed in the window front almost gave him hives when he had to look at it.

Lucille asked, "Did you like the jam?"

"Yes, I did." His blood suddenly felt like it flowed with jam—thick and sweet and stuck on Lucille Prescott.

"That's nice to hear. I fiddled with the recipe, so I don't know if you got some of the last batch or the new."

"I'll buy another jar and see if I can tell the difference."

"You don't have to do that."

"I want to."

Her earlier nerves seemed to have settled and her smile lit up the stars. She was even more stunning at night with the moon's milkiness crowning her pale hair.

Lucille smoothed the neckline on her sweater, her fingers without rings. A gold wristwatch and a string of cultured pearls were the only jewelry she wore.

Gazing at him, she grew solemn. "I should have said this sooner, and I apologize for not doing so. But I wanted to thank you."

Confused, he replied, "Thank me—for what?"

"For keeping Lanie safe when she was in the department. She wasn't happy with you for assigning the duties you did, but I think I know why you did it. It's family over there and you were protecting her. After Ray died I didn't want Lanie anywhere near that station. But you see how headstrong Lanie is and she has a mind of her own. She's determined to be something important. I'm grateful for the way you kept her out of harm's way. Thank you so very much."

Rarely did Dutch receive verbal appreciation, and Lucille's profound gratitude touched him. Being in command of a department where law and order had to be kept was demanding, and something he was up to, but the field he had to play left very little room for praise. When he went out on a call, it was never because somebody wanted to say thank you. There was always a problem to be solved. Always hot tempers to be cooled.

He had never grappled for words before and now cursed the fact that he had to collect himself. He clenched his molars so hard he could chip a filling.

What he felt deep inside was almost disturbing because it involved emotional sentiments. He was *not* a sentimentalist. He did not hug people and he didn't need a pat on the back. A beer bought for him at the White Horse Saloon was enough of a satisfying thanks.

But what Lucille said to him was better than any beer. "I appreciate you saying that, Mrs. Prescott."

"You're welcome, Chief Deutsch."

"Herb," he responded, hearing his heart thundering in his ears. "My name is Herb."

"I know that." She smiled, her whole face enchanting. "It's just that you don't look like a Herb to me. It's so...if you'll forgive me...old-fashioned."

"Most people call me Dutch."

She mulled over his request. Then to his relief said, "Dutch suits you much better. I'm Lucille to my friends."

"Good enough—Lucille."

Dutch slowed when he saw the lights of the station ahead. He wished they could walk longer.

He held the door open for them both to go inside. She pulled away, the dusting of rosiness on her cheeks waning. "No. No, I'll wait out here."

"Then I'll be right back."

Dutch slipped through the door. Lucille kept her distance, concealing the distress that was causing her to tremble. She would not, *she could not,* go inside. Not now. Not ever again.

She hadn't set foot in the station since she brought Ray his lunch on the day he was killed. After Lanie took her deputy's oath, Lucille never once visited her daughter on duty. She couldn't do it. She and Lanie had an unspoken understanding about it.

Waiting, Lucille berated herself. Coming down here with Dutch was crazy. The station only reminded her of every single reason why she should have sought out Ken for help. She had to get her misguided feelings back in order; priorities needed to be defined.

Dutch returned holding an unlocking device. "This'll do it."

They retraced their steps to her pearl Eldorado.

"It was silly of me to lock the keys in my car. I don't know how I could have done such a thing."

"We all get distracted."

Dutch had the door open before she could blink. He reached in and pulled her keys from the ignition. They felt reassuring in her hand, and she once again chastised herself for being so clumsy.

"Thank you."

"Any time."

"I hope there won't be a next time."

From the way he looked at her she got the impression he wanted to say something. She wasn't blind to his rugged, masculine features. It was okay to acknowledge that he was handsome, but not wise to explore that line of thought any further.

Feeling the moment's awkwardness, she verbalized a question that had been on her mind. "Are you taking up bingo?"

"Not a chance."

"Then why...?"

"I wanted to see you."

She was instantly flustered.

Here was the truth. She knew it, she'd felt it—she just hadn't wanted to accept something like this could happen to her, to them. Of all the men in Majestic— she couldn't explore her feelings for Dutch.

"Lucille, if I thought you and Burnett were a hot ticket I wouldn't be putting myself on the line right now. But you should know I'm attracted to you and I have been for some months now."

"But you can't be."

His mouth twisted. "Then I'm mistaken about you and Burnett?"

"Ken and I...we..." She shook her head. "We're comfortable."

"Comfortable doesn't put a light under our fires, Lucille."

"It does mine," she said in a rush, then sat inside her car. "I have to go home now."

Turning over the ignition, Lucille pulled out of the parking lot space and didn't look back. It was pointless.

She could never become involved with him. Not in a million years.

Eight

Almost ready to go off shift, Paul could have used a bit to eat and some company. He thought back to the dinner he'd had with Lanie and Lucille, and wished he had the same to look forward to tonight. The company had been good. Both women were friendly and their high regard for each other was apparent.

Paul had never understood the meaning of "do your caseload and go home" until now. In Miami there was always a case pending, a file always needing attention. You went home and came back and the desk was just as you had left it—unorganized and chaotic—and stacked with a half-dozen new reports to be followed up on.

Clocking off the boneyard shift at three in the morning, Paul opted to finish paperwork at the station rather than head out. There was no point in leaving. He wouldn't feel ready for sleep until the sun came up, anyway. Since he was Duty Officer until 6:00 a.m., when Deputies Griswold and Ridder came on, he might as well stick around.

At this hour the images behind the station's window glass fogged into muted darkness and it was a strange feeling to be inside and not driving on Washington Avenue, with a cell phone clamped to his ear getting the prelim details on a battery case.

The police station had been dead since just after 1:00 a.m. this morning when Paul had been called on a barking dog complaint. Now the electric motor of the station's mini-refrigerator was the only noise to keep him company.

He hadn't anticipated the sense of misplacement he'd feel without Miami's waterfront strip. He hadn't counted on missing the energy of South Palm Beach and the highways with water encompassing both sides.

To a native Floridian, Colorado didn't feel like home just yet. He kept expecting to see a flock of seagulls, smell the salty ocean in the air when he woke and feel a tangy breeze on his face.

The area surrounding Majestic was spotted with grazing cattle herds stretching out for miles. Telephone poles towered, their wires swinging in the breeze like jump ropes held up by rows of wind-bent pilings. Tall green grasses roiled, their tops tufted like wheat. Sagebrush filled the thin air. A river meandered. Wildlife thrived.

It seemed as if every window in town had a view of mountains. He'd studied the street grids and had most of them memorized. North and south or east and west—pretty much no-brainers. Street names were simple.

Glancing at the large analog clock on the wall, Paul noted the hands had finally crept off five-thirty. He rolled back his chair, having finished the last report of the evening. He handwrote the pertinent information into the thick book log. At Miami-Dade, everything was entered into a computer software form that was networked with other departments. They did things the old-fashioned way in Majestic.

In the weeks since he had arrived, the new changes he'd created in his life were beginning to create a distance from the weighted feelings he'd succumbed to at Miami-Dade. But sometimes, just when he thought he'd put all the bullshit behind him, a memory or a feeling resurfaced and he became caught up in the past again. He reminded himself he was going through an adjustment period. Not only was he regrouping in terms of his job, he was learning a new lifestyle. A new place.

One more glance at the clock. Fifteen minutes to six. He was out of here.

Paul grabbed the portable radio and his set of keys. He locked the station and walked across the street to Rooster's Place Café where two black and white Explorers were parked in the lot.

He breathed in the coffee smell that greeted him as he made his way through the restaurant and took a seat at the last booth. The chief, Deputy Gordon T. Griswold and Deputy Delroy Ridder blew steam off cups of joe.

"Morning," Dutch greeted him in a deep morning voice as he slid down the semicircle of red giving Paul room to sit.

"Mornin', Evelyn," Paul acknowledged, while nodding to the waitress to add another cup of coffee on the tab.

Long seconds of silence enveloped the table while those coming on duty seemed to be waiting for the caffeine to hit their bloodstream.

Ridder asked, "Did anyone watch the Rockies game last night?"

"Caught the last inning." The red in Griswold's mustache took on a brassy shade from the light fixture over the table. "That relief pitcher was the worst ever."

Dutch complained, "I wouldn't have put a reliever in. The starter was doing all right. He was only behind the count on fouls, not strikes."

Ridder said to Paul, "We go to some Rockies games in September. You'll have to come with us."

"*Us?*" Dutch ribbed. "Last year Tracy wouldn't let you go."

The tops of Ridder's ears reddened. "I'm going this year and my wife can kiss my lily-white butt if one of her relatives decides to plan a September wedding again."

"I'll tell her you said that next time I see her," Griswold said.

"You do, Griswold, and I'll be having the chief swap out my graves when Paul's done with them, for your day shifts. Or better yet—I'll have Dutch make you tag meters and put you on swings."

Swing shift officers handled the most calls, given the hours of the day they worked—usually three to midnight. Bars were open, tempers flared and fists were swung.

Dutch merely laughed, apparently knowing he held all the power so he didn't get into the argument. "What did you log, Cabrera?"

"Disturbance of the peace—Sim Johnson left his trash cans out at the curb and his neighbors wanted him to bring them in. I talked to him about it. Barking dog at Tenth Avenue, and I investigated gunshots near Laramie Ranch." That call had gotten Paul's attention, and he'd burned up the highway with lights flashing. "When I got there the shooter was gone, but twenty-two casings were on the ground by the roadside. Pranksters."

Dutch swore, "Jesus Christ."

"Them boys up over at the camp," Ridder said somberly, taking a drink of coffee. Then to Paul, he explained, "We have teenage boys who stay up at the youth camp on Ridge Flat. They get some beer in them and leave the campground looking for trouble. They've bullet-marked the road signs for sport before. The fifty-five mph has been replaced, what—Dutch, a half-dozen times?''

"At least. Mile markers are targets, too.''

Dutch said, "I'll take a drive up there and talk to the counselors. If I'd've ever done anything stupid like that when I was their age, my daddy would have kicked my butt from here to next week.''

"Is that when you had a skinnier butt, Dutch?'' Griswold asked, then ducked when Dutch pitched a sugar packet at him.

"It's a good thing the Rockies didn't send you in as their reliever last night,'' Paul said, enjoying the male conversation. "You had a left hook to that throw, Dutch.''

Laughter rose from the table, Dutch told him where to go and Paul knew right then he'd been accepted unconditionally into the group.

After he left Rooster's, Paul mowed the lawn, then stripped down to his briefs and lay down on the bed with a floor fan oscillating air over him. He napped until he heard a dog barking and kids squealing as they jumped on a trampoline behind the backyard fence. He dozed back off, his brain falling into a deep dreamless state.

When he next opened his eyes he was surprised by the time on the bedside clock. 11:00 p.m. He'd overslept. His body must have sensed he had the night off. He hadn't slept this hard for a long time.

Paul got up and took a long shower, soaping every inch of his body. He worked his fingers into his short hair and scrubbed deep. Cutting the water, he toweled off and dressed in faded jeans and a much-laundered white tank undershirt. He decided to shave in the morning rather than now. Barefoot, he went downstairs.

He couldn't remember what he'd bought at the grocery. Some hearty man frozen dinners had to be in the freezer somewhere along with his gallon of strawberry ice cream. He couldn't help remembering the chicken dinner he'd had at Lucille Prescott's house last week. It was one of the best meals he'd eaten since arriving in Majestic.

Walking past the counter, he glanced at his cell phone. The *New Voice Message* function was activated. Punching buttons, he retrieved the message.

"It's Sid." The man's discomposure was evident immediately. Paul's eyes closed, his breath held, and he listened for the slightest sign of slurred speech. "I fucked up, Paul. I couldn't save him. I tried, but he was a stupid punk and bought a gun. Christ Almighty. Ah, Jesus…I should have been there. I was in court. I could have delayed it. I'm feeling shaky. God help me. I'm tempted, kid…really tempted. I want a drink. Call me when you get this message. I need to talk to somebody."

Paul punched the memory dial immediately.

The phone was picked up on the first ring.

"Sid, it's me."

"Aw, Jesus. Paul, everything's screwed up." For the long minutes to follow, Paul remained quiet as Sid sliced open his heart, draining pain from a situation gone bad.

One positive thing did become apparent—Sid hadn't taken a drink.

"I had him in juvie custody. He was waiting for me to get there and talk to him, but the courts let him out.

Twenty-four hours later, he's on the morgue table. Dammit. If I'd have been there for him—''

"Sid, you can't live with them every second. I was once that age and you couldn't tell me shit until I was ready to hear it. Even if you'd reached him, choices have to be made eventually.''

"He wasn't ready. I swear to God, we have to get the guns off the street corners or these judges are going to send more kids to their graves. It's a load of bullshit. If I had one more day, I could have made a difference. I was close, so close.''

"You did your best. There's never any blame in that.''

"The best wasn't good enough.''

"The best is all you have.'' Paul leaned into the counter, his hand on the sink's edge. "You did the right thing to call me.''

The silence on the phone line stretched taut.

"The bottle's sitting in front of me.''

Paul's nostrils flared. "Get rid of it. Flush it down the toilet. Go do it now.''

"I know what you're saying, kid. I know it's what I have to do, but I don't think I can. It's hard....''

"It's easy. Pick it up, take it into the john.''

"Jesus Christ...son of a bitch. Goddamn booze. It'll kill me.'' The sound of the toilet flushing brought a flicker of a smile to Paul.

"Good deal, Sid.''

"Yeah, kid. Good deal.'' But the words were strained and Paul kept him on the line long enough to be certain Sid wouldn't go buy another bottle, and would attend an AA meeting instead.

When Paul finally said goodbye it was after one. He nuked a microwave dinner, but the hunger he'd felt earlier was gone. He threw half of it out, then drank a glass of milk to settle his stomach.

Bracing his hands on the counter, he stared at the drain. Being this far from Miami, Paul worried there would be a time when his friend would not rethink the booze and pick up the phone. A time when the caseload of the Juvenile Assessment Bureau would prove too much, and Sid would fall into a relapse again, just like he did when his wife left him.

Paul had chosen to put his life back together over keeping a watch on Sid. Sometimes Paul questioned his decision to bail but, deep inside, he knew he had done the right thing for himself. Sid had to stand on his own two feet—nobody could hold him up.

Paul was only a phone call away and tonight proved it could work.

The house was cloaked in grays. Only the light from the stove hood illuminated his surroundings. He moved into the living room, hoping some television would occupy his mind—at least until the newspaper hit the front door.

Sidestepping some of the moving boxes he'd yet to unpack, he sat on the sofa that was too short for him and picked up the remote. But he didn't turn on the tube.

The windows were thrown open and he heard noise coming from next door. Spilling onto his side of the veranda, flickering light from a television picture intermittently lit up the railing.

Lanie Prescott's nocturnal habits were as unpredictable as his own. They'd talked about it over dinner last week. Sitting across from her had felt comfortable and pleasant with Lucille adding to the conversation. Bright, resolute and sometimes sardonic, Lanie was a woman he wanted to get to know better.

Since it appeared they were both awake, he stepped outside.

The night air was balmy with the smell of damp earth, flower nectar and sun-warmed tar from rooftops. Cricket chirps rose from cracks in the walkway and the planters. The yard was nicely manicured. Lucille kept it alive with a flourish of color.

He went to Lucille's screen door and saw Lanie sitting on the couch. The stacked outline of moving boxes along the walls and the white of her cast were illuminated by the television signal. She sat as relaxed as he'd ever seen her.

A pillow cushioned her cast. Her left leg was bent, her wrist casually resting on her knee, and the remote control held in her hand.

"Lanie—hey," he said through the window, but she didn't reply.

She seemed almost trancelike as she sat in front of the TV.

A red T-shirt rode up her leg, her thigh a supple curve of golden skin. She had a great body that was perfectly proportioned for her height. Long hair tousled on her shoulders in a soft silhouette, creating a breath-catching beauty. There was something defiant about her, but the stubborn will and strong attitude just made her more attractive.

He knocked. Her head turned toward him with a start. Recognizing who he was, she waved him inside, but motioned for him to be quiet. Her gaze was fastened on the movie she watched.

The actress, Frances McDormand, was on the television in the white and wintry setting of the film, *Fargo*.

The grinding wail of a wood chipper overpowered a policewoman's call, "Police!"

The chipper's evil intent pervaded, the suspect clueless.

"Hey, hands up! Police!" the woman repeated, her drawn weapon steady in both hands.

The suspect looked up, startled, recognition dawning in his eyes.

"Police!" Police Chief Marge Gunderson motioned to the badge on her woolen hat.

"Marge Gunderson is brilliant," Lanie commented. "Whenever I watch this part, my heart beats faster. It's like this..." She shook her head, a lock of hair falling over her brow. "I don't know. Indescribable rush. She doesn't accept any boundaries or intimidations. She truly is brilliant."

"So are you."

Lanie laughed. "Oh, yeah. I'm so brilliant I have a broken leg." She set the volume to mute and lowered her leg, conscious his gaze was on her thigh. "Why aren't you sleeping like everyone else?"

"I'm off tonight. I won't sleep anymore today—tomorrow. Whatever day it is. I'm up until my next shift. And not everyone is sleeping. You're up."

"I was working on the Policy and Procedure Manual." A laptop and files were spread out on the coffee table, along with papers and folders that were stacked haphazardly on top of each other. "I needed a break. I've been at this all day."

"Dutch mentioned he'd hired you."

"Not in the capacity I was hoping for."

He sat in the needlepoint chair across from her. He barely fit in the delicately carved frame, but Lanie occupied the entire sofa. Besides, this way he had a full view of her.

The words *Bring It On* were printed on the front of her shirt. With a twist, she knotted her hair and it held in place off her shoulders. She was antsy—her good foot wiggled, the one wearing a bunny slipper. The fuzzy pink ears bounced.

"What've you got there?" he queried, folding his arms over his chest. He was pretty sure he already knew, having caught the metallic glint from the door before coming inside.

Almost with a look of embarrassment, she said, "My handcuffs." Then she drew her hand out of the sofa cushion. "It's a habit I have. I open them, click the lock closed, then swing them open. Watching *Fargo* always puts me in the mood." She groaned. "I can't believe I just told you that."

"We all have our vices."

"Oh, please. You're perfect. You look great in your uniform, you're smart and you're a chief-deputy. If you have a vice, I haven't seen it."

She was way off base to form that opinion of him by sight alone. It wasn't that he had a vice—at least not now anyway. He'd quit smoking a couple of years ago and drinking had never been an issue for him.

His failings were more like rarely leaving his work unfinished, or bringing the caseloads home—*if* he even made it home that morning. The joke around the metro station was that Lieutenant Cabrera was never off shift.

Resting his hands on the carved arms of the chair, Paul lifted an ankle to his knee. "You asked me why I quit the Miami-Dade PD." After a long pause while he searched Lanie's face, he decided to be honest. "I started to feel like all I did in my life was work. But the thing is—I liked my job. At the same time, it was smothering me.

"The DC Unit is a burner. I almost think cops in homicide last longer because they deal with bodies. The victims are already lost and remaining detached comes easier. I'm not saying detectives in that unit have it easy; it's all relevant to the job. There's a dark side to every division. It's just that being on domestics is a mind-burner. You take the same calls from the same people. You try and help them leave a bad situation, but they don't listen."

Paul shook his head, his mind clouded with memories. "Dealing with that day in and day out took the life out of me. I needed to make a change. I was so hot to get out of there that I resigned with an open case in my file."

Compassion softened her features; the shape of her mouth and color in her violet-blue eyes. "That's not terrible."

"It was for me. I promised a mother I'd find her little girl and I never did. I followed leads for over a decade and wasn't able to bring her home. She's still out there somewhere. As long as I'm living, I'm going to make sure her case remains open."

The movie continued to play, actors moving through scenes without sound. Words spoken, but unheard. The low hum of the VHS tape moving through the player created the only noise in the room.

When she didn't say anything, Paul wondered if he'd said too much.

"I think I just fell in like with you, Cabrera," she confessed, her voice a gentle whisper. "That was not a comfortable thing to admit. Thank you for telling me you're human."

His muscles released the tension that gripped his body. He smiled suggestively. "If I knew you'd feel that way about me, I would have told you sooner."

"Don't think I'm going to start baking you pies like the other women in this town. My idea of winning a man over has nothing to do with food."

"Then how do you win him over?" he asked, stimulated by their light flirtation.

In the dim light the soft blush across her cheeks set off her skin tone. "I don't even try. That's something that has to happen on its own. Forcing a relationship never works."

"I agree."

She regarded him thoughtfully. "He speaks from experience."

"Yeah—I was married once for nearly two years. It didn't work out. She was a new sergeant assigned to my unit and we had a lot in common. It turned out we had too much in common, because nothing outside of work held us together. A marriage can't be based on departmental hours and the same working styles."

There was a noticeable note of indecision in her voice as she asked, "Do you have any children?"

He'd always pictured himself having kids one day, but the timing had to feel right and he wouldn't have a child without marriage. "No."

After his divorce four years ago, Paul had only seen women casually and hadn't pursued anything serious. He'd been fine with his personal life up to a point, but then he began to think about having more, filling in voids. Time moved forward and he wasn't getting any younger.

More recently, sharing what he had with a woman

and making a home seemed more possible than impossible.

Gazing at Lanie, he couldn't recall the last time he'd felt this relaxed. But his relaxation was contradicted by how his body reacted to her when he watched the smile on her mouth, saw the alertness in her eyes and listened to her laugh. Being sexually aware of her was something he'd felt from the moment he'd seen her in that dress with legs that didn't quit.

But she was no one-night-stand woman and he was starting to believe he was looking for more than that.

Her eyes didn't break the connection with his, and after long drawn-out minutes, Lanie looked away. "Did you hear that Karen went into labor this morning?"

"Coyote told me at breakfast."

"She had a boy this afternoon at three-fourteen. Eight pounds, a half ounce. Her fifth baby. Three boys, two girls."

"I always wanted a brother."

"And I always wanted a sister. I have a best friend, but that's not the same thing." Lanie adjusted her pillow. "Do you have family in Florida?"

"My mom and stepdad."

"Will you see them much?"

"They travel a lot in one of those motor homes. Mom said they'd come this way in July."

"Are you close to her?"

"I am now. For a long time, I wasn't. Then my dad died and things got better between us." That was rocky history he wouldn't visit right now.

The ending credits for the movie rolled up the screen and Lanie rewound the tape with an aim of the remote. A questioning thought held Paul, something he'd wondered about since seeing Lanie fixed so intently on the film.

"I watched how you followed that scene in the movie. Could you fire your weapon on a suspect fleeing a crime?"

She licked her lips, then bit on the lower one with a soft catch of her teeth. Her plump mouth looked like rose petals. "I could, yes. Drawing a gun isn't what a police officer wants to do unless it's necessary, but I could if I had to."

"No hesitation."

"Cabrera, you insult me. Yes—I could."

She shot a pillow at him. The soft cushion bounced off his chest. He remained motionless, a smile stretching across his face.

"You proved your point," he said, his fingers loosely knit and locked over his navel where the thin shirt he wore molded the impression of his flat stomach. "Next time I see you holding a pillow, I'll duck."

"Funny."

"What other movies do you have to watch?" he asked, thinking that living next door to his landlord wasn't a bad deal.

"All my favorites are packed and I don't know which box they're in. My mom doesn't have a DVD player so we're stuck with whatever she has on VHS."

"She had *Fargo*. That's a good one."

"My friend, Kevin, brought his copy over for me."

There was no reason Paul should wonder about her "friend" Kevin, but the thought didn't release easily. If she was dating, the guy wasn't around much or else Paul would have seen him at some point. Paul thought about the idea that she could be involved with someone.

Why that hadn't crossed his mind before he didn't know.

Lanie grabbed her crutches from the floor and used them to help her stand up.

"Hey, sit down." Paul was beside her. "I can get the movies. Where are they?"

"That's okay. If I don't stand up every so often, my good leg goes to sleep."

Traces of soap and flowery mint shampoo clung to her, and the smell aroused his senses and him. He was pretty sure she wore a sports bra, but it was fairly useless at keeping her breasts firmly in place. They moved with her steps, a soft gentle quiver beneath her tee. The hem brushed the backs of her curved thighs. It covered just enough skin to leave the rest of her to his imagination.

Semi-hardness pushed against his jeans when Paul sat back down and his fingers curled over the arms of the chair.

At a tall cabinet, she glanced at the titles and recited, "*State Fair, A Letter to Three Wives* and *Leave Her to Heaven*. Mom likes Jeanne Crain."

A low huskiness barely cloaked the desire holding him in its warmth. "How's the job search coming?" he asked, reminding himself they were at different places professionally. He'd found the direction he needed to be going in, but she was still searching for where she wanted to go. Starting something between them would only lead to a dead end.

"I'm impatient that it's taking so long to hear something. After working for Dutch, all my patience is tapped out. But when I do get a call, I'll pass the interview. I know it. I *can* prove myself. All I need is to get this damn cast off and take my life back. If only that Ludlow offer wasn't on hold I could... My mom's friend is a lawyer. He said I don't have solid ground to sue because they haven't rescinded their offer—just postponed it.''

Lanie brushed the knot of hair off her shoulder and it loosened to fall down her back. ''Either way, I'll be all right.'' A sparkle came into her eyes that he envied.

She was everything he used to be. Determined and hungry. The need to feel the passion from her pulled strong. He wanted to feed on some of the spirit she possessed, taste what she tasted. Bring her enthusiasm to his mouth like a wedge of lime sucked on after a shot of tequila.

Lanie paused from reading and quizzed, ''Why are you looking at me like that?''

His eyes must have been blazing, revealing too much about his wants. He had to remind himself he expected nothing. ''Keep going.''

She returned her attention to the videos. ''*White Christmas* and *Gidget Goes Hawaiian*.'' She studied the box. ''I didn't know she had this one.''

''I'm up for some surf scenery.''

''You really want to watch *Gidget?* I didn't think that would be a guy movie.''

''It'll have surfboards and half-naked women. Close enough.''

Lanie slid the cassette into the player and rearranged herself on the sofa once more. The beginning beach scenery rolled onscreen and they settled in to watch the movie.

Paul said, ''I have some strawberry ice cream at my place. You want some?''

''I would. Thanks.''

Lanie glanced in Paul's direction as he stood. The

sight of his body in motion, the tan skin on his arms and the carved swell of biceps sent the blood coursing through her veins like liquid heat. She was extremely aware of him and had been ignoring the warning signs that she was interested. She just lost that battle when tingles erupted across her arms.

Before today, staying on with the Majestic PD had been something she might have considered—with the right options. Now, staying felt dangerous. She couldn't complicate her life more than it was.

A guy like Cabrera was a pit in a cherry pie. You never knew when that stone would turn up—but the pie was so delicious you didn't care. It was only after you chipped your tooth that you realized you should have stopped after one spoonful.

When he'd asked about her job search she hadn't been altogether truthful. She didn't have a good feeling about her prospects. Offers weren't burning up her phone line. Ludlow was her best hope.

Paul was halfway through the door when she asked, "Cabrera, do you know anything about civil rights cases?"

"Just that they take up a long time in court."

"That's what I thought. Better bring the whole carton."

Nine

Lanie sat in Cookie Baumgarten's chair getting her hair foiled, a treat paid for by her mom who was under the dryer after her soft set. Her mom's friend, Myrtle Sanders, waited for her comb-out and style in the next chair.

Cookie Cutter's hair salon was a great source for gossip and it was spread thicker than her mom's jams. Myrtle and Cookie were two peas in a pod. What you told one, you told the other—from there it was free for all the world.

"Lucille," Myrtle said, over the purr of the hood dryer. "I heard that lemons are going on sale for a nickel each at the grocery store tomorrow. I'm going to buy several and bake a custard pie before they go back up in price."

"What are you entering in the Founder's Day bake-off this year?" her mom asked, glancing away from her magazine.

"My snowball cookies. They're a sure thing." Rows of tiny blue-and-pink plastic curlers were pinned on Myrtle's head. "Lanie, you'll be visiting often, I'm sure. You should bake a cake and enter it."

"I'm not a very good cook."

"With all this free time on your hands, you could do some practicing."

Lanie bit the remark riding on her tongue because Myrtle didn't mean the advice maliciously. She gave her opinions freely and most people didn't object, since she was the first one there to lend a hand when someone was in trouble. She was well regarded for the famous chicken soup she brought to those who were laid up with an ailment—or if you were just plain in need of some old-fashioned comfort.

What Myrtle didn't understand was that Lanie hadn't been sitting around. The P&P manual had been a huge project and she had completed it within a relatively short amount of time. This morning Sherry collected the finished Policy and Procedure pages and took them down to the station.

When Lanie was done here at Cookie's she was going to speak with Dutch about something. If he could swallow his pride and come to her, then she would do the same and go to him on his turf. She had an offer to put on the table for his consideration.

The job search wasn't coming along the way she had hoped. The follow-up calls she'd made hadn't resulted in anything useful. No doubt about it, her physical limitations were hindering her progress. Nobody wanted to interview someone who couldn't start right away. She went to the Internet and made inquires on Hot Jobs. Hinsdale County was looking for a Patrol Deputy with an open application extension to September 1. That would buy her some time and she submitted her application to them. Scrolling down the list, she read that Aurora required a police dispatcher. The timing of the last entry had been ironic given the Majestic PD's current situation with Karen.

"And do you know what else I heard?" Myrtle asked, her crisp blue eyes wide with information. "Barbra is going to be singing at the Mirage this September and she might pass through Majestic.''

"My Barbra?'' Cookie queried, as she dabbed color on Lanie's hair. "She doesn't give concerts anymore. She wouldn't go to Vegas. Are you sure you aren't confusing her with Celine Dion? Celine has a show at the Colosseum in Caesar's.''

"I can tell the difference between Celine and Barbra, Cookie,'' Myrtle insisted. "I'm just telling you what I heard.''

Barbra Streisand's distinct voice sang "Don't Rain On My Parade,'' through the shop's speakers. Cookie Cutter's played continuous Barbra on the sound system.

Handing off another foil strip to Cookie, Lanie gazed at her reflection in the mirror. A tinfoil halo shone from her head and pieces of hair stuck out every which way. A plastic cape kept color from getting on her blouse. Her bulky cast rested over the iron foot bar of the chair. Her leg felt like a dead weight.

She'd gone to her scheduled doctor's appointment yesterday and her hope of getting the cast off was shot down as soon as he spoke to her. He said the E.R. physician had informed her incorrectly. While it was possible to have the cast off in three weeks, he preferred to leave it on for four with fibula fractures. She was stuck for another week.

"Have I cooled down enough to take out my rollers?'' Myrtle asked.

"Go ahead, but don't pull on them. You'll stretch your curl.''

The door opened and the delivery boy from Majestic Floral carried a large bouquet brimming with an assortment of colored roses. There had to be at least two dozen.

"Oh, my goodness me!" Cookie gasped, dropping what she was doing. "They're gorgeous. Who could have sent me these."

"Nobody," she said with a squint. "The card reads 'To L.P.'"

"L.P.," Myrtle repeated. "Lucille Prescott! I didn't know Ken was a romantic."

Lanie's mom laid a hand over her heart, lifted the hooded dryer off her head and stood to collect her flowers.

The gesture was incredibly nice of Ken, Lanie thought, as she watched her mother's cheeks grow red. Maybe he wasn't so dull after all.

The delivery boy left and the ladies stared at the arrangement, wistful smiles on their older faces. "Ken really is a gentleman," Cookie said. "Open the card and read it to us, Lucille. We all want to live vicariously through your romance."

Lucille slipped the card from the envelope, read it, then gazed at them with a puzzled lift to her eyebrows.

"What?" Myrtle pressed, her face like that of a Pekinese, eyes wide and ears twitching. "What does it say?"

"It says... 'To L.P. Thinking of you. Signed, Your Rescuer.'"

"Oh, my goodness," Cookie gasped once more. "Did Ken rescue you from anything?"

"No..."

"They aren't from Ken," Myrtle said, leaning forward to read the card for herself. "Whoever sent these has a reason he can't come forward or else he would have signed the card with his real name."

Lanie asked, "Mom, do you have any idea who they're from?"

"I...I don't know." But Lucille's face paled and she turned away.

Myrtle drew in the fragrant scent, sticking her nose in the flowers and coming out to exclaim, "Wait! Lucille, these might not be for you. Lanie, you have the same initials as your mother!"

Lanie's heartbeat went into high gear. "Nobody would send me something like this."

"Who's to say," Myrtle argued. "You're an attractive young lady. A lot of men in this town could be in love with you. The thing is, which one of them rescued you?"

"Nobody."

Cookie's eyes sparkled. "Paul Cabrera did when you broke your leg. That was a knight in shining armor moment, Lanie."

Lanie countered, "If he wanted to send me flowers because he was thinking about me, he would have done it before now."

"The element of surprise," Cookie elaborated.

Myrtle threw her attention back toward Lucille, mouth pursed with speculation. "Lucille, about the other night when you left the bingo game early. Herb Deutsch followed you outside. I didn't think anything of it at the time, but just yesterday Juanita Hart told me she saw you two walking together just after you both left."

"You were walking with Dutch?" Lanie questioned. It was news to her. Mom hadn't mentioned anything.

"First of all," her mother said, seeming very flustered and out of sorts judging by the way she fidgeted with the floral card, "I locked my keys in my car and he had a device at the station that could get them out.

I took him up on his offer. Secondly, he knows I'm seeing Ken and, therefore, unavailable.''

''You'd be unavailable if you were married, Lucille. He's grown too comfortable with your relationship and I think whoever this secret admirer is, is somebody who's telling you to put some spice in your life. *Orrr,*'' she enunciated the *r* with a conspiring wink at Lanie, ''maybe it's that Latin lover boy living next door to you.''

Cookie's observation dropped in a moment of silence over the room.

''I'm calling the florist to ask who sent them!'' Myrtle said, yanking the phone into her grasp and punching numbers faster than a speed dialer. She was on and off the line in less than a minute. ''The mystery man asked to remain anonymous. Both of you have investigating to do. There are ways of finding these things out.''

Lanie and her mother shot Myrtle a look at the same time.

Myrtle pulled off her cape. ''I'm sorry, Cookie, but I can't wait any longer for you. I wish you wouldn't double book. I'm in a very big hurry this afternoon.'' She tied a scarf over her head to cover the white lines of scalp showing through the many rows of uncombed curls. ''I have a book due at the library that I have to take care of right away.''

She rushed out of the beauty salon without closing the door.

''They've given the son of a bitch a nickname.'' Dutch rested his foot on a chair bottom as he addressed his officers during their afternoon update meeting. ''Since this guy's modus operandi is asking the clerk to change the battery on his watch, he's being called Mr. Tick Tock.''

"Interesting handle," Paul said from his seat, arms over his chest.

Dutch knew Paul was a hell of a big guy, and if the Tick Tock Dick came here, Cabrera would get on him.

"Is that the slam-and-grab guy that hit up Montrose a couple of weeks ago?" Coyote asked, his boots propped up on the conference desk.

"And Telluride last week," Dutch said, skimming the rest of the short report. "We have to be on alert for this damn time bandit. We're hot in the middle of summer and the town's full. Bad publicity is the kiss of death for tourism. That's all we need—some idiot trying to heist Liz Taylor's diamonds.''

Griswold bit into an apple. "She's in town?"

Dutch clarified, "Figure of speech. Why do you ask—did Liz Taylor ever come to Majestic? She's a looker, even with the gray hair," Dutch said, flipping over the paper to the next sheet. "I never heard any of you talk about her being here.''

Gordon Griswold summed up his reasons. "Because a classy dame such as La Liz skips small places like Majestic and goes to Switzerland.''

"Shirley MacLaine stayed at the Motor Inn." Coyote bit into a day-old donut, still in the box from Sissy's. Thanks to Cabrera, they'd been getting a dozen sent over in the mornings.

"That wasn't Shirley Maclaine," Griswold argued. "I spoke to her and she said she was a reincarnation of Shirley.''

"All right, all right." Dutch took back the meeting. "I want drive-bys of Plum Jewelers and Lemar's jewelry store several times a day. Coyote, you're on grave

tonight. Do a midnight alley check on both. I don't have
a good description of him—seems he wears disguises.
They've got witnesses who've seen him in a beard,
mustache and long hair—and all of it changes colors—
so don't count on anything.''

He finished the Hot Sheet items, then said, ''We've
got a completed Policy and Procedure manual that Prescott cleaned up. Most of you don't have to refer to it,
but it's here for anyone who needs a refresher. As for
dispatch, the temp I had lined up can't start for another
week. Karen had the baby a week early and threw the
whole damn schedule off. So I'm putting Ridder on the
front desk tomorrow.''

''He'll be happy about that,'' Griswold said with a
grin.

''We're going to rough it for the short haul until the
temp can come in.''

Other business was wrapped up and Dutch excused
the officers. He stayed behind, his attention drawn to
the P&P manual. Prescott must have killed herself to
complete it in such a short time.

He flipped through the pages, and found the updates
were perfectly inserted and paginated. He had to give
her credit for doing an excellent job, although he hadn't
told her that. Her friend dropped the box off and he
supposed he should telephone her as a thank-you.

Yes, maybe that was just what he needed to do. Lucille might answer the phone.

She was a hard woman to figure out. Since she'd left
him in the dust after he recovered her car keys, he
hadn't talked with her. He'd seen her at the grocery
store the other day buying milk, and he rolled his cart
past the dairy case, but she made brief eye contact with

him and turned the corner to where her lady friends were congregated at a display of detergent.

The old cat and mouse game—women running and men chasing. He wasn't that kind of player, but he also didn't want to botch things. A woman like Lucille would take a different tack and Dutch wondered if the plan was already in motion. It took him all morning to decide on his attack.

"Chief," Paul said, breaking into his thoughts. "Lanie Prescott's here to see you."

Dutch drummed his fingertips on the table. "Tell her to come into the briefing room." Now that she was here, he had no reason to call Lucille. Disappointment showed itself in the form of irritation.

She came into the room on her crutches giving Cabrera a long stare as she hobbled past. She took hold of herself and let the moment slip away, but not before one last puzzling look at the guy.

"Sit down, Prescott. Take a load off," Dutch said, sliding the P&P to the left. "What's on your mind?"

"Well…hello to you, too."

In short order, he replied, "Hello, then." While he had the thoughts in his head, he added, "Top-notch on the P&P. It must have been a nightmare sorting through everything. Appreciate it."

Her eyes lightened. "I think that's the first time you've ever said that to me."

He was sure he had given her the thumbs-up before, but right now he couldn't recollect what for exactly. Somewhat annoyed that he was unable to cite an example, he asked, "What can I do for you?"

"It's what I can do for you," she said, her posture tall and sure. "Since Karen went into an early labor, you're short a dispatcher. Put me on the front desk. I've worked on dispatch before and I did a great job. I know what to do and it doesn't take two good legs to do it. You need me, Chief.''

Leaning back, he folded his hands and cradled them at the back of his head. She was right about that. He could use a body for a week.

"I'll give it to you for a week."

"Only a week?"

"I've got a temp lined up."

"Let her go."

"Why?"

Lanie put her hands on the table top. "Why? Because I'm asking you for the job. Because coming to you for help isn't easy for me. Because doing desk duty when I've been in uniform stinks, but I have to take care of myself and pride won't stand in my way." She went on in a reasonable tone that crackled with conviction. "Because you owe me."

The room rang with those words and Dutch knew they covered a four-year history of stormy arguments and blame for his not taking her seriously. He could see she was very serious now.

She was right, he did owe her something and it wasn't a position or spot on the payroll. It was respect. She never thought she'd had respect from him before, even though his regard had always been there. Anyone who could pass the POST and willingly put their life on the line for others was good in his book. She was a woman and that's where the complications came into effect. There were various ways to show respect for a person, and keeping Lanie Prescott out of the action on meter maid and crossing guard duty had been his way.

She may have felt shorted because of his decisions,

and she may have just cause to feel like he owed her, but there was no humbling himself when Dutch said, "All right, Prescott. The job is yours. Be here at eight o'clock tomorrow."

Ten

Two deputies were in the field and Paul remained at the station desk. His schedule was sporadic, something he preferred so he didn't have empty time on his hands. Policing was a serious job, and at some point, the hours spent on cases had to be lightened up.

He learned early on that Chief Deutsch and the deputies had a sense of humor and their practical jokes kept the atmosphere upbeat. No wonder Delroy Ridder had tested the salt and pepper shakers that first morning they met for breakfast at Rooster's Place. Griswold had gotten him a couple days before and Ridder ended up with a black mound of pepper on his sunny-side-up eggs. Keeping with the spirit of things, Ridder reprogrammed the speed dial numbers on Coyote's phone to ring through to phone sex lines. Coyote paid him back by hiding one of those continuous playing electronic greeting cards in Ridder's office. The notes to "Evergreen" wore on Ridder's nerves and he tore through his desk yanking out drawers. He finally found the card taped to the back of his framed commendation on the wall.

Lanie didn't join in on their pranks. She was pretty serious about her work; she clocked in on time and gave all her attention to the business at hand. She had been working mostly days, but on the weekends she volunteered for extra duty and Dutch put her on swings to handle the influx of evening calls.

The position of Paul's desk in relation to the front reception area gave him a view of her at work. She'd answer calls and dispatch deputies with ease and efficiency.

The office ran seamlessly when she was here, not that Karen had been a bad manager. Lanie just approached things differently. Files were where they should be, and if you needed a document she knew where it was. For all her abilities, she drew the line at making coffee. She contended that if they wanted a pot they could perk it themselves. She wasn't a waitress and they didn't have a broken leg—she did.

This morning she came in wearing a black walking boot. The plaster cast had been removed and she was in great spirits. She looked really great, too.

Rolling his chair back, Paul contrived a reason to ask her something.

At her desk, he stood over her. "Lanie, where's the folder on traffic stops for last month?"

Her lips were colored in a soft pink. She had the longest eyelashes he'd ever seen; they framed her eyes which were a unique mix of blue-violet he never got tired of staring into.

The light from the front window set off her hair color, fall tones of brown and blond. Its texture appeared soft and silky, thick and satiny in its pinned up roll held in place with a hair claw.

"Filed under July in that tall cabinet, third drawer down."

Her eyes never left his, steady and with an often puzzling gleam to them. She'd been acting strange toward him for almost a week—ever since Dutch had re-hired her.

The way she looked intently for reactions from him with a heated smoulder in her eyes, as if she were X-raying him clear through to his briefs, made his mind swim with sexually charged ideas.

If he wanted that kind of gratification, he could have had it discreetly with Raine Ithaca who'd made her intentions clear. But sex just for the sake of sex wasn't what he was after. Not when he saw Lanie.

Her ability to draw thoughts out of him he didn't normally talk about left him desiring more than a night in bed. But that didn't mean he stopped appreciating her feminine qualities.

The sensuous curves of her breasts covered by her blouse left little to his imagination. She wasn't wearing anything overtly sexual—a crisp white blouse and khaki pants. Dutch gave her the okay to wear her uniform, but she'd been adamantly against his suggestion, commenting she wouldn't wear it for show.

The slash of exposed skin at her throat teased, and had him thinking about what she'd look like with one more button undone. Two or three. The beat of his pulse pounded in a deliberate rhythm in his ears. Looking at her was like drowning in something indescribably good.

He grabbed a manila folder from the cabinet—it didn't matter which one—and turned to stare at her when he felt her eyes on his back. "Do you have a problem with me?"

"No." Her tone was flat, a contrast to the sharp assessing look in her gaze.

"The hell you don't." He slapped the file on the cabinet top. "You've been looking at me differently for days. I want to know why."

She tossed down her pencil, the throwing of the gauntlet, so it seemed. Something he didn't understand—what in the hell had he done to her?

Lanie spoke with quiet, but determined firmness. "Did you or did you not send me roses at Cookie Cutter's beauty salon?"

He gave her a blank look. What she was saying left him clueless. If she was trying to draw some kind of response or admission out of him, she was mistaken.

"What the hell are you talking about?"

"The arrangement of roses to 'L.P.' from 'Your Rescuer.'" Her stare drilled into him, waiting for an answer. "And the single white rose that has been delivered to my mom's house every day since then. Seven of them to be exact. If you have some...*feeling* for me, then just come out and say it. Don't hide behind the florist."

Paul dipped his head closer to hers. "I'll say this: I don't know what you're talking about."

He could almost feel her stomach sink as she said, "You really don't know?"

"No," he said, the word sounding tight.

"You're the only one who's rescued me...so they have to be for my mom." Her hands cradled her cheeks and then her elbows dropped onto the desktop. Almost trancelike, she mused her thoughts aloud. "She's certain Ken isn't the one sending them. That's why she hid the vase in the laundry room last night when he came over. 'Your Rescuer' can't be Dutch. Something this secretive isn't his style. If he wanted my mother's attention, he'd be on the doorstep with his club and caveman suit. Which, thank God, he's not."

The pieces fell together for Paul. "You mom has an admirer?"

"Yes, and it's not her boyfriend…gentleman friend—whatever she calls him. He keeps sending a rose a day with the same note."

"Ask the florist who's sending the flowers."

"We tried that. They won't budge. It's a confidentiality issue. You'd think with so many loose-lipped people in this town, the information would leak out. Not even Myrtle Sanders has been able to crack this— and she went to work right away."

"Leave it alone," Paul advised, his hip braced against the edge of the visitor's counter. "The guy will come forward eventually and spill his guts. Unless his deliveries turn obsessive. Then I want to know about it."

"I can handle things. I once wore a badge and I will again." She set her hand on a sheaf of paper and pulled it from a stack. "Which reminds me—I need Dutch to sign this private citizen weapon permit. Put it on his desk where he can see it when he comes in, would you?"

Paul took the paper. "You want to keep a gun in your purse?"

"I've carried a concealed since the day I swore my oath. I feel light without my Sig Sauer .40 now that I'm out of the house."

"Be careful with it. The thought of you holding that much magazine capacity makes my gut clench. Always keep the safety engaged."

Indignant, her mouth dropped open. "Would you have said that to Ridder or Griswold?"

He smiled, a lift of his mouth that was slow and crooked. "Neither one of them has a purse."

"You know what I meant."

"And I think you know what I'd say."

She jabbed his leg off the counter. "You wouldn't have said anything to them because you're shortsighted. Go have your eyes examined."

The length of his laugh was cut short when Ida Strom-Corbett burst through the door and blurted, "I want to report a crime."

She was a regular with the same complaint. One look at her dress and Paul saw this would be the same report. Third one this week.

Ida Strom-Corbett was mid-sixties, gray-haired and somewhat of an over-exaggerator. He had followed up on her story and it was true, but his hands were tied. There was no law against keeping a dog in a pickup truck cab at a place of employment as long as the dog had ample water.

"Skeeter," Paul said, folding his arms.

"That damn dog, Skeeter. I want you to arrest it."

"I told you, Mrs. Corbett—I can't arrest a dog."

"Then I want Toby Stillwell put behind bars. The dog's owner should be held accountable."

Toby Stillwell was the night clerk at the Gas 'N Go and he brought his black lab with him wherever he went. The dog was perfectly content to wait out the hours Toby was behind the register. Most of the time he slept, keeping low on the seat until—for some reason—he got a scent of Ida when she walked by. Then he went nuts barking through the open window.

Lanie was already working on the report and changing the dates. "Is your account of the incident the same?"

"I was leaving the Gas 'N Go at five-fifteen. I bought the newspaper and a coffee." Ida brushed at the brown stain on the front of her dress. "At the end of the day, my mind's on going home and glancing at the headlines. I don't keep track of what car I'm walking past, and just like it happened the other day, I'm walking by Toby Stillwell's pickup truck and the dog hops up from the seat and barks at me. Scares the holy wits out of me every damn time and I spill the coffee.''

"I'll talk with Toby tonight," Paul said. "In the meantime, why don't you buy the coffee someplace else?"

"I shouldn't have to change my routine because of a dog." On a huff she grabbed the report, signed her name and stormed out of the station with as much force as she had when she entered.

"She'll be back tomorrow," Lanie predicted, sticking the complaint into her filing tray.

Paul noted the hour. It was after six o'clock. Lanie had been off for a quarter hour; her mom wasn't outside waiting in the Eldorado. With her leg in the walking boot, Lanie couldn't drive and she'd been reliant on Lucille.

"Is your mom coming?"

"She'll be late."

"Call her. I'll take you home." Paul saw by her expression she was mulling it over. He sweetened the offer. "Dinner wherever you want. My treat."

She pondered his offer. "Margaritas and chips at Fiesta Mexicana."

"Works for me."

A short while later, Deputy Griswold came in to pick up the radio and walkie-talkie. Just as Lanie and Paul were leaving, she answered the phone and told the caller they were on their way.

Grabbing her crutches, she explained as she progressed out the door, "A swimmer at the Motor Inn refuses to get out of the pool. The manager wants a unit over right away. I said we'd—*you'd*—handle it.''

''Is it after swimming hours?''

''The pool doesn't close until nine.''

''Then what's the problem?''

''There's a naked man singing 'Are You Lonesome Tonight' in the deep end.''

''Thanks for the dinner and the ride,'' Lanie said, letting go of a long and content sigh, then breathing in the summer night.

Getting out of the house and back to work had been really good. She felt like her old self in the station except for her demotion to dispatch. That was something she struggled with, but being in the thick of things made her all the more determined to line up interviews elsewhere. She would be back in uniform.

''Any time,'' Paul said beside her on the veranda. They stood together in the dark, the lights off inside except for the one on the end table. It must have been after ten. They had talked forever in the restaurant about everything and nothing. He was pretty familiar with Majestic by now and his comfort with its slower-paced lifestyle was apparent. She'd doubted it at first, but she saw he fit in. In some ways, she envied his ability to adjust so quickly. She didn't think she could have been this comfortable so soon. Whenever she thought about starting over with a new set of friends and a new set of co-workers, she talked herself into being fine with it all. She knew she would be, but more and more, leaving Majestic felt like the wrong thing to do. Why she thought that, she could only speculate. Each time she did, one answer seemed to come to mind.

Paul Cabrera.

He was the only thing to change for her since she'd decided to move forward with another department and strive for better opportunities. It was Paul coming into town who made her thoughts uneven, Paul's face and his imagined touch that interrupted her sleep.

She was out of her mind to be thinking like this. Alone with him, her awareness of his masculinity was heightened. His black hair was cut neatly and it beckoned her to run her fingers through the sides. She loved the color of his skin; a tan that wasn't brought on by sun but by bloodlines. Looking at him elicited a sigh deep within her throat. He towered over other men and when he was with her, he made her feel protected, safe.

While she hadn't been sure and didn't think he had been the one to send flowers, his admission he knew nothing about the roses was a letdown.

"Did you want me to send you flowers?" he asked, the uncanniness of his question unnerving.

"No...I mean, not unless you wanted to. I mean— no." She shook off the crazy ideas in her head. Her heartbeat slammed against her ribs in a low rhythm. "Why would I want you to send me roses? We don't feel that way about each other."

"A man can give a woman roses because he wants to see her smile, or because he thinks she's special. There doesn't have to be any motive other than that."

The deep qualities in his voice made everything racing inside Lanie slow down.

She spoke in a broken whisper, "But then she'd start thinking there was more to her smile. She'd start smiling whenever she saw him. She'd lose her thoughts and think only of him and how he made her feel."

Paul tucked a wisp of hair behind her ear, the touch sending tingles down her back, and she shivered. His face was above hers, his hand laying flat against the wall behind her head.

"That's the whole point," he said, his words wrapping around her. "I know that's why I'd do it. To make you crazy about me."

Maybe I'm halfway there already....

She suddenly felt light-headed. She wasn't thinking clearly. The day had been long and tiring and—

"Paul...you're talking crazy."

"Now she calls me Paul."

Had she? Calling him Cabrera put distance between them she didn't want to shorten.

But she couldn't help herself remembering how good his hand felt on the small of her back when he walked her out of the restaurant. Or how the warmth of his fingers encircled hers in the E.R. Such simple things, but he'd made her feel wonderful.

Lanie struggled for composure. It was late, she was tired...and she longed for him to remove her hair clip and ease the tension tugging on her scalp. Longed for him to loosen the severe office hairstyle from its tight twist and let her hair fall across her shoulders.

Pearly light enveloped the veranda in a dim haze cast from the lamp.

If he leaned in any closer his teeth could nip at the lobe of her ear or his mouth could crush hers. The length of his thighs were long and with a small step, she'd be standing against him.

Nothing separated them except the beats of their hearts.

Without another thought, her hand lifted and touched his face to discover if his cheek felt as smooth as it looked. He held still for her touch, swallowing slowly.

Her fingers were whisper-close to his mouth, his cheek in her palm.

If he wanted to make her crazy for him, he didn't need any roses to do it. This, right here and now, was a moment of lunacy. She shouldn't be like this with him, but she couldn't help herself. From the first second she'd seen him, she'd lost her senses.

Her thumb stroked his full upper lip and, with that, his big arms came fully around her and pulled her into his embrace. His mouth covered hers and swift heat curled through her belly.

With a will of their own, her arms draped over his shoulders and held him close, the thud of her heartbeat strong as she melted into him. He was solid and warm, her breasts heavy and yielding to the hard strength of his chest.

The firmness of his lips was intoxicating and she allowed him to consume her mouth with a kiss. A kiss so passionate, she responded without inhibitions, pressing into him and taking the groan that passed through his lips onto hers. His tongue glided and slipped into her mouth, a full open kiss that made her shaky.

She knew she'd regret this, knew it and didn't care. The moment felt uncontrolled and exciting at the same time. Fire spread and the involuntary tremor of pure physical arousal began.

It had been so long since she'd been with a man, been held or kissed and made to feel this way. Everything inside her unraveled and she let it go, welcoming the sensations.

Paul smelled good, the warmth of his skin heating the scent of him to fill her breath. Her hands rose to stroke his neck, the short hair at his nape and the collar of his uniform.

The uniform. God…it reminded her of everything. He was the new chief-deputy and she was—

She sucked in air, his lips softly against hers.

—wasn't ready for this. Her feelings were out of control and shattering. She wasn't prepared for her reaction to him. It frightened her, yet excited her and it sobered her muddled emotions. Once she had been hurt deeply by a man. She couldn't, wouldn't let it happen again.

And this was the perfect setup for disaster.

She broke free of Paul's delicious mouth, but was still gathered in his arms by his hold around the curve of her waist. Unfulfilled and aching, she wanted more. Her body felt as if it were half ice, half flame. Her nipples were tight and peaked, longing to be touched by his hands. The satin of her bra was confining, feeling a size too small.

She resisted him—this was a mistake.

No, it couldn't be a mistake if it had felt so right.

She breathed between parted lips, unable to meet his eyes. He eased her out of his arms, steadying her as if she couldn't stand without him. It was almost true. She disliked the weak helplessness of wanting more.

"I have to go inside," was all she could manage to say.

Slipping inside the house, she laid her cheek against the raised door panel and wondered how she could face him tomorrow.

More devastating…she wondered how she could be around him and not want this again.

Eleven

Dutch knew precisely how long Lucille Prescott took at the beauty parlor. Fifteen minutes before he anticipated her exit, he stood out in his front yard.

The afternoon wasn't overly warm, the sky an endless span of blue with white airbrushed clouds looking like something Hollywood had whipped up from a computer program.

Dutch's new dogwood tree had gone into a little bit of shock after he had planted it and the last few scorchers hadn't helped. The leaves were yellowing. He'd applied some of that miracle plant food, but he hadn't seen a miracle yet.

Holding on to the garden hose, his gaze constantly drifted across the street. He watered the tree, shooting the stream of water at the trunk in a random manner until a hole started carving a dip in the dirt. His concentration was lacking.

The tree was a lost cause.

For the last week he'd gone through different scenarios in his head on just how he was going to ask Lucille out. His strategy would depend on the way their conversation went today. For starters, he'd compliment her on her hairdo. After her visit to the beauty parlor, she always came down the stairs of Cookie Cutter's with that Candace Bergen glow he found so appealing.

Not many women could do something with shoulder-length hair and make it look good when they were in their late fifties.

Lucille was an exception. He'd never seen her hair stacked into one of those—what were they called?—bouffant styles. That overly puffed hair reminded him of a football helmet.

Dutch checked his watch. Any time now.

He'd been thinking about where he could take her. Dinner would be expected, but so ordinary for a first date. He might have gone for a movie, but some sappy romance was playing at the Egyptian. Just as well it was a dame movie—he wanted to showcase his best assets since they hadn't spent time together before.

Ultimately, he settled on bowling. He was great at that and had the right clothes to wear without getting his gut in a twist over argyle or plain socks, a suit and tie or a sports coat. Bowling wasn't too exerting and the pub inside the lanes served beer and wine.

Dutch watered his tree for over forty-five minutes. He knew Lucille was inside Cookie's. Her Eldorado was in front of the beauty parlor and he'd seen her go in. What was taking her so long?

When Lucille finally appeared in the doorway, Dutch lost his train of thought. He would have sworn he'd prepared to go through with this, but all of a sudden he felt real anxious. Not like him. He was a regular rock when it came to pressure. Nothing fazed him.

Nothing except seeing Lucille Prescott wearing a rose colored linen top and slacks with pumps. Her golden hair gleamed, loose curls sweeping over her ears and touching her neck.

Pretending like he had a purpose in watering the tree, he smiled at her and waved. "Hello, Lucille."

One of her slender hands lifted to shade her eyes against the glare so she could see him. No friendly smile touched her lips, nor did she speak.

"Hello," he repeated cheerfully, worried she hadn't heard him.

She turned toward the big car, unlocked it and opened the door.

His heart fell into his stomach. He cut the water to the hose bib and dropped it on the grass, ready to go after her.

But he only got halfway to the curb when she closed the car door and walked straight for him.

"Just what did you think you were doing?" she asked, drawing up to him wearing a light mist of the most fragrant perfume he'd ever smelled on a woman.

For a flicker of a second he wondered if this was a trick question, but he didn't take her for a jokester. "What do you mean?"

Her eyes were summer blue, full of ire and annoyance. "I know it was you. Why are you doing this to me?"

The roses. His gift to her. Two dozen brilliant colors for beauty, one white rose each day for admiration. The inspiration came to him when they were walking that night and he smelled the roses blooming from the gardens. He would forever remember the smell of roses and Lucille in the same thought.

She lowered her voice and said, "You've got to stop sending them."

"You don't like roses?"

"Whether or not I like roses isn't the issue."

"The white ones have petals as pale as your skin," he said, finding he fell into the observations of a poet— something that didn't come natural to his thinking.

"I mean it. You have to stop this nonsense. Ken came over and I had to hide the bouquet in the laundry room. I didn't want to explain something that I can't explain anyway."

"Is it the roses you don't like—or me?" he dared to ask.

She licked her lips, her mouth temptingly soft. "I like you just fine when I don't have to think about you. But each time a rose is delivered to the door, that's all I do is think about you."

"That's what I hoped."

"Why?"

"Because I want to get to know you better."

Exasperated, she claimed, "But I'm seeing someone."

"You're not married to Ken Burnett, and if I thought you were madly in love with the guy, I wouldn't be cutting in. All I'm asking for is a turn on the dance floor." Without a breath, he said, "So how about tonight me and you go bowling?"

She didn't outright tell him to forget about it. But she did gaze at him with indecision flitting across her expression. After a long while, she came to a decision.

"I've got to be honest with you, Herb."

"Dutch," he corrected.

"Dutch," she emphasized, making his gut clench with a bad feeling. "I was married to a man who put his life on the line before and it cost him. I'm not giving my heart away to that hell ever again."

So that was it. He should have guessed or at least assumed. She was afraid—not of him but who he was. The chief of police. Taking the news wasn't something he would do lying down because he wasn't Ray Prescott. However devastating, however sad the death,

Dutch commiserated with her. But it didn't mean the same thing would happen to him.

"Lucille, I understand where you're coming from, but please hear me out. Anyone, at any time, can have something happen to them. Cars wreck, a heart attack strikes and sometimes plain old bad luck can take something ordinary and turn it disastrous. That's life. We don't stop living it because we're fearful crossing the crosswalk will leave us vulnerable. I'm sorry you lost your husband, I deeply and truly am. But life marches on. You should march on. And I'd be grateful if you gave me a chance to see if we have the same beat to our steps. I'd like to take you bowling tonight. Please say you can come."

Then he waited, holding his breath in a way he hadn't done since he'd been in simulation training at the police academy, anticipating a bank robber coming out with guns blazing.

Lucille, with her ivory complexion and pearl necklace strung around her neck, wouldn't give him a smile. "I'm sorry, but no."

Dutch took the hit as if it were an uppercut to his chops. His recovery was swift, his expression hardly changed. "Me, too, Lucille. I won't bother you anymore."

Without another word, she got into the Eldorado and turned over the engine.

Driving away, Lucille dared herself not to look in the rearview mirror.

It was a dare she couldn't keep.

She saw Dutch standing in the yard like a proud bear, yet with broad and strong shoulders slightly hunched forward.

She'd hurt him.

If he only knew he was one of the few men she'd met in her life who could weaken her knees.

Ken Burnett was seeing another woman.

Lucille was dressed and ready with no place to go. She and Ken were to have had dinner this evening, but a moment ago he had called to cancel. He'd always put another woman ahead of her in their relationship—his mother.

One crook of Mrs. Burnett's finger and Ken came running, dropping what he had to do like a hot potato. Oftentimes, Lucille was left out in the cold.

Having a close relationship with Lanie, Lucille forgave a lot. She put Lanie ahead of Ken and understood a child or parent came first. It was just that Lanie wasn't a helpless twit. Mrs. Burnett required assistance choosing what to take out of the freezer for dinner. At eighty-two, she wasn't senile by any means, but she was downright manipulative in her son's life. And he let her get away with it.

While nobody was perfect, and Lucille had her own character flaws, it was becoming increasingly more difficult to accept Ken as a whole package—because Mrs. Burnett came along as the trim. She was the string that bound everything in a knot.

Lucille sat in her needlepoint chair, fingertips touching the stitchery on the arms. The house was quiet. Lanie was working and Lucille was by herself.

She felt an antsy unsettling, a stirring and longing.

She was lonely.

Having Lanie in the house had filled voids, but a daughter wasn't the same as a man to snuggle next to in her large bed. How many times had she awoken, wishing Ray was beside her to stroke her hair and stroke her cheek. To touch lips to hers.

She missed the feelings he brought from inside her heart. Missed the sound of a masculine voice in the dark. Missed flowers on her anniversary.

Lucille left the chair and went to the dining room table. The vase of roses stood in the center. Only the white ones now. She caressed the petals and some rained onto the table like fat snowflakes.

She studied the bouquet for a long moment, then she took her purse, locked the door and started the car. If she gave too much thought to where she was going, she'd turn around and go home.

Once inside Bowlwinkles, she went straight for the telephone book and looked down the column of last names for a number. Holding on to the pay phone receiver, she put aside everything she feared and dialed.

When the line was answered, she simply uttered, "I'm at the bowling alley."

Then, without saying anything further, she hung up.

Frozen to the spot, she fidgeted with her pearls to keep from running. She turned toward the loud noise of pins dropping and heavy balls smacking the alleys.

This was the first time she'd been in here. She'd bowled in high school, but rarely since. The pastime didn't particularly lure her attention; although she recalled enjoying it. Even so, she hadn't had on a pair of lane shoes in at least thirty years.

Lucille's immediate friends weren't bowlers. No chance of bumping into them, but she recognized several people. The checker from the grocery waved and Lucille tried to appear casual. She focused her interest on the games being played, as if she were here rooting for someone.

"What made you change your mind?"

The raspy sound of Dutch's voice was oddly reassuring as she turned toward it. He held on to a bowling bag handle almost as tightly as he must have been holding on to hope.

Lucille touched her pearls and swallowed the heaviness in her throat. His handsome face was reserved, but his light blue eyes revealed more. He gazed at her with heartrending tenderness. Whether intentional or not, it moved her more than the roses.

"You were right. I have lost step with others."

He came closer and said in a confidential murmur, "That can be fixed. All you have to do is put the right foot forward to get back into the swing of things."

To her ears, her voice sounded unsteady, but she'd ventured too far to retreat now. "You'll have to show me how to do this."

"First, we rent you some shoes." He smiled and took her by the hand, his fingers rough and warm. "Then I'll pick you out a bowling ball. We get a lane and order a drink; then we're set to bowl. Do you like wine or beer?"

She didn't drink much, and when she did, she ordered wine. "Beer."

"You're my kind of girl, Lucille."

He winked and she realized, without her being aware of it, she'd been waiting for this moment.

Twelve

Saturdays were always busy and for Lanie, the most normal thing to happen today was Juanita Hart's report of her dress store mannequin being removed from the Dumpster in back of her shop. Lanie had taken the information down over the telephone. Juanita didn't want the mannequin back, she just thought it was odd that a plastic figure would disappear soon after she tossed it in there. She felt the police should know.

Juanita's report was tame in comparison to the rumors that were flying with Danny Glover newly arrived in town. Some insisted he was here scouting locations for the next installment of the *Lethal Weapon* movies and others said he was searching for a tree to chain himself around for his latest activist cause.

Not since the Sheen and Estevez brothers had been in Majestic back in the nineties had so much speculation abounded. It was still an unproved fact whether or not Heidi Fleiss had been with Charlie and Emilio or not.

The dispatch line rang again. Lanie took the call, then sent Paul to the scene. He was the patrol officer in the field with Ridder and Coyote tonight. Saturdays were almost impossible to keep up with in the summer. She used her skills to multitask and get things done. At least she was more able to do two things at once now that she'd had her cast removed.

It felt wonderful to run her hand across her shin for the first time in four weeks. She'd been given her freedom and put into a walking boot. The black boot was just as ungainly as the heavy plaster but at least she could get around now without crutches.

Lanie was able to bear weight on her leg for small increments of time and build toward becoming more mobile. But the orthopedist cautioned that the walking boot was only a structure to support her weight. Her leg was still broken and traumatizing the fracture would prolong the recovery, so she had to be conservative.

She didn't know how she could be any more conservative than sitting behind a desk and watching her replacement get all the action she never had. She hated to concede sour grapes, but working this way alongside Paul was a challenge to her dignity.

Even so, they'd fallen into a pattern of going home together on the days their schedules closely paralleled.

Not since that night when they'd kissed and she'd felt drugged by a heat that blossomed low inside her belly, had she allowed her thoughts for him to get carried away. She told Sherry about it, but she hadn't been able to bring herself to tell her mother. She couldn't pinpoint why not—she always told her mom pretty much everything. Maybe because Lucille seemed to be in a place all her own these past few days.

Last Friday after her mom's usual day at Cookie Cutter's, she'd acted differently. There wasn't any one thing Lanie could explain. It was just that she was different. She sounded different, she moved different and she looked different.

When Lanie asked her mom if everything was all

right, she only smiled. A soft and bemused smile that Lanie hadn't seen in a long time, so she left it at that. Whatever made her mother content, Lanie was happy for her. It did seem strange that it took Ken so long to make her feel this way, however.

By the time midnight came, Lanie had intercepted three calls from the Majestic Motel with complaints of loud noise and arguments in room eight. She'd sent Ridder twice, and would have a third time if he'd been available. Lanie always tried to send the same officer to a callback because they knew what was going on already.

The rock group, Shaved Ice, was in town for a gig at the White Horse Saloon, and apparently the husband and wife band members weren't getting along this evening. Ridder said the two claimed to despise one another, and each wanted the other arrested for mind games.

There was no law against annoying each other; causing a disturbance at the motel was another matter. A unit had to be sent to calm them down, and to remind them that if they got combative, one or both of them would spend the night in jail.

Since she and Paul were walking out together, she went along with him to answer the call. Sitting on the passenger side wasn't something she could get used to, both in her personal and professional life. She liked to be in charge. She liked driving herself and not depending on anyone.

The Majestic Motel was off the beaten path, closer to the edge of town than the center of it. Once a ski lodge, the current owner had revamped it into a discount motel. With its reasonable rates, a different clientele was attracted to the plain accommodations. Some travelers were willing to forego HBO and a continental breakfast to save a few bucks.

When they pulled into the parking lot, they could hear the music before they even got out of the unit.

"How many times was Ridder out here tonight?" Paul asked, his arms at his sides but slightly curved to reach either his gun or handcuffs in a fast second.

"Two."

"That's one time too many."

Under the meager row of outside lights attracting moths, Paul looked tired. He'd been on for ten hours and tension lines showed on his face. He took his chief-deputy position quite seriously; sometimes she wondered if he put too much of himself into the irregular pace he'd created. It almost seemed as if he didn't want time on his hands. She often wondered what was troubling him when he stared hard at a report but didn't follow the text.

She tagged along, her normal walk out of step, while he hunted down the music. The sounds of Led Zeppelin guided him to room eight.

Once there, she folded her arms beneath her breasts and leaned against the wall.

"Knock on the door," he said to her.

Shrugging, she pushed away and gave the door a knock, but it wasn't loud enough for her to hear on the outside, much less anyone on the inside with Zeppelin blaring.

"Knock again," Paul said, his eyes fixed on the doorknob. "Louder. Tell them the police are out here."

Lanie knocked harder. "Police department, we would like to talk to you."

That produced a reply from inside: "Whadda what?"

Paul edged his shoulder to the door. "Stand back,"

he warned her. He hit the door with the butt of the shoulder—hard enough to make the window shake.

"Who is it and whadda want?"

"Police department! Open the door before I rip it off the hinges!"

The music went completely dead. The door swung inside and a man and a woman filled the opening. They both wore tight clothes, black mostly. She had on a lot of eye makeup—so did he. Eyeliner. He had a goatee which was braided. They couldn't have been older than their midthirties.

The man said pleasantly, "What can I do for you, Officer?"

"Keep the music off for the night."

"He's the one who turned it up," the woman complained. "Thinks he can play that guitar riff from 'Stairway to Heaven,' but he can't."

"Shut up, Sigrid."

"Officer, I was trying to get some sleep and he won't back off." She gazed at Paul with a glitter to her eyes and an appreciative curve to her lips. "Aren't you the tall one? You're the tallest cop I've ever met. You should come down to the White Horse tomorrow night and listen to us play. I'm the drummer."

"And she sucks," the man commented.

"Shut up, Andy."

Andy went into the room, picked up his guitar and moved the strap over his head. "If you want to hear some good playing, then listen to this."

He was plugged into an amp and electric music shot out the speakers.

Paul went inside the room to pull the juice, with Lanie right behind. She kept close to the exit wall. The toggle from the light switch dug into her shoulder blade.

Sigrid went to her drum set, sat and began belting out beats of a tune herself. The two songs clashed and Andy told her to shut up. She threw a drumstick at him, he ducked, and it sailed across the room. Lanie couldn't dip her head fast enough.

The wooden drumstick nailed her on the forehead. It wasn't all that painful—it just sort of smarted for a minute.

Paul came unglued, yanking the electric cord from the wall. She'd never seen him so fired up.

"Get away from the drums," he ordered Sigrid.

She rose and shot Andy a look. "If we go to jail, it's all your fault."

Paul turned around to her and replied, "And that's just where you're going, darlin', for assaulting a police officer."

He was in the process of taking Sigrid with him when Lanie, as much as she was loath to say it, stated, "I'm not a police officer."

Paul's teeth gritted. "She hit you with a blunt instrument."

"I'm fine."

"Lanie, she assaulted you."

"She was aiming at Andy," Lanie offered.

"Yeah," Sigrid put in. "I was aiming at Andy."

Paul rubbed his jaw and shook his head. "This is a bunch of bullshit and you two shouldn't be together if you cause each other this much grief."

"I want a divorce," Sigrid declared. "I can't live with him for another day."

"What do you think I want?" Andy shot back. "We just can't afford a lawyer."

"Then come here," Paul growled, "so we can go

home. You—'' he said to Sigrid ''—put your hand on my badge.'' Then to Andy, ''You, too, buddy.''

The couple hesitantly put their hands on Paul's six-point tin star. As they stood there with uncertain looks, he recited, ''By the power invested in me by the State of Colorado, I now divorce you.''

''Wh-what?'' Sigrid said, backing away. ''We're divorced now?''

Andy's eyes narrowed. ''Wait a damn minute—we are?''

''Isn't that what you wanted?'' Paul asked, walking toward the door.

''Well, yeah,'' Andy said slowly, then gazed at his wife. ''I'm sorry, Siggy-baby.''

''Andy, I didn't really mean it. Officer—marry us back.''

''I don't think so. You'll get into another fight, the music will bother the guests and I'll be back.''

''No,'' Sigrid assured. ''We won't. I want to kiss and make up.''

Paul declared them married once more, reversing the process by the same sequence of events. ''So that's it.''

''Thank you, Officer,'' Sigrid said, giving his arm a squeeze. ''You don't know how much this means to us. You made me see the light. I'm mind, body and soul in love with this man.''

Lanie left the motel room with Paul, glancing over her shoulder to see Andy and Sigrid in a passionate lip-lock in the doorway.

''Jesus H. Christ,'' Paul said as he climbed back into the unit. ''There are days when I think I've seen it all and I'm always wrong.'' He turned on the overhead light. ''Let me see your forehead.''

''It's fine.''

He disregarded her, his fingertips moving gently over her forehead, feeling for a lump.

Tonight Lanie had seen a side of Paul that she'd never seen before. He'd been edgy, his brown eyes layered with a darker color while his words were abrupt and clipped. The set to his jaw was rough, and a suggestion of annoyance had hovered over him. Perhaps this was the first time she'd seen a trace of cynicism tightening the muscles in his body.

"That divorce/wedding thing you did in there was…" She wasn't sure what it was, short of inspired. "That was, well…I've never seen that approach before. Did they teach you that in the Florida Academy?"

"Nothing as complex. I took it from life. I have a degree in psychology and it comes in useful."

The admission shocked her. She had no clue. "You're kidding me."

He engaged the motor and backed up. "Sometimes you have to play along and let them find out for themselves that what they want isn't really what they want."

Lanie pondered the philosophy behind that, then said, "Jeez, Cabrera, I hope you haven't been analyzing me."

In the darkened interior, the flash of his white teeth was her answer.

Paul strode through the house without turning on the lights and rid himself of the belt around his waist. The holster with its police arsenal was laid on the kitchen table. He removed his wristwatch and tossed it next to his gun.

At the refrigerator, he pulled the door open and grabbed a long-neck. He popped the cap and brought the bottle to his mouth.

The first swallow of cold beer was always the best.

He ended up in the living room where he removed his boots and dark socks. The earth tone rug was soft and worn beneath his feet. Shrugging out of the black tunic with its badge on the breast pocket, he tossed it on the sofa's back, then propped his feet on the coffee table's edge.

The front door was open to bring a cross breeze into the stuffy house that had been locked up all day.

The night was still warm, or maybe his body just ran hot. Sometimes he felt as if he were suffocating. The muscleman T-shirt he had on was thin and cool.

The only light in the living room came from the computer screen on his laptop and whatever spilled in from outside. The sheer curtains behind the couch were held back by ivory cords; he had never closed them, liking the way they looked as is. Lantern light from the yard bathed the window and curtains in muted yellows.

His gaze traveled across the shadows of gray in the room, his mood just as gray.

He'd spoken to Lavenia Torres this morning.

In the days and weeks following Angel Torres's disappearance, Paul chased down leads and hit dead ends. He buried himself in a mountain of paperwork and spent long hours on the phone. Nights blended into days; weeks into months. While investigators gathered all the information they could, he felt isolated in his quest to find Angel because none of them had made the promise he had.

In hindsight, it was arrogance and an assurance he could fix anything that had caused him to speak carelessly.

He had been fresh out of the academy, less than a year on the force, and he was the first officer responding to the scene. His blood was pumped and his heartbeat could barely keep up with the energy in his body. Immediately, he felt it deep in his bones—a mother's fear. Her child was missing.

Through Lavenia's tears, he promised he'd find Angel and bring her home. It was a promise he shouldn't have given.

Dammit, he knew better now than to ever give an assurance with a guarantee—and in his line of work, there were no guarantees.

The crime had been the top story on the evening news, and the media continued to carry updates for several months. Then other segments began to take precedence and, little by little, the young girl was forgotten. But not by her mother and not by Paul. Never. He would always carry a photo of Angel, always wonder where she was.

Lavenia forgave him his premature vow and they spoke every once in a while; he assured her the case would stay open as long as he had breath in his body. She liked to talk about her daughter, mostly he listened as she laid open her heart. He felt her pain in a way that few could.

A light knock caught on the doorjamb and he turned toward it. Lanie was silhouetted in the dark. "It's me, Paul. I'm worried about you. Tonight you were—are you okay?"

"Today was not a good day."

"I'm sorry."

"It happens." The bottom of the narrow bottle rested on his thigh, his fingers around the neck. "Come on in."

The screen door hinges creaked softly.

"It looks different in here." She scanned the room.

"I haven't changed anything. Same furniture."

"But your things are on it." Her hand glided across the sofa back to the fabric of his uniform. "I miss this sofa."

"You want to sit on it?" he invited, a corner of his mouth lifting in a half smile.

She sat beside him and leaned into the cushions. A soft breath passed between her lips as she turned toward him. "Mmm."

The low sound of her voice, content and laced with a sigh, wrapped around him. Hers was the scent he breathed when he lay down alone and closed his eyes.

"And I thought women weren't easy to please," he teased. "Just give them a sofa and they're happy."

"Not just any sofa. This is my favorite one. It's all worn in a cushy sort of way, and the arms are just the right height for my head."

Paul laughed quietly. "You want me to get up so you can lie down?"

"No," she replied, not very convincing.

Cool air coming into the house drifted over him, soothing and taking the tension from his tired muscles. He liked this. It felt comfortable sitting in the dark talking with Lanie.

Lanie's blond hair fell on her neck and caressed her breast. Silver hoops dangled from her ears. Straight teeth cut into her lush lower lip and he suppressed the urge to touch her mouth with his finger.

Kissing her had been reckless and wild. The fire reawakened and he envied the man she would marry. She had a sensuality that his entire body responded to. He felt more intimacy with her than he had for other women he'd seen. Theirs was a relationship he couldn't measure or define. They weren't dating, but neither were they just friends.

Lanie mattered to him, more than he had thought possible.

She sat up a little and regarded him intently. "I know guys aren't into talking about their feelings, but what's the matter?"

Men kept things bottled inside—she was right. He was no exception.

Sid had been with him from the start and knew the full extent of his emotional involvement regarding the Torres case. Paul had no one here to rely on when he needed to unload or just hear himself thinking.

Taking someone into his confidence wasn't easy, he never wanted to reveal too much. Especially weaknesses or vulnerabilities. He thought of himself as immune, but he wasn't.

Lanie's hand touched his. Comfort was a rare thing he accepted.

"There's a block of houses on Northwest Twenty-seventh in Miami," he began. "They're all the same style built in the same year. Same bland color paint, same matching composite roofs and the same white front porch. Everyone socializes on the porch, it doesn't matter the time of day. People who live on Twenty-seventh sit around and trade stories. Some of them work and some collect welfare. It's the middle balance for the system. It's where you go when you want to step up and it's where you stay when you don't want to step down and lose government subsidies, because Twenty-seventh is on the cusp. Low-income enough to get aid, but a nice neighborhood when you're making it on your own."

He ran his hand under his jaw, his knuckles brushing

the rasp of skin that needed a shave. "Magnolia trees grow from the sidewalk along the street. Back in the seventies, a renovation project broke concrete to make the planters and give the street appearance more of a Florida feel. Those trees are big and wide. The pride of the street when the flowers are in bloom."

Lanie straightened and propped her elbow onto the sofa's arm. "I can picture everything."

"I got the call at eight-fifty-six on the evening of May the tenth. I was heading across Seventeenth Street and was the first one on scene."

"Domestic violence?"

He spoke quietly and clearly. "Missing person."

In the half light he couldn't read the subtleties in her features nor see if she had clued in to the change in his voice.

"This is the case," she said, her voice whisper-light. "The one you resigned with an open on it."

"She was at the curb wearing a yellow dress that brought out the gold in her brown skin. She had a scarf on with black braids poking out from the hem. She was jumping up and down, and I could sometimes see the pale pink undersides of her bare feet. She frantically waved me over while screaming in horror as the neighbors began to gather around. I asked her to state her name and she said Lavenia Torres. I knew heading in that it was a missing child call and my gut was already twisting.

"Lavenia was a good witness. She was able to tell me detail by detail what happened. She and her daughter, Angel, were sitting on the porch when the ice cream truck drove past the house and Angel begged to have money to buy a fudge bar. Lavenia gave her the money and Angel chased after the truck. The whole time,

Lavenia sat on the porch and watched until her daughter left her view—obstructed by the full branches of the magnolias. The truck's music faded as the kids returned home with ice creams in their hands. All of them except Angel. She never came back.''

Lanie's breath caught in her throat, a sound so tight Paul could literally hear the hitch.

"Lavenia gave me a flawless description of the truck—white with blue, the menu painted on the side in both English and Spanish. Dent in the rear bumper and a Florida DMV plate. One of the neighbors was able to supply four of the numbers. The truck was apprehended minutes away from the scene. No Angel Torres. The driver's name came back with a clean record. He swore he never saw Angel, never sold her an ice cream. We didn't have a probable cause to arrest him so he was let go.''

"What about fingerprints? Couldn't they dust the truck? What if she'd been there and he'd had an accomplice?''

"Later into the investigation, we exhausted every inch of that idea. No matter how hard we tried to pin the driver as the perp, he didn't pan out. He even took a poly. Came back so clean, you could have eaten on it.''

"Then how could she have disappeared on a street where other kids were heading for the truck at the same time? It doesn't—''

"Make sense," he finished for her, his chest heavy. "I know. And damned if I haven't tried for thirteen years to make it make sense. We went after gang bangers, known offenders living in the area, suspects in a larger metropolitan grid—all nothing. Every lead dried up.''

"That poor mother..."

"Lavenia lives with something I'll never fully understand or be able to feel. She watched her daughter walk away, smelled the last trace of her hair in the breeze and felt the warm touch of her skin in her hand when she gave her the money. She wasn't a bad mother, she was doing really good as a single parent. Lavenia was right there, not in a bar looking for men to show her a good time, but right on that street with her daughter. If only those fucking magnolia trees hadn't been planted, Lavenia could have seen what happened."

He blinked, his eyes dry and burning. "So that's what changed my life. That's what brought me here. You can only live with so many cases like this before you have to distance yourself from them. I wasn't a good enough cop to find Angel."

"You can't say that," Lanie said softly. "Sometimes the answers aren't there."

"But I keep looking for them," Paul returned in a monotone. "I search the Internet for similar cases across the country. A few years ago, I ran across a case in Indianapolis that set off a warning. When I investigated it further, I found out the suspect in that case had been in jail at the same time Angel had been kidnapped."

"It could have been something else," she offered. "You have to check every lead to get a match. FBI profilers, DNA samples and local testing. Watching cases and looking into arrests."

"I did all that. I'm to the point where I have to refrain from letting it take over my life. It almost incapacitates me when I let it. I can't dwell on the case anymore. I searched for a suspect to no end, then I gave the file to my superior when I retired from Miami-

Dade.'' Paul leaned his head back on the sofa and gazed at the ceiling. ''Maybe one day something will turn up, but it's not going to be because of me. Lavenia understands it was time for me to move on, but we keep in touch. We always will.''

Lanie's hand went to his, gently prying his fingers open and meshing hers together with his. ''Paul, I'm so sorry I asked you now,'' she said with sympathy. ''I didn't mean for bad memories to surface.''

The comfort she offered curled around him and he lifted his free hand to play with a lock of her hair. Its satiny feel wound around his finger, silky and sweet.

''They're barely beneath the surface no matter what I'm doing,'' he said. ''It doesn't matter if you asked me or not, Lanie.''

He slid his hand down the back of her neck and stroked her nape. She sighed, long and drawn out. Using gentle circles with the pad of his thumb, he gave her a massage.

''Mmm...you're better than the sofa,'' she whispered as he softly stroked her skin. Leaning languorously toward him, her head tipped forward, she closed her eyes. His touch was no heavier than a caress.

Countless seconds passed. Her slender fingers still locked into his, a reminder of her comfort and concern. Heat settled low in his belly without bringing him to sexual arousal.

Unbelievably, this was enough for him. Just being with her, touching and feeling the muscles in her neck slacken gave him pleasure.

Lanie's contented sighs dwindled and he heard steady breathing, light and peaceful. He didn't stop, not even as she dozed.

After a while, she stirred, then sat up, momentarily

disoriented with her hair tumbling over her shoulder. Looking into his face and glimpsing the room, she mumbled, "I fell asleep. I'm so sorry."

He smiled. "That's okay."

"It's not. You were talking to me and it felt so good and I just—"

"Don't apologize. I wanted you to feel good."

She stood and brushed the hair off her face. Her blouse was wrinkled from where it crushed next to his arm. "Let me make you something to eat. I bet you haven't eaten all day."

"I had some snack cakes and two Cokes a couple of hours ago."

"Then anything I fix will be a step up."

Paul stretched his arm over the back of the sofa and extended his legs. The recollection of her telling him she wasn't a cook came to mind. "I don't know if I have any frozen meals in the freezer."

"I can do better than that." She sent him a smile that filled him with a lazy warmth. "My mom's got leftovers in her fridge."

Dutch drove his Explorer past Lucille's house on the pretext of a routine perimeter check. Nobody was around on a Monday midafternoon.

Neighbors were at work and schoolkids only had two weeks left of summer vacation; most of them spent it up at Cascade Lake before the season came to an end.

Lanie was on duty and Lucille had come back from the community center an hour ago. He had a rough idea of her routine from having talked with her at Bowlwinkles.

A vague smile came into Dutch's eyes.

Lucille Prescott was a pretty good bowler for not

having been on the lanes in so long. When she captured her house ball from the lift, tucked her fingers into the holes and studiously approached the alley, her behind had a cute little shimmy with her walk.

She drank two glasses of draft beer, nibbled on a bowl of peanuts and recorded his strikes on the Accu-Score once he showed her how it was done. So to speak, she took the ball by the holes and didn't disappoint him.

He always suspected Lucille was an amazing woman. Now he knew for sure.

His unofficial neighborhood watch was concocted to try and catch her outside. After walking her out of Bowlwinkles he asked for another date, but she said the night had been fun and they should leave it at that. She didn't want complications.

Dutch begged to differ. He wasn't complex. He said what he meant and meant what he said. His argument was that she couldn't get a more straightforward guy.

Lucille didn't see his side of things and thanked him for a good time.

He'd thought about crashing her bingo game last night, but dabbing ink on a card wasn't his idea of a sport. Besides, Burnett went with her and Dutch preferred not to see them together.

He cut the engine and walked to her front door, knocking officially with his heart knocking just as loudly in his chest.

She opened the door and he couldn't contain the grin on his face. She looked wonderful. Just like sunshine and peach blossoms. She wore peach, his favorite color. A trace of lipstick shone on her lips and her eyes were a nice shade of blue today.

"Hi, Lucille," he said, clearing the scratch out of his

throat. "I was in the neighborhood so I thought I'd check on you and make sure you're okay. There's a jewelry robber on the loose, grabbing and running with anything that sparkles. The thieving son of a dog hasn't struck residences, but we can't be too sure these days. You think you've nailed the MO and they go and change their pattern on you." He took in a gulp of air, moving right along to the point. "That's not the only reason I stopped by. I was hoping that tonight—"

"Thank you so much, Chief," she cut in after gazing nervously behind her. "It's not just any town that can have a conscientious chief of police who makes house calls to check on the residents. But as you can see, I'm safe and sound."

"That's not really why I'm—"

"Safe and sound," she reiterated firmly.

Ken Burnett appeared behind her and Dutch felt as if he'd been hit in the gut.

"Burnett," he said through a stiff jaw. "I thought you had a restaurant to run."

"I've got employees who take care of the afternoon shift, Chief. As settled as I am in business, I'm ready to kick back and enjoy my retirement funds. I'll reap the benefits from the Steakhouse with somebody else managing it." Ken put his lanky arm around Lucille and gave her shoulder a squeeze. "We're not getting any younger."

Lucille's posture went stiff, her eyes fixed on Dutch.

Ken Burnett continued, "Lucille and I were just talking about what she wants for her upcoming birthday. She's a special woman and not just anything will do."

"I don't want any fuss," she said in a subdued voice. "Chief Deutsch, it really was thoughtful of you to stop by."

"Don't mention it," Dutch replied tightly, his eyes leveled on Ken. The man's tan complexion reminded him of a manila envelope. What did Lucille see in Ken Burnett beyond the fact he was a nice guy, the president of the Chamber of Commerce and did volunteer work at the Clinic?

Inhaling sharply with a tight flare of his nostrils, Dutch adjusted the angle of his cowboy hat that went with the uniform. "Well...I'll be going now."

"See you around town, Chief," Ken said, still glued to the spot next to Lucille. They looked like a mismatched wedding cake topper and the whole image gave Dutch indigestion.

He got back into his Explorer, twisted the key and accelerated with a heavy foot on the pedal.

Halfway down the block he determined this was only a setback and the immortal words of Clint Eastwood came to mind.

"Do you feel lucky?"

Yes, I do. Yes, I do.

Thirteen

Paul drank his fourth cup of coffee at the wheel as he cruised swiftly across Main Street. Behind the cloudless reflection of his sunglasses, his eyes were strained. This was his third shift on daytime and he was feeling the effects of an interrupted sleep schedule. His internal mechanism ticked better during after-dark hours, and it took more than three days to reset his body clock—more like a month to reverse dinner with breakfast again.

He had just left a video meeting at the department. Every one of the Majestic deputies had been in attendance, leaving nobody in a field vehicle. This was something new Paul had never seen before, given the large area his former precinct covered. If the Miami PD pulled in all their force to watch cops on the TV, crime would have enjoyed the holiday.

During the movie, Dutch stood to offer his opinion every now and then by pointing at the visuals. Over the years, Paul had viewed these types of police procedural tapes that showed how other cops handled situations. They were informative, but the dramatic scenarios never played out like that in real life. A criminal didn't engage his weapon in exactly the same way the fictional action was portrayed. It was useful to a degree, Paul guessed. But nothing was better than training that actually got you out on the street and working the unit to see things firsthand.

When the video was over, Dutch handed out the bi-yearly report on major and primary offenses. The arrest summary was average for a town this size. Majestic could have been the manual for textbook incidents.

Lanie was off today and the station had an unusual thirty-minute lull, just long enough for Dutch to cover the Hot Sheet after the officers watched the film on the briefing room television. As he dismissed them, an indecent exposure call came in and Paul had to take it.

As he sped through town, lights flashing, he thought about where he had been less than two months ago. His belief about his abilities in Miami had a profound effect on his performance. Here, in this breathtaking setting of Majestic, he was realizing people could bounce back from failures by *not* focusing on what had gone wrong.

Lanie was a perfect example.

Seeing the fiery determination in her reminded him of his early years on the force. Her drive and ambition brought back the reasons he'd taken the oath in the first place.

Protect life, protect property, be involved with the community and make people feel safe—that's what being a police officer was all about.

He wanted to see her eyes alive with the honor and dignity she strived for, even if she had to go elsewhere to get it. But damned if he wouldn't miss her when she was gone.

He slept in her bed, could swear he smelled her in the room with him. Her presence was everywhere in the house. From the flowery wallpaper and old lamps with fringe, to a misplaced sock he found in the back of a bureau drawer.

Lanie's house had started to feel too comfortable, as if she came along with the furniture. His furniture remained in storage—along with his life. It was time to look for a place of his own, to unpack boxes and settle in. Time to quit thinking about the ways she fit into his days and nights, to quit having dinner with her and sitting on the porch. To get away from talking about things he never talked about with other people.

He should go out and do something with other women, but there was only one who captured his interest.

The taste of Lanie's mouth, the touch of her skin and the feel of her curves beneath his hands made him want to explore feelings that went beyond friendship. She fit snugly against him when he'd held her in his arms for that kiss. A kiss that made him realize what an emptiness he had inside him. She made him want more than he could have from her. Each time he saw her, the pull was stronger. But she was determined to begin elsewhere and he was where he needed to stay. Those two definitive lines of thought left no room for middle ground.

On most mornings at Rooster's Place, Paul ran into a Realtor who ate breakfast in the next booth. Joe Fieland was friendly and kept offering to show him some properties on the market. Paul was building a collection of the man's business cards. He should give Joe a call and take a look.

Making a right turn at Wooded Creek Road, he bore down on the only school in Majestic where grades K–12 were taught. Fall classes would be starting next week. It was a nice school—one he might have enjoyed if he could go back in time with the life-educated brain he had today versus the punk mentality he had way back.

His school years hadn't been great.

Paul stole lunches in grade school. Not because he was hungry—although sometimes a lift came with a reward like a chocolate cream-center cupcake. Stealing was a high for him. A rush of adrenaline that he used to get through the day. Going home came soon enough and he didn't want to be there anyway. So getting in trouble at school seemed a way to pass the time. Students would dare him to walk out of class and he would. The principal's office and detention hall were a lot better than his living room where that dick-head of an excuse for a father would sit tuning in a boxing match and hating life.

Whenever his father had to come down to the school, he played it cool like the concerned parent. Antonio Cabrera sat like a big man in a dilemma about what to do over an uncontrollable son, a guy who cared and wanted to make things better. It was a load of bullshit. A liar's act.

Paul knew he would be in for a mouthful of Tabasco or a belt across his shoulders when they got home—if his father could wait that long. More often, Paul got slapped on the back of the head in the car as they left the school. Physical punishments only lasted until Paul developed a thick skin and lost his fear.

The day he quit fearing Antonio was the day Paul became a man at the age of twelve. Puberty came early for him, his height superceding the other boys in the classroom in the fifth grade. Paul's strength grew rapidly. He "pumped iron" with whatever tools in the garage he could find, turning his biceps into brawny weapons. Using fists was the only way Paul could win against the prick.

God, if he ever had kids he'd *never* treat them the way he'd been treated by his father.

Driving around the back of the school he saw the yellow bus and the cars parked beside it. Children remained onboard and the driver stood in the doorway speaking with the small crowd of parents who'd come to pick up their kids—kids whose arms and faces hung out the windows when he cut the motor to his police vehicle.

The Lake Bus left the school grounds for day camp Monday through Friday at eight in the morning and returned at four in the afternoon. Kids were supervised by adults and taken to Cascade for swimming and waterskiing lessons on a summer pass that cost next to nothing.

An older woman jumped out of her car and came toward him. "He's that one! Right there at the back of the bus." She pointed, her gaze turning accusing and narrowed. "He's ducking and those boys are hiding him, but I know what color his swim trunks are. They're light blue with a white stripe at the waistband. I was shocked. I *still am* shocked. What kind of manners did his mother teach him—obviously not good ones. I'm appalled."

Paul radioed in that he was on scene, then addressed the woman. "Ma'am, slow down."

"I don't want to slow down," she declared. "I was following the bus and I saw that…horrible…horrible sight."

The driver of the bus, Margaret Peterson, left the bus stairs appearing flustered. Her cheeks were colored, her walk concise. She wore a straw hat and white capris.

Parents questioned her, but she offered no answers other than to say she had to talk to the officer.

When the group of kids tried to follow her, she about-faced and blew on the metal whistle dangling from a ribbon around her neck. "Get back on the bus and *sit down!*"

The corner of Paul's mouth twitched. She could have been one of the nuns at the local Catholic parish he'd attended as a boy.

The children filed back inside to reposition themselves on the seats, but most of them were on one side of the bus—waiting to see what was going to happen.

"Officer Cabrera," she said, her cheeks as red as apples from the heat and her distress. "I didn't see it, but she claims there was an incident at the back of the bus with one of my passengers."

"What incident?" one of the moms asked. "What is going on?"

"That boy in the blue trunks," the woman insisted. She looked to be in her late sixties, very uptight and with a thick crop of white hair. She had Wisconsin plates on her Oldsmobile. "He's the troublemaker. Are you his mother?"

"No," the other woman vehemently denied. "My *daughter* is wearing pink. And what difference does that make anyway? Officer Cabrera, I'd like to pick up Ellen now. She's got a five o'clock piano lesson."

Paul shifted his weight, hand at his hip. "I need to find out why I was called here on an indecent exposure violation. Join the other parents and we'll get this cleared up."

The Wisconsin woman said hastily, "My husband and I are here for a nice vacation and I didn't think we'd be subjected to this kind of thing. I pulled over as soon as it happened.''

"You almost ran me off the road getting me to stop," Margaret said crossly. "I heard you honking. Officer Cabrera, isn't there a violation for almost running a bus off the road?"

"One thing at a time." He asked Wisconsin Woman, "What's your name, ma'am?"

"Ethel Farber. We're staying at the River Run Bed-and-Breakfast."

"All right. So what happened? Tell me *calmly*."

Ethel plunged in, "I was on my way back from the John Wayne gift shop and I was driving behind this bus. I like children," she went on with an empathetic note, "so I smiled and waved. We did this for several signals. Each time we stopped at a light, I smiled. Well, this—*this boy*—he was in the back seat and he stood up and dropped his shorts." The wrinkle lines on her face deepened as she grimaced. "He mooned me."

Paul bit the inside of his mouth. "And you called the police for this?"

"Of course! I want him taken in for indecent exposure."

"Margaret, you didn't see what transpired?" Paul asked.

She ruefully shook her head. "I glance in the mirror every so often, but my eyes are mostly on the road. I didn't see him do it."

"Trust me, he did it," Ethel snapped, her voice high-pitched. "His buttock cheeks pressed next to the glass. If you dust for prints, you'll get two round circles."

"We don't dust for that kind of print, Ms. Farber." To Margaret, he said, "I'll go talk to him."

"I want you to do more than talk to him. I want him punished."

Paul said evenly, "I'll personally bring him home to his parents and we'll take this further. I'm not going to haul him in for horseplay, but I'll make sure he's going to suffer some consequences."

"Be sure you do, Officer. I'm going to speak with your superior and make certain you follow through."

Ethel Farber stormed to her car and drove out of the parking lot with a shake of her white head.

Paul approached the school bus and braced his foot on the step. "Get him for me, Margaret."

She disappeared down the aisle of laughing kids and came back with a boy whose chestnut hair was parted down the middle and whose nose was dotted with freckles.

"Here he is," Margaret said, holding the shoulder of his T-shirt in her fist. "He's given me nothing but trouble all summer and I have to say it doesn't surprise me. I didn't see him do it, but the girl he sat next to ratted him out."

"That's my Ellen," her mother said. "She never fibs. If she said she saw him do it, then he did it."

Sherry's son, Mark, jerked away from Margaret, a smirk on his mouth. "I thought it was funny. And anyway, they dared me to do it."

"You'll be thinking it's real funny tonight," Paul remarked.

"I'm supposed to take him home," a woman's voice offered. One of the mothers came forward. "His parents are working today and I said I'd bring him to the car wash."

"The car wash?"

"Dirty Harry's Car Wash. His father owns it. Sherry's working today and I said I'd help out."

"Okay, Mark, we're going to see your dad." Paul steered him away from the bus.

The kids shouted at him through giggles and several of his friends hollered:

"Dude—run for the hills!"

"Butt boy!"

"Call me later, Mark!"

"Oh—wait a minute, he's got his water ski in the cargo." Margaret used her key and opened the hatch.

Paul carried the ski to the Explorer and had Mark sit in the front seat, then he sat next to him. Mark had a scrape on his elbow and the laces of his skater tennis shoes were missing.

Now that he was away from his buddies, his face turned a little paler.

"Aw jeez," he mumbled, his shaggy hair in his eyes. "My dad's going to ground me for life. I wasn't supposed to get in trouble for the rest of the summer."

"You should have thought about that before."

"Can't we forget about this?"

"I don't think so." Paul engaged the gear column and turned through the parking lot.

Mark said nothing, his lips tightly together.

As Paul cruised the short blocks to the car wash, he commented, "Did it ever occur to you that maybe nobody wants to see your skinny white butt?"

"Ha ha. Very funny. Is that gun loaded?" His gaze was fixed on the Glock.

"Yeah, it's loaded."

"Have you ever shot anybody with it?"

"Fortunately, no."

"Then you must not be a very good cop if you let 'em get away."

Paul turned into the car wash, the sign above it reading: *Dirty Harry's Car Wash: Brushless Automatic Service.*

The day was sunny and hot, and a line of cars waited for service. Air blowers and the sudsing machine whirred from the open building.

He saw Lanie sitting at one of the bistro tables out front, drinking iced coffee from a plastic glass. The newspaper and some other papers were before her. The flat of her wrist kept the paper corners from being picked up by the faint breeze. Lifting her head his direction, she gazed at him through sunglasses.

As Paul stepped out of the Explorer, Mark went ahead, passing the bistro tables with their angled umbrellas.

"Hey, Mark," Lanie called. "What happened?"

"Nothin'."

To Paul she asked, "What's the matter?"

"I need to talk to his dad."

"I hope he's not here," Mark said, with a snort over his shoulder. "My life is over. He's gonna take away my skateboard, my TV and I'm gonna be tortured by Hailey 'cause I won't have anything to do."

Lanie gave him encouraging words. "Whatever it is you need to work out, your dad's a pretty reasonable guy."

Mark's tone was flat. "If you think he's such an okay guy—then why did you divorce him?"

Paul cocked his head at Lanie, his lips half raised in a startled smile. "Looks like I'm not the only one with an ex."

Lanie mulled over her response and ended up muttering, "Looks like it."

Although she failed to see why it was an issue. She'd never mentioned that Kevin was her ex-husband because her marriage was ancient history. And besides, everyone in Majestic knew. There was no reason to dredge things up. Sherry and Kevin had been happily married for twelve years. The pain of that time in her life when her ex-husband and her best friend had married was gone.

She hated to have her past history book opened in public. It hadn't been an easy time. She was glad she could be here, talk with Sherry in the office and be friendly with Kevin without getting emotional. It had taken time and practice to get to this point.

Lanie preferred not to walk down memory lane—and certainly not with Paul Cabrera.

"Kevin's in the office," she said, refocusing her attention on the job applications before her. But after Paul was gone, she couldn't help feeling she'd let him down. She had no reason to feel this way. Just because he'd told her he'd been married before didn't oblige her to return the favor.

Mark's comment about Kevin and her splitting up sullied Lanie's concentration. She gathered the application forms she'd been filling in and tucked them inside today's newspaper.

Lanie began to walk home since Sherry was busy. Sherry was to have driven her, but if Lanie kept her pace unhurried, she could make it back to her mom's in the walking boot. She only had to go ten short blocks to get there.

Passing the building that used to be the Burger Barn

and was now Fiesta Mexicana, Lanie couldn't help but be pulled by old memories....

Kevin Mooney was new to the school in the tenth grade and the girls tripped over themselves vying for his attention.

Cocky about his sex appeal in those first several months at school, he went through plenty of girlfriends before breaking off with the last one to take his time picking out just the right one to ask to the winter dance.

Lanie never thought she had a chance so she had never bothered to flirt with him. She was tall and awkward, not pretty in the way other girls were with their petite statures and less on the top than Lanie.

Sherry, one of the smaller girls, said she'd never fall under Kevin's spell, and Lanie and Sherry huddled at lunch hours listing all the reasons why he was conceited. But somewhere around Halloween, the game turned to listing all the reasons they thought he was the most desirable guy in school.

Lanie was on a hall pass delivering a note when she ran into him by the lockers. He asked her if she wanted to hang out at the Burger Barn after school. His invitation couldn't have shocked her more, especially after so many months of him not acknowledging she existed. She muttered a nervous okay.

When the bell rang he was waiting for her at her locker and it was the beginning of their inseparable relationship. It also marked the beginning of friendship tension between her and Sherry, until Sherry got a boyfriend and the two couples started double-dating.

Lanie fell in love for the first time at the age of fifteen.

In their senior year, Kevin and Lanie were crowned

Prom King and Queen. The night was special, bringing her a happiness that escalated on their wedding day.

Lanie heaved a sigh, clutching the newspaper closer to her chest as she turned down 3rd Avenue.

After her divorce, she'd had to get herself back on track—which had been beyond difficult since Sherry and her ex-husband married less than three months after her quickie, no-fault decree had been granted.

Sherry tearfully confided she was two months pregnant.

Their friendship was strained and fell apart. It had taken months to put it back together. She repaired things with Kevin first—perhaps that had been easier since she'd once been in love with him and the hurts that they'd lived through had been jointly constructed. They'd married too young and too quickly out of high school.

Mending fences with Sherry had taken her longer but slowly, by bits and pieces, they came to terms with what had happened and Lanie was there for her friend at the hospital when she delivered Mark, Kevin's son.

Kevin and Sherry were doing well and that made Lanie happy for all of them. They were good parents to Mark and Hailey, and they had a stable family life. When Kevin's father died, he handed down Dirty Harry's. The only car wash in Majestic was a respectable business and did nicely. Kevin had thought about changing the name, but Dirty Kevin's just didn't have the ring.

Lost in her recollections, Lanie didn't hear the car approach. Paul drove the Explorer alongside of her, the window down.

He slipped mirrored sunglasses from his face and

rested his forearm over the steering wheel. "I'll give you a ride."

Every time she resolved not to let him affect her, he did. Just when she thought she was immune to him something happened to change that. In this case, his gaze on her felt like velvet. She had to remind herself to breathe.

"I can walk," she replied, gazing over her shoulder and wishing he'd drive away. She really didn't feel like filling in the blanks.

The vehicle accelerated slowly, keeping pace as she walked the residential street with its canopy of elm branches. Sunlight dappled the sidewalk.

"Kevin is the friend who loaned you *Fargo*."

"He was more than a friend," she replied, preparing for more questions. Maybe she did want to talk about it.

Notwithstanding their devotion to police work, their divorces were another thing they had in common. Failed marriages that ended years ago weren't optimum things to share, but the similar situations were something they could talk about with understanding.

"How long were you married?" Paul's voice was steady but Lanie's pulse was not.

"Four years." At the time, she'd found the last year unbearable. Now looking back it was stupid to have been bothered by his mowing half the lawn and saving the other half for another weekend. And his leaving the cap off the toothpaste now seemed inconsequential. He was a good man—they just didn't work well living together.

Paul questioned, "How long have you been divorced?"

"Twelve years."

He nodded and she assumed he went through the math given he knew Mark Mooney's age. She felt compelled to prove she was okay. "I'm fine. People make decisions that sometimes hurt, but time moves forward and we learn from the past."

Lanie chastised herself for feeling that she owed Paul an explanation. In her frustration, she resorted to cool sarcasm when pointing out, "And by the way, I don't recall you telling me your ex-wife's name and where she's employed now."

"Sergeant Julie Windham, formerly of the Miami-Dade DC Unit. She works in Property Crimes."

That's right. A police marriage. Two officers living in the same house resulted in the highest number of divorces within the law enforcement community. It was also hard being married to somebody outside the department.

Lanie felt badly for him, for herself…and for the whole sorry history they had with loving people they were no longer with.

She had been in love once in her life and she wondered if she would ever feel that way again. She had had other relationships, but nothing special. There had been the reserve officer she dated when she worked dispatch before entering the academy. When he was reassigned, their seven-month romance didn't weather the separation.

While she'd had casual friendships with men, nothing had developed into that heart-stopping-have-to-be-with-him feeling. No one had interested her in a way that left her wanting to be together—until now. Just when her life was packed in boxes and she was picking it up and moving elsewhere, she had to meet Paul Cabrera.

He reminded her of his Glock. Big. Powerful. Something she should avoid at all costs. But the sight of him sent a flutter to her heartbeat, a thrill to her mind and body. The way he looked at her sometimes made her feel like the last chocolate left in the box. A treat to be taken and savored.

It was her own fault she reacted to him like a high-school girl with a crazed crush. She was helplessly fascinated by him.

He was all male with a beautifully sculpted body and perfectly carved facial features. The available women in town tripped over themselves to get his attention, and sometimes she felt like she could be just like them.

She had to constantly refocus and redirect her thoughts.

"What's over is over," she replied in a rush of words. "I'm happily single and you're happily single. We survived."

"Are you really happy or have you talked yourself into it?"

Just when she was fighting back, he had to ask that.

"Is this a psychological question? Most of the time, yes," she tossed back, her misgivings increasing by the second for ever having begun this conversation. "I am *very happy* with my personal life."

The statement tasted bitter in her mouth. She wasn't being honest and she hoped he couldn't tell.

No—she hadn't been happy lately. Especially when Paul came in and out of her days and nights as if he belonged there. His living next door was very disadvantageous. Seeing him all the time at home, and then at work, made her realize just how starved she was for the sound of his voice, the touch of his hand and the expressions in his eyes.

But she'd never admit that to him because she could

barely admit it to herself. "I'm not saying no to re-marriage, but saying 'I do' doesn't guarantee forever."

His voice was thick, measured by steady but pronounced breaths. "Nothing guarantees forever."

The way he said it implied something else—something she was left to consider as he drove away.

Fourteen

"I invited Paul over for breakfast," Lucille said to her daughter, a spatula in hand and the aroma of pancakes filling the kitchen.

It was almost eleven on a Tuesday morning and Lanie had just woken up. Her progress down the stairs halted with her mother's announcement. Paul sat at the table enjoying a short stack and watching embarrassment fan color across Lanie's cheeks. She clearly hadn't expected to find him here. Her thick hair was brushed into a messy ponytail.

"I see that." Lanie flashed him a smile that was about as excited as a shoplifter being caught on camera.

She continued down the stairs wearing PJ bottoms and a T-shirt with *Shooting World Target Range* and two smoking pistols silk-screened across the front. His gaze roamed down her neck and lower to the images of guns over her breasts. Interesting sleeping attire theme.

Lucille turned her attention to the griddle sizzling with pancakes. "I hate to think of Paul next door without anything to eat."

Proceeding into the kitchen, Lanie's voice was scratchy from sleep as she observed, "For a man who's starving, you look fit."

"I'm all out of beer," he remarked with a grin.

She pulled down a plate from the cupboard and let her gaze linger on him. He welcomed her study.

He wore a microfiber pullover shirt; the navy-colored knit stretched across his broad chest, flattened next to his abs and contrasted against a pair of bleached jeans. His upper arm muscles filled out the sleeves without any extra room.

Paul drank his coffee, then set the mug down. "I once knew a guy in college who poured beer on his cornflakes."

"Why?" Lanie opened the fridge and grabbed the orange juice.

"He liked beer."

"Lanie, your pancakes are in the oven staying warm."

She took the tray out and fixed herself a few, then sat across from him. He could smell warm sheets on her hair and the sweet fragrance of her skin.

Temptation didn't begin to describe what he felt when he looked at her. She made him need, want. She could bring something special into his life that was missing. Something he hadn't felt in a long time.

The intense pull toward her scared the hell out of him.

A windstorm had swept through town last night moving anything that wasn't anchored. When he left the station after three, he came home and sat on the porch to watch the storm.

Drinking a beer, he saw himself in the leaves tumbling down the street and a pop can clinking its way into a storm drain. Maybe he wasn't as solid as he thought.

He'd thought he had it all figured out. Come here, rebuild his career and focus on his future.

He hadn't counted on Lanie mixing into the equation.

He lingered over his coffee, in no hurry to leave. He liked Lucille Prescott. She'd been telling him about her water garden in the backyard. He offered to mow her side of the grass today and she took him up on the offer.

Lanie swirled a bite of pancake through the syrup puddle on her plate. His eyes followed her fork as she brought it higher—his full attention on her mouth. A mouth he'd kissed and wanted to again. The pulsing beat of her heart rode in the hollow of her throat.

He wanted to lose himself in the sweetness of her mouth, the touch of her lips next to his. The color of her eyes darkened, then with deliberate slowness she ate the next bite.

"Taste good?" he asked in a low tone.

"Very." She ate some more, but couldn't stand him watching so she set her fork down. "Are you almost done with your coffee?"

"Do you need a refill, Paul?" Lucille had the coffeepot in hand and was pouring, failing to notice that Lanie's question was meant to get him to leave.

Lanie rose to her feet and walked around him. He caught another trace of her floral shampoo, breathing it into his lungs and remembering what her hair had felt like his hands. He resisted the urge to touch it now, to feel the glossy smoothness with his fingertips. If her mother wasn't in the room, he would have pulled the scrunch from Lanie's hair.

Paul remained seated. "Do either of you know Joe Fieland?"

"He's a Realtor," Lucille supplied. "Very hard-working and honest."

"He wants to show me some houses."

Lanie gave him an unblinking stare. "Are you going to buy one?"

"I'm thinking about it."

"If you think you're going to buy a house," she said through the ring of a telephone mounted to the wall, "you better give your landlord a month's notice. You can't just bail out without a thirty-day written— Hello?" She held the phone to her ear and listened. A slowly emerging smile caught on her entire face. "Yes. I will. Thursday. Of course. Ten o'clock. I'm so glad it's not. Yes. Thank you so much."

She hung up and exclaimed, "I have a job interview!"

"Oh, Lanie," Lucille said, wiping her hands on a towel and giving her daughter a hug. "That's wonderful. Where?"

"Pike's Peak. They're about an hour beyond Grand Junction."

"I'm happy for you, sweetie."

Lanie smoothed her hair out of her face. "Finally! I was beginning to think I'd never hear from anyone. That was the commander calling. He read my resume and he's got an available sergeant's position working patrol. *Patrol.* That means a squad car and uniformed street assignments. He was understanding about my leg, saying my recovery wouldn't be a detriment. I can't believe this."

Paul got to his feet and set his empty cup in the sink. "That's really good, Lanie. I hope you get it. You deserve an opportunity to prove yourself as an officer. You'll do well." His words were strong and direct, as honest as he'd ever spoken. He knew what they meant to her and he put aside what he felt, what he would have preferred, and gave his full support.

"Thanks, Paul. I appreciate that coming from you."

Lucille's emotional state was transparent. She said one thing, but she was obviously wishing for another outcome. The forced smile she gave her daughter was encouraging, but she excused herself and left the room.

"She's worried for me," Lanie said in the quiet. "Because of my dad."

He nodded his understanding. "I know."

"I'll be careful."

"I know."

"It's right for me to leave and do this," Lanie said, as she smoothed a washcloth over the counter and began to wipe it down. "She knows I'll be fine. I will."

"You will."

"Quit agreeing with me," she said with a shaky laugh. "You're being too…nice."

"I'd rather have been something else." A corner of his mouth pulled upward and his voice lowered. "If you stayed here I could have been your best fantasy."

Momentarily lacking words, she eventually replied, "Fantasies are just substitutes for the unattainable."

"Wrong. If you ever had the fantasy, you wouldn't think that. You don't know what you're missing."

Tomorrow was Lanie's big interview. She had a hard time focusing at work, her thoughts zeroing in on how badly she wanted to make a good impression. This was so important to her, she couldn't make a mistake.

It was difficult at home for her mom and Lanie wished she could take away Lucille's worries. Mom hadn't been herself lately, more so since the call from Pike's Peak.

She'd gone on about what a nice day it was yesterday, but the sky had been overcast with the threat of a summer thunderstorm.

Lucille had recently been absentminded. The other day, Lanie found the butter in the freezer and the ice cream in the refrigerator. She was easily distracted; her concentration just wasn't there when she made her jams. She had mislabeled the last batch.

Planning a surprise party for her mother's fifty-eighth birthday was a good idea, now more than ever. Sherry was helping organize the event for Friday evening. Invitations had gone out and Cookie Baumgarten had a plan to lure Lucille away from the house so they could decorate and hide the guests. Her mom needed something exciting in her life to take her mind off Lanie's possible departure.

If all went well tomorrow, and Lanie was confident it would, she'd be on her way to a job with infinite possibilities.

Deputy Griswold walked past her desk. "Where's the chief?"

"In his office talking with Officer Cabrera," she replied, straightening documents for Chief Deutsch's signature. Hopefully she wouldn't have to be a fill-in secretary for too much longer. She would be doing what she was trained to do.

Paul came out of the chief's office when Deputy Griswold went in to speak with Dutch. As Paul walked past her desk, he gave her a look. A kind of hesitation as if he were considering saying something, but changed his mind. He went to his desk and she let it go. Until half an hour later, when he stood at the coffeepot pouring an afternoon cup, he gave her that look again.

Moving past her desk with Griswold, Dutch said

halfway out the station door, "I'll be in the field riding along with Gordon if you need me. And if you're gone before I get back—break a leg tomorrow, Prescott."

"Bite your tongue," she said, turning back around to watch Paul again.

They were alone and she confronted him. "What? Why have you been looking at me funny?"

"I never look at you funny."

"Well it seems that way to me. You came out of Dutch's office and ever since you've been staring at me like you wanted to tell me my blouse was on inside out or something. Since I know it's not, whatever is on your mind has to be bothering you or you'd have dropped it. So spill."

He set the coffeepot back on the warming burner. "Don't think so."

"Why not?"

"Because there's nothing to say."

"I don't believe you. Something happened in Dutch's office. What was it? Did he say something about me?"

Paul's eyes fastened on hers. "He talks about you."

"And says what?" Her pulse sped. She didn't think she was going to like this.

With a crooked grin, Paul replied, "He says you file accurately."

"Oh, that's not what I meant."

"I think you have to let this go, Lanie."

"Let what go? I don't know what's going on."

"And leave it at that."

She marched toward him and stopped several inches away and set her hands on her hips. "Look me in the eyes and say I don't have anything to be concerned about."

Paul's grin faded and the set of his mouth became a grim line. Brown eyes locked into hers and his expression turned serious. "Whatever happens tomorrow at your interview, remember you're qualified and you're smart."

Puzzled, her brows lifted. "Is that all?"

"That's all."

She didn't believe him. He alluded to something more and it made her wonder. "It's not all. What's going on?"

Before she could gather her next breath, he had her in his arms and was kissing her fully on the mouth. She had no time to catch herself and resist given they were at work—she didn't want to resist. She wrapped her arms around his neck and kissed him back.

Their kiss was unexpected and passionate. The feelings she'd had for him that had been on the back burner were suddenly aflame. The texture of his mouth, soft and warm, yielded beneath her lips. He felt so good next to her, he smelled good and his arms held her next to him as if he didn't want to let her go.

The kiss ended and left her desperately wanting more.

In a ragged breath, Paul said, "I'd like to have you around and explore things between us—I'm not denying it. But I know why you're so adamant about leaving here and I'm not going to say anything that might hurt you."

Confused thoughts swam in her head. "What could you say?"

His fingers wrapped around her arms and set her away from him. The heat in his eyes burned through to her soul. "Nothing. Leave it at that."

He snagged his keys and walkie-talkie, then left to get into his Explorer.

Lanie was left alone in the station, dazed and wondering what had just happened between them. She went through the motions, answering calls and finishing her paperwork.

She brought some documents into Dutch's office, a place she preferred to avoid. A stuffed moose-head was on the wall and its glass eyes gave her the creeps. Next to the mounted head were framed photographs with Dutch mugging for the camera. Each one was of him and a different dead animal: ducks, fish, deer and a turkey.

She looked for an open place on his desk to set the papers so he'd see her signing instructions.

He should clean up in here and store half this stuff. The basement stockroom was busting at the seams with police documents, storage boxes and an old whiskey still that had been confiscated in the 1970s.

Shoving aside a manila folder she cleared a spot, but paused. A piece of paper, a letter to be exact on the Majestic PD stationery, caught her attention, because her name was on it.

Frozen in limbo, Lanie debated her next action. She'd never read his private correspondence before, but this was right on top—right there staring her in the face. It wasn't as if she'd gone fishing for it.

Lanie leaned forward and began to read, gazing out the doorway once to make sure she wasn't neglecting anyone who might have come in.

The addressee was the Pike's Peak commander whom she'd spoken with this week. Maybe Dutch was being a big person and writing her a glowing letter of recommendation.

She scanned the lines, feeling guilty for doing so but unable to help herself. The letter was dated last week.

To Commander Zach Studder—

Deputy Lanie Prescott is a four-year veteran of the Majestic PD and I can vouch for her work record. She's performed top-notch in her duties for parking citations, funeral processional and dog licensing as needed.

She is the perfect candidate for you. She's eager to participate in the non-aggressive street duties necessary to keep a department well-oiled.

I'm faxing her records to follow. She's exactly what your department is looking for to fill that vacancy we discussed on the telephone. Female, experienced and enthusiastic.

Yours,
Chief Herb Deutsch
Majestic PD

Infuriation scorched through her blood and elevated the pressure in her veins until she felt a physical throb in her head. While it was illegal to come out and state that a department was looking to build its minority hires, it was never hard to read between the lines.

Lanie was sick.

She faltered in the silence of the room. Every piece of confidence she'd had in the past forty-eight hours was shredded. She hadn't been assigned an interview because she was the best qualified—she got the interview because she was a woman.

''Forgot my sunglasses,'' Dutch said, startling her as he came into the office and shifted folders to dig out a pair of aviators. "The damn sun is so bright it could blind a person."

Swallowing, Lanie calmly said, "Chief Deutsch, I always thought you were a real jerk. Now I know for sure."

"What? What did you say?" Dutch's jawline clamped hard and the cleft in his chin grew pronounced. His narrowed line of vision followed hers to his desk—to the letter to be exact.

"You only built me up to them because I'm a woman and they need a woman."

Dutch held his head tall. "What did you want me to tell them? You're a man?"

"No! But you could have had some respect for me as an officer and a—"

"Gentleman?" Dutch finished for her. "Prescott, you're a lady. And I mean that with all respect. I'd take that as a compliment if I were you."

"I don't want to take anything from you." Lanie struggled to keep her composure. "Certainly not a recommendation you don't mean."

"I meant everything in that letter." Starting at the neck and flushing upward, his face turned red. "And no matter what you want to believe, I wrote it because I thought that's what you'd want." He put the sunglasses on. "Griswold's waiting for me."

He was gone before she could say anything more.

It wasn't trespassing. Not really. She had a key and it wasn't as if she'd let herself inside her own home for malicious reasons. Paul was working the graveyard shift and she'd be gone before he got back.

The house was quiet, dark and introspective. She scaled the rickety pull-down ladder to her attic.

Lanie sat on the dusty planked floor, her leg stretched out in front of her. An iron-banded trunk with memorabilia was lifted open. She'd laid out many of the newspaper clippings and photos of her dad.

Touching her fingertips to his academy graduation picture, she felt her eyes fill with tears. He looked so young, so full of life. It was painful to see the joy and hope on his face. There were photos of Dad and Mom at a party they'd thrown in the old house when Dad got assigned to duty. A few of the pictures showed them dancing in the kitchen, smiling and in love more than any couple Lanie had ever seen.

Certificates of honor, copies of *Walking The Beat* magazine and various correspondence sifted through her fingers. She dug through the trunk further, certain what she wanted was inside. She knew it had been put away in a black dress sock, rolled and tied with a remnant of ribbon her mom had had in her sewing basket.

At last, in a nook beneath a high school sweater, Lanie found what she sought. She lifted the sock as if it were a living, breathing, delicate creature that needed tender care. She unwrapped the ribbon and held the sock at the toe. A star-badge fell into Lanie's open palm. Tarnished, it held no gleam under the attic's artificial light. Etched in the tin was ornate leaf-work and a solitary eagle with spread wings. The lettering, blocky and simple, in the star's center read:

Chief of Police
United States
Majestic

Dad's dress uniform and hat were neatly boxed, protected against aging, in another trunk. The U.S. flag the department had given them on the day of Dad's burial was in a shadow box in the hallway. But the badge was not. Mom hadn't been able to bring herself to display it.

Lucille hadn't wanted these things at the time of Ray's death because of her overwhelming grief so Lanie had kept them. There had been a few times since that her mother had come up here and looked through the trunk herself. Once on her father's birthday, the second on their wedding anniversary, and the third had been this year on the anniversary of the day her father had been shot. Her mom had been solemn and quiet, fingering the belongings as if they'd turn to dust if she didn't touch them gently and reverently.

Lanie held the star in her hand, its cool metal growing warm from the heat of her skin. She remembered all the times she'd seen him wear it, the pride shining in his eyes, and the jovial manner in which he talked with those he passed on the street. Chief Ray Prescott had been very much beloved.

A tear slipped past Lanie's closed eyes and she leaned back.

Air caught in the rafters, stifling and heavy; it felt cloying. She drew in a breath almost suffocating from the warmth collected by the summer afternoon.

She listened to the beating of her heart.

The rhythm was a slow, almost a defeated sound— as if the beats of hopeful enthusiasm were failing. She was going into cardiac arrest, she thought with a sarcastic smile. She was trying—honestly. But how much of a setback could one woman endure?

Rudolph the Red-Nosed Reindeer stared at Lanie, its plastic face a little battle worn. They'd had him since she could remember. Rudolph and his reindeer buddies—all looking at her with silly grins.

"Stop smiling. What do you know?" She whacked them, and they tumbled down in chain reaction—legs and antlers falling like dominos.

She sat up, grabbed her hair and tied it in a knot. Pulling hard, to the point of tugging, she wanted to *feel*—anything but this stupid, stupid self-pity.

Paul's face popped up from the attic floor's opening, momentarily scaring the daylights out of her.

"It's you," she breathed in a rush.

"Were you waiting for Santa Claus?"

"Santa doesn't have what I want in his sack of toys. What time is it?"

"It's after three."

She'd lost track of the hour.

He must have just come home from his shift. He had removed his uniform tunic, wore just the trousers and a black undershirt that left no imagination as to the density of his muscles. A St. Michael's medallion, patron saint of law enforcement officers, hung from a silver chain around his neck.

"What are you doing?" His gaze traveled over the mementos.

"Looking at stuff that belonged to my dad."

Paul hunkered down by the trunk and picked up several of the old photographs. "How long was he a cop?"

"Twenty-two years."

"Long time."

"Yes."

She wanted to do her dad's memory proud, but more important, she wanted to be a police officer for herself. Keeping that dream alive had been too damn hard lately and she didn't want to fall apart in front of Paul.

"You knew," she offered in a voice choked with reserve. "You and Dutch talked about it in his office and you didn't want to tell me why I got the call from Pike's Peak."

"Yes." His reply was steady, unlike her emotions.

The single word of confirmation was her undoing. She shuddered, losing the battle. First one tear fell, then the next until more followed and she was dabbing her eyes with her knuckles. "I'm sorry. I don't mean to be like this."

"It's okay."

"You know, I think I've done a really good job of bucking up. I took the Policy and Procedure job, I went back to dispatch, I've been doing okay. Until now. Now I..." She gazed at Paul, blinking against the old-fashioned crying spell that could really suck her under if she let it. He came into focus—a blurry, rugged man kneeling closer.

"It's really hard to keep myself together day after day. I'm tired of pretending everything is all right. Maybe all these road blocks are a sign I'm just not cut out for police work. My dad" —she opened her hand and stared at his tin star— "had what it took. I wanted to do well, too."

Paul sat closely beside her and tucked his arms over his chest.

She took comfort in his presence.

Lanie sighed and slipped her father's badge back into the sock.

A disquieting expression crossed Paul's features—as if he truly did understand what it was like to want something better, only to find out the pursuit of it was all screwed up.

"What are you really looking for, Paul?" she asked,

seriously wanting to know. In this second, she felt something more than sexual attraction for him. He felt like he was a part of her destiny. Like somebody who knew what it was like to want something so badly but not be able to have it.

"A good life," he finally said, thoughtful and introspective. "I want to do my job right and live without regret."

"You have regrets?"

"Many."

"Tell me one."

He leaned back on his hands. "Being detained off and on as a juvenile offender for a four-year period."

"You were in Juvenile Hall?"

"Elected officials call it the Youth Guidance Center. Sometimes it was better than living at my house." The line of Paul's mouth tightened. "My mother worked on an assembly line for a die-casting factory and my father was a house painter—when he was working. He roughed her up and it got ugly. The police came out so often, they should have set up an office in our front yard."

"That's terrible."

"The prick would be arrested, spend the night in jail, but she always took him back the next day. He had her under his thumb, like a bug he was torturing with a slow death. I couldn't watch it anymore. I moved out when I was seventeen. It's amazing I even graduated high school with all the crap going on."

Slowly exhaling, Paul pinched the bridge of his nose, bending one leg and resting an arm on his knee. "He died after falling off a scaffold."

Lanie couldn't imagine going through such a dark

youth. Hers had been filled with color and light, love and warmth.

"He was my father, but I was glad he was gone. My mother, the day after his funeral, became another person. It was the first time I think I'd ever seen her truly smile. She wasn't afraid anymore."

"You said she still lives in Florida," Lanie offered, brushing a smudge of dirt off the bottom of her shorts.

"Yes. She's great now. Married to a hell of a nice guy who treats her right. They're both retired and do a lot of traveling. They have one of those big motor homes fully equipped with AC and a color TV set. She's happy."

A reflective moment passed. Then Lanie commented, "You did well, Paul. You pulled yourself up out of a rough spot. I don't see that as a regret. Look at where you are. You're somebody important."

"When I was nineteen, I was a Class C misdemeanor criminal in the county system. I had a party-boy problem, but a cop named Sid Cisneros wouldn't let me waste my life. He helped me out. He got me a scholarship to college and because of it, I changed my outlook and attitude. So my regret is not realizing my potential soon enough. You know you have potential and you're doing something about it right now."

Paul's long legs stretched out before him, his boots large and dull from campground dust. He must have taken a Ridge Flat call—a pang of envy assailed her at the thought. She had potential—but she didn't have a badge. There was a wide gap between the two.

"Are you quitting before you even start?" he asked.

That was a moot question.

"I can't go on that interview now. It's a fake."

"Bullshit. There's a viable position open."

"For a woman," she reminded.

"And you're a fine-looking one," he drawled. "Look, you know as well as I do they can't hire based on race, sex or religion. It boils down to abilities and who they think will fit in."

"They want me to fit in because I wear a bra and panties. I just don't think I can lower myself to—"

"Recite it to me." A feral gleam lit in Paul's eyes beneath dark angry brows. Gooseflesh rose on her skin in a shivering cascade of both fear and intrigue.

"Recite it to me," he demanded once more.

The strength radiating from him wound around her, possessing and demanding. Lanie felt hypnotized.

Flushed, her hands suddenly grew cold. She could barely think much less breathe. "Recite what?"

"The swearing-in oath. You've got a killer memory, what did you say the day you got your badge?"

She could remember the two-paragraph oath with its honor-bound duties exactly to the letter.

Lanie wet her dry lips and sat taller. Their eyes locked. She'd play along, although what for— "I do solemnly swear that I am duly qualified, according to the Constitution of this State, to exercise the duties of the office—"

"That oath is from the wrong school, Prescott," Paul cut in with a dissatisfied shrug. "Frank Serpico said there are two lines of thought in police work—respect and disrespect."

The cynicism in Paul's remark grated.

She accentuated his annoyance with her own. "Are you saying I don't respect my job?"

"Don't drag your feet," Paul lectured. "Officers have a deliberate walk. If you want to play cops and robbers, you've got to walk the walk. Go on the Pike's Peak interview and kick some butt.''

"I can't," she said stubbornly. "It's a matter of pride. They don't want *me*. They want a *her*."

A hot ache filled her throat.

"Get tough, Lanie. I know you are. I've seen it in you." Without backing off, the steely edge to his voice was cutting her in two. "I think you're losing respect for yourself when you sit up here and stroll down memory lane and say 'Poor little old me, I'm not like my dad.'''

Her heartbeat plunged then soared, slamming hard and nearly choking. Images of her father's funeral colored her vision.

Lanie drew her hand back to strike him, but he caught her wrist.

In one forward motion, she was locked tightly in his arms. His mouth came over hers, sending her stomach spiraling into a wild swirl of heat. The kiss was volatile and harsh, devouring. She fought, pushing at his chest and nipping at his lips. But he wouldn't surrender his claim. His demanding lips seared with an urgency that confused her.

His tongue swept into her mouth, searching and commanding. She didn't want him to take what little resilience she had left. She felt stripped and raw, yet filled when she'd been so empty.

The strong hardness of his mouth chipped away at her defenses. She succumbed to the forceful domination, allowing herself to feel all that he offered within every fiber of her body. His mouth clinging to hers was a kiss for her tired soul.

The weight of her breasts grew heavy and sensitive in her demi-bra, the nipples tightening. She clasped her body tightly to his, kissing him back and taking what he gave. She wanted to use him, suck him dry. Take all of his power and keep it for herself.

The swell of his biceps exposed in the tank shirt drew her touch. She discovered his skin felt as smooth as it looked. Fingers splayed, fanning out to take as much of his strong arms into her palms as she could. He felt like glass on a warm summer afternoon.

She melded into his chest as his hands slid down her back and up again beneath the light cotton of her tank top. His hands felt so good on her bare skin. Warm and calloused. Rough, yet gentle. She could lose herself in the way he touched her. The way his hand skimmed over her waist to the swell of her hips.

She wanted to drown in these feelings and think of nothing else.

A ragged gasp escaped her when the kiss ended. Her heartbeat throbbed with the lust for pleasure left unsatisfied.

Paul's forehead touched hers, his breath mixing with hers in a hot and moist merging of spent air.

She fisted her hands against the brawn of his chest. She hated the inexplicable feeling of emptiness and the squeezing hurt. Fury over her vulnerability sharpened her voice.

"Wh-what are you trying to do? Get me off your conscience because you didn't tell me what Dutch was up to?"

He laughed, a low and guttural sound. "You're banging the wrong drum, darlin'. I can shake a conscience off the bottom of my boot and not step in it. I don't give a damn what Dutch did. Neither should you. It's a hell of a thing to be asked to appear in front of a review board and you should be honored. Your emotions are sloppy right now or you'd have seen that.''

He was right. She'd been hideous, she'd been stupid and she'd been blind. Of course she'd go to the interview. What did it matter how she got there so long as she did.

''It's for patrol,'' she said aloud, biting the flesh on the inside of her lower lip in contemplation. ''They wouldn't just say that and then stick me on meter maid duty?''

''Damn straight.''

''Damn straight.'' She smiled, somewhat reluctantly. ''So how come you're a police officer instead of a professional Kleenex dispenser?''

''Not everyone cries in counseling, Lanie. Being a shrink wasn't what I was after. I had to major in something for my degree and the human mind is a lot more interesting than other subjects.''

''I asked you this before…um, you haven't been keeping a notebook on me or anything?''

He smiled, wickedly indulgent—she assumed for her sake. Towering over her, he bent forward and held out his arm to help her up. ''No. Come on, Lanie, scrape yourself off the floor.''

Once she was standing she gingerly returned her father's items to the trunk, closing the treasured memories off until the next time. When the keyless metal lock clicked into place, the sound of it caused her to shiver.

She was on her own. She was her own destiny—not Ray Prescott's.

''Weakness of attitude becomes weakness of character,'' Paul said as he helped her down the stairs.

It was creepy how he could read her thoughts. She

hoped he didn't carry her around in his subconscious making mental notes.

"Did Frank Serpico say that, too?" she asked, almost flippantly and expecting the answer to be yes.

"No. Einstein did."

Fifteen

"Surprise! Happy birthday, Lucille!"

Lucille brought a hand to her heart, speechless. She was ushered into her house by an excited Cookie Baumgarten and taken to a festive birthday bash. The ceilings were decorated with streamers and balloons and the table was covered in Myrtle Sanders' best crocheted tablecloth and piles of gifts in colorful paper.

"I thought...but you said you needed my help getting your cat into its crate...and we just dropped him off at the vet," she managed to protest.

Cookie chuckled fondly. "That was all an act. I'll pick him up tomorrow."

Lucille skimmed her gaze over the people in her home. Everyone from the community center was here; Haskell Ehrlich the lawyer and the only man in her swim aerobics class, the ladies from Cookie Cutter's salon, some of the bingo crowd, Lanie, and Paul Cabrera from next door.

It looked like the whole town had been invited. Everyone except—

"Come look at your cake. Myrtle made it," Lanie said, taking her by the hand and bringing her to a double-layer white frosted birthday cake with red roses and her name written across the top in a handwritten script.

And two candles. Those number kind that were huge—**58.**

"We wanted to celebrate in style," Cookie said. "We're going to keep the party alive all night. Hit it, Myrtle!"

Myrtle Sanders turned on the CD player and Elvis began crooning.

Distressed, Lucille knit her fingers together and kept them at her waist so she wouldn't wring her hands. She wasn't up for a celebration.

For her birthday she'd just wanted the day to be normal without any fuss. But she couldn't disappoint these people after the trouble they'd gone to so she pinned a smile on her face.

"This is wonderful," she said. "Thank you all. I'm so surprised."

"That was the plan," Lanie said, laughing.

Lucille enjoyed her daughter's happiness. Yesterday she'd driven to her interview and she'd come home feeling good about it. The thought of her leaving again brought Lucille on edge once more. She hated the idea of her only child moving away and putting herself in a police car. But she kept up her good spirits to encourage Lanie.

Paul stood beside her, and Lucille thought they looked nice together. She wished that something would happen between the two of them, then Lanie wouldn't want to leave and everything could fall into place here.

Her daughter would be happy and Lucille would be…content.

That's how she'd begun to think of her life lately. Simply content. Nothing more, nothing less. Ever since she'd gone bowling with Dutch, she kept thinking she was missing something. She tried to put him out of her mind, but he would sneak back in when she least expected him to.

It wasn't fair to Ken to harbor an unsettled longing for another man so she'd put her energies into making this relationship with Ken better. She had him over for dinner last week. He raved, as he always did, about her cooking. The evening was going along fine until Ken mentioned his favorite dessert was Dutch apple pie and he'd love it if she baked him a pie next time he came over. After that her concentration was lost.

"For you, Lucille," Ken said and he offered her a box of Whitman's chocolates.

His hair was ultrablond and combed neatly off to the side. He wore a tropical print camp shirt and the fabric draped across his upper body. Few men could pull off pineapples and not look fruity.

"Thank you, Ken." Lucille accepted the box. "They're my favorite kind."

"I aim to please. That's my present on the table. The big one with the silver bow. You want to shake it and try and guess what it is?"

"That's all right," she murmured, fingers sliding over the pearl-chain anchoring her glasses around her neck. She wasn't dressed for a party, but she didn't feel like being at one so it didn't matter.

Ken said, pointing to the cake, "So how does it feel to be the big five-eight?"

"No different." Lucille approached the table with the white cake in the middle. She'd swear the red wax 58 was so tall its digits cast a shadow across the floor.

The evening moved along and Lucille forced herself into the spirit of things as the hours ticked off. She was sung, "Happy Birthday," encouraged to open their presents and she had a slice of cake and ice cream.

She did not release the smile locked on her mouth until the last guest left and Lanie went to bed. When she was alone, she stood in the room and felt...old. And alone.

She reflected on what she had accomplished in her life this past year versus the year before, and the year before that.

Her conclusion was: She was reliable like a watch that never needed winding. She could be counted on for having the same time day in and out. Nothing she did was beyond the ordinary. Except for...

...bowling.

Going to Bowlwinkles had drawn her out of comfortable and into a little bit of the wild side. She'd drunk beer, something she'd forgotten she preferred over wine. Ray had enjoyed wine so she'd acquired a taste for that, but an ice-cold beer on tap had been utterly refreshing.

So had Dutch's humor.

Herb Deutsch was so blunt, so exposed. He wore his feelings on his shirtsleeves and made no apologies. She wished she could do that. She wished that for once she could just let her hair down and do something for the sake of wanting to do it just because and for no good reason at all.

She glanced at the clock. It wasn't yet midnight. Her birthday was still today. How long had it been since she'd ordered a dirty martini? So long, she couldn't even recall.

When had she gone into the bar of any establishment by herself? The thought petrified her. A lady just didn't do that sort of thing unless she was trolling for company. But who made up that rule anyway?

The next thing Lucille realized she was holding on

to her purse and walking into the White Horse Saloon
on a Friday night at nearly midnight.

The room was dark and smoky, the bar long and
polished. She kept her head high and walked toward it.
Once at the counter, she hopped up onto a bar stool and
tried to compose herself. This was so unlike her. Oh,
she should just turn around and go home.

How does it feel to be the big five-eight?

"It feels damn good," she said aloud.

"Excuse me?" the bartender returned.

"Um, oh. I'll take a dirty martini please."

"Put it on my tab," said a voice from the end of the
bar.

Lucille softly gasped and turned.

Dutch sat on one of the stools. "Good evening, Lucille." His voice was humble, deep and level. She liked
the sound of it. The last time she'd spoken with him,
she'd been somewhat short. She'd run into him at the
bank after determining to try and be a couple with Ken
who posed no complications at all.

But Ken didn't make her heart beat like this. Not by
a long shot.

Seeing Dutch threw most of her resolve out the window.

"Mind if I join you?"

She nodded. He took the stool next to her. The cleft
in his chin had a very young Kirk Douglas look—but
not exaggerated. He smelled manly without any cologne. The precision flattop haircut he sported tempted
her fingers. She refrained, but that didn't stop her from
wondering if his hair would feel soft or bristly. A black
polo shirt emphasized the breadth of his burly shoulders.

Having him beside her was dangerously wonderful.

His sense of protection cloaked her in its web. Dutch made her feel safe and taken care of. While she was slightly taller than him, everything else about him was synonymous with one hundred percent male. He was heavily built—not overweight, but like a bull with a muscular frame. Would his arm feel as iron hard as it looked?

"I was surprised to see you walk in," he said as her martini was served. "I was glad, but surprised."

"It's my birthday."

His face fell. "Ah, Christ—excuse me. The date slipped my mind. I knew it was today, but—I didn't get you anything."

"I don't want anything."

But she did want something, only it didn't come in a box or fit inside a card. It was something not tangible and yet she could feel it whenever she was near Dutch.

Heaven help her…it was his face she'd begun to imagine before she turned the lights out in her bedroom at night.

Lucille tested the martini. It packed a wallop, her stomach burning as the alcohol slid down her throat. Other than that, it was delicious.

"Too strong?" Dutch questioned. "I can have them make you another one."

"This one's fine." She took another sip and this one wasn't so startling. She felt Dutch's gaze on her and she stared ahead at the row of liquor bottles on the wall.

Dutch thought Lucille's blue eyes looked like sapphires. Her hair was its usual golden crown of curls, but a few tendrils had gone flat. She was still the best-looking woman he'd seen all day. All week. Hell—in a very long time.

Her shoulders were erect and she stared into her

drink like a fairy-tale queen wishing on a dream. He would have given up his entire bullet collection to know what she was thinking.

"Lucille…" he said, venturing closer.

"How did you know it was my birthday?"

True confession time. There was no good way of organizing the thoughts inside his head. "I looked up your small business permit and your driver's licence information."

Giving him a puzzled gaze, she asked, "Why?"

"You know why." Holding his breath, he dared to take her hand in his. Her skin felt like creamery butter—soft, smooth and delicate. She felt better than he had ever imagined.

She grew tense, her arm stiffening where it met his. "Lanie told me what you did about the interview."

He felt as if he'd been hit with a bucket of ice. "It was in her best interests and—"

"Sending them a letter of recommendation for her was nice. Hiring her back at the station was nice. Letting her do the Policy and Procedure manual was nice. Every time I turn around, you're doing something quite nice."

Dutch could take a compliment as much as the next guy, but he was no damn saint. "Lucille, I didn't do those things to be nice. I base what I do on the person. Well, maybe I did give her the P&P manual to impress you."

"Your roses impressed me more," she admitted softly.

"There's more where those came from. Just say the word."

"I…I want to."

He waited for her to elaborate, his body alive in

places he hadn't felt in a long while. He took her hands in his big bearlike ones. Gazing into her eyes, he had a premonition that what he was about to say would change their lives forever.

Rubbing her knuckles with tender strokes, he said, "I want to see you, Lucille. Publicly. Socially. Privately. That means you'd have to break it to Burnett you're no longer an exclusive with him. You'd have to give me a chance to show you what I'm made of. Are you willing to give me a shot?"

Lanie was worried to death. Her mother wasn't home and it was after two in the morning.

When she heard her mom's Cadillac pull into the garage, she'd never been more relieved.

"Mom!" she said when Lucille came through the kitchen door. Her mother looked up, startled to have been discovered. "Where have you been? I've been worried. I went to bed and I thought you had, too. I was going to tell you one last 'happy birthday' and your bedroom was empty. I've been up for hours waiting for you."

"You shouldn't have worried, Lanie."

"But it's practically three in the morning." Lanie smelled the distinct smell of barroom smoke on her mother's cardigan sweater. "Where have you been?"

"The White Horse Saloon."

"You never go there. What happened? Did Cookie and Myrtle make you go there? Were they with you?"

"I went alone." Her mom looked her in the eyes. "But I didn't stay alone."

Lanie was lost. Her mother wasn't making sense. "Mom, are you all right?"

"I'm fine. In fact...I'm—" her smile was eager and

alive, filled with affection and enthusiasm ''—I'm fantastic.''

Her mother's infectious grin caused her to return a smile of her own. ''Did Ken do something? Did he have a secret surprise for you at the White Horse—''

''Herb Deutsch and I have decided to try dating and see how it works out.'' Lucille Prescott's chin never lowered, never quavered or showed a single sign of uncertainty.

Lanie, on the other hand, felt as if the floor had just been pulled out from beneath her. ''Are you out of your mind?''

''Not even remotely.''

''But why?'' Lanie gasped. She couldn't believe this. Her mom and Dutch? It was a disaster, a catastrophe. ''I'm aware Ken isn't your ideal man—but Dutch?''

''I'm attracted to him, Lanie,'' she said, as she moved into the kitchen and set her purse on the counter. The very admission tightened the muscles in Lanie's stomach. ''This isn't something I'm jumping into. I've thought about him for a while now. Ever since we went bowling.''

''You've been out with him before?''

''I had a wonderful time. And I had a wonderful time tonight. He taught me how to play pool.''

''Pool? But you like needlepoint and bingo.''

Lucille started up the stairs. ''I like a lot of things I didn't know I liked.''

Lanie's heart sank and in desperation, she blurted, ''You can't do it, Mom. You know how I feel about him. He's a Class A—as in Ass—Jerk and you're too good for him.''

''Lanie, my eyes are wide-open, and for the first time in a long while, I'm beginning to see things differently.

You told me to find somebody who knocks my pearls off and I think it could be him.'' Her shoulders were erect and she had that look to her that said she wouldn't argue about it further. "I'm going to bed now. Good night, sweetie, and thank you again for the surprise party.''

The soft click of her mother's bedroom door shutting was the end of the subject.

Feeling the biggest headache of her life coming on, Lanie took one of her leftover pain pills. Two, actually. Her leg hurt—sort of. The walking boot chafed below her knee and... Never mind. She needed something to dull the pounding in her head. How in the world had this happened with her mom and Dutch?

They were an unlikely couple. He couldn't make her mom happy, he didn't have it in him. Sometimes he showed his good side, but it wasn't all that often. What did her mom see in him?

Lanie dropped onto the sofa and wrapped her mocha throw around her shoulders. As she tried to make sense of things, the medicine worked through her and she began to feel more relaxed. She needed to confide in someone about what had happened with her mom and...Dutch.

Groaning, she found herself on the veranda going to Paul's door.

She stopped shy of knocking. What was she thinking? She couldn't run to Paul with her problems at three in the morning. He already thought she was lame for putting pride ahead of common sense with the Pike's Peak interview. Thank God she'd listened to him and gone.

Her muscles relaxed as the painkiller took effect in her blood making her so sleepy she could hardly keep her eyes open; she fought the drowsiness that clawed at her.

The night, warm from the aftermath of the day, sluiced over her and Lanie sat on the wicker porch bench with its cushioned padding. She felt better just getting some air.

She lay down, telling herself it would only be for a minute, with the blanket over her shoulders. Remarkably, she was comfortable with her leg hanging over the edge in the boot.

In spite of her resolve to get up, she began to drift off, the memory of her kiss with Paul in the attic her last conscious thought before waking to a woman's voice declaring:

"Irving, there's a woman sleeping on Paul's porch."

Sixteen

Paul stood next to his mom and stepdad. He knew his parents were coming this morning, but finding Lanie out here was unexpected.

Her eyelids opened to slits against the early morning sunlight. She lay on the wicker lawn furniture, a blanket draped across her shoulders.

"Who is she?" Oleda Goldberg asked, hovering over Lanie's prone body.

"She's my landlord," Paul said, trying to figure out if she'd slept there all night.

"She came with the house?"

"She lives next door."

"What's she doing on your porch, Paul?" Irv asked, his accent very Southern-Jewish.

"I don't know." He touched Lanie's shoulder. "Lanie, are you all right?"

Lanie stirred and rested an arm over her forehead. She licked dry lips and her gaze slipped over each of them in turn. "I needed some fresh air."

Paul imagined the view from Lanie's angle—three faces looking down.

Irving Goldberg was a year into his seventies with a thick head of shining silver hair. A salt-and-pepper mustache hid his upper lip; he kept the rest of his face clean-shaven. The dominating size of his brows overshadowed kind eyes and a long nose. Contrasting against his gray hair, his Florida complexion made him look younger than he was.

A foot shorter than Irv, his mom wore exaggerated black-rimmed eyeglasses. Their shape was a thick rectangle, the temples heavy. The color of her glasses matched the midnight black color of her hair which seemed to be natural.

As far as he knew, her hair had always been sleek and dark. When she'd been married his father, she wore it in a long braid to please him. After he died, she cut her hair and kept its length brushing her shoulders. She had wrinkles—had gotten them too many years before she should. But she looked good, great in fact. Never wore any makeup except for deep red lipstick.

Lanie's gaze drifted past them to the street where a Winnebago the length of the Gator Bowl field was parked in front of Paul's house.

"Where's Aerosmith?" Lanie asked, her voice thick with sleep and, Paul suspected, a pharmaceutical hangover.

"That's not an Acrosmith tour bus, darlin'," Paul said. "It's my mom and stepdad's home on wheels."

"He calls his landlord 'darling,'" Oleda commented with a shrug and a wink to Irv.

"Paul, let's bring her inside and your mother will make her some coffee," Irv suggested, the nylon of his windbreaker swishing as he bent to help Lanie sit up.

Twenty minutes later, Lanie sat at the kitchen table—much more alert—drinking a cup of coffee his mom had fixed. Oleda kept the motor home stocked with the ingredients for her special Spanish coffee recipe. She used Kahlúa, cherry brandy, sugar, nutmeg, whipping cream and a maraschino cherry. The drink did the trick in bringing a person around.

"You still look peaked," Oleda said, sitting across from Lanie and sliding a bowl of freshly cut fruit forward.

Irving was to Lanie's left and Paul sat to her right. His arm rested on the back of her chair and his hand brushed her shoulder. Having her in the company of his family made him feel closer to her.

She was beautiful in the morning. Her eyes and her face. Her mouth. She'd slept in regular pajamas with a top and matching bottom. Even with a walking boot on she had the sexiest pair of legs he'd ever seen.

"What's in this stuff?" Lanie asked over the cup's rim as she took another sip.

Irv shrugged with his hands that were peppered with liver spots. "I never question Oleda. She knows what's good for a person."

"Were you at a wild party last night?" his mom asked, brows lifting high enough to surpass the frame of her glasses.

"Her mother's birthday party," Paul supplied, absently rubbing his knuckles across her back.

Oleda's brows rose. "Her mother has wild parties?"

"No, it broke up at eleven," Lanie said. "My mom and I—" She bit off the thought, her gaze taking in the faces watching her. "I just sort of wandered out on the porch and accidentally fell asleep. I took some painkillers. I never take them on an empty stomach." She raked a hand through her messy hair, tying it into a knot without a hair band. The improvised knot stayed in place. "They must pack a double punch when they're burning a hole through your stomach lining."

"You have to be careful," Irv tutored somberly.

"Medicaid tells seniors to check the labels for inter-actions. Sam even said the same thing."

Oleda slanted a gaze at her husband. "Sam? Sam Bloomfeld?"

"No. Good Sam—in the *Highways* magazine."

"I missed that issue."

"It was there. By the campground directory."

"I never read that page. You figure all that out, my love."

Their banter was kindhearted and genuine, and Paul was happy to have them here. They'd been married for nearly twenty years and their relationship was cemented in a bond of love and affirmation. Their differences gave them strength.

Irv was a practicing Jew and his mother was a prac-ticing Catholic. They respected each other's religions and they'd had two nontraditional ceremonies because of the politics involving interfaith couples.

Paul wanted Lanie to see a good part of his life. He'd mostly painted his past as dark. His mom and stepdad were the light—positive influences that made him a bet-ter person.

He felt at home sitting here, Lanie next to him and his family joining in to catch up on what he'd been doing in Majestic.

"Hey, Paul," Irv asked with an expressive smile, his upper lip eclipsed by his thick mustache. "How's the Porsche running?"

Paul eased back into the chair, a leg crossed and his foot resting on his knee. He slowly shook his head, still smiling. "It's great. When are you going to admit you were wrong?"

"Hah!" Irv laughed, creases at the corners of his eyes. "Oleda, what do you think of that? So, Paul, did you get good gas mileage on it when you opened it up on the highway?''

"Very efficient. I told you I got a good deal. The used price was the same as a new Honda."

"There's nothing wrong with a Honda," Irv said.

His mom put in, "I think you two will never agree about that car. He wanted it, he earned it. Paul, I like the Porsche. It has pizzazz."

Irv took a bite from an orange segment, compliments of the refrigerator in the Winnebago. "But, dolly, cops don't drive Porsches."

"Don Johnson drove a Ferrari," Lanie pointed out and Paul turned toward her with a smile. A tiny amount of whipping cream was on the bud of her upper lip. Without the gloss of lipstick, her mouth looked like a slice of untried fruit—something his mother didn't have on the table. Paul was half tempted to lean over and kiss the cream from Lanie's mouth.

"That's right," Oleda said. "The show never explained where Don got all his money. Irv, do you know?"

"No, dolly. I never watched that show." Irv stood, and as he passed behind Paul's chair to get a second cup of coffee, he gave him a few manly pats to his shoulder—a physical gesture that had never been given to him by his father.

"Maybe Paul knows about Don Johnson." Irv ruffed the short hair on the back of Paul's head, the gesture not offensive to him. Irv had come into his life when he was eighteen, up to no good and beyond stupid. He'd missed out on a lot because of mistrust. It took a few years for him to see that Irv was the best thing to ever happen to his mom.

"Sonny Crockett was a Colombian drug lord," Paul

answered after picking up an orange segment and popping it into his mouth. "He could afford to buy anything."

"And Tubbs was his dealer." Irving didn't buy his fabricated *Miami Vice* story, adding two bits of his own.

"I didn't know that," Lanie said, her gaze fastened on his mouth as he licked the sweet taste from his lower lip. He felt her unflinching stare seep through his skin and clench his belly. Then lower, the heat slid and wrapped around him.

Chuckling, Irv said, "Paul, you're a good man. You know I'm just giving you a hard time about the Porsche."

Positive reinforcement was the most basic of all psychological components and Paul knew it for its simplicity. Even so, it made him glad to have Irv as his stepdad. The guy made you feel like you mattered.

Lanie quietly drank her coffee, but Paul saw the spark in her eyes. A silent enjoyment perhaps over hearing him being wisely counseled by his stepdad.

"I was twenty-eight," Paul said lightly, his mouth curved. "I had to have something flashy to buy with my return."

"A revamped portfolio would have been flashy." Irv's grin made his cheeks redden as he took his seat at the table once more, a spoon clinking against the side of his cup. "I hope you're keeping one up. You can still make money in a downward moving market."

"You didn't put sugar in there, did you, Irving?" his mom questioned. "Sweet'n Low. I had it by the pot."

He gave her a loving smile. "I got the Sweet'n Low, dolly."

Turning to Lanie, his mom asked, "What do you do?"

Lanie cleared her throat. "I'm, ah, right now I'm working temporarily at the police station."

"You're a police officer, too?"

"Not at the moment."

"She's a deputy," Paul said, proud of that fact. "She's moving and making a career promotion."

Lanie glanced at him. He loved the color of violet in her eyes when she first woke up. "Thanks. Your son is very encouraging."

"How did you hurt your leg?" his mom asked.

Toying with the cup's handle, she said, "Pursuing a car stereo thief. I broke my fibula."

"Really! Well, my goodness. She goes for all the action," his mom exclaimed. "I think it's so admirable for a woman to be a police officer. Your mother must be proud."

"Actually my mother would prefer I was not a deputy, but she's still supportive." Lanie's face hid emotions from his parents, but Paul read through the facade. She was upset about something else.

"Are you okay?" he asked, his voice low.

Tension crept into her tone as she sat forward. "I'm all right. It's just that I didn't sleep very well last night and this coffee is—what did you say was in here?"

"I didn't," Oleda replied, filling a glass from the sink faucet. "You need some water. You could be dehydrated."

"Paul, show me where the hookups are for the Winnebago," Irv said. "Your mother will take care of your landlord."

When they were gone, Lanie dropped her head in her arms on the table and wished she could die and curl up in a coffin. She didn't feel ready to go home and face her mother, but staying here was like climbing a rope backward. The uncomfortable moment of being found on Paul's side of the porch and meeting his parents—what must they think of her?

"So, you like my son," Oleda stated, without preamble.

Lanie looked into brown eyes behind predominant glasses with lenses like the bottoms of her mother's jam jars. "Is this a trick question?"

Oleda laughed. "You're delightful. You've got whipping cream on your upper lip. I saw Paul staring at you—which he does a lot."

Completely thrown by the observation, Lanie swiped a napkin across her lips and sputtered, "Gone?"

"Yes." Oleda slid the fruit toward Lanie. "Have some citrus. You need it."

"But I have to be going—"

"Stay for another minute. We'll talk about Paul."

That piqued Lanie's interest. Childhood stories, secrets revealed and pasts uncovered. Like a soap opera, Lanie was drawn to the details about Paul. Had her attraction for him been that transparent?

Lanie took a small bite of orange slice in anticipation. Maybe she did need citrus. "It's good."

"It's a Florida." Oleda's lipstick was dark and red; her teeth were perfectly straight—most likely dentures. "My son is a good judge of character and I can tell he likes to be around you."

"We're co-workers. I work as the dispatch operator so I see him almost every day."

"He's a wonderful man, my son," Oleda said, sipping coffee. "He grew up with a rough childhood. My first husband wasn't a prince and I wasn't woman enough back then to stand up to things I shouldn't have put up with. Paul protected me and I know he bears the burden of guilt for not doing more. Sometimes he doesn't let himself smile.''

Lanie had seen his smile. And she loved it.

''I named him after Paul McCartney,'' Oleda said, ''of the Beatles. I always thought Paul was the cutest. My Paul, he was the only Spanish boy in school who could say he wasn't named after a saint but rather a British sex symbol. He's good-looking—don't you think?''

The question threw her, sinking into her subconscious thoughts of yellow submarines and Chief-Deputy Paul in mirrored sunglasses with a mandarin collar. She much preferred him in a dark ribbed undershirt, the slabs of his pectorals visible through the thin knit. That night in the attic, the way he'd looked…smelled. And kissed.

''Yes,'' she said coming back to reality. ''I'd be blind not to notice his looks. All the women in town notice. He gets free donuts and haircuts.''

Oleda laughed and squeezed her hand. ''You're really delightful.''

Lanie pondered that a moment. She wasn't sure how sweet she had been to her mother last night. What a disaster. She had to go home and make amends.

''It was nice to meet you. Thank you for the coffee.'' Lanie stood.

''We'll be visiting Paul until Friday. You have to come over and taste my paella.''

''Oh, I'll try.''

As she let herself out of her own home, Lanie felt like she was going the wrong way. She took a last glance at her furniture mixed in with Paul's belongings. It felt strange to be a guest in her own home with her pale sofa, richly woven tapestry rug, trusty table and chairs—and know that she was a stranger in her mom's house, too.

Where's my place? she wondered.

Her life had turned into a big drifting mass of upheaval.

She just had to get that Pike's Peak job.

Majestic had Victorian homes on its quiet streets, but as the town spread out into the mountains the houses were newer and custom built. Some were more modern, some rustic. Each of the homes Paul had seen today had their own individual character.

While his mom and Irving were sightseeing this afternoon at Canyon Falls, Paul decided to go looking at houses to get a feel for what he could buy.

Paul followed Joe Fieland in his Porsche, Lanie sitting next to him.

"If I had to be by a phone a minute longer, I think I would have gone a little nuts," she said, the wind blowing through her hair. "It's been four days. Why haven't they called?"

"Review committees have to meet and discuss the other candidates."

"I was hoping there weren't any others." With a punch of her finger, she switched the radio station. "I really want this job. It's going to be my stepping stone and give me the experience I need." She rapidly changed the station once more.

He'd never seen anyone so dissatisfied with songs one right after the other. She was going to cut Pearl Jam short and he grabbed her hand as she reached for the knob once more.

"I like this one," he said.

"It's an oldie."

Holding her wrist in his fingers, he'd felt her pulse beat in an uneven rhythm. "I'm not that old." He put his hand back on the wheel. "How are you and your mom doing?"

Lanie told him about Lucille Prescott and Herb Deutsch trying out the dating thing. Whatever made them happy was Paul's thinking. But Lanie had a differing opinion for obvious reasons.

"We don't talk about it unless we have to. I can't tell her what to do. She's fifty-eight." Lanie's profile grew despondent, her shoulders slumping forward as she groaned, "She's out somewhere with him right now. She left me a note on the kitchen table."

"She's trying to include you."

"I know...." Lanie sighed. "It's still hard. I think about all the grief Dutch has put me through and—what am I saying? It doesn't matter. I love my mom too much to let him put up a wall between us. Hopefully she'll see the worst in him."

"There's optimism for you."

Lanie shot him a sarcastic smile.

Paul followed Joe Fieland on Pine Ridge Road and turned behind the Realtor's sedan as he went down a wooded drive.

The arts and crafts style immediately caught Paul's attention with its long sloping roof and a wide, sheltering overhang. Earth tones had been selected as the exterior paint on both levels and the woodwork was square and simple.

They got out of their vehicles for a closer look.

Paul viewed the surrounding area from the flagstone drive. Pine trees grew taller than his Florida condo. The mountainous setting was secluded, woodsy. Different hues of greens created a natural fortress in the landscape. The only sounds came from wind whispering through boughs and the gurgling creek that ran alongside the drive.

"I've always wanted to see the inside of this one," Lanie said.

To Paul's amusement, she'd been uttering that comment all day. Lanie took the expansive and wide steps to the double front doors. They were dark oak, massive and spanning ten feet in height. As tall as she was, she looked short in front of them. She also looked really good. She had on a dark pink T-shirt with laces loosely crisscrossed in the deep V displaying a tease of cleavage. Shorts showed off her legs. The walking boot was fastened on one leg and a white rubber flip-flop on the foot—little yellow daisies stuck around the toes. Her hair was pulled back in a long braid, the kind that captured hair from the top of the head down. The different colors of brown and blond in her hair were emphasized as they wove between each strand.

Wrought-iron knockers lay against each panel and Lanie gave one a test, rapping twice. "I like the sound. Does it have a doorbell, too, Mr. Fieland?" she asked.

Joe held on to an MLS book, cell phone and ring of keys. "Yes—it plays the first four bars of 'Claire de Lune.'"

That would be the first thing to go if I bought this one, Paul thought.

The broker drew up to the door, got out his pass key and opened the house.

"My God, it's incredible!" she said, passing through the door and disappearing inside.

Slipping his sunglasses into his shirt pocket Paul followed them.

The entry instantly felt comfortable. The floors were

dark oak and dominating, darkening the area to give the house a sense of dignity. But the walls were a light-colored paper, brightening the space and making it feel inviting. He strolled through the lower level, taking in the features. The rooms were deliberately set at irregular heights and the main living area contained a large flagstone fireplace. Somewhere in the house, he heard Lanie's declaration of loving something. For a woman with a bad leg, she traveled fast.

Paul found Fieland and Lanie in the kitchen. Light streamed in from a loft window and everything in the area was generous in scale. A built-in sideboard took up one wall, a sink and counter on the other, and the lighter colored woodwork lessened the formality. Moss green paint covered the walls.

"I can't cook worth a darn," Lanie said with a flourish, "but this kitchen makes me want to get out pots and pans and do something."

"The oven is state of the art. The last owners had it put in." Joe went to the appliance and highlighted its features. "The refrigerator is built in, as well as the dishwasher and trash compacter. There's a wine rack here. You've got lots of room to move about if you're cooking with guests."

A corner of Paul's mouth lifted. He could only envision one guest right now and her head was in the oven checking out the racks. In that position with her behind curved into a supple contour, her top fell away from her skin. He saw into the crisscrossed opening, and admired the full swell of breasts in a lacy bra. "It's huge," she said.

That's what he would be if he kept his eyes on her.

"And of course the laundry room is on this level, powder room, a dining room and closet space. It comes with a study—or home office as we say in the business. You'll be amazed at the upstairs. It's got—'' His cell phone rang and he checked the number in the ID. ''It's my office. I've been trying to get a matter straightened out all morning.''

''Go ahead,'' Paul said. ''We'll take our own tour.''

''I might be a few minutes.''

''Not a problem.''

Joe clicked on the line, began talking then let himself outside into the backyard through a glass door in the kitchen.

''Do they clear the roads up here in winter?'' Paul asked Lanie as they went into the entrance hall.

''Yes, but you should have a four-wheel drive.'' She paused at the base of the stairs after taking the first one, her hand on the railing. Turning toward him, she said, ''Your Porsche is great, but going down this road when there's ice could turn it into a German snow sled.''

Paul's laughter filled the foyer.

Lanie's eyes set off the delicate features of her oval face. With her standing on a stair and him on the floor, they were at eye level. She smelled like mint and maybe something else. Roses.

''I wonder what's up here?'' she said breathlessly.

He liked the look of her lips. The gloss on them was sheer pink and shiny. Just a touch of soft color and a whole lot of sexiness.

He grazed her mouth with the heel of his thumb, enjoying the way she shivered and sucked in her breath. Low and composed, he phrased, ''Your upper lip and your lower lip are exactly the same size.''

Whether nervous or taunting, she licked them, the pink tip of her tongue briefly appearing. What he could do with that tongue. And how that mouth would feel against his naked skin.

"Everyone's lips are the same," she replied, the jagged hitch in her breath giving away her slipping composure.

"Mine aren't."

She lowered her lashes, studying him longer than he thought he could stand without taking her into his arms and crushing his mouth over hers.

"They look fine," she said at length, a slight pique in her tone as if she thought otherwise. "Don't you want to come upstairs now?"

He laughed, low and seductive, at the play of words. "I would like nothing better."

She took the risers and he was right behind her. "Do you like the house?"

"I love it. I could see myself living here."

"It's pretty big for just one person," he said, not realizing what his thoughts were. This was a great house, but he couldn't picture himself in something so big without a special woman to share it with.

"I could manage," Lanie said. "I've lived alone for years. I can put up my own Christmas lights. I'm not afraid of a ladder."

Paul laughed again, his gaze on her cute derriere as she made her way to the top of the stairs. Heat coiled in him. "Lanie, darlin', I don't think you're afraid of anything."

She scowled at him. "I'm not your usual type, am I?"

"I don't have a type."

"I think you do and I'm definitely not it. Is that why you find me challenging?"

He drew closer, touching her cheek. "I find you beautiful."

She groaned and ducked out from beneath his arm. "Don't say that anymore, Paul. I'm not hiring and you're not volunteering."

Unclear about her intent, he questioned, "For what?"

"To be my...boyfriend."

That captured his full attention. "Interesting. Go on."

"Okay, so I like it that you think I'm pretty. I'd be a fool not to be flattered and be" —her voice lowered as if Joe Fieland was just around the corner— "*attracted* to you in return." The inflection in those last words were as if they were too hard to get out. Or too hard to own up. "But we both know that anything between us would be a waste of time. I'm not sticking around Majestic and you are. We can't get past that so let's look at the rest of the house and—"

"Why did you come with me today, Lanie?" He folded his arms over his chest and leaned a shoulder into the paneled wall, liking the sunlight that poured over her skin turning it golden. "What's the real reason?"

"I needed to quit waiting for the phone to ring. This was something to do." She shifted and her fingers nervously moved over the light switch. With a click, she turned on the overhead hall light. "It works."

He said nothing. Simply watched her every fidgety move as she examined the molding around the door and then flicked the light off.

In a disgruntled tone, she flung out, "You want the truth. Fine." She smoothed wisps of hair behind her ears where silver hoop earrings dangled from the lobes.

"I came because I wanted to prove I could spend the day with you and not be preoccupied with the way you kiss."

Pushing himself away from the wall, Paul closed the distance between them. With her mouth full and stubbornly set, he looked into Lanie's face and smiled. She had the most beautiful eyes, the nicest skin and smelled so damn good. He cupped her high cheekbone in the palm of his hand. Her expression changed from defiant to submissive, making his stomach curl with need. "That's the best thing you've ever said to me, Prescott." Her sensual mouth beckoned. "And I'm going to kiss you for it."

His mouth crushed hers. He tasted and explored, running his tongue through her. Sleek and velvety, she made his body heat. As he pressed into her hips, she leaned into the wall. She gave no resistance, a gasp of anticipation melding into his mouth with a moan. He felt her knees trembling as she swept her tongue through his mouth returning what he gave—a mutual pleasure that demanded more.

Slender hands came round his neck as she clung to him, kissing and nibbling on his lower lip. She was eager, sexually aroused. He was on fire, burning and wanting to be consumed by the woman in his arms. The kiss made his heart pound. If this was something she was trying to prove to herself, she was either a good actress or she wanted every bit of him.

She stroked the nape of his neck, her fingers smooth against his skin. The full swells of her breasts burned an imprint on his chest, her tight nipples straining against her bra and through the light knit of her shirt. His muscles went taut, his groin stiffened. He wanted her naked. Wanted to feel every inch of her sweet-smelling skin. It would be so easy to delve his hand beneath her top and learn every curve and valley of her breasts. His hand would slide to the apex of her legs, to stroke and excite.

Dragging his mouth off hers and trailing kisses across her cheek, he held on to her and breathed next to her ear. "You make me want to forget about everything but you."

The curve of her cheek nuzzled his jaw, her nose and mouth next to the hollow of his throat. He could feel the fringe of lashes, the hot air expelled from her lungs. Slight and light, her hands hooked behind his head.

Pliant and melted against him like a pool of hot liquid, she only stayed that way a moment longer before stiffening, apparently catching her breath and realizing what she was doing.

Sidestepping him, she stumbled out from his reach with lips soft and tempting, wet from their kiss. She laid the back of her hand against her forehead. "Don't make me look lame, Paul. I can get you off my mind just like this." She snapped her fingers and irritation welled inside him. Maybe she could snap him off, but he couldn't snap her off.

Lanie was becoming more to him than he'd expected. He wasn't sure how to handle that. Right now, he chose to ignore the ache in his body and forgo sorting out what he was feeling beyond the physical.

"Let's look around," he said, closing off the parts of him that only wanted to take her in his arms again and damn everything else.

Managing to pull herself together, Lanie went down the hallway and peered into the doorways of rooms. Suddenly the new penny luster had dulled and she wasn't consumed by the house's allure. At the guest bath, she absently admired the fixtures and light, then went to the last room.

The master bedroom. Very large. Floor to ceiling corner fireplace with glass and brass. The walls were painted burgundy, navy and sand. Colors that were masculine, yet a woman could lose herself in the room on a satin-draped bed with the right man and—

She turned to get out of the room quickly and nearly rammed into Paul's chest as he filled the leaded glass double-door entry. She liked how his inky black hair was clipped short, slightly spiked, and gave his entire face a chiseled and angular appeal. The bridge of his eyebrows was serious, his half-closed eyes deep in thought. Their deep color was magnificent and overtly sexy. Rich and dark brown like espresso.

His lips…she loved them. Loved their look, loved their feel next to her own. Loved how he kissed and made her breathless. She'd lied when she said they were simply "fine." His lips were perfection. They were better than watching *Fargo* and pretending to be Chief Marge Gunderson.

"What do you think of it?" he asked, his voice showing either extreme control or indifference toward her. She hated to think it was the latter, that he could turn off his awareness of her so easily. Contrary to what she had said, she couldn't snap her feelings away.

"It's a bedroom," she commented, holding on to the hitch in her voice. "It'll do."

His expression became questioning, his tone growing amused. "I meant the house. What do you think of it?"

Frantic to hold herself together, she acquiesced. "I like it. I love it."

"So do I. Maybe I'll make the owners an offer."

Incredulous, she blurted, "Really?"

"I'm thinking about it."

They went back downstairs to wait for the Realtor. Paul rested his butt on the foyer windowsill; the dial of his watch picked up a slant of sun and it gleamed next to his tan skin.

"I get my walking boot off tomorrow," Lanie said, forcing general conversation, anything to keep her from remembering how great their kiss had been.

"It's been a long time," Paul said, laying his hands on the sill and crossing his legs at the ankle to recline quite casually.

"Seven weeks of hell."

"I wouldn't say it's been all bad. You got to know me."

"Yes," she agreed. "I didn't think I was going to like the man who came in and took my job and my house within the same week."

"You can come over to my side whenever you want company," he said.

A dangerous invitation. She always wanted his company. He exuded such a virile masculinity he could curl her toes.

She ran a hand through her hair, her fingers snagging on the rope of braid and unraveling a section. Since he lived next door and she worked with him, she had a window into his life, but she wasn't with him all the time. She had no right to ask, but she couldn't stop the words, "Do you ever have company besides me?"

Calmly, and without drawing breath, the muscles in his arms flexed as he revealed, "I haven't been with a woman since I came to Majestic."

Since an intimate guest would have been his for the asking, she was curious. "Why not?"

"Because when I have sex, it has to mean something.

I'd have to care about the woman, know what she likes and doesn't.'' Eyes as brown as coffee and just as satisfying, never faltered from hers. ''She'd have to be someone I'd bring ice cream to in the middle of the night.''

Lanie's heart beat in her throat.

Joe Fieland came around the corner, pocketing his cell phone with a cheery smile. ''Sorry to keep you waiting. What did you think of the upstairs?''

''I liked it,'' Paul said as they stepped outside. ''I'm going to give this one some serious thought.''

The bright sunlight caused Lanie to squint as she battled to control her erratic pulse. Paul slipped the mirrored lenses off the bridge of his nose and put the glasses on her face. Every hair on her head tingled at the root.

''This was the last one I had to show you,'' Joe said. ''I appreciate you coming out today.''

Lanie didn't gaze at Paul but she felt his eyes still on her as they went to the Porsche.

She'd have to be someone I'd bring ice cream to in the middle of the night.

Going with Paul today had been a mistake. How could she have known that going house-hunting would end up in a conversation about sex? My God, did men really go without it because it didn't mean anything? Lanie found that terribly hard to believe....

...terribly attractive if it were true.

Paul Cabrera was turning her life inside out. She didn't know which way was up—this way or that way. No, that wasn't true.

He had alluded to taking their relationship to another level because she meant something to him. Meant what exactly? A female body that felt good next to his? She couldn't deny that, because kissing him was the best thing shy of heaven.

Somehow, without her being aware, he had become a permanent fixture in her life when she desperately needed someone to lean on.

It was awful living out of boxes with uncertainty hanging over her head. She wanted to know something about that Pike's Peak job. She was tired of being displaced and kept on hold. Maybe it wasn't in the cards for her to leave Majestic. Surely anything and everything that could have gone wrong had done just that.

She sat in Paul's car and slanted her gaze on him. Maybe staying was just what she needed to do. But what would she do? She was not cut out for dispatch. If only...

But there were no "if onlys" for her.

She had to leave. And the sooner she got out, the better, before she did something foolish—like fall in love with Paul Cabrera.

Seventeen

They decided to pick apples at Ashford's Orchards so Lucille could jar apple butter for the Calico Corner.

Dutch was an excellent driver on the two-lane winding road that took them forty minutes away from town. The scenery was colorful and the day was cloudless. She wore a parchment-colored pair of pants and a blouse in a slightly darker shade. She carried a tote she had hand-embroidered, a project she'd just finished last night. The mood had struck her to get it out and she rushed to finish to bring it along today.

A pair of black-striped chipmunks bolted in front of the car from the roadside. A fast reaction and the Jeep's responsive tires prevented a near disaster as Dutch swerved and recovered the steering.

"Oh, my goodness," she gasped, a hand over her heart. "I thought we were going to hit one."

Dutch's firm grip on the wheel lessened. "Don't you try what I just did, Lucille. If something like that happens don't jerk your steering wheel."

"But if I didn't swerve, I'd run over the chipmunks."

Dutch's square jaw was hard, his mouth a line. "Do you know I get called out to more accident scenes because of small animals. It's better to mow them down, Lucille."

"I couldn't do that."

"You've got a soft heart," he said, momentarily putting his hand on hers, sending heat to her pulse. "But you're more important than a couple of rodents."

The dirt lot at Ashford's wasn't full. The aroma of sweet fritters and caramel apples scented the day. A concession stand by the corn maze sold hot dogs, chips and soda pop, as well as coffee, hot chocolate and fresh apple cider.

"I never knew you had a car of your own," she mentioned after Dutch came around to her side of the Jeep and held the door open for her. "I'm so used to seeing you in an official Explorer."

His eyes lit up with the reflection of the sky in them. "There are a lot of things you don't know about me. Today you'll find out a few."

The prospect brought a smile to her lips.

As Lucille walked, dust puffed around the light color of her step-ins, marring the bottoms with dirt.

Dutch's flattop was spiked up and the shave across his face was baby-smooth. He truly was a handsome man; a bit debonaire yet with that candid gruffness. She suspected he'd take care of all her needs and never let anything harmful happen. Living alone, she sometimes worried about being by herself in a time of crisis if Lanie wasn't around.

Dutch rummaged in the back of the Jeep and came up with a picnic hamper he'd packed himself. He'd insisted on doing the cooking, another delightful surprise.

They made their way to the booth and paid. They were given baskets and access to the crops of Paula Red and Red Baron apples. Dutch led the way through the rows of trees, their fruit fragrant and honeybees drifting through the branches.

Each time the trail grew rough through the orchard

run, he'd say, "Watch your step" or "Be careful for that branch, Lucille."

He was so mindful for her well-being. She was affected pleasantly by his manners. He was a real gentleman. Whenever she felt her heart being pulled toward him in a way that warmed her soul, she remembered he was the Majestic chief of police. Getting past that was very difficult, but she rationalized that it wasn't as if they were getting married.

When they reached a nice spot, he spread a woolen blanket on the ground and helped her sit down. His hand was warm and smooth, like the apple she'd picked along the way. She recalled how it had felt over hers in the Jeep. Tingles rose across her arms. She inconspicuously rubbed them away.

Once she was beside him, she tucked her feet by her side debating whether or not to remove her shoes. They were smudged with dust. She should have worn tennis shoes, but she didn't have any.

"Do you want to eat now or pick apples?" he asked, considerate of her preference.

She couldn't eat a bite just yet. This was so new to her, so different that she felt strange. *This* felt strange, being out with a man other than Ken. When she told him that she was going to be seeing other people, he'd been shocked and hurt. He wanted to know who the other man was and when she confessed it was Dutch, Ken said it would never work out between them because Dutch was all wrong for her.

Lucille knew there were no sure assumptions about anything. She wasn't sure how things would go with her and Dutch, but if they were going to be seen around town, she had to be up-front about it with Ken. Cookie and Myrtle knew and both of them just about fainted dead away. It was Myrtle who jumped out of her chair at Cookie's and said Dutch had been the one to send her the roses. Lucille filled them both in.

"Pick apples," Lucille said at length, still nervous and not yet hungry for lunch. She hoped if she set her mind on the apple picking she could relax.

"Whenever you're ready for lunch, Lucille, you let me know. I've got it covered." His rugged face beamed, certain he would please her. "And I think you'll like what I have."

She liked him for thinking of her comforts. If she'd come on her own she'd be eating a hot dog and cider instead of whatever mystery he'd put together.

He extended his arm to help her up and she gripped his strong hand. Standing so close to him caused her heart to flutter. "Can you give me my basket?"

"My pleasure."

He gave her pleasure all right.

Lucille hooked the handle through her arm.

"These look nice down here," Dutch said and she followed.

Tiny granules of dirt slipped inside her shoes. She shook her foot to kick them into the toe area.

"I haven't been apple picking in years. Not since I was a kid on the farm," he said.

That surprised her. She plucked an apple. "You grew up on a farm?"

"Mill, Illinois. Nothing big. My dad didn't make his living off the land. My mother was a homemaker."

"And your ancestry is Dutch?" She maintained the conversational tone, as pleasant and warm as the day.

"German." He grabbed apples from the lower branches, dropping them into his basket as if he'd done this dozens of times. "And you?"

"A little bit of everything, mostly Danish."

A wooden ladder stood next to the tree trunk but she wasn't planning on going up. Dutch took the rungs and, for a man who was compact with muscle, he was steady on his feet. *Pluck-pluck-pluck,* the apples continued to fill his basket. When it was full, he climbed down.

"Looks like I'm at my limit. Give me your basket and I'll help you out." He'd set his basket down and had taken hers, and was back up that ladder very quickly. "Do you like apple pies, Lucille?"

"I love them."

"I can bake one anytime you want."

"Really?"

"I can cook just about anything."

"That surprises me."

"Why? Because I'm a man?"

"No...well, yes. I suppose I never thought of you in a kitchen. I can't get the image in my head."

Whatever he'd packed for them to eat must have been something he was proud of because he grabbed and picked with speedy efficiency. She thought his tactic was rather endearing.

"I think any man can cook." He gazed down at her through the green foliage. "If he can read, he can read a recipe."

She shaded her eyes and stared upward.

He had the kindest eyes, so soft in color yet with a touch of black...black in the center. He went on, "I'd love to cook dinner for you sometime."

"I'd like that." She laughed. "All this talk about pies and I'm getting hungry."

He sped up his apple picking, taking two apples at a time and dumping them into the basket until it brimmed with red. It was evident he was on a mission to pick their share then sit under the sky and eat whatever it was he'd brought.

She was touched, honestly. Ever since that night at the White Horse Saloon, she'd been thinking about him. He made her feel pretty.

"Done!" he declared, climbing down and spilling apples galore as he took the last rung. He had an apple blossom stuck in his hair and he smelled like musky men's soap and pollen dust.

With the two baskets on the ground, and Dutch standing with his legs spread and hands on his hips, he meant business. The pullover he wore was a deep blue and lay flat next to his chest and stomach which was anything but sloppy. The ridge of his chest was as bulky as a bulldog's, tight and fit. She wondered how he would feel should she press her hand against his ribs, over the beat of his heart.

Flustered, Lucille touched her pearl necklace and toyed with the strand. "So what is it you've made for lunch?"

He began pulling things out and as each container was set on the picnic cloth, he said, "Crab salad, pear cole slaw and blueberry crumb cake squares."

Lucille's mouth fell open. "I'm truly amazed. You did all that?"

"I hope you'll like it, honey."

The romantic endearment caused her to blush. Her heartbeat was speeding out of control, beating so fast she could barely catch her breath. This was so sudden, so fast. She was falling for him by the second. How could this happen to her when she barely knew him?

Growing light-headed, she drew in deep gulps.

"Lucille, Lucille." He held her by the shoulders. "Relax."

"I can't." She could barely swallow. "I'm wondering if this is the right thing to do. Me and you. Us. Everything is happening so quickly. I feel excited and edgy at the same time."

He lowered his head. "I have a way of taking the edge off."

Then his lips were on hers, gently pressing. Firm and offering a new sensation, something she hadn't felt since her husband died. The feeling was purely physical, with the longing and the maturity of an older woman's heart.

When he broke the kiss, she held on to him as if she'd collapse.

"Feel better?" His face was a breath from hers, mixing and mingling with the scent of apple blossoms surrounding them.

"Yes," she whispered. "But, I..."

"Don't say anything more, Lucille."

And he kissed her.

Eighteen

Paul cast his fishing line and stood on the banks of the Cottonwood River. Insects skiffed across the water's surface where the current was slow-moving. Yellowing leaves drifted intermittently from trees, a sure sign autumn was approaching in the coming weeks. The last time he fished for anything, it was off the side of a boat out in the Atlantic during one of the twice-yearly Miami PD fishing excursions. He and Sid had shared good times and laughs over the green faces of the burly officers who were hard as nails at the station, but who were weakened with seasickness out in the ocean.

Irving and Dutch dug through the tackle box. The chief had joined them late in the afternoon after a full day at the station before giving way to Griswold and Coyote on the swing shift. Since the month had rolled into September, vacationers left daily and the town had almost returned to the locals. Rooster's Place had calmed down from the summer and you could get a seat at Ken's Steakhouse now without a wait.

"Paul, do you have any more of those pink marshmallows?" Irv asked.

"The jar's down by those rocks."

The three men had caught sixteen trout between them so far. They were nice-sized rainbows. But it wasn't the size of the fish they were after when they cast their lines, it was the time spent talking, having a beer and watching the water roll by.

Dutch had a lot of outdoor gear. He came prepared with waders and a trout vest, a stocked tackle box and a cooler filled with Bud. He soaked up the last remnants of a warm afternoon and stood out in the water, a cigar clamped between his lips.

"Irv, what kind of engine do you have in that Winnebago?" Dutch asked around the cigar.

"Three hundred and thirty horsepower turbocharged."

"And you climb mountains in that okay? I've always wanted to hit the road and go to Alaska. Fishing for salmon would be the ultimate vacation."

Irving baited his hook. "It's got a six-speed electronic transmission for plenty of hill-climbing power. And what's with the vacation?" he said, standing on the sandy bank and throwing out his line. "How old are you?"

"Fifty-six."

"How long on the job?"

"I'm into my thirtieth year."

Irving waved him off. "Oy, long enough. You ought to retire."

"Hell, I'm too young to retire."

Paul sat on one of Dutch's camping chairs, took a drink of beer and breathed in the clean air. "If I were you, Chief, I'd be retired and enjoying this river every day."

"I can fish on my days off." Dutch's face grew ruddy and he rubbed his jaw with his knuckle. After a moment of thought, he confessed, "I never wanted to consider retiring because I don't want to get that useless feeling."

"I never feel useless. Oleda's always got something for me to do," Irv chuckled.

"I don't know about giving up the job." Dutch reeled in his line for a second cast. "I've done it for so damn long, I don't know what I'd do without it."

"You'd have the freedom to come and go as you pleased, live off your pension plan, and do all the activities you kept telling yourself you'd do one day—that's what you'd do with your time. Soon you'd have no time at all and you'd be having the ride of your life. That's the way it is for me and Oleda. We always have something going on. She's active in Good Sam and she sets up activities for us. We're meeting up with a group from Silver Springs when we leave here—big pinochle tournament." Irv's hair caught the last rays of sunshine and cast it in a silver light.

"You've got a good woman to share your retirement with," Dutch said. "Me, I'm not married."

"How are things going with you and Lucille Prescott?" Paul rested his beer bottle on his thigh.

"She's a peach," Dutch said, slugging his way back toward shore with another trout.

"Nothing sweeter than a peach," Irv commented. "My Oleda, she's an orange. A regular Florida dolly."

Dutch cracked another beer and Irv sat down on the cooler. They let time wander by without talking, each wrapped up in his own thoughts.

Daily, Paul felt more and more at home in Colorado and was settling into somewhat of a sense of belonging. Looking at houses convinced him he'd never fully be relocated until he had his own place. It was time to bring out his things from a storage facility and fill a house with them. Time to surround himself with possessions that represented who he was and what he liked.

"Prescott hear anything from that Pike's Peak job?" Dutch asked, breaking the silence.

"Not yet," Paul replied. Lanie's mood was up and down with waiting. She'd hinged all her hopes on that call and he hoped for her sake she got it but for selfish reasons he was hoping she wouldn't.

Irving brushed grass off his leg. "She's a sweetheart. I like her, Paul. You look good together."

"She's got plans of her own, Irv. She won't be around."

"That's a shame." Irving called to Dutch, "Herb, don't you have any extra positions in the department you can put her on?"

Dutch shook his head, the fishing hooks on his camp hat swaying. "I can't hire her back on in that capacity. The city ordinance says we've got an allotment for four deputies. Paul's the fourth, and even as a chief-deputy, his slot still counts as plain old deputy. There'd have to be a vote to change it, and it's just not going to happen with our city budget. When the tourism dies, we don't need to be a five-officer department."

Leaning into the chair back, Paul ventured to say, "She would have never quit if you'd have considered her a real officer."

"I did, Cabrera. She had a uniform and gun just like the rest of them."

Paul should have let up, but he didn't. In his time with the Majestic PD, he'd seen through Dutch's motives. The man didn't have a leg to stand on. He'd purposefully given Lanie the mundane assignments. To a point, Paul knew where the chief had been coming from; but it still didn't make it right. "But you didn't make Ridder or Coyote ticket cars."

"That's the way it worked out." Dutch cracked his

neck, a jerk to the right and left. "They're doing it now."

"Out of necessity."

"Are you getting at something, Cabrera?"

A thin layer of tension built between them. Paul never pushed his superiors into a debate, but this felt personal. If Lanie had a place on the Majestic PD she wouldn't be going elsewhere. Then again, if Lanie was there, there would be no position for Paul. It was a losing situation.

"You run a damn good station, Dutch," Paul replied, toning down his argumentative voice. "You're involved and you get out there with the rest of us. That means a lot."

"How about we call it a day?" Irving jumped in as he stood. "We've caught more than enough trout for dinner. I saw you have a barbecue on the patio out back, Paul. We'll fire it up and grill fish."

"Sounds good," Paul said rising to his feet. "My mom's got some black beans on the stove. She was showing Lucille how to make them."

Dutch's eyes brightened. "Then I'm going home first to shave and change my clothes."

Fish sizzling over cedar chips scented the air with a mouthwatering aroma. The globe of sun descending in the western horizon left elongated shadows in the backyard from the fence and trees.

Paul didn't do backyard barbecue since all he had was a condo balcony. He left the chef duties to Dutch who attacked them with enthusiasm. Lanie was in the kitchen with his mom preparing salads. Lucille was outside on a lounge, her gaze rarely straying from Dutch. He talked to her while flipping fish, giving her the low-down on how to grill a trout without overcooking it. She listened raptly while smiling.

The girls had been planning on making dinner for them all and the trout was an added bonus. As soon as Dutch's name was mentioned and that he'd be along in thirty minutes, Lanie grew quiet. She was diplomatic enough not to say anything, but Paul sensed she was not happy about him being a part of the barbecue.

Since the day she'd found out Dutch had faxed information on her to Pike's Peak, she'd kept things between them businesslike and professional at the station without being overly chatty.

"I wouldn't have pegged you for a guy who could cook, Dutch," Paul said, taking a potato chip and popping it into his mouth.

"A man's got to survive and I'm not the type who can live out of a can or a box."

"He's an excellent cook," Lucille said, holding a platter out to him so he could take the finished trout off the grill. "He made me crab salad and it was wonderful."

"I don't have the patience to cook." Irving arranged paper napkins and silverware on the outdoor table with its red and white oilcloth cover. "Oleda enjoys cooking, so it works out well for us."

Paul's mom came out with a large bowl of greens and she sat down to relax. "Everything is ready except for what I have on the stove. And Lanie's mixing a pitcher of lemonade."

Inside the kitchen, Lanie felt restless and nervous at the same time. She brought the cordless phone from her mom's and set it on the counter, just in case it rang. Not hearing any news from Pike's Peak was constantly on her mind. Couldn't she get even the simplest of jobs?

She didn't want to make a follow-up call. Not yet. Week two had barely begun. Besides, she wasn't in a good frame of mind to hear their response. If the news was bad, it would be yet another devastating setback. *Setback?* Not quite, since she had no *set forward.* She lived in a constant state of not knowing and of just going through the motions.

Heaven help her if she didn't land this patrol detail, because her days were numbered as the dispatch operator. Karen would be off her maternity leave soon and that would leave Lanie out in the cold. She couldn't stand it if not only did she end up handing over her deputy position, but her dispatch one as well.

She was ready to move on and have solid ground beneath her, now more than ever since she was no longer tied to that awkward walking boot. She'd never been more relieved to hear she was done with it. She had to be careful with limited weight on her leg for the first few days. Those test runs in the doctor's office had felt strange—supporting herself on two feet—but she was determined to get strong quickly. She started physical therapy next week, grueling three-days-a-week sessions to get her back in shape so she could tackle anything.

Stirring the freshly squeezed lemonade, she was lost in her thoughts and didn't hear someone enter the kitchen until two strong arms encircled her from the back. She loved the feel of Paul's chest next to her, the smell of his skin and the heat from his body.

"Hello," she said, the spoon in her hand growing still.

"Hello yourself." His deep voice wound around her,

making her feel warm inside. "Is that done? I'm thirsty."

"Sure. Get a glass."

He reached above her head to the cupboard. The dishes weren't hers. He'd brought in his own and it felt odd to be in her kitchen with differences everywhere she turned.

Imagining how her own things would blend in here, she saw her cups next to Paul's. It was strangely reassuring, but wholly unrealistic.

She poured cold lemonade into a glass and he popped a straw into it. Crushed ice floated with lemon slices as he drank. The way he sucked on that straw, his lips sensuously firm, was downright sinful. She imagined him giving her an openmouthed kiss, capturing her tongue with his, then lowering his face to the sensitive skin at her collarbone.

He turned the straw her way. The flavor was just right, but more than that, it was the intimacy of sharing the same straw and looking into his eyes as she drank. She could drown herself in his gaze and how he felt beside her.

Without thinking it through, she stood on her toes and brushed her lips across his. He tasted like sugar and lemons. She let her mouth linger over his, his arms sliding around her and holding her close. It was a subtle kiss, stolen through the sounds of laughter in the backyard—anyone could come in at any time.

And of course, someone did. Stepping out from Paul's arms, Lanie turned away from him and pretended she hadn't been kissing him at all as Dutch went to the sink and washed his hands.

He cleared his throat and announced in that tone that

was gravelly and rough, "Dinner's ready. Your mother wants that pot brought outside."

"I'll get it while you finish with the lemonade," Paul volunteered and was out of the kitchen before she could say anything to the contrary.

The lemonade was done, he knew it. His words were just a ploy.

Being left alone with Dutch was beyond uncomfortable and she had a feeling Paul had left her here on purpose so they could talk things out. But there was nothing to talk out. She couldn't say anything she hadn't already said to Dutch, and vice versa, or he would have said it by now.

Both of them were too stubborn for their own good. She recognized that. But take the Pike's Peak position out of play and she still had a hard time reconciling him being romantically interested in her mother. And her mother being romantically interested in him.

He dried his hands on a plain dishcloth, slowly as if he were stalling for time. She felt obligated to make small talk as she tossed lemon peels in the garbage.

"Things are quieting down now at the station," she said, not looking directly at him when she spoke. "Soon we'll be in November though and it'll pick back up with the ski season."

Dutch shifted his weight from one foot to the other, standing like a wall of compact bricks. "Yeah, I heard that popular rapper was going to check out our skiing this winter. The rental offices told me he'd signed a lease for the Sky Lodge."

"What rapper is that?"

"Puffy P. Diddly."

Lanie bit on the inside of her mouth to keep her smile

from showing. "I think he's calling himself P. Diddy now."

"Why the hell can't he make up his mind?" Dutch asked as he neatly hung up the towel. She observed him and was surprised he was thoughtful enough to hang it straight. "What's with names like that anyway? They're not real, that's for sure. You take a good name like Clint Eastwood or John Wayne—those are real men names."

She wiped off the counter, rinsing out the dishcloth. "I guess it's dinner…" she said, thinking he'd take her cue and go eat. She felt flustered with him watching what she was doing.

He didn't leave. He didn't do anything but stand there and look at her until she looked at him. He was such a proud man with statements that were often blunt and without apologies. In a way, she envied him that ability to be so sure of himself.

"How does the leg feel?" he asked, as if forcing conversation.

"It's a little bit painful. I don't put all my weight on it when I'm just standing at the counter. But I'm getting better."

"Good…good to hear." He glanced out the back-door half window and saw her mom sitting in the sun-set. The golden hues of the late-day sun painted her with honey tones. She'd never looked more beautiful.

Lanie knew her mom was on Dutch's mind and her hunch was proven as he said, "About me and your mom, I know you don't like me, Prescott. I might have given you cause to feel that way a time or two."

She met his eyes, a quick connection before she looked the other way.

"All right, so more than a time or two. But when I

think about it, and I'm being neutral, there's not much of anything I'd change. Hell, maybe I'd have put you on patrol more, but Griswold and Coyote and Ridder— we all thought it was better for you to stay in the safer jobs.''

''There's never a safe job in our line of work,'' she said in her defense, an ache welling in her heart. ''We all know it, but we do the job anyway because we're willing to take that risk.''

''Prescott—''

''No, please. Let me say this.'' She drew in a breath and forced her pulse to calm. ''My dad told me that serving as a police officer takes a very special person and it's an invaluable thing to do for one's community. He never once regretted his decision to put himself out there. He knew I could be something special, too. But I've never had the chance to show anyone just how valuable I can be. From the first, you didn't take me seriously. I was ready from day one to take the risk, but I wasn't given the chance.''

''Maybe I was wrong.''

His statement surprised her. ''Seriously?''

''I was raised in the old school where women cooked and cleaned and the men went out and brought home the bacon. Times are different now and I'm not so sure for the better, but the fact is we're living a whole new life philosophy now.'' He rubbed the back of his neck and admitted, ''I'm not a man who changes easily. I'm set in my ways, I like things done how I like them done and maybe—'' he nodded ''—maybe I should have seen things from your point of view more often.''

The back door opened and Paul's mother came in. She peered at them through the heavy black frames of her glasses. "Come on now, you two. Bring the lemonade and your cheery smiles to the table."

Lanie didn't know how "cheery" her smile was, but she found herself at the long table eating dinner with Paul's parents, her mother and Dutch on the opposite side from where she and Paul sat side by side.

The impromptu Thursday evening get-together lingered on well after the dessert was served. Oleda and Irving were card lovers and they brought out a deck and suggested a game of poker.

Lanie observed the four suits of five cards in her hand, her mind not fully concentrating on the game. Dutch conceding he could have been wrong to treat her the way he had felt sincere and she knew he didn't say something he didn't mean. His words weren't a tactic to win her approval toward him and her mom. They were from the heart, a regret that perhaps had been on his mind and he'd finally spoken it to her.

She wasn't paying attention to the three-of-a-kind she had when Irving declared a full house and won all the poker chips in the center of the table.

A new hand was dealt.

"I've always wanted to go to Florida," her mother said as she picked up her cards. "I envy you your sunny weather all the time. I like beaches. I'd love to go to Hawaii one day."

"Is that why you have the *Gidget* movie, Mom?" Lanie asked as she sorted her cards.

"Oh, that, I saw it on sale one day and I thought it would be cute. I've enjoyed watching it. Maybe I'll get over to Waikiki sometime and go to the Beachcomber and hear Don Ho sing."

Dutch asked for one card then said, "Maybe somebody will take you."

They shared a brief smile and Lanie drank a swallow of lemonade to quench her dry throat.

"I ran into Julie the other day," Oleda said over the rim of her glasses. "She looks really great. Working too much, but I think you all do."

Julie. Lanie's attention picked up on the name. Paul's ex-wife.

"I saw her before I moved," Paul commented. "She's putting in for a promotion and I think she's got a good chance of getting it."

The ever-so-vague sting of jealousy touched Lanie. She didn't have a single right in the world to feel this way, nor give the mention of his wife's name a moment's thought.

"Oh, and we had dinner with Sid Tuesday before we came," Oleda added. "Paul, you don't have to worry about him. He's holding up. He's going to meetings and was in good spirits. He said you'd spoken recently."

"We talk a couple times a week."

Irving sang under his breath as he dealt cards. He was a very happy-go-lucky man, an endearing sort who could make a person smile even if they didn't feel like it. "Sid's got a good head on his shoulders. He was telling me about the time you broke up a domestic dispute at the Floridian trailer park. He said the husband was busting up the place and you pointed out that when they divorced he'd get all the destroyed stuff and the wife would get the good stuff. That stopped him but good."

Paul smiled. "I remember that night. After Sid told him that the guy started cleaning up the mess. We never received another domestic dispute call from those two again."

"What about this Mr. Clock bandit?" Paul's mother questioned as she sipped on her lemonade. "Paul mentioned him."

"Mr. Tick Tock," Dutch corrected. "He asks for the time and a new battery in his watch, then he takes jewelry. We'll catch the guy if he comes into my jurisdiction. I've got all my deputies on alert. Prescott does a good job at the dispatch keeping us up to snuff."

Lanie met Dutch's eyes only briefly, then looked back at her cards. She tossed her three-chip ante into the game and ventured, "I was ticketing an illegally parked Mercedes one day in front of Rooster's Place and I'd just finished writing it up. My hand was on the wiper blade and here comes this man who's got to be at least seven feet tall. I've never seen anyone as tall as him. He was very pleasant about the whole thing, he didn't try and talk his way out of it. In fact, he said he knew he'd let the meter expire because he didn't have enough change. He played for the L.A. Lakers."

"Good team," Paul said, his hand straying beneath the table to rest on her thigh for a moment. She gazed at him and he smiled.

What she'd thought would be a difficult night was turning out to be the most enjoyable she'd spent in a long time. Through their laughter and the stories they told, she forgot about her pressing life and simply enjoyed herself.

Especially since she just won and took delight in it.

"Royal flush!" Lanie declared to the groans around the table. "I can't believe it! Irving dealt me the hand right out of the deck. All I was missing was the jack of hearts and I just got it. I can't believe this," she repeated, a smile on her lips.

"Aren't you the big winner?" Paul said, munching

on a carrot stick. The sight of him made her heart turn over. She loved spending time with him like this, with everyone. Damn, even Dutch wasn't so bad tonight.

As she raked the chips from her winning hand toward her, the phone rang inside.

"Not mine," Paul said, glancing into the kitchen.

Lanie recognized the ring as her cordless. She rose and answered the call, bracing her hand on the counter as soon as the voice on the other end identified itself. She mostly listened, adding a yes or a no, her heartbeat in her chest flitting around like butterflies. When the person on the other end was finished, she said, "Thanks," and hung up.

Returning her attention to the group, she stood in the kitchen doorway and announced, "That was Pike's Peak PD."

Expectant faces stared at her, her mom hanging on what she would say next.

It wasn't with the great fanfare that she'd practiced when she added, "I got the job and they want me relocated there by the end of the month."

Nineteen

The old deserted Gold Spur mine was one of many gold finds near Majestic. Past Milepost Forty-Four, the ghost town of Red Forks was surrounded by sage and outbuildings long since abandoned. Their wood frames were barely standing, roofs depressed and ready to crumble. The flat terrain was littered by rusted-out mining equipment and the skeletal remains of wagons with gray-wood yokes and missing wheels.

Paul got a call about a shooter near Ben Hermann's place. And since it wasn't two in the morning, Ben wasn't after a can of tuna for his cat and some company. Griswold, who was taking a turn at dispatch, said Ben thought the gunman was a poacher targeting his cattle.

The boys from Laramie Ranch wouldn't have made it this far from their campground unless they'd stolen a car. And a poacher would have to be pretty stupid to pick a place with so little cover to do his dirty work.

The gray highway gave way to dirt as Paul turned onto the stretch of washboard road. Dust fanned behind the Explorer as several split-log buildings came into view. He saw the Trailblazer parked by a creek next to the mill.

He knew who owned the vehicle without running a check on the plates. The Blazer belonged to Lanie.

Cutting the engine, Paul went around to the back of the mill. He spotted his suspect thirty feet away from a sunken wagon bed. Spread-legged, she extended both arms and was shooting cans off the wagon's planked side. The hubbed wheels were missing on the front end, giving her a slanted target line of ten metal cans to aim at.

She picked off one, nailed it clean in the center, then watched as it spun into the sky and dropped onto the brown grass.

"Hey," he hollered. "It's me."

Whirling around, she said, "Hey."

He went forward, the brim of a Stetson shading his gaze. "We got a call from Ben Hermann. You're making him nervous."

"I'm not doing anything illegal. Everybody comes up here shooting. Go ask Dutch. His shell casings are by that building." She squinted in his direction. "What's that on your head?"

"A cowboy hat."

He'd paid good money at the Western wear store for the black felt hat. Ridder told him only wanna-be citi-fied cowboys wrapped something around the band like snakeskin or turquoise conchae. Paul didn't think he'd take to wearing a cowboy hat, but the harsh high-altitude sun took a beating on him when he was on the day shift and he needed something more than a pair of sunglasses.

Lanie gave him a long appraisal, then smiled. "An authentic Stetson. You are making the complete trans-formation, Paul. I might not recognize you anymore."

"You'll recognize me," he said, shoving the brim higher with his thumb. "I'm the guy who lives next door."

"But I won't be for much longer." She refocused, squeezed the trigger and hit the next can with a *ping*. The ricocheting echo of the revolver's discharge claimed the expansive area.

"I remember you saying you shoot at tin cans to relieve stress." Paul stood several feet behind her, his words low. "Darlin', what have you got to be stressed about?"

"Nothing. Everything. Watch out, I'm aiming."

She hit another can dead center.

Her brassy nerve had him shaking his head while admiring her at the same time. She was right about this place; Dutch and Griswold had bragged about taking practice shots here. There wasn't anyone around, cattle free-ranged over the ridge and the property was managed by the land agency.

She reloaded, opening the barrel with a single flick of her wrist as she slipped bullets into the chambers. The slick maneuver was a turn-on. She had an efficiency to her that spoke louder than words. She knew damn well what she was doing.

"I thought you were glad to get hired," Paul said, leaning into the gray trunk of a tree that had been struck by lightning many years ago.

"I was. I am. I'm just a little anxious," she revealed, her pouting mouth ripe and full for kissing.

"Having second thoughts?"

"Never." The soft features on her oval face compelled him to stare. Her mouth, moist from a frosted-like gloss, was sheer and pink.

He watched a hawk soaring high with its full wingspan.

"I think you might be," he remarked, reaching down and picking up a rock. He threw it and knocked off one of her cans. Folding his arms over his chest and crossing his legs at the ankle, he said, "I think you were having a great time the other night and you were wishing you could stay here. With me."

"Is that what you really think?"

"Yes, that's what I think whenever I have you in my arms. Lanie, I want you. Maybe too much to be fair to you. So what do you really want?"

She heaved a sigh, didn't meet his eyes and replied, "Right now I just want to shoot cans. Let's see what that Glock of yours can do."

"Can't. I'm on duty."

"That's too bad. We could have had a contest." She repositioned her legs and held her arms together in front of her body. One through six, she knocked the cans from the wagon in a succession of direct hits.

"Oh, yes!" she cried happily, lowering the hot Sig Sauer .40. "And Dutch had me ticketing cars with expired meters."

"It's his loss. Mine, too."

Lanie faced him, hand on her hip. "You aren't making this any easier on me. Yes, I'm stressed. About you, me, the whole move. That's why I'm shooting tin to make me forget I ever—never mind."

Walking over the rough ground, Lanie went to the wagon and got the cans that had fallen inside the bed. The tin on them was shiny and several still had the labels on. She'd nailed the Campbell's smack in the C. She'd opened a dozen cans from her mom's pantry, put the food in plastic containers for the refrigerator and driven up here.

She should have been elated, thrilled, happy beyond compare to be leaving and hiring on with Pike's Peak. It's what she wanted, what she'd held out hope for.

Almost two months of stalling and she'd finally gotten the green light. She could be on with the Pike's Peak department as soon as she passed the Lateral Recruit. While she was working with their physical therapist, the commander was willing to put her to work in the station. It would be desk duty, but she'd be there as an official sergeant. This was her step up.

Everything was going in the right direction for a change, everything but her thinking. She was thinking in the past, looking backward instead of forward. Paul was on her mind, in her thoughts. Whenever she talked herself out of wanting to be here with him, he'd smile at her and make her feel as if she'd miss him like crazy when she was gone.

This was pure lunacy on her part. She had to get over these feelings, she had to get over him.

But it wasn't easy. Not by a long shot.

Lanie lined up the cans, needing to go for a second round. Needing to feel like she had control over something.

She backed away and reloaded. As she took aim, Paul said, "You need to get out and have some fun, Lanie."

"I am having fun." She fired and hit the can.

"I mean some good old-fashioned small-town fun." The Stetson on his head shadowed half his face. She thought he looked like one of those cigarette ad men scorching the magazine pages clear through to the binding. The hat fit him, made him fit the part of Chief-Deputy.

He had so much going for him.

"Come to the Founder's Day picnic with me," he said in a drawl that went along with his smooth-looking hat.

She'd already been planning on going. She never missed it. Few in town did. The celebration was the last big event at the end of the summer season; people came into town to see the lumber-cutting contest and eat good food. And there was always a local band playing in the bandstand.

"I'll go," she said, pushing her hair out of her face.

"Good. It's time I spent some money on you." He moved his hand over her hair, smoothing the wisps through his fingers. She was never able to stop shivering when he did that. His touch was deliberately designed to throw her mind into a tailspin. It worked every time.

Her breath vanished and she imagined the two of them licking on the same chocolate dip vanilla cone and watching the egg toss.

"In fact, I want to start the date tonight. You and me—dinner and a movie. Then my place afterward for some ice cream."

She gave a sideways gaze. "I should warn you, I haven't been out on a date lately."

He grinned. "Should I be worried?"

"I don't know. How much money do you keep in your wallet? I'm in the mood to indulge myself."

The strength of his laughter resonated. "Indulge all you want, darlin'."

Paul and Lanie sat in the park, the moon a white sickle in the sky.

Majestic Municipal Park rose on the hip of Wooded Creek Road at the top of a hill overlooking the valley which was now dotted with lights. Behind them, a swing set stood motionless in the calm evening air.

With a blanket to protect them from the damp grass

and an open bottle of wine, Lanie and Paul watched the sleepy town below.

"This is definitely romantic," she said, raising her glass and taking a sip of blush wine. "So were the flowers and the dinner."

Paul had brought her a bouquet of mixed flowers, then they'd eaten by candlelight at a restaurant in Silver City. It felt good to get out of town for a couple of hours.

Before taking her home, Paul surprised her with the wine and a stop at the park. She hadn't been up here in ages, not since Chief Deutsch had her checking for abandoned vehicles to tow, and that was during the day. She forgot how beautiful Majestic looked at night.

Paul brought his arm around her, bringing her close. "Cold?"

She shook her head. Although the nights were getting cooler, she wasn't cold in the sundress she'd worn. She was warm, and was loving how strong Paul felt beside her, how protected she felt whenever he was close.

"I like this," he said, indicating her dress.

She had on a simple sleeveless dress in ice blue fabric with thin white ribbon that tied in a bow beneath her breasts. She'd bought it from a small shop in town, having nothing like it in her wardrobe. She knew tonight was going to be special and she wanted to look that way, too. She painted her toenails dark red and wore a simple pair of open-toe sandals. Although with Paul, she could add on six inches to her height before she was taller than him.

She reminded herself that wishing for anything more than this wasn't going to happen. Sitting in a park, watching lights was the closest she'd come to anything long-term with Paul.

The new sergeant job was going to be great and she should have been on a cloud just thinking about it, which she'd done most every day since receiving the news. Then there were those times when she felt as if she would be leaving something behind that mattered to her as much as her mom, and her home, and her friends.

Paul Cabrera.

It was futile to even second-guess her decision to leave Majestic. This is what she'd been working toward. So what if they were looking for a ''female'' officer. She was female but more importantly, she would get in the hours on the beat in order to move onto bigger and better opportunities.

Don't look back, she told herself.

But with Paul next to her, she didn't want to look at anything but him. He, more than anyone she'd ever known, understood what it was like to move away from everything familiar and comfortable—away from friendships, family ties and that feeling of ''home.''

''Do you miss Miami?'' she asked, playing with a blade of grass.

''I have my days and it's usually when something connects for me that I didn't know was different. Like I've never heard leaf blowers revving up here, or the sound of multiple lawn mowers. It was so routine to hear that at my condo every Wednesday morning when the gardeners were there. I miss things that I never thought I would—like buying a shirt at the shop on Washington Avenue that I can't get here. You don't think about it until you're wanting the shirt.''

''We've got plenty of Western wear,'' she said with a smile.

''Not what I had in mind. The Stetson is as Western

as you're going to get me." Paul stole a look at her, his white teeth flashing in the dark. "I talk with Sid frequently. He lets me know what's going on in the old neighborhood. If it weren't for him, I might not be so inclined to make things work here. He keeps me remembering what it was like where I was and why I'm better off where I'm at."

"He's important to you."

"Like a father, brother and priest all in one." Paul laughed with a shake of his head. "Last night he was telling me the department busted a major Armani and Versace illegal importer at one of the European stores, and one of the clubs we used to patrol was closed down because a black Range Rover drove through the front plate glass window. When the sun goes down, the bad guys come out to play."

"We don't have anything nearly as exciting."

"And I'm damn content with that."

The signal on Main Street changed from red to green, a semiblur of color that caught Lanie's eye. "I remember when they installed the first traffic signal and people slowed down just so they could catch a red light."

"Big news, huh?" The smile in his voice was evident.

"It was pretty big news," she confirmed, remembering back to how her dad had been so proud to roll traffic through the first sets of lights.

Melancholy consumed her in its wave of nostalgia. This was her home; it would always be her home—she was going to miss Majestic. The small-town feel, the familiar history that had been created over the years. She knew everyone.

While the town was her foundation, her future was elsewhere.

Before she realized she was speaking aloud, she said, "I was just spinning my wheels here. I *have* to move on."

"You have to do what you think is right, Lanie."

"You don't think I'm right to leave?"

"I think you have to find your place or you won't be happy."

She could be happy. She could be very happy with Paul Cabrera if only... There was no point in wishing for something that wasn't going to happen—not so long as Chief Deutsch was in charge.

Paul cautioned, "A bigger city department is a lot different than what you're used to. Pike's Peak has a sizeable population and it's more susceptible to hard crimes, so be careful. Officers I knew didn't wear their wedding rings on patrol because it made them vulnerable on the streets. When criminals get it into their heads that you've got something to lose they'll use it against you. Women officers never wore their rings, either."

"That won't be an issue for me." She mulled over all the reasons why not, then ventured to ask, "Why haven't you remarried?"

"Most women can put up with a lot from a cop's erratic schedule, but falling asleep on a date just didn't cut it. I like working the graveyard, but it never left me time to find a special woman."

She felt his eyes on her, dark and questioning. "So why haven't you remarried?"

"I haven't fallen in love again."

Have I?

God, where had that thought come from? Dangerous territory to visit. Put it out of your head, Lanie. Just let this night be what it is. No false hopes.

Resting her cheek on his shoulder, she smiled with contentment. "This is nice."

"It is. When I was a little shit, I went to parks. But not to look at the view. I met buddies there and we'd figure out how we were going to get somebody to buy us some beer."

"How old were you?"

"Sixteen or so."

"That's so young, Paul."

"But it's what made me who I am today. I wouldn't change any of it." He paused, then asked, "Do you want kids, Lanie?"

"Yes." She didn't have to think about it. She'd always envisioned herself having children. She loved it when Sherry brought the kids over, and Lanie had always had a soft spot in her heart for Hailey. Lanie wanted to have that kind of stability and life. A loving marriage. But finding a man to fall in love with, to settle down with wasn't easy for a woman in uniform. Men were intimidated by her height and her occupation when they saw her coming at them wearing a holster.

It figures, when she'd been looking she never found anyone. Now that she wasn't looking, she had found Paul.

"Do you want children?" she returned.

"Eventually, yeah. I think I'm more ready now than I have been. I just need to find the love of my life first," he said into the darkness.

She felt heat like a zap of lightning bolt through her. A rush of desire made her dizzy and she took another sip of wine to steady her beating heart.

They sat beside each other, as close as possible, gazing at the stars and lights below. Paul meshed his fingers with hers. Warmth seeped through her skin, his hand firm and comforting.

Each was lost in their thoughts, perhaps thinking about what might have been....

"Lanie," he said her name so quietly it was like a wisp of air. "I'm going to miss you more than Miami."

He drew her onto his lap with an easy scoop of his arms. Her right hip met the front of his jeans, the side of her breast squeezed next to his chest. With an easy abandon, she put her arm around his neck, her long hair brushing over his hand while he stroked her cheek.

Wine and Paul, they created spontaneous combustion. Fiery heat collided in her. A touch of his mouth and she'd—

He kissed her deeply and hard, drawing the breath from her body as she shuddered in response. His tongue entered her mouth, brushed and traced the fullness of her lower lip. Her nipples swelled to tight points. Kissing him was erotic, wild. He filled her with intense pleasure just by a mere kiss.

With her caught on his lap, he took full advantage of their position and she welcomed every sense that thrilled to life. Her hand came over the wide span of his chest, the muscle hard beneath his shirt. Sculpted and firm, he was magnificent. He palmed her breast and she was over the edge. Lost.

She panted softly, working her hand beneath his shirt. He made a strangling sound, wrapping her long hair in his fist and holding her face close. She felt a primitive flame curl inside her and a shameless energy sizzled through her body. It was like this with him whenever they kissed and held each other. Nothing else around her existed.

He teased her lips lightly, speaking in a ragged voice, "Let's go home."

Home suddenly felt like wherever Paul would be.

Once they were in the living room, they kissed in the dim shadows with the fragrances of a late summer night spilling in through the window.

"I like how you look in this dress," he said huskily.

"Hmm. I painted my toes, too."

"I noticed."

"You did?"

His eyes were deep brown, gazing down onto her so wonderfully she could melt. "Lanie, I notice everything about you."

She brought her arms around his waist, her hair falling over her shoulder. "And I wore my hair down today, too," she added softly.

"It's beautiful."

"I didn't buy the dress for me," came her whisper. "I bought it for you."

She felt his body tighten, grow heavy, and he deliberately said, "It's not my size."

"That's not what I meant."

"I know what you meant." He tucked her long hair behind her ears. Her breath came in a jagged pant touching his face. "You feel good." His hands slid downward over her behind, cupping the swell and fusing her to him. She fit perfectly next to his legs, his belly. "I want you...."

She pressed her mouth lightly over his, tasting the sweetness of wine. Her tongue traced him and he nipped her lower lip with his teeth.

"I want you, too," she said through their kisses.

Paul held out his hand and took her up the stairs to

the bedroom. It looked the same, but different. Pocket change lay on the dresser; a pair of jeans were tossed onto the floor as if he'd shrugged out of them on his way to the shower. The Stetson's firm crown was cradled on the mirror's top. Sitting on the nightstand, a hardcover book on emotional intelligence.

The bed was neatly made.

He turned and took her into his embrace. Her arms fell over his shoulders and she kissed him, sweeping her tongue through his mouth. His hands wove through her hair, holding her close to him and taking as much as he gave.

They kissed until she was softly panting. His lips were soft, almost like silk, yet firm and hard.

He moved his hands to the small of her back, running them down her spine to cup her behind and bring her to his erection. The barrier of clothes made the moment feel more urgent. She wanted to savor, but she wanted to be satisfied. She smiled, wrapped up in a heavenly cloud when she kissed him. He sensed the satisfied curve on her mouth because he kissed the corner, then traced her lips with his tongue.

His hand ran down her shoulder, her arm, beneath her breast. He was much taller than her and she had to stand on her toes to fully meet his mouth.

She felt herself walking backward to the bed.

"Does your leg hurt?" he asked, breaking his mouth from hers.

"No, but I'm not supposed to bear any stressful weight on it," she whispered in a soft hush.

He nudged her to lie down on the bed and he fell back with her, his arms lifted over his head. He was so startlingly gorgeous, all male and bringing her to an edge beyond reason. She focused on one thing and one thing only.

Paul.

His hair framed his face perfectly, his mouth was wet from her lips—he was perfection, simply incredible—and he was hers for the night.

"I should probably be..." She lay on top of him. The rush of breath that left him gave her a feeling of pure bliss and little inhibition.

"You won't hear me complain," he said roughly, his hands caught in her hair as it teased his chest. She lay over him, arms on either side of him.

Lanie kissed him hard as he moved his hands up and down her back, gently in soft strokes that inadvertently tickled her sides. She giggled and caught his lip gently in her teeth. "Stop it...no, don't stop."

His lips brushed the column of her neck, kissing the shell of her ear, his teeth nipping at her earlobe. She let out a moan, her skin prickling with tingles. His hot breath made her feel as if she'd come in two pieces, shatter and let out a moan of pleasure. His hands slid up and down her stomach, a tantalizing massage and rasp of knuckles across the fabric.

He pressed the hard length of himself against her and she wanted him, now, filling her and satisfying, but this exquisite torture was too sweet to abandon so soon.

His hands slid over her bare thighs, slowly under her dress to rub her skin. Blunt fingertips traced patterns, elicited shuddering contractions in her body. The bottom of the dress crept higher, bunching around her waist. The air in the room peaked her nipples into hard points, her breasts heavy. In this position, they almost spilled from her neckline as she leaned over Paul to drop a kiss on his mouth.

Nudging her back, Paul sat up and unzipped the dress. Lifting her arms, she let him pull the fabric over her head and the pool of ice blue was tossed over the side of the bed.

In that same instant, she was tugging on the buttons of his shirt, stripping him out of it and baring him to her view.

Paul without a shirt and she in nothing but her bra and panties. It was a stimulation better than touching. Just looking. Just wanting.

He wore his bronzed skin like a Greek god meant to be worshipped. He was smooth, beckoning her fingers to glide over him and feel the tiny amount of black chest hair spread between his nipples that were flat as dark pennies. He was all sleek muscle and definition.

He stroked her navel, making light little swirls with his fingertip.

She felt Paul's breath quicken and grow short. She could die looking at him, feeling him beneath her. She'd never been filled with such need for a man. She wanted to bring them over the edge and come together.

His hand slid across her stomach and he hooked his thumbs into the elastic of her panties. Her breasts, full and round, were shaped in her bra. He reached around and unhooked her, the bra gliding off his hand. For a long moment she watched him as he looked at her, at the pouting shape of her breasts, their fullness. The rosy nipples were in tight beads, puckered and swollen. She should have been self-conscious, but she wasn't. He touched her, a gentle pressure that made her mouth fall open in a cry and catch in her throat. Her head tilted back, her hair brushing down the length of her spine. It felt intensely good to have his body against her. Sharing body heat, feeling each other's breathing. She was alive with heat and hunger and desire.

She nestled her head into the crook of his neck as he stroked her back and the sides of her breasts. She loved the feeling, but she wanted more.

And he knew it.

She unzipped his pants and shifted her weight enough for him to take them off. She helped him rid himself of his briefs until he was naked beneath her.

She lay on her back, left leg bent with her arms above her head while he removed her panties. He stopped for a second, admiring her body again.

Tall and curvaceous, she felt she'd been created especially for him.

He trailed his fingers down her belly and over the apex of her legs, causing her to let out a whimper. She felt shaky and somewhat out of control. The power he had over her, the feelings he evoked—they were immediate and demanding.

He barely touched her center, just lightly traced, then circled. She arched her back, reaching out for Paul's arm. She let out deep breaths of air, just barely catching her breath to roll with him onto his back.

She took him into her hand, bringing her fingers around him. "Do you have…?"

"Yes," he said, reaching into the bedside drawer and getting a condom.

Dipping her head to kiss his collarbone, she nuzzled his skin while he put one on.

She lowered herself onto him and let out a moan as she pushed. He was large and the sweet-hot friction of him made her cry out. He slowly rocked his hips and she felt the throbbing heat of him fill her completely.

He cradled her close. The tempo increased and she

leaned over him, her knee bent to keep the weight off her leg.

In this position, he fondled her breasts, sucking and tasting, then holding her hips with his hands to keep her moving to a rhythm he set.

Her hair curtained them as they moved as one.

"Look at me," he said. "I love watching you."

He pushed himself all the way inside her and she gasped as he thrust harder and harder. She was on the brink, waiting for him to meet her. On a growl, he sought his release and she let go in a contraction around him that she felt deeply inside her body.

The moment was explosive and shattering, both of them catching their breath as she fell on top of him, cheek to his chest. The thud of his heart filled her ear, a steady beat that flowed through his blood.

They lay there for a while relaxing and he stayed inside her. He pulled her closer and kissed her on the mouth, brushing her hair away from her cheek.

Paul found her in the kitchen by the coffeemaker. She wore one of his shirts, the hem barely covering her butt and pretty underwear. Her hair was tousled and she yawned while she waited for the last cup to drip into the pot.

He snuck up on her and kissed the side of her pale neck, nuzzling and breathing in the smell of her skin.

"Who's this?" she sighed, leaning into his chest, her arm coming under his and keeping him snug against her body.

"The man you made love to all night."

"Oh, that would be—" she turned in his arms, wrapping her own around his neck "—yes, it is you." She giggled, then kissed him full on the mouth.

Next to her plump and sweet lips, he murmured, "You've got that Sunday morning read the paper look."

"Hmm." They kissed for a long moment. Little kisses, playful and light.

She poured him a cup of coffee, he drank a sip and tried not to gag. The stuff was bad. She stuck her head into the refrigerator, rummaged around for food and ended up scrambling eggs for breakfast.

He sat at the table.

"Coffee?" she asked, pot in hand.

He cracked a smile; he couldn't help himself. "Is it supposed to be?"

"What's the matter?"

"Darlin', it's lousy."

Lanie shoved the pot onto the warmer. "You were out of coffee so I re-brewed what was in the filter."

"I have coffee."

"I didn't see any."

"I keep the coffee in there." He pointed to the cupboard by the utility closet.

She opened the cabinet by the sink. "Well, I keep it here. All you have is paper towels in this one."

"That's where I like them."

Lanie whirled around, his shirt hem teasing the backs of her long legs. "This is really weird, you know that. It's funny to be in my house with your stuff and see your moving boxes here while mine are next door at my mom's. How come you haven't fully unpacked?"

"I knew this was only temporary."

And with those words came a truth that made Lanie's smile fade:

Their relationship was just as temporary.

Twenty

Despite his opinion of bingo night, Dutch found himself once more seated at a table playing the game. He went through the motions of holding his marker, trying to make it look like he was having a good time when all the while he would have rather been reading the latest issue of *Guns and Ammo*.

The only redeeming factor was Lucille sitting beside him.

Unfortunately, Ken Burnett was on her other side.

Dutch had a feeling this evening would be a test of his patience. God knew he had a lot of it, but this was above and beyond the call of duty. Lucille said she didn't want to hide from her friends and bringing him to bingo was the best way to show there were no hard feelings for anyone.

Lucille was wrong.

Ken Burnett shot him more dirty looks than a prisoner waiting to have his mug shot taken. The man wasn't taking her decision not to see him calmly. Dutch couldn't blame him. Ken was fired up, provoked and mad as hell. It was evident by the redness of his skin, brought on by boiling blood pressure that washed out his tan.

The only reason Dutch came tonight was to prove to Lucille he was accommodating. He'd do things she liked so long as she did things he liked. He would draw the line, however, at wearing the *Born to Bingo* shirts Myrtle Sanders, Cookie Baumgarten and some of the men wore.

"*O-65,*" the announcer called.

Dutch had it, smacked his card and looked across at Lucille. Ken glared in his direction.

"Do you have that one?" Lucille asked Ken, trying to maintain an air of calm.

"I don't know. I might," Ken snapped, then lowered his tone. "Does it really matter? Lucille, how could you bring that man with you tonight?"

"It's a public bingo game," she replied in equally hushed tones. "I'm not hiding from anyone. I can go where I want and with whom I want."

Dutch said, "It's a free bingo night and I'm here to play, which is more than I can say for you. With all your talking, I can't hear the numbers."

"I don't think our talking has anything to do with you not winning," Burnett said across Lucille's card. "You aren't dabbing."

"Dab this." Dutch smacked Ken's center square with his marker.

Ken Burnett slid his chair back and rose to his feet. "Step outside."

Lucille's eyes widened and she stood as well.

Dutch was already halfway out the front doors.

The evening air held a bite to it. He raked his hand over his hair and waited for the two of them to come outside, hoping they'd be alone and not dragging the roomful of players with them.

Lucille and Ken appeared with Cookie Baumgarten and Myrtle Sanders in tow.

"That was quite an impressive show," Cookie said,

"if you're trying to prove to the town you three *can't* get along."

"I get along with everybody," Dutch remarked. "I don't have a beef with Burnett so long as he leaves Lucille alone when she asks him to."

"She hasn't asked me any such thing," Ken insisted. "There wasn't any trouble between us until you came into the picture. I'm sure she's flattered, but you won't last. You're not right for her."

"And you are? You've had a year to make her fall in love with you and apparently you haven't or she wouldn't be seeing me."

"Enough!" Lucille said, hands nervously fingering her pearl necklace. "This isn't the right time or place."

"When is the right time?" Ken held his ground.

Cookie put an arm around Lucille. "Are you okay?"

"I'm fine!" she said strongly. "I'm just wondering what I've gotten myself into. When I'm with him I don't think clearly."

Dutch gave a "who me" face, thinking that she'd acted pretty clearly on their picnic.

"That's why I think you're rushing into something, Lucille," Ken said as he moved toward her. Lucille's chin was level and resolute.

"No, Ken. I'm not rushing. Dutch is right. You and I had plenty of time to decide if there were more than sparks between us. We didn't sizzle, we never had fireworks."

"I could try again."

"I'm afraid you can't force it."

"I agree," Dutch added.

"Who asked you?" Ken snorted.

Cookie and Myrtle surrounded Lucille as if she needed protecting from both men.

"Do you want us to drive you home?" Myrtle asked. She replied, "I came with Dutch."

"And you should go home with me," Ken said, not backing off. "So we can work things out."

"I honestly don't think there's anything to work out." Lucille went to Dutch. "I'm ready to leave now."

He took her by the elbow and guided her toward his Jeep. Ken wasn't taking things lying down and Cookie had to subdue him.

"Now, Ken. Settle down. Myrtle and I will take you to the White Horse and buy you a drink."

Once in the Jeep, Dutch turned over the engine and they drove home in silence. At her house, he quit the motor and they sat quietly with their own thoughts.

At length Lucille said, "Maybe we are rushing."

"I don't think there's any rushing at all. We both know how we feel when we're together. There's a definite fire there and you know it."

"Yes...but I'm not ready to have it burn out of control."

"I understand that. We haven't been seeing each other that long. But you think about all the times we've been together since we decided to give this a go and you won't find a single time when we didn't connect. Every moment with you, Lucille, is the best I've had in a long time. I like you in my arms, kissing you and holding you close. I don't think that's something either of us can deny."

"I'm not denying it. I'm just thinking it might be too fast."

"Life is short," he reasoned. "I know what I want and I go after it." He touched her hand, holding it and rubbing his fingers over her smooth skin. "But if you need time, then we'll slow down. I can wait until you catch up with me, honey.''

He leaned in and gave her a soft kiss, her breath catching on his lips.

"Whatever it is keeping you from me is something that can be worked out. All I can do is reassure you that I would never hurt you. You have to know that."

"I do, Dutch...I do."

Lucille let herself out of the Jeep on her own, requesting that he not walk her to the door. Only when she was safely inside did he pull away and head for home.

He was going to win her if it killed him.

So maybe they should slow down and savor the moments. Maybe it was time for him to dust off his dating skills; after all, it had been a while. He'd start by taking her dancing. They played Sinatra and Tony Bennett at the Mile High Room. They were real men who could sing a woman right out of her shoes. Next, he'd cook her the best homemade dinner in his entire repertoire.

Dinner, music and the right mood at his place. Low lights. Candles. Wine. Roses. Lots more than the first bouquet he'd sent her.

He'd have his house spotless, the gun cabinet glass gleaming, furniture polish on all the wood and his magazines in order on the coffee table to show he had class. He better make sure he bought the latest issue of *Time*.

Pulling into his drive, he cut the motor and opened his front door. The house wasn't in order; there were empty cans on the sofa table and laundry in the basket by the heating vent. Dishes were in the drainer and dust was on the globe light above the dinette. His cleaning girl wouldn't be here for two more days.

Making plans on how he'd win over his girl's heart,

Dutch stripped down to the raw, took a shower and was sitting in front of the tube wearing his robe and skivvies by the time a rerun of *Gomer Pyle* came on.

Lanie wasn't home yet, giving Lucille plenty of time to think about what happened this evening. Contrary to Ken's assurances he'd give her time to sort through her feelings, he wasn't. The scene at the community center was something she didn't want to repeat. She was so sure that they could all get along.

She was wrong. Wrong to think Ken wouldn't protest and wrong to think she wouldn't favor one man over the other.

She sat at the table with a cup of decaf. She'd spilled sugar next to her cup and the spoon left a caramel colored ring on the table. She didn't wipe it off. Normally, she was so careful about staying neat and orderly.

Her world was tidy, uncomplicated and organized. But what she was considering...

It would upset everything she'd created for herself and wreak havoc with her life in ways she could never get back. But she didn't really want to fall back on her old life. Her old routine.

And Dutch in her life was anything but routine. Every moment with him, she felt alive. He was right— a person was only on this earth one time. Chances were fleeting. Opportunities missed were opportunities never tried.

Heaven help me—I'm rationalizing.

Smoothing her hair, she gazed at the clock. If only Lanie would come home then her decision, at least for tonight, would be made. But Lanie was on the late shift tonight with Paul and she wouldn't be home for hours.

As the clock ticked off the seconds, Lucille made a

decision that would forever change her life. It was now or never.

She grabbed her purse and car keys, then halted halfway to the garage.

What was she thinking?

She couldn't drive over in the Eldorado. She might as well honk the horn all the way over if she did that. What to do...

The garage door was up, and as she proceeded inside an idea came to her that was completely crazy.

Careful of her clothes, she rolled the one-speed bicycle out of the garage and tested the air in the tires. Full enough to ride ten blocks. Hooking her purse through her arm, she hopped onto the seat and pedaled across town, hugging the curb and lurking in the shadows.

This was asinine, completely crazy. She should turn around, and yet she pedaled forward, taking a short cut across the alley and down East Filbert.

Once in front of the house, she hid the bicycle in the bushes. Her hair was windblown and she hand brushed it with her fingers. Then she applied another light coat of lipstick.

Dragging in her breath, she crept to the front door. There was no going back.

She knocked, softly. She hoped he'd hear her. She didn't want to have to muster her courage to knock twice.

The door swung open and Dutch filled the entry. He wore a robe, the sash loosely tied. She gazed at his chest, the light mat of hair. Her breath quickened.

Chivalry might have been part of his appeal, but there was something more. He knew it. She knew it.

With Dutch, there was more than enough kindling to light the spark.

"Lucille," he declared, his voice riddled with panic. "Is everything all right?"

"I think so."

"Then what—"

"Let me in, please, before someone sees me."

He stood aside and closed the door.

She didn't dare take a moment to look at the decor. Turning toward him, she said, "I'm fifty-eight, Dutch."

"I'm aware of that."

"I thought about what you said. You're right."

"About what?"

"About everything."

"Everything—you and me? Lucille, are you—"

"Don't question me. I know what I'm doing."

With that she put her arms around his neck and kissed him soundly, passionately, as if she'd waited a lifetime for this.

Twenty-One

The officers were ordering their usual breakfasts at Rooster's Place Café when Lanie, who'd come by early to join them for a meeting Dutch had called, sat down in the booth and began talking to Ridder about a report he'd filed.

Paul gazed out the window as Coyote reached for the sugar packets.

The sky no longer had a pink tint to it at five-thirty in the morning due to the days growing shorter. Sunset came earlier, the nights stayed darker longer, and the temperature fell to the freezing mark overnight.

Time pushed forward. The leaves began to change, turning from green to yellow to gold, drifting from the ancient elms along Main Street to fill the curbside gutters. Barren and twiggy, the deciduous skeletons were slowly revealed by fallen foliage. The Rake Roundup volunteers bagged the leaves as fast as they fell, but soon dormant lawns were covered once more with multicolored fall carpets as September turned the air crisp and honey-sweet with fall.

Soon there would be snow on the ground, and for the first time in his life, Paul would experience a white Christmas. Irving and his mom were coming in to spend a week with him during the holiday. He'd have a house by then, something comfortable for a bachelor.

Bachelor. The sound of the word didn't sit well in his thoughts. But that's what he'd be. Lanie was leaving in less than two weeks. She'd found a place in Pike's Peak to rent, a small one-bedroom apartment. Her physical therapy was helping her get stronger every day. She'd received some kind of refund from her extended stay apartment in Ludlow that helped put her on track financially to be able to make the move.

The seasons were changing and Lanie's time in Majestic was almost over.

He wanted her to stay, wanted her in his life like she was now, but neither of them were making commitments. He always knew he wanted to remarry, but he also knew the statistics for cops to have a failed second marriage were very high. The next time he spoke his vows they were going to last forever.

He had strong feelings for Lanie. Whether he was physically with her or not, her presence warmed his soul. He'd connected with her and she created feelings inside him that held tight to his heart and wouldn't let go.

Being with her was the best part of his day and he could get used to the way they were now. Her touch scorched his skin, her scent filled his mind, and her body fit next to his with perfection. She was like the piece of him that had been missing. With her, he was a better person.

She was everything he desired, everything he wanted. But she was out of reach, unattainable because her heart was taking her elsewhere. So Paul had to be content with the present, to satisfy himself with what he had now.

Certain words and thoughts remained unspoken between them as they acted as if nothing would be changing, even though everything around them was changing.

Sitting at the table with Dutch and Coyote who were busy with their plates of eggs and bacon, Paul ordered only coffee.

Lanie blew steam off her cup, her long hair pulled away from her face. An ivory sweater fit tight enough to outline her figure. She wore a pair of jeans and tennis shoes. For this hour of the morning, she looked amazing.

Dutch said, "I wanted to catch you three first thing so we can get on the same page with breaking news." He set down his fork. "I got a call last night about another hit by Mr. Tick Tock. At three in the afternoon on the fifteenth, he robbed a jewelry store in Telluride. He's getting braver and I swear the guy has no fear of being caught. He's got to know we're all on alert around here."

"Not that high an alert if he hit another store," Coyote commented. "I hope he comes here. I'll get the son of a bitch."

"Take a look at these sketches—the eyes are similar, but that's about it. We're getting different composites from different clerks and, you know as well as I do, a person who's been traumatized doesn't necessarily get the details right. These drawings are a guide for you to remember what he looks like."

Paul studied the drawings, then passed them onto Lanie.

Dutch tucked the papers back into his folder when they were through. "Also, Karen's coming back on the first of next month so the rest of you won't have too long to take rotational turns on dispatch once Prescott is gone." He turned toward her, cleared his throat and said frankly, "You did a bang-up job for us in a pinch."

"Thank you," she murmured, her expression closed off.

The atmosphere between the two of them was still thick and tense. It had been several weeks since Dutch and Lucille had been seeing each other and there was no indication their relationship would be growing cold.

These days, Dutch joked around a lot. Broad and hooked high at the corners, the smile on his mouth was almost a permanent fixture.

"One last thing," the chief announced. "Founder's Day tomorrow. I want all the deputies on duty. We'll have our last full house in town before Thanksgiving hits and the ski season really starts. Everybody will clock in at nine o'clock and be prepared to work a twelve-hour shift."

"I was planning on it," Coyote said.

Breakfast was over and Paul was officially off the night shift. He got into his vehicle and followed Lanie in her Trailblazer, both of them turning into the same driveway.

A deep sense of foreboding claimed Paul as he walked to the veranda. He couldn't sort out why. It was just there in the background. A feeling, an uneasiness that he knew a hot shower and sleep wasn't going to cure.

"Come in with me," Paul said, after opening the door.

"Sure. Are you all right?"

"Yeah. It was a long night."

"You need some time off, Paul." Her hand touched his shoulder as they passed through the door. "You've been working really hard."

"I'm fine." But he couldn't shake the dark feeling off his mind.

The house was quiet. He set his keys on the countertop and their cold metal sound reverberated off the walls.

Without being fully alert to his surroundings, he stood in the kitchen with the shades drawn. He was here, but not here. His mind was in a fog.

"Paul…" Lanie's fingers meshed with his as he held her hand and took her upstairs.

They showered together, the warmth of water running down their bodies in the stall. She grew silent as he held her from behind, enfolding her in his embrace, his chest next to her slender back and his hands flat around her midriff.

"I need to hold you," he murmured. "I have to smell your skin, your hair." Lowering his face into the crook of her neck he closed his eyes. He was convinced these feelings were with him because Lanie was slowly disappearing out of reach. "I want to take you inside me when I breathe. Fill me, Lanie…God…I need to feel your heart beating next to mine."

"Me, too." She turned around and slid her arms over his shoulders, hands touching to stroke and soothe him. Her fingernails rubbed the short crop of his hair at the base of his neck where the muscles were tight with tension.

The quiet power of her fingers was gentle as she cradled his face in her hands. Water ran down her face and droplets spiked her lashes. He looked deep into her eyes, losing himself. He kept her close, her warmth seeping through to him in the cascade of water.

Tenderly, Lanie kissed the column of his neck, her wet hair brushing beneath his jaw. Expelling the breath he'd been holding, he leaned into her, drinking in her life energy. She was so alive, so real.

He studied every detail of her face. The pale complexion and the shape of her nose. The whisper of her thick eyelashes as she slowly blinked. Her face reflected everything he loved about her. Courage and determination. Spirit and desire.

Heat surged through his veins, inflamed his need to feel anything but the odd premonition filling his mind.

Lanie lifted her face to his, sensing his loss in a way he could feel, but not explain. Their mouths came together, a rush of white-hot arousal catching hold of his body. His tongue glided over the seam of her lips, drinking and taking. He swept through her mouth with silky strokes, his erection hard and aching.

The kiss was more than a mating of mouths. She ran her open palms up his arms and skimmed her fingertips over the smooth and warm skin of his biceps. Each muscle jerked and tensed as she felt the contours.

Her hands cupped him and he let her explore, gritting his teeth and dragging the breath from his lungs. All he could think of was Lanie. He had reached that place in his mind where nothing mattered but them being together. Everything else ceased to exist.

He skimmed his fingers across her belly, flat and satiny. The soft weight of her bare breasts, full and pear-shaped with rosy peaked nipples, fit into his hands as if they'd been molded just for him. Hands glided over her ribs before his right palm rested between her breasts.

Her heart beat steady and fast.

She trailed her fingers into the dark hair that lightly covered his chest. His breath sucked in with a hiss as she traced a path between his flat nipples, around each one, then down, to the corrugated plane of his stomach and lower to circle his navel.

He tipped his head to hers, their foreheads meeting. A deep and masculine sound rose from his throat; a kind of moan and cry for what he wanted. For what he would have. His hand trailed down the curve of her back, pressing her against him. She touched her lips to the side of his jaw where his beard was spiked and rough.

This woman was so beautiful. He knew her mind and body, and wanted them both in this instant. He brought her to him, her leg hooked over his arm, and he kissed her while entering.

A cry broke from her mouth as he withdrew and returned in a slow and deliberate pace. She moaned as he rocked her pelvis with long, hard strokes.

Fire and intensity assaulted him, along with it an urgency that he frantically sought to quench. Her fingers tangled in his hair, bringing his head closer to hers for a kiss. She gripped his shoulders hard, a climax flowing through her like an electrical current that sizzled into his bones. His senses were alive, their heartbeats filling the shower.

He waited for her to find her pleasure before claiming his release in a guttural cry. Paul shuddered and low sounds vibrated in his throat. Nothing coherent except for the soft utterance of her name.

He held onto her, his chin burrowed in the moist hollow of her neck, his nostrils next to her skin. Their breath came together in ragged pants.

Emotions flooded, and with Lanie he found a momentary peace.

Lanie curled next to Paul on the bed as he slept, exhausted from the night shift. She lay awake, absorbing his warmth and listening to the sound of his breathing.

She'd forgotten what it felt like to anticipate being with a man. To have him in her thoughts every second of every day.

She could get used to this. Him. Them together.

Being with Paul and having him fulfill needs she had long since left behind made her complete. Made her feel like a desired woman. She loved that about him, but she feared loving him.

Lanie watched him sleep. His face was peaceful and sated. His eyes were closed, the lashes dark and blunt. The shape of his nose was strong, the nostrils slightly flared. She was tempted to trace the outline of his mouth, but she didn't want to wake him.

She could get used to this.

She bit her lip, thinking about possibilities. Pike's Peak wasn't that far away. Several hours. Why couldn't they—there was no reason not to. They could have a long-distance relationship if he was willing. There would definitely be hurdles with their schedules and getting the same day off together would be difficult. Still, it could work.

She closed her eyes, drifting off to a light sleep only to have a phone ring and wake her. She rose, quickly stumbling for the cell phone lying on the bureau. Paul was so beat, she hated to have him wake.

She answered the call as he stirred on the bed, an arm thrown over his forehead.

''Hello?'' she whispered into the receiver.

''I'm looking for Paul Cabrera,'' a woman's voice on the other end said.

"He's here...." Lanie glanced at Paul. "Um, he's sleeping."

"Can you tell him it's Julie? I have to talk with him and it can't wait."

Lanie felt uneasy as she walked to the bed and put her hand on Paul's forearm. "Paul, it's Julie. She says it's important."

He took the phone and sat up while uttering, "Julie, what's up?"

Lanie didn't feel jealousy, only something strange and unsettled. She could almost feel the fine hairs on the back of Paul's neck stand on end as he listened.

"Ah, Christ..." he moaned. "Oh, God. When?"

His face grew tight, his eyes squeezing closed.

All she could do was touch his knee and sit beside him. But for all she knew, she wasn't even here. Nothing else existed for him, but the sound of his ex-wife's voice on the telephone. He was lost in whatever she had to say.

His voice was carefully reined, and a cold chill spread over her body as he asked, "How did it happen?"

He sucked in his breath, rose from the bed and gazed out the window into the backyard. Pinching the bridge of his nose, he remained quiet for a long time. Finally, he said, "I'll get on the first plane out of here. I'll call you from the airport."

When he hung up the phone, the room had a chill to it. A sense of doom and despair.

"Paul...are you all right?"

It took him a moment to find words. "Sid Cisneros was in a vehicle accident last night while en route to a crime scene. An SUV blew the signal and entered the intersection."

Grief held her, an ache for Paul settling in her heart like a steel weight. "Oh, Paul."

"He—" Paul paused to correct the waver in his voice. "The impact occurred on the passenger side of the unmarked car where Sid was sitting. He's in critical condition. Julie said the doctors don't think he'll make it."

"I'm so sorry. Is there anything I can do?"

Almost in a trancelike tone, Paul said, "Sid was my life's turning point, the man who became my father. When I was sinking to my lowest, Sid was the one who told me to start bailing or I'd drown. Because of Sid Cisneros, I'm a police officer. I could have ended up in prison for God knows what if it weren't for him."

"I'm sorry," she repeated, the words not seeming like they were enough.

"Losing Sid is incomprehensible. I just can't." Paul moved from the window and began taking clothing from the bureau. "Jesus Christ, my heart's pounding in my chest." A vague look filled his eyes. "I just spoke to Sid two days ago."

Lanie didn't know if it would help or not, but she ventured, "Then I'm sure you're on his mind while he's in the hospital. He may not be awake, but he knows you care."

"We always joked around saying that if the booze didn't kill him, the job would," Paul said quietly. "When he quit drinking he said he'd survived because he was too tough to die with his badge in his pocket. I can't accept this. He's got to pull through."

"Let me help you, Paul. What can I do?"

He grabbed a small travel bag from the closet. "You can tell Dutch I won't be around. I'm going home— back to Miami."

Twenty-Two

Paul landed at Miami International Airport as dawn colored the sky in a palette of pinks and oranges. Moving around travelers with a purposeful stride, he walked through the airport on the moving ramp. Multicolored decorations brightened the passageway. Around him, Spanish was the predominant language.

The carry-on he'd packed was thrown over his shoulder by a strap and as he made his way toward the exit he reached for his cell phone and called the hospital once more.

He spoke to the charge nurse who told him there'd been no change in Sid's condition. He'd been awake when they brought him in, but he'd lost consciousness and hadn't come out of it since.

As Paul passed the baggage carousel, he looked for Julie. Instead, he found Lavenia Torres waiting for him. She was tall and slender, midforties with black kinky hair that hadn't begun to gray.

"Paul," she said, embracing him and holding him tight.

He put his arms around her and lowered his face into the crook of her neck, closing his eyes tightly.

The moment was brief, yet profoundly touching.

When she pulled back, he questioned her with his gaze.

''You've always been there for me. Now it's my turn to be here for you.''

''I appreciate it,'' he replied, his voice thick.

''Julie's in the car waiting for us. She's parked in the red zone so we've got to hurry.''

The closer they got to the large double glass doors the more he felt the humidity rolling toward him like a blanket.

Once outside, a stickiness instantly coated his skin and left him damp. The air smelled of exhaust and mustiness and the traffic was backed up to the exits. The temperature must have been in the high eighties and the sky was perfectly cloudless. He'd just left weather that had been dipping into the mid-thirties at night.

Julie pulled up to the curb and they got in; the air-conditioning going full blast was a luxury.

''Paul,'' his ex-wife said, leaning over to give him a fast hug before she merged into the taxis and buses. ''I'm really sorry about Sid.''

Seeing Julie and Lavenia reminded him of his former life and the different feelings he'd held for both these women.

As they drove to Baptist Hospital, thoughts about Colorado were left far behind.

Julie got them to the hospital in less than twenty minutes and Paul hopped out and strode toward the elaborate building.

He made it to Sid's room, stopped in the doorway and was devastated to see his friend, his mentor and longtime partner hooked up to tubes and machines.

All through that night, he kept vigil by Sid's side. The driver of the unmarked, Garv Holloway, was on the next floor down, his injuries not life-threatening. He was wheeled into Sid's room and spent time talking to Paul about the man they both cared for. Sid's visitors were those of his police family. He had never had children. He always said the juveniles he straightened up were his kids. Sitting in a metal hospital chair, Paul put his hands together and pressed them to his forehead.

Julie and Lavenia stayed and brought him coffee throughout the night. Around midnight, Paul drifted to sleep.

He woke when the sound of a raspy and dry voice spoke. It was soft, muffled and brittle, but the word was unmistakable:

"Kid..."

Dirty Harry's Car Wash sponsored the annual Mullet Contest at the Founder's Day picnic. Whoever took a photograph of the best mullet would win a free detail and wax. Last year, Toby Stillwell won with his entry of a woman's high and tight cut in the front with the length as long as one of Cher's wigs.

The day began with a parade on Main that started at one end of town and ended on the other. The procession would have lasted all of twenty minutes, including the fire truck brigade, except that the horse for Miss Majestic took off before its saddle was cinched. The mare ran through the crowd, left a present in the Pay and Pack Grocery parking lot, then walked over to Cookie Cutter's and grazed on the front lawn before being caught.

Once the parade broke up, the crowd moved to the former rodeo grounds where the turtle races began. The Wild Bunch band, a quartet of fiddles, played a crowd favorite, the "Orange Blossom Special."

Lanie walked through the crowd as kids ran all over

the place, their faces smeared with candy and colorful paint. She was given smiles and nods by parents and tourists as she passed. There was a definite respect that came with wearing her uniform.

She was officially on duty.

The thick cloth of her uniform felt right. It changed her when she had it on, she had to be in a different place with a tin star on her breast pocket and a gun on her hip. Handcuffs in her belt. The weight of everything rode smooth and heavy.

Being reinstated to the department for the day had come without any advance warning. She'd been shocked when Dutch told her the news.

She'd telephoned him late last night after Paul left for the Montrose airport to catch a small plane into Denver en route to Miami. Dutch didn't say anything at first when she told him Paul had left and why, then he told her to be at the station at seven o'clock the next morning and to bring her uniform.

Once there this morning, with just the two of them in attendance, he asked her if she wanted to work twenty-four hours as a Reservist Deputy for Founder's Day. She'd been taken aback, but figured something was up since he told her to bring in her uniform. She agreed to come back on board for the day, holding up her right hand and swearing the oath once more. It was very simple and quick.

And here she was, walking the grounds with her head held high, with Dutch next to her looking like he meant business—law and order would be kept—Founder's Day or no Founder's Day.

It was a little awkward being on duty with the same Chief who had made it impossible for a promotion.

"Hold up right here," Dutch said as two boys from

Laramie Ranch approached. "I saw you boys over by the stables earlier, and I hope for your sakes there aren't any leftover fireworks hiding over there from the Fourth of July."

"Not us," the one boy replied stoically.

"Where's your counselor?"

"Right there," the other supplied, pointed to the man coming toward them.

Dutch introduced himself and Lanie, as if they were partners, then proceeded to tell the counselor, "It's an ongoing battle between us and the youth camp that's got to give. Last week my deputies found some shell casings and liquor bottles by the mile marker. Some cans of Bud and an empty fifth of J.D. Cigarette butts."

"I hear where you're coming from. We can talk to the director. He's over there by the apple dunking booth."

The chief went off with the three guys, leaving Lanie to look for suspicious activity on her own. The problem with Founder's Day was, most of the time, nobody really did anything until several hours before it was over. By then, those who'd been consuming liquor were bolder with their talk and fistfights usually broke out. During the day, it was mostly families with younger children.

Lanie came across Karen and her husband with the new baby. "He's adorable," Lanie said.

Karen grinned. The glasses riding on the bridge of her nose slipped down and she pushed them up while saying, "Look at you back in uniform. Does this mean you're staying?"

"No. I'm just filling in."

"I got all hopeful for you, hon. You be sure to say good-bye to me before you leave."

"I will."

Walking along a little further Lanie saw Deputies Ridder and Griswold eating hot dogs slathered with mustard and onions. They stood by the food pavilion, their radios turned on to intercept direct calls from the station's forwarding service.

"How does it feel, Prescott?" Ridder intoned in a caring voice. "How do you like wearing the uniform again?"

"It's really good." There was no hiding the honesty there. It did feel good to look and be important. Pike's Peak was going to give her more days like this very soon.

Though each time she had that thought her pulse slowed down to next to nothing. But she didn't want to think about other things right now except for the duties she'd been assigned. Lanie wanted to make sure everything went smoothly today.

Ridder wiped his mouth with a napkin. "We're going to miss you, Lanie."

"Thanks, Ridder."

"And you're all set up there?"

"I'm good." She'd received her refund from Ludlow over a week ago and that money had come at a perfect time.

"Have you heard from Paul?"

"No." She hadn't heard anything from him, but he'd barely just left. She could only imagine the turmoil he must be feeling as he made his way to Miami. There, he had friends and family waiting for him. Oleda and Irv. Julie…

The idea of Paul's life being centered on another city hit Lanie with a revelation. He had more in Florida than he had here, and he always would. Or so it seemed.

With a mom and stepdad who cared deeply for him, and with Lavenia Torres and her open file—a connection between an officer and a victim would never wane if it was strong from the start. And then he had Julie. Lanie didn't think of her as someone she should worry about. She had had Kevin and she understood that a bond between former spouses could remain strong even though both of them had moved on.

Lanie felt more alone and left out than anything else. She felt a little lost, too, without Paul here. She missed him terribly.

Deputy Griswold swallowed his meal with a swig of root beer. "My wife is helping out at the egg toss," he mentioned, the bristles of his red mustache foamy from the soda pop. "Last year she roped me into giving her a hand. I'm not going near that venue today. You don't know how hard it is to get raw egg off your clothes until you've been nailed by a couple."

Lanie smiled, nodding. Static came over Griswold's radio, then a call rang and Ridder picked up his transmitter. Dutch's voice came over the speaker reporting disorderly behavior over by the wood chopping event, most likely involving beer. Ridder said he'd respond before Lanie could offer to go.

Standing tall, Lanie offered, "Deputy Ridder, I can go to that."

"Got it covered, Lanie," he insisted.

Just like old times, she thought wryly.

"See you two around," he said before hastily leaving.

After Ridder left, Griswold pitched his plate into a cardboard trash can. "Let's see what trouble we can find."

There wasn't any trouble. Just a crowd of people having a good time. Griswold ended up going over to talk with a group of women and Lanie kept walking on alone.

Kevin and Sherry came toward her with Hailey who was holding onto a balloon.

The little girl exclaimed, "Lanie. Look at my balloon."

"What a pretty pink color, Hailey."

"Hi, Lanie," Kevin said. "You look good like that. I heard you were on duty."

She explained, "Just for today."

Kevin and Sherry stood next to each other, casually dressed and easygoing. They looked right together, like they belonged. They had a solid marriage, a good foundation and a happy life.

"We're looking for Mawk," Hailey added in a little voice.

Sherry rolled her eyes. "He was supposed to meet us by the egg toss and he's a no-show. Who knows what he's getting into."

"I'll go look for him, Sher," Kevin said, picking up Hailey in his arms. "See you around, Lanie."

"Bye, Kevin."

When he was gone, Sherry and Lanie went toward the drink stand, walking in step with one another.

Sherry asked, "Have you heard from Paul?"

"Nothing yet."

"I'm sure he'll check in with you. How awful for him. He's got so much on his mind right now. I bet you hear from him soon."

"I'm worried, Sherry. I don't know if he's coming back."

Speaking the words aloud pressed a heavy weight

against her heart. The sounds of happiness and laughter around her diminished.

"Of course he'll come back." Sherry stopped. "This is his home now."

"He calls Miami home. I heard him say it. I really don't know if he'll come back here. He's got so much there and nothing here."

"You're here."

"Not for long. I'm gone a week from Monday. What are we going to do when I'm in Pike's Peak and he's here?"

"You can call each other, see each other on your days off. You'll find a way to work it out."

Lanie sighed, and then confessed, "I'm thinking about giving everything up for him."

"Everything—what? How?"

"My position." Lanie shook her head. "No. I don't know why I said that. I can't. I worked too hard to get it. I'm going—but why am I afraid to leave?"

Her friend stated simply, "Because you're in love with him."

"I can't be," she returned, denial flaring swift and strong. "I have feelings for him, yes. Very strong feelings. I just can't let myself give in to something more. It's there, I feel the pull. I want to, but I can't."

"I wish you would, Lanie. I think he's right for you and you're right for him. If you two thought about it, you could work something out."

"He's not here so I can't work out anything."

Just then Lanie's attention was diverted to a bench where her ten-year-old paperboy and his teenage brother were laughing so hard their faces went red. The younger boy was under the bench pulling on strings to make a mannequin move and jerk. Several children passing by with balloons got scared and the balloons went sailing off.

"I think I just found Juanita Hart's stolen mannequin." Lanie gave Sherry a smile. "Thanks for the encouragement. Have fun today. I've got to go talk to two smart alecks."

Later that night, when the Founder's Day events were over and Lanie was home, she was still smiling over the prank those boys had pulled. She and her mom sat in the kitchen drinking cups of decaf.

"Juanita had reported the thing had gone missing from her rubbish bin. Now I know who took it," Lanie said over the rim of her cup.

"You didn't go hard on them, did you, Lanie? It's awfully funny. I'll bet Juanita doesn't care since she did throw it away."

"I told them not to scare the little ones and, aside from that, to do what they wanted with it. There's no law against having a mannequin at a public event."

The women smiled.

"This is nice, the two of us," Lucille said. "We haven't done this in a while."

"I know. I didn't see much of you today."

"I was with Cookie and we stayed near the white elephant sales. I got a new clock."

A farm clock sat on the counter, its dark maple needing some polish and shine. The face had a slight crack in it that could be repaired with a new circle of glass. Lanie could imagine her mom fixing it up as good as new.

"And did you find Dutch?" Lanie asked, forcing a pleasant expression.

Lucille didn't readily respond, as if unsure as to how

best to answer. "A couple of times. He was working so we didn't talk much."

A silence dragged through the kitchen, the sound of Lucille's new clock ticking from the countertop.

There were many things Lanie wanted to know, but just as many she'd rather not know about. Still, she loved her mom and her happiness was foremost.

"Is it very serious between you two?" Lanie asked. She'd always been able to ask her mom how she felt about things and this shouldn't be any different.

Lucille stared into the depths of her cup, then licked her lips. "It's all happened so fast. It scares me."

"Then take it slow," Lanie replied, running her fingertip over the coffee cup's handle. "Don't rush anything."

"I'm not...it's just that...yes, I have feelings for him."

Lanie toyed with the spoon beside her cup. "I can tell."

"I'm sorry, sweetie," her mom said softly. "I know you don't like him and I—"

"Don't, Mom." Lanie touched her hand to her mother's. "You don't have to justify yourself to me. You've waited a long time to find somebody. I want you to find what you're looking for. I know it wasn't with Ken." A tentative smile touched Lanie's mouth. "I was just hoping it would be someone else who...well, someone who I liked more than a trip to the dentist."

"Oh, Lanie. You're funny and wonderful...and I think I have fallen for him." Her mom's hand rose to fuss with her pearl necklace as was her habit, but the necklace wasn't there. She ended up fidgeting with the point on her blouse collar.

"Where are your pearls?" Lanie asked, pushing back her chair and going to the sink to rinse out her cup.

"The string broke this morning. I've got to take them in and have it fixed." Her blue eyes focused on Lanie. "What about you, Lanie? What's happening with you and Paul? I know you're close...."

"Paul is a good man. My heart breaks for him right now."

"We should call Oleda and tell her we're concerned. I have her phone number. She left it for me."

"That would be a nice gesture, Mom. We'll do it tomorrow. Right now, I'm tired and it's very late on the east coast."

Her mom stood and gave her a spontaneous hug. Pressing a kiss on her daughter's cheek, she said, "You look like you belong in the uniform, Lanie. You really do."

Those words were the best Lanie had heard all day.

When Paul pulled up to Lanie's house, the same moving trailer that had been at the curb months ago was back. She was leaving as planned. He'd lost track of the days while in Miami and the end of the month had come so quickly he had hardly been aware of it.

Sid's funeral had been three days ago. His friend died the morning after Paul arrived. He never fully regained consciousness. All he'd done was utter one word—one word that spoke volumes. Sid knew Paul had made it back. Paul stuck by him through the long days until Sid simply drifted away.

The loss was hard on Paul, and he wouldn't have been able to get through the next day without the support of his family and former officers. The Miami-Dade department pulled together during the tough time and organized the funeral. Many of the detectives and officers who visited Sid in the hospital were his pallbearers.

A graveside service was completed with a twenty-one gun salute, the hardest thing any officer ever has to hear in his career. The moment was somber and filled with respect and gratitude for a man who had served his community well.

Paul spent some time with Oleda and Irving, who told him they had been in touch with Lucille and Lanie. Normally Paul would have called himself, but there were too many emotions holding him together and he preferred to keep them to himself just now. He was a very private man when it came to feelings and he wanted his resolve to remain strong.

The day after the funeral, Paul spent time in Sid's apartment, sorting through personal items with Sid's ex-wife and brother. There were police commendations on the walls, memorabilia and photographs—memories of good times.

The time away had had a changing effect on Paul.

There was never any doubt in his mind that he'd be going back to Majestic. It was his new home and now, oddly, he felt more like he was part of the small-town setting than he ever had been.

He got off the plane in Montrose and retrieved his car from the garage. Driving back to town, the air was sweet and clean. The sky was a blue that was indescribable and the grasses had turned a rich umber color.

Seeing Lanie's house with the Victorian architecture and the paint in plum and rust was something like a homecoming. He hadn't realized until he was walking up to the veranda with the house key in his hand how deeply he had missed her.

He let himself inside, tossing his carry-on onto the sofa she loved. The one he didn't fit in, but he smiled knowing she was so fond of it. Paul didn't take the time to check the mailbox or phone messages. He went next door to find Lanie.

After knocking lightly he stepped back and waited. She opened the door and her gaze drank him in.

Seeing Paul, a wave of relief washed over Lanie, weakening her knees.

"You're back," she managed to say around the heaviness lifting from her. To have him here where she could touch him was the best.

"I'm back," he concurred. "Come here."

Paul encircled her as tightly as possible without crushing the breath from her lungs. Tucking her into his chest, he locked her in his grasp. He was like iron, like steel. Strength she needed.

"Are you okay?" she asked.

"Good now that I'm home."

Home.

He kissed her softly, then took her hand and brought her next door where he gave her a far better welcome-home kiss. She dissolved in the warmth of his mouth and the feel of his body.

When he pulled away, she swiped fingertips beneath her eyes, angry that she'd cried from the emotions welling inside her. The man before her could make her happy with a simple smile, a carton of ice cream or a night snuggled together to watch a movie.

Paul was the best thing that had ever happened to her and she wasn't going to walk away from him without trying to make it work. If only it could be here in Majestic.

"Come here, darlin'." He took her to the couch and

sat down, bringing her onto his lap to hold her. "I missed you."

"Me, too." She kissed him lightly. "I'm sorry about Sid, Paul. Losing my dad was the hardest thing I've ever gone through and I know how close you were to your friend."

"Yeah, it's been a rough time." He stroked her cheek, tucking her hair behind her ears. "I saw the moving trailer, Lanie. So you're a go for Pike's Peak?"

She wished she could have had another answer, but she'd made a commitment and she couldn't not go because her heart was pulling her to stay here. This should have been the most exciting time in her life, yet she was torn.

"I leave Monday morning."

"Lanie, is there was any way you could stay?"

"How, Paul?" She laid her head on his shoulder. "When you were out of town, Dutch rehired me for Founder's Day. Putting on that uniform and having the respect it represents reminded me how important my job is to me. Even if Dutch had another opening for me here he wouldn't let me do the kind of work I was trained for. I can't achieve what I want in Majestic. I wish I could." Half joking, but half serious, she added, "If you could come with me, then we wouldn't have a problem...."

Paul caught her chin in his fingers and turned her face toward him. "If I could, I would, but I have an obligation to the Majestic PD. I owe Dutch my loyalty. This is where I have to be." He stroked her hair. "We can see each other, just not as often as we'd like."

She knew then that that was all there could be for them. They both had other priorities. They were both on different paths and that's where they'd stay.

That night, Lanie slept beside Paul and absorbed his warmth and the tenderness that lay deep in his heart. They'd made love and afterward, he held her close with his arm wrapped tightly around her, rubbing her back until she'd dozed off.

It had been a long and dreamless sleep where the future before her was in a cloud. But in the dawn light, she knew one thing beyond a doubt.

She was in love with Paul Cabrera.

Twenty-Three

The Elk Grove Lodge was secluded and rustic—the perfect getaway for a romantic weekend. After all the love and excitement of the past couple of weeks, Dutch decided a weekend with Lucille would be a real treat for both of them.

Herb Deutsch had never been more surprised than when he found Lucille Prescott on his doorstep one late night not so long ago, silently offering more than he could have expected. He'd been raised to be a gentleman about such things and Lucille was definitely a lady who a man of his character wouldn't press. But she was right, she was mature and levelheaded—and so was he. Making love with her was beyond words. He loved the feel of her in his arms. She was his Lucille and he'd never known another woman like her.

She was on his mind constantly. He lived for the waking hours when he could be with her, hold her hand and cook her dinner. He loved to surprise her with a nicely set table and flowers. They'd gone bowling several more times and she seemed to enjoy that. Pool at the White Horse was next on their ticket since she'd liked that as well.

Dutch couldn't think of a better life's mate than Lucille Prescott and he was in love for the last time in his life.

He had known from the onset of their relationship
that he'd like to take it all the way to the altar. Lucille
was the woman for him and he'd envisioned them saying their ''I dos'' and living off his retirement. He'd
always wanted to travel, but hadn't had the opportunity
to do much of it. Seeing Germany was something he'd
always wanted to do because of his ancestry.

Talking with Irving Goldberg had really got him
thinking about why he hadn't retired up to this point.
He never wanted to be just a label on the AARP mailing
list, or ''putter'' in the garden and make small talk with
the clerks at the grocery store.

Retirement meant a new phase of living life. He still
had so much to do and he wanted to do it with Lucille.
If she'd have him.

She came out of the powder room having freshened
up for their dinner in the main dining room. She wore
a pale pink two-piece dress, its color complementary to
her complexion.

Smiling at him, she said, ''I'm all set, Dutch.''

His heart about stopped, then pumped triple speed.
The back of his throat felt thick and he wanted nothing
more than to envelop her in his arms and never let her
go.

''I swear, Lucille, you are the best-looking woman I
ever laid my eyes on,'' he declared, rising from the
corner chair where he'd had the television set on, but
wasn't paying attention to the football game.

''I love when you say that, Dutch.'' She came into
the room, a pink cloud dream. ''It makes me feel special.''

''You are special. What we have is special, honey.
Don't you feel it, too?''

''Yes...I do.'' She came toward him and hooked her

arms around his neck. She kissed him, softly and tenderly.

"Lucille," he uttered, feeling every ounce of joy welling in his heart for her. "Grow old with me."

"I'm already old," she teased.

"No, you aren't. You've got a lot of years left in you. We both do. I want to spend them with you." He brought her flush against him in a bearlike hug. She was delighted and gave him a soft peck on the lips.

"I've got this moment, that's all that matters to me right now."

"But what about tomorrow when we go back to Majestic? I want those moments, too." Bracing her shoulders, the soft fabric of her dress beneath his palms, he declared, "I love you, Lucille. I *love* you. I *love* you!"

She gazed into his face, her eyes glistening with moisture. "I love you, too. Heaven help me, I do."

The words warmed him to the core and they shared a kiss.

Lucille, caught up in the moment, breathed next to Dutch's warm lips. "I'm attracted to you like no other man after Ray's passing. Any time you were nearby, I knew it. I could sense you were there, I can feel you by my side. All you have to do is look at me and I'm putty in your hands."

"Oh, honey…I feel the same way."

Touching Dutch and having him touch her was like nothing she had imagined. She didn't think she could feel this way, could want more than she had. But she did. She wanted him. And she wanted him forever.

Gone were the cautions of what the job could do to him. She hated to think about that, she couldn't do it. Every time she worried she'd be getting into a love affair with a man who could be gone in the line of duty, she tried to stop her feelings for Dutch. But it was futile. It was useless. She could no more stop herself from loving him than she could stop the sun from coming up tomorrow.

She loved him—*Yes, I love him!*—so much she couldn't ask him to resign from the police department. It was his life, what he'd invested all his years doing. He was a leader and the Majestic PD needed him.

She needed him.

He steered her onto on the bed and sat her down, taking her hands in his. His lashes were stubby and dark blond. The short spikes of his hair were something she never tired of touching. His eyes were so kind; when he was with her, hc was different from the man Majestic knew.

Dutch knelt in front of her, his hand diving into his pocket. He came up with a simple diamond ring. She gasped, putting her hand over her heart and holding her breath.

"Lucille," he began, wetting his lips with his tongue. "I love you like no other. I know it's been a whirlwind, but when something is right, you know it's right. I want to be your life partner, your friend and your lover, honey. I would be honored if you said you'd be my wife."

Lucille fought back the tears welling in her eyes. She never thought she'd hear these words again and want to answer them, want to commit herself heart, mind and body to another man.

"Dutch, this is the best time of my life and I can't lose it. Yes." She nodded. "Yes, I will marry you."

He kissed her mouth, her cheeks, her forehead. They held each other, locked in an embrace that spoke of cherishing and love. He put the ring on her finger and kissed her once more, a seal of their promise.

She smoothed the neatly shorn hair above his ear. "I'm very happy."

That brought a loving smile to his mouth. He wrapped a curl of her blond hair around his finger. "Me, too."

He looked into her eyes for a long moment, then said, "I wanted to make sure of something before I told you what I'm about to say."

Her brows lifted. "It's nothing bad, is it?"

"No. I think it's good. But I had to know if you accepted me for the man I was and not the man you wanted me to be."

Confusion held Lucille. "I don't know what you mean."

He held her hand once more. "I know how hard it was for you to put your faith in us because I'm the chief of police. The fact that you accepted me for who I was, Lucille, means the world to me."

Lucille's chest ached.

"That you love me unconditionally is something I'll take to the grave with me." He rubbed his thumb over her palm. "So I think you're going to be happy when I tell you that I'm going to resign as the chief."

Lucille couldn't have been more unprepared. "But...you love what you do. You aren't going to resign just for me?"

"No. I've been thinking about it. Irving's onto something with that RV of his, the time he's got and the freedom. I'm not getting any younger. Why not live off the pension and enjoy my life—our lives. I've made up my mind."

"Dutch, this is such a big step for you."

"Lucille, I'm ready. I've got thirty years under my belt. I'm turning in my paperwork on Monday and I'll stay on board until the town council can find a replacement for me. I'm going to recommend Paul Cabrera if he wants it. Without tipping anyone off, I felt out the other deputies and they don't want the extra responsibilities."

She instantly thought of Lanie and how she'd fit into all this.

"Well, this certainly will change things," she said. "Lanie might not have to go to Pike's Peak. She could stay here and hire back on. We could all—"

"Not while I'm in command, Lucille," he interrupted gently. "I just don't have the room for her and I don't want the added headache."

Lucille stiffened. "I thought you said she was a good officer."

"She's good at the simple things, but I'm not convinced a woman is a better deputy than a man. I don't see it happening. She's just not the same as the men on my roll call."

"But she tries hard. You just never gave her an opportunity."

"I thought you didn't want her in dangerous situations."

"I don't, I didn't…but that's what she wants." Lucille touched her brow. "I'm confused. I thought this could be the answer for all of us."

She rose to her feet and looked out the window at the snow falling in fine white flakes. "Dutch, I need to know something. It's been weighing on my mind for a long time now. At first I overlooked it because part of your appeal is your chivalry. You're definitely a man's man and I feel safe and protected when I'm with you.

I also liked the fact that my daughter was on meter maid duties and menial tasks instead of doing more dangerous work.'' She faced him. ''But do you honestly believe that because Lanie is a woman she's inferior?''

Dutch's expression was unflinching. ''I'm from the old school. If a guy can't cut the mustard, get out of the ballpark. If a woman can't tackle a two-hundred-pound suspect, then she shouldn't be wearing a badge. I trust Lanie to cover my back, I just don't see her as the same calibre of officer as Paul and the other deputies.''

Nodding slowly, Lucille replied, ''I think we're about to have our first argument.''

Twenty-Four

Lanie's purse straps were slung over her shoulder, and her hands were stuffed into her coat pockets as she walked to Plum's Jewelry. She needed to get out of the house, to do anything other than anticipate tomorrow. See a change of scenery, take a walk, order a milkshake at the drive-in. Anything.

She decided to take her mom's broken pearl necklace to the jeweler for repairs while she was out of town. Holding onto a groan, Lanie tried not to think about who her mom had gone with to the Elk Grove Lodge. Lucille would be back this afternoon and they'd spend the evening together. Paul was coming over, as were Sherry and Kevin. It wouldn't be anything like her first going-away party. Just cold cuts and rolls, and it would be a small gathering of her closest friends.

All her things were packed into the moving trailer again and she'd worked her last day on dispatch on Friday. Tomorrow she'd be on the road. Paul was driving her Trailblazer for her and coming along to help her unload.

She tried not to think about how it would be when he had to leave and come back to Majestic without her. She was going to miss how he sat on the sofa and read the paper on Sunday mornings. How he stirred his coffee and cooked eggs over easy. The way he shaved.

She loved his handsome reflection in the steamy mirror after they'd taken a shower together. He'd stroke a razor under his jaw, smoothing away the cream and leaving his skin smelling good, feeling soft for her lips to trace kisses against. When he walked across the bedroom wearing nothing but a towel, she loved how his body moved, how his strong physique dominated a crowded room when they entered it together.

She'd miss the way he drank a bottle of beer holding on to the neck with two fingers and a thumb, so sexy. She never tired of sitting against him on the sofa, fitting perfectly into his chest, to watch a movie or talk.

She had to hold on to her resolve. She couldn't become more conflicted, and she had to remind herself that even when she got to Pike's Peak, it wasn't going to be ideal.

She'd be working inside, assigned to a desk for the month of October until she could enroll in the next Lateral Recruit program. A program like that, since she was moving from one police department to another in a different county, took eleven weeks.

Lanie opened the door to the jeweler's. The store lighting was soft against walls painted pale gray with white trim. The cases were illuminated to show off the gems, gold jewelry and watches. Grace Plum ran the store. She was the owner, and she kept a steady clientele for weddings and anniversaries, birthdays and just plain because days.

"Hi, Lanie," Grace said, looking up from the case where she was arranging cocktail rings. She was in her sixties, and was a transplant from Los Angeles. "It's so nice to see you on both feet."

"I'm getting around really good now." Through a

laugh, she said, "I can wear two of the same shoes. I love it."

"That's wonderful!" Grace smiled. "What can I help you with?"

"I brought my mom's pearl necklace." Lanie stuck her hand into the big purse, moving her handcuffs aside. The cool metal of her gun weighted her handbag. She had a permit to carry it and she felt comfortable about keeping the weapon with her.

She held out the silk jewelry bag. "The string broke and she hasn't had the chance to bring it in herself."

Grace wrote up a claim ticket. "I can have it for her next week, if that's okay."

"That would be fine."

Lanie's gaze strayed to all the sparkling items in the case. She'd never been one to mull over what kind of wedding set she might want, but now...unbidden she looked at the solitaires. Then she chastised herself for doing so.

"I've got new pictures of my granddaughter," Grace said with a proud smile. "She's on the computer screen in my office. My son-in-law sent me the file. Would you like to have a look, Lanie? She's just precious."

"Sure." Going into the office, Lanie gazed at the computer screen image of a tiny pink-wrapped bundle.

"Darling little thing, isn't she?" Grace called out to her from the store.

"Very cute," Lanie answered, sitting on the chair and studying the photograph.

Her mind drifted.

Lanie had had a scare last week. Her period had been late by five days. The day Paul left for Miami, they hadn't used protection. The moment in the shower had swept them away. When she missed her due date, she was terrified because she was so regular. If she'd gotten pregnant she would have been in a panic. But as the first day turned into the second and the third and fourth, she started to imagine what it would be like to have a baby. To have Paul's child.

When her period came, she became emotional and cried. Paul was gone when this happened and she never told him about it. How could she explain to him what she'd felt when she couldn't explain it to herself?

Breaking into Lanie's thoughts, a man's voice from the store area caught her attention. "I need the battery on this watch changed while I wait," he said in a humorous voice. "You got any for this brand?"

Lanie was instantly alert. By sixth sense she knew who the man was and a chill crept through her body.

Rising from the chair, Lanie quietly went to the office door and stood behind it, out of sight. Lanie watched the scene through the hinge cracks.

She could tell right away that Grace knew who she was up against. The police had advised both her and Lemar's Jewelry to do as he said, and not try to subdue Mr. Tick Tock if he ever came in.

"I—I think so," Grace replied, her tone cautious without its usual merry inflection. With trembling hands, she struggled to open the watch back with a jeweler's tool.

The man had his back to Lanie. He was of average build and had long dingy red hair, no doubt a wig. As he turned his head briefly toward the main entrance, Lanie noted his scruffy gray beard. He wore a royal blue plaid jacket and workman's boots. The disguise concealed him perfectly and he was nothing like his composite sketch.

Lanie reached for the butt of her gun, gripping it

tightly in her hand. Without making any noise, she withdrew her weapon.

"Having trouble with that, lady?" he asked.

"It seems to be stuck," Grace said. "Perhaps—"

"I'll get it." The man withdrew a hunting knife from a sheath on his belt. Lanie barely had a chance to suck in her breath, as he poked the tip into the watch and popped the back open. "There."

Thoughts raced in Lanie's head. She could go to the phone and call the station, but she'd risk being discovered in Grace's office. The element of surprise was best. She had no option other than to wait and watch.

And apprehend.

Grace took the watch back, her fingers shaking. "I'll just see if I have this battery in stock."

"Don't leave this counter, lady. Forget the battery if you're not sure." Then he ordered, "Everything in the bag, and I mean right now. Get me those diamond earrings from that case."

To Grace's credit, she didn't hesitate or look toward the back to tip him off that he wasn't the only one in the store. She removed the jewelry from the case and dropped it into his open bag.

Mr. Tick Tock studied his knife. "You know, I've killed a lot of animals with this. It's a good skinning knife. Really sharp."

"I don't care for hunting," Grace said, standing at the far end of the counter.

"If there was no hunting, we wouldn't eat."

"I buy my meat at the grocery."

The knife was still in his hand, but not raised. He put the point into his palm, as if examining its sharpness.

It was the way he held it that caused sweat to bead

on Lanie's skin, her down coat too hot in the heated air.

"Somebody's got to kill it first," he said. "It gets bloody if you don't do it right…those right there—the dangling diamonds and pearls. Yeah, I like those."

Grace dropped the earrings into the bag.

"I—I don't like the sight of blood," Grace said, making small talk as Lanie motioned her from the doorway to keep talking. "If it comes on the television, I change the channel."

"Well," he said, matter-of-fact and without inflection. "You can't change this channel, lady."

Adrenaline slammed through Lanie as she bolted from the office, gun raised. "Don't move. Keep your hands where I can see them."

He disregarded her request and turned to see who'd approached without his being aware.

Lanie got a good look at his face. Weathered and lined, he wasn't as old as he looked. Not like the sketches. There was youth in his eyes, but a hard life had aged him.

"Who're you?" he asked without fear, the hunting knife still in his grasp.

She'd played out this scenario many times in her head. Stay cool, stay focused, be brave. Holding her breath a second, she ordered, "Put the knife on the counter and take five steps toward me."

He didn't do as she asked.

This was the instant in time when an officer had to make a split-second decision. She knew he wasn't going to cooperate and he had a weapon. Foremost was disarming and restraining him.

His arm rose, knife blade shining. "Come and get it, pretty lady."

She threw her heavy purse at his hand, stunning him just enough so he dropped the knife, but made a lunge for the front door.

She attempted to tackle him and, in the struggle, he caught her on the side of the face and hit her cheek with his elbow. She saw stars, blinked them away, and jerked her knee, with a burst of physical strength, into his groin. He shifted away but her effort had not slowed him down.

He squirmed and fought her, breaking free after snagging the knife off the floor and dashing out the door. She'd drawn on every ounce of strength in her body, but she hadn't been able to subdue him.

Lanie Prescott had failed in her attempt to capture a suspect. For the second time.

Standing, she favored her leg which had taken the impact of their fall. *God, please don't let me have broken it again.* Shoving hair off her forehead, she stood back and caught her breath.

"I called the police!" Grace said, her face ghostly white.

Lanie would have to face Paul and the others and admit she had let Mr. Tick Tock get away. She was mortified beyond words.

"My goodness, Lanie, if you hadn't have been here," Grace said. "It could have been terrible. He might have— Oh my good Lord, I don't want to think about what he could have done to me!"

The wail of a siren grew louder and an Explorer jolted to a stop in front of the store's entrance with its lights flashing.

Chief-Deputy Paul Cabrera appeared through the door. He gazed at Grace, then at Lanie.

All she could do was helplessly say, "I tried to get him, but the guy got away. He pulled a knife on Grace."

Paul was first in command at the station while Dutch was gone. There hadn't been anything out of the ordinary that morning—until Grace Plum called in a robbery in progress at her jewelry store and said Lanie was involved.

After taking Grace's statement, Paul had Lanie come with him to the station where he took her statement and had her fill out her citizen's report.

"My desk looks different from this side," Lanie commented, taking a sip of water.

She had pulled her hair back into a ponytail with a rubber band she'd fished out from the dispatch drawer. Pale pink color touched her cheeks, but it was the darkening bruise on her cheekbone that had him narrowing his eyes.

He kept his voice tight while asking, "Did the guy hit you?"

She blew the bangs from her brows, easing back into the chair and exhaling. "Does it matter? I let him get away."

"It matters to me."

"Forget about it, Paul. We have to go after him."

"I've already radioed Coyote and Ridder, and as soon as I make sure you're all right, I'm out of here."

"I'm fine. Go."

"The right side of your face is swelling."

"I'll put ice on it. Do your job, Paul. I know you can get him." The color of her eyes darkened to violet, her voice breathless as she talked. "I almost had him. He overpowered me."

"You did fine. You're all right and so is Grace."

Paul thought Dutch was mistaken to have accepted Lanie's resignation. The chief should have given her a fair shake at an opportunity to grow in her position. While she might not have captured Mr. Tick Tock, she had kept the situation from escalating into something much worse.

It should have been apparent to Dutch that he had a good thing going with Lanie Prescott. But the chief could be too bullheaded for his own good.

Paul's radio went off and he answered. "Majestic PD, what's your emergency?"

"Cabrera—it's Coyote." Wylie's voice rasped from the speaker.

"Go ahead, over."

"That suspect from the Plum's Jewelry store, we scouted the perimeter of Main. No sign of him, over."

"He couldn't have gone far. I'm heading out now. Over."

"Copy that, Paul. Cruise Pine Ridge Road, Ridder's over there on a tip."

"Will do. Over."

Paul went swiftly into his office and collected his radio. Lanie had followed him. "I can help. Let me come with you. I saw his face. You're shorthanded with Dutch gone."

He paused, eyes locked on hers.

"You know you can do it, Paul. You're acting chief. Dutch already deputized me once and you can do it again. I'm within the six month time frame and all it takes is an oath of office, a new application—which I filled out the other day for Dutch, and then I get my privileges back. You need help. You need me."

In that moment he came to a decision without hesitation. "Raise your right hand. I'm swearing you in," he said, slipping into the dark blue down coat with police insignias sewn to the front.

She lifted her hand, positioned her fingers and repeated after him so fast that, in a matter of seconds, she was once again Deputy Lanie Prescott of the Majestic PD.

As she slipped on her coat, she asked, ''What do you think Dutch is going to do when he finds out you re-hired me?''

The door to the station opened and Chief Deutsch filled the entryway with his compact form. ''What do you think I'll say?''

Lanie's brows knit together. ''When you find out why, I think you'll say—okay.''

''Then fill me in.'' Dutch pinned his badge onto his shirt pocket. ''I'm back in charge.''

Dutch and Lucille had returned early from the Elk Lodge—they could not find common ground after their disagreement. Their first conflict didn't ride well with him, but right now he didn't have time to think about how he'd work things out with her.

An hour had passed since the Plum Jewelry store had been hit and luckily the merchandise had been left behind, but there were no signs of the suspect. Dutch called his officers into the meeting room of the station, his nerves chaotic.

He did not like a robber on the loose in his town and he'd catch the bastard. Agitated, he cracked his neck, hoping to rid the tension at the base of his skull.

''All right, listen up,'' Dutch said, looking tired and running a hand through his short hair. ''I had a brief chance to get up to snuff. Ridder and Coyote, I want you to patrol the forest road.''

Dutch shifted through a roster book and gazed at Griswold. "I want everyone on walkie-talkies." Then to Paul, "Street patrols. Do peripherals. I want a drive-by on Plum's Jewelry in case that jerk-off comes back trying to collect his goods. Grace is safely at home and the store is locked tight, but I don't want to leave anything to chance."

Lanie waited for her assignment, teeth set on edge and her heartbeat picking up speed. She knew what she'd get stuck with—dispatch duty. She just knew it and she wanted to pummel his chest.

"Prescott, in my office." Then Chief Deutsch left the room and Lanie was the last one sitting after Coyote, Ridder and Griswold filed out.

Paul remained. She gazed at him and shrugged with a smile on her mouth. "I guess we know where I'll be."

"I'll go in with you and talk to Dutch."

"That's okay. I can handle myself." It had taken her over six weeks to get back on her feet and she could stand on them without any help.

She took a seat in Dutch's office, the chair cool beneath her while she crossed her ankles. Disorganized papers and file folders cluttered the desk. She observed him as he shuffled through piles of notes, stacking and sorting. She appraised him, trying to see what her mother saw in him. Yes—he was strong and militant, and women were attracted to men who could protect them in such a fashion. But Dutch, he was more than militant. Rigid, uncompromising, cold, filled with so much machismo he could have been the inspiration for the word.

His hair, his face, the jaw—angles. Everything was flat or clipped tight or square. If there was anything soft about him, it was his eyes. Their color was pale, a light blue. Lanie could almost see her mother in them, feel the reflective warmth of Lucille Prescott in Herb Deutsch's gaze.

It couldn't be true. He couldn't actually be in love with her mom.

He leaned his stocky weight into his high-back leather chair and folded his fingers over his wide chest. If he thought he could browbeat her, he was wrong. She would hold her ground.

"You were in the store when it happened?"

"Yes."

"You saw the guy?"

"Yes."

"Can you describe him for me?"

Lanie did.

"So we don't have much to go by. He's probably ditched the wig and I'd bet that's a false beard."

"I would say you're probably right."

Dutch rummaged through his papers, finding a particular envelope. His eyes leveled on her. What he said next caught her by surprise. "Then let's go prove it now."

Incredulous, her mouth opened. "Excuse me?"

The chief was on his feet. "Do you want to ride along with me so we can catch this guy?"

He was leaving the decision in her corner—a chance she had wanted for so long. Perhaps there was a thimble of goodness in him somewhere. There had to be for her mother to have fallen for him.

If she failed in front of him, she would never forget it. Neither would he.

Silence loomed and stretched into a buzzing note that filled the room. Dutch folded his arms over his chest, his breath barely rising and falling beneath them. His facial features and body language gave no clues as to what he was thinking. It unhinged her, unnerved her.

"Yes. Let's go."

"Then shake a leg and keep up with me."

Twenty-Five

When Deputy Griswold radioed the call details to the Explorer, Paul was driving on Fourth Street several blocks away from the Mini Mart where a clerk had spotted a suspicious person coming out of the alley.

Paul switched on the lights and gunned the accelerator. He turned into the parking lot and cut the engine.

Ridder and Coyote drove down the fire road in their vehicle, and a moment after that, Chief Deutsch and Lanie showed up.

Dutch took immediate control, dividing the officers into territories to cover the area.

"What did you two find on the fire road?" Dutch asked.

Coyote moved the brim of his hat to shade his gaze from the sun. "A few shoe impressions, some cigarette butts, nothing obvious."

"Go back up there and fan out," Dutch said, radioing a directive to Griswold back at the station. Then to Ridder, "You two, head in a southern direction and cover that part of the hillside." His face grew hard-edged and his eyes became crystal-clear. "If you see anyone you don't recognize, stop them. I want to talk to anyone you find."

Deputy Coyote Jenkins and Deputy Ridder took off

in the police vehicle, climbing the road and spewing dust in their tracks.

Lanie was next to Dutch and whatever they'd talked about at the station was not now apparent to Paul. Her eyes met his, and quiet and unspoken thoughts were exchanged. That she was here in an official capacity was something she'd hoped for. He knew what this meant to her, and he was aware of the feelings that must be going through her mind as she worked side by side with the man who'd sent her elsewhere to seek career satisfaction. Yet she remained professional and alert, listening and observing.

Dutch rubbed the underside of his jaw. "Cabrera, give me what you have."

Paul briefed him and Dutch nodded with an inhaled jerk of breath that expanded his chest. "Check with the convenience store again. Go into the johns—both of them. You never know. Look in the trash bin out back, see if there's anything that matches Lanie's description of our perp."

"Prescott, come with me. We're going to do a walk-around on the backside of the building, taking it fifty feet into the woods. You see even a thread, you call me. You take south, I'll take north."

"Yes, Chief," she replied, marching forward in a strong stride that took her around the store building in one direction while Dutch went in the other.

Pinecones dotted the ground on a bed of needles that were russet and stiff. Lanie looked for anything that shouldn't be here. She spotted a torn and weathered, faded grocery receipt that had seen some rain. She read the blue ink date. February 22—seven months ago. Pocketing the receipt, she made the decision that it was nothing to call Dutch for. She poked in the earth with the toe of her tennis shoe, then moved on. Boughs rustled overhead, the sunshine dappling through. The autumn air had the crisp bite of an apple.

She wasn't in uniform, but she was prepared. Her badge was pinned on her shirt and her gun was tucked inside the breast pocket of her coat.

Pervading nature's quiet, the static on her radio hissed and Dutch spoke, "Prescott, don't do anything stupid. Copy that?"

Brows furrowing, she clicked on the receiver. "Copy."

"You spot him, you don't do anything. You call me. Over."

She broke etiquette and questioned her commander. "Why?"

No reply, just dead air.

Then a hiss. "Because if something happened to you, your mother wouldn't forgive me. The guy's got a knife. You can't handle this. *Copy.*"

Lanie bit her lip, turned in a slow circle as wind moved everything surrounding her and nothing was still. Not her heart, not her thoughts, not her hand as she held onto the butt of her forty-caliber pistol.

"Prescott—copy," Chief Deutsch called through the small radio.

Barely audible, she responded. "Copy."

She trudged west, alert, her gaze darting across every inch of the terrain. The hairs on the back of her neck rose, stiff and prickling at the edge of her collar.

Green and brown everywhere. Trees and earth. Then a flash of color. The ragged sound of someone out of breath; the pound of heavy feet covering the forest.

There it was again!

Off-white, like parchment. A shirt. Long-sleeved. Jeans and long legs darting through the pines. Strawberry-blond hair flowing as he ran like a rabbit, hopping and jumping, faster and faster.

Lanie's legs pushed her hard. She pursued, never thinking to call for Dutch as she chased the suspect into the woods.

Her heart thumped in her ears, her legs burned from the burst of energy.

"Police!" she shouted.

He kept running, deaf to her call. She kept after him, her right leg sparking with sharp pricks of pain from the abuse.

"Hands up! Stop! Police!" she panted breathlessly, leaping over a fallen tree.

He turned back once and she saw his face, and the chalky color of his complexion. Breath he expelled from his nostrils glistened moisture on his mustache.

For sure, it was him! It was Mr. Tick Tock—the robber she'd tried to subdue at Grace's store. He'd gotten rid of his plaid jacket.

"Police!" She slowed, panting and pointing to her badge.

Recognition filled his eyes, his thoughts plain on his face. He doubted she could do him harm. He considered her insignificant and tore off, jumping over the bulky skeleton of a dead tree.

A bitter struggle consumed her entire being. She was supposed to call the chief. Was she hesitating? What to do?

He saw her as no threat, she knew it. Felt it. She could almost hear him saying, "You couldn't catch me once, you can't catch me now."

"Police!" she hollered, arms raised and rigid.

He disregarded her command.

The Sig Sauer .40 was grasped in both hands, her index finger on the trigger. "Stop!" she hollered so loudly, the back of her throat grew sore and raspy.

She kept seeing Marge Gunderson of *Fargo* play across her mind. Marge never faltered—she knew what she had to do, and she never hesitated. Not once.

Lanie gritted her teeth, aimed and fired.

Mr. Tick Tock staggered and fell.

Lanie couldn't move. Time ebbed past, uncalculated. Only the steady inhale and exhale of her breath measured the seconds that crept forward. She was lost in this moment that she had viewed and reviewed dozens of times in her life.

Only there was no movie to rewind.

This was real. This was real. This was real.

Chlorine perfumed the community center pool room where the last aerobics class of the day was getting ready to begin. Voices from the women echoed off the wall tiles contrasted by the baritone call of Haskell Ehrlich, the only man in the class.

Lucille wore a black one-piece bathing suit and a rubber swim cap with daisies etched into it. The suit was the only thing she owned in the dreary color, but even she had given way to its slimming disguise. The latex kept her hugged in tight, breasts pushed high and waist and hips squeezed into curves.

She almost didn't come today. Just hours before, she'd been dropped off at home by Dutch. She'd fretted around the house for a short while before deciding to come to her class. She had to think about what happened between them and sometimes she thought better in the water.

Dutch. The old bullheaded mule. Why did she have to love a man whose mind was in a time warp?

Haskell entered the center wearing his Speedo with a towel thrown over his shoulder and a bottle of Evian in his grasp. As always, she didn't quite know where to look when he came at her with a bulge in his suit that was impossible to avoid. Quickly lifting her gaze to his face, she put on a stoic expression.

"Hello, Lucille," he said, his smile bright white. "We missed you at bingo. I heard you were out of town. Glad to have you back."

He dunked into the pool. Haskell scissor-kicked and splashed over to the edge. "Are you coming in?"

"I will."

The instructor appeared, a young woman with a stick-thin figure and a lime green suit that contrasted against her red hair. The rumbling loud motor of the filtering system distorted her voice as she said, "Oops, I forgot the keys to the filter room."

She always shut off the filter during class so people could hear her instructions. With the noisy splashing in the pool during jumping jacks, extra noise coming from the maintenance room was a handicap. One time the instructor told everyone to form a "pike" position and Haskell called out, "Who has pie?"

The teacher said, "Everyone get in the water and warm up. Jog in place. I'll be back with the keys in a moment."

Lucille grabbed a noodle and entered the pool. Haskell went into the lap lane. He didn't really follow the aerobics class; he liked to talk and flirt with all the women. With the water waist-high, he splashed it across his hairless skin. The man shaved everything.

Cookie came over wearing full makeup and a shower cap. "Hi, Lucille."

"Hi, Cookie."

They began warming up, legs marching and splashing. Lucille drifted to the spot by the lap lane. The truth be admitted, she wasn't comfortable in the deep end without her floating device. She needed that noodle because when she couldn't touch the bottom, she sort of panicked.

Marching without much thought, she gazed ahead at the women and the white foamy water cresting on the pool's surface. Haskell goofed off and she heard him laughing at something Cookie had said. Then he took off down the lane and began swimming.

It was half a minute later that Lucille became aware of something else. Haskell Ehrlich was no longer swimming laps behind her. The lane was a vast stretch of nothing but rippling water. Slowing her jog, Lucille poked her head under the water's surface. Through the murky water, she saw him on the pool floor.

"Oh, dear God!" she screamed inside her head, shooting up to her feet. Without further thought, she sucked in a lung full of air and dove back under.

She gave no attention to the deep water and her fears. She kept pushing toward Haskell, legs moving with thrusting tight kicks. Where she got the strength, she didn't know. She simply moved.

Once she reached him, she grabbed hold of his arm and brought him to the surface. As she broke free of the water, she struggled for air and shouted at the same time.

"Girls! Help me! *Help!*"

Cookie Baumgarten's voice rose over the splattering water. "Lucille, oh my goodness! Girls!"

Women descended toward Lucille and she quickly ordered, "Get him to the side! Put your noodles under him, roll him up! Hurry!"

There was mass confusion for a moment and nobody thought to run and find the teacher—they were propelled into action from jolts of hormone replacement therapy and sheer will.

Amid the chaos, some semblance of order came into play as they got Haskell to the edge. Lucille jumped out of the pool and she grabbed his arms and pulled, the noodles keeping him on the water's surface while the girls shoved him up. Myrtle Sanders gave the final push that sent Haskell onto the cement.

Lucille leaned over Haskell and looked to see if his chest was rising and falling. Nothing. She listened for his breath. Nothing. Felt for the flow of air on her cheek. Nothing.

"He's not breathing."

Haskell's lips were blue.

Lucille had taken CPR classes several times and the knowledge was in her head. But at the moment, the instructions were scrambled into a ball like a twist of knitting yard.

"Do something, Lucille!" Cookie said, her voice strained.

Looking briefly at the faces watching her, Lucille log-rolled Ken onto his side, her knees and body holding him into position. Thankfully, a trail of water began flowing out of his mouth. As the fluids slowed to a trickle, he made no gurgling sounds.

"He's still not breathing," Myrtle said. She'd climbed out and was next to Lucille, helping hold Haskell onto his side.

"Lay him back," Lucille said firmly.

She leaned over him, tilted his head and pinched his nose. From within the chaotic pages of her mind, she gathered what she needed to know and began CPR. Compress, ventilate. Puff-puff breathe. Repeat. Compress, ventilate. Puff-puff breathe.

A sputtering cough escaped from his mouth. His eyes fluttered open and Lucille had never been happier to see Haskell Ehrlich's over-tanned face and wet-lashed gaze.

The ladies gasped and cheered.

Lucille's shoulders slumped and she sat down in exhaustion.

"Is he breathing?" the instructor called, dashing toward them.

"He is now! Lucille saved him!" Cookie declared, the lipstick on her mouth smudged.

Their teacher ran to the red wall phone and dialed 911.

Haskell came around, his breath short and his eyes dazed. The women kept him calm while Lucille rose to her feet.

She was shaky, the adrenaline still flowing through her body. Her heartbeat pumped steady, but thinking straight and coherently was emotionally difficult.

Cookie was beside her and put her arm around her shoulders to comfort her. "Lucille," she said softly. "You did a good thing."

Unstrapping the chin strap from her swim cap, she swallowed and gazed at Haskell who was growing pinker by the moment. Relief flooded through her.

He was going to be all right.

She had saved a man's life today.

Twenty-Six

That evening at five o'clock, Lucille and Lanie Prescott were the headline features on the nightly news broadcast out of Montrose. The story was so unique— a mother and daughter both performed Special Commendation tasks in the same day. It was picked up by all three Denver networks and broadcast on their six o'clock news programs.

A camera crew had been in town all afternoon getting the story on Lloyd Antill, alias Mr. Tick Tock, and the way Lanie had taken him down with a clean shot to the calf. Incapacitating, yet not life-threatening. He'd go to trial for the robberies he'd committed.

Lucille and Lanie had come home to the constant ringing of the telephone and ended up letting the machine answer. Sherry and Kevin called to see how Lanie was holding up. The women from the aerobics class had sent flowers and balloons for Lucille. Needless to say, tonight's going-away party had been cancelled.

Back in Lucille's house, the women had their first opportunity to be alone since all hell had broken loose earlier in the day. They smiled at one another, then fell into each other's arms and talked at the same time.

"Mom, I was so worried when I heard!"

"I was, too! Lanie, my God."

"What you did, Mom—you're a hero."

"I'm not. I was just— Oh, Lanie!"

Worries were conveyed and sentiments of love and being proud were uttered.

"Lanie," Lucille choked on a sob. "If anything had happened to you. Lanie…I love you so much."

They sat at the kitchen table, fingers locked together and tears in their eyes that spilled down cheeks.

"Mom, I don't feel bad about it," Lanie confided. "I'd do it all over again."

It was true. Lanie held no regrets about shooting Lloyd Antill to stop him from running.

He'd pulled a knife on Grace and he wouldn't have stopped. She had no choice. After the incident and the other officers came in to assist, she was taken back to the station where Dutch treated her as if she were glass.

"The chief was nice to me," she whispered, the emotions coming back. "He asked me if I was warm, if I wanted water, if I needed to use the rest room." Lanie smoothed her hair away from her face, the length caught in a ponytail. "I've never seen Dutch like that. When he called to have you come down to the station and be there for me, and heard what happened at the pool, he kind of got a blank look on his face. Like he was going to—I don't know."

"Imagine how surprised I was to hear about you. Is everything all right now?"

"I gave my statement. There was so much going on. Paul was out at the scene with Coyote and Ridder. It was Deputy Griswold and me at the station. Dutch said I need to have psychology consultation within a forty-eight hour period. I kept waiting for Dutch to read me the riot act, to tell me what an idiot I was—but he didn't. I've never seen him like this before."

"We don't have to talk about Dutch," her mother

said, giving her fingers a squeeze. "Do you want me to fill up the tub for you, Lanie?"

"No...I'll be fine. And you? Mom, what you did with Haskell. I'm so proud of you!"

Haskell Ehrlich had suffered a heart attack. The man didn't have an ounce of extra fat on his body, but three of his four arteries were clogged worse than tree roots in a mainline. He would be spending time in a Montrose Hospital for bypass surgery. He was recovering in a comfortable room without side effects from his near drowning. Lucille still rode on a roller coaster of ups and downs from it.

She sat on the fragile side of life, viewing things in a way she had never viewed them before. Suddenly many things became clear.

"Lanie," she began, her heart swelling with awareness. "Today I reacted without thinking. I forgot about my fear of the deep end when I saw Haskell in trouble and I knew I could save him. I realize now that you love to help people and there are times when you might be in a dangerous situation, but somebody has to be there and ready to help. Not just anyone can do it. But you can. And Ray could."

An emotional smile touched Lanie's mouth.

Lucille's features were loving and tender. "I'm not going to be afraid for you anymore, Lanie. You need to do what you're doing. I see now that it's a part of who you are. You're so much like your dad. You did him proud today."

"Thanks, Mom. Thanks so much for believing."

They embraced in the comfort of the kitchen's warmth. A long moment passed when Lucille pulled back and said, "So when are you going to see Paul? You need him tonight more than you need me."

"I'll stay with you. You've been through a lot, too."

"You need to be with the man you love, Lanie. Not your mom."

Mothers were intuitive and Lanie must have worn her feelings on her shoulder.

Lanie quietly intoned, "And what about you, Mom? You're in love with Dutch. Why don't you ask him to come over?"

"Maybe...yes, I might." Her mom's eyes widened. "You won't be leaving tomorrow. You can't. Not with everything that's happened."

"I've already called Pike's Peak and told them I'd be delayed. They gave me all the time I need."

"I wish you could have all the time you need here and never have to go anywhere."

"Me, too, Mom...me, too."

Dutch hadn't had the chance to talk with Lucille. There was so much paperwork to organize, relevant issues that had to be followed up on, along with the task of holding a press conference. He barely recalled his statement.

Every time he tried to put his effort into something, he saw Lloyd Antill's face as he lay on his side hugging his leg with Prescott standing over him. The woman had balls.

Deputy Ridder came in with boxes of pizza. The night was going to be long. Antill had been taken to Montrose for medical attention; he was in police custody while, in Majestic, Dutch was in charge of settling the dust.

"Six o'clock news is coming on, Chief," Ridder said, picking up a slice of pizza.

Griswold and Coyote grabbed wedges while Paul Cabrera sat off in the background, a cell phone against his ear.

"Here it comes," Ridder said. "There you are, Chief."

Dutch stood somberly at the crime scene. "I'm honored to say that an officer in my charge has apprehended the jewelry bandit known as Mr. Tick Tock. She bravely tracked and subdued him without making a lethal shot and now we can take the criminal to trial."

"Chief, what about the officer? Will she be placed on leave? Will she be coming back?"

"I have no further comment."

The picture jumped back to the newscaster who said, "In a rare turn of events for this small Colorado town, the officer's mother was also involved in her own excitement today. For that story, we go to the community center."

Dutch stared at the television, watching and listening to Lucille. She was vibrant as she relayed what happened. He noted her nervous energy, the quiver in her tone as she spoke.

"She looks good on the television," Ridder commented.

Dutch thought she looked better than Betty Porter. No one could hold a candle next to his Lucille.

"Cabrera, in my office," Dutch said, "I need to talk with you."

Quietly rehashing his thoughts, Dutch had made up his mind. He had already talked with the men in his department and learned that both Coyote and Ridder were happy to stay in their present jobs with less responsibility and more flexible hours. Paul was a sure thing if he wanted the job. Dutch had no doubts the town council would vote him in.

Paul sat across from him. His facial features were rock hard. The man was solid and dependable. "What's on your mind?"

"My retirement and you taking my place as the new Chief of Police for Majestic."

When Paul came home, Lanie was sleeping on the sofa in his house. She must have let herself in with her key. Quietly, he set his keys on the counter and went to her. Unbound, her hair was a cloud as her head rested on a throw pillow; the mocha blanket draped over her shoulder, her bare skin and the thin strap of a bra visible. She was sleeping in her underwear and her hands were together on her cheek.

Delicate was not a word he associated with Lanie but, at this moment, that is exactly how she looked.

He was in love with her.

He wanted to be with her every day of his life. He wanted to envelop her in his arms, slide his hands over the small of her back and bring her to him. He couldn't let her go.

He moved away to let her sleep.

"Paul…"

Coming back, he sat down beside her on the sofa. She rested her hand on his thigh. "Yeah, darlin'?"

"I missed you."

"I missed you, too."

The blanket fell as she rolled onto her back. The hollow in her throat was creamy, the pulse point beating life through her body.

Gazing at him through violet-blue eyes, she said, "I did it, Paul. I could shoot."

"I know that, darlin'. You did good."

"Would you have fired, Paul? Tell me...what would you have done?"

"I would have done exactly what you did."

She smiled weakly. "You're not just saying that?"

"I never say anything I don't mean."

The room grew still, the tick of his wristwatch beating.

Paul said, "I love you, Lanie."

He did. Within every fiber of his body, he loved her more than he thought possible. It filled him, gave him each breath he took and made him the man he was right now sitting next to her.

"Today," he unbuckled his service belt and set the heavy weight on the coffee table, "when I heard about what you did, I was never prouder knowing I was the one who'd sworn you back in."

"If it weren't for you..." she whispered.

"No, Lanie. If it weren't for you making the decision to take him down, he would have gotten away. How's your leg?"

"It's all right."

"Do you want to talk about what happened? Dutch said you're on psych evaluation. That's common practice, okay?"

"I know. No—I don't need to talk about the shooting right now." She sat up, the blanket pooling in her lap. Her breasts were cradled in satin the color of plums, the valley between in a tantalizing shadow. "I don't want to give up my job, Paul...but I can't leave you. I want to be with you wherever you are.

"Paul," she said reaching for his hand. "Can't you put in for a transfer and come with me? We can serve on the same department. I love you. I love you so much it's an ache in my chest. I don't think I could go unless I knew you'd come with me and we—''

''Lanie,'' he interjected, putting a fingertip to her lips. He leaned in and kissed her, sealing his mouth over hers in a way he'd wanted to do all day but there had been no chance. ''Herb Deutsch is retiring, effective immediately. I'm going be promoted to chief if the town votes me in, which he thinks they will. Stay. Stay with me. I'll put you on as a deputy as soon as I'm sworn in.''

''Paul…'' She smiled with all the love she felt welling inside her. ''That's such an honor to be promoted to Chief.''

She threw her arms around him and gave him a kiss. He cupped her face in his hands. ''Will you tell Pike's Peak you aren't available anymore?''

''Yes…yes. I'll stay, Paul. Not because I want a job from you.'' She smiled. ''I want to watch you take your new oath of office.''

Not even counted cross-stitching could keep Lucille's mind busy. It was late. David Letterman was over and she'd clicked off the TV. If she drank one more cup of sleepy tea, she'd float away. She might as well accept not sleeping tonight.

She set aside her sewing and rose from the chair.

A knock brushed against the front door and she started.

She gazed out the sheer curtains and saw a man's silhouette on the porch.

Dutch.

She let him inside and his masculine scent drifted into her living room. He smelled of fireplace smoke and the deepest hour of the night.

"Have I come at a bad time?" he asked, his hands stuffed into his coat pockets.

She pulled the corners of her housecoat closer together. "No. I was up."

"I saw the light on."

"I was working on some stitchery."

He shifted, his hands reaching out to unzip his coat. "Lucille, do you have anything to drink?"

"Would you like me to make coffee?"

"Something that'll knock the wind out of my sails, Lucille."

"Whiskey?"

"That works."

She poured him a glass, neat. He drank it in one swallow and sat down on the carved chair in her living room. The golden oak frame was so slight, he felt like he'd bust through the floral cushion. For the first time he paid attention to what was in here.

All around were crafty things that could have put the Calico Corner out of business. Plant holders with roosters on them, quilts on racks. There were even handmade coasters.

Growing overly warm, he slipped out of his coat.

"I'm putting in for my retirement now, Lucille. It's time for me to go," he managed in a compact voice.

"You're leaving town?" Lucille asked, with a note of concern in her voice.

He disregarded her query and went on with what he had to say—in order to set things right in a way that only Lucille might understand. "I didn't see something that was as obvious as warts on a bullfrog. I missed it because my thinking was too narrow." He gazed at her where she sat across from him. "I've lost the edge, the broad scope of the job. Maybe I never even had it."

"Of course you did—you do."

He felt the burn of emotion in his chest and cursed it.

"Dutch...what is it?" Lucille's voice was like an angel's. So fine, so soft, so feminine. She was everything he wanted in a woman.

Lowering his head, he stared at his hands. Hands that had seen the grip of a gun and the cold metal of cuffs. They'd seen a lot, his hands. They'd seen more than his eyes which had been blinded to truths that existed around him, yet he had not seen them for what they were.

"I was wrong about Lanie," Dutch said in a choppy voice. "She's got what it takes. Maybe if I'd seen that before now I wouldn't be feeling like I was taking her away from you. I've asked her to withdraw her application from Pike's Peak because she's got a job here with our department—if she'll have it."

Lucille was quickly on her knees in front of him. "Dutch, my darling, I don't know what to say. You'll hire her back?"

"It's not really up to me, but I have clout. I can make it happen."

She rose to her knees and reached hers arms around him. "Oh, Dutch. Thank you. Thank you for giving me Lanie back!"

"Lucille...my Lucille. I love you so much."

"Oh, Dutch, I love you, too."

He sucked in a long and jagged breath, but one look into her lovely face shining up at him and he forgot to be manly. Men felt things, too, and they got emotional. To hell with it, letting everything out made him feel better.

"You saved Haskell Ehrlich's life today," he said, touching her cheek.

"It wasn't anything much. Anyone would have done it."

"You're not just anyone, honey." He smiled, shaking his head in awe at the woman before him. "You're brave and you have one hell of a daughter who takes after you. I'm sorry we fought today. I shouldn't have pigeonholed you into my idea of a woman. Because you are my ideal. It's you. You're everything I want, just as you are and don't change anything."

He scooted from the chair and got onto the floor on bended knee, holding her hand. "Will you be my wife, Lucille?"

No hesitation, no considering. She said, "Yes, Dutch. I will."

He kissed her hard on the mouth, soaking in the feel of her in his arms and knowing he'd die happy and loved.

"We'll never fight again," she insisted, raining kisses on his face.

"Never."

"And we'll always agree, even when it's to disagree."

"Right."

"And we'll never try and change one another. Except I might take some issues with all this...what do you call all this stuff you decorate with?"

"You adorable man," she laughed and gave him a big hug. "You'll get used to it."

Twenty-Seven

The Majestic Police Department awarded Lucille Prescott and Lanie Prescott special commendations for acts of bravery. City Hall was brimming to capacity as the women posed for photographs with their engraved plaques. Retired Chief of Police Herb Deutsch awarded them a certificate of honor and the mayor gave them each large brass keys.

Lanie smiled throughout the ceremony, proudly wearing her Majestic PD deputy uniform. She thought back to the time when she had been the crowd control enforcer at the Pay and Pack Grocery Mart; now she had a key to the city.

She gazed at Paul in the front row, the new chief of police who had bowed out from participating in the ceremony. He said that this was on Dutch's watch and he should have the pleasure.

She had come a long way.

The Pike's Peak PD had been very understanding and they'd found someone else.

In Majestic, she might only be a third-year deputy with some meter maid days shared with Ridder, Coyote and Griswold—but she was happy. Happier than she'd ever been in her life.

That day her mom came down to the station for the first time in four years and they'd shared sandwiches in the meeting room, Lucille had fully accepted Lanie's new position with the Majestic PD.

For weeks afterward the talk in town didn't die down and both women stayed in the limelight. Everyone had a story to tell, whether they'd been there or not.

As for Ken Burnett, he'd been seeing Cookie Baumgarten and he looked a lot better these days.

Lanie's official coming-back party wasn't planned until November at Rooster's Place. The big bash had to be postponed until Lucille and Herb Deutsch returned from their honeymoon in Hawaii.

The night of the party, Paul came to Lanie's house to pick her up; she was back in her house and Paul was living in the house on Pine Ridge Road. The one where she'd fallen in love with its kitchen—and the bedroom.

At the door, she greeted him with a half smile. "You're early."

"You're gorgeous."

"You're all mine," she laughed.

The cold winter weather poured into the warm interior. She wore a simple cocktail dress in cranberry red and the very same pair of black evening shoes she'd worn the night she'd met Paul. Her hair was swept into a soft roll, anchored in place with rhinestone pins.

"You look good enough to kiss," he said, coming inside and taking her into his arms. He kissed her slowly, delightfully, thrilling her to her toes. She was made for indulgence, for long hours languishing in an unmade bed.

"So do you," she murmured against his mouth.

She wove her fingers through his hair. She loved the feel, so silky and sleek above his ears. It was short and tightly cut, black as midnight and wonderful. He was the handsomest, kindest man she'd ever known. She fell in love with him more deeply each day.

Seeing him in a suit with a tie and white shirt caused a flutter in her stomach. She flushed and seriously wished they were spending the evening at home.

Lightly brushing her lips, he spoke against them. "I'm early for a reason."

"Hmm?" She gave him butterfly kisses.

"You're beautiful, Lanie. You look great and you smell great, but I can't take you to the party like this."

She gazed into his face. "Like what?"

"You're not altogether. You're missing something."

"What?"

"A piece of jewelry."

She touched her neckline, the skin warm beneath her palm. She wore a tiny gold chain with a heart on it that her mother had given to her recently.

Paul took her hands, and in the wildly unpredictable seconds that went by, she felt like she was in a dream.

"You know I love you, Lanie," he said, his eyes dark brown, the brows above leveled sincerely. "I love you like no other."

"I love you, too."

"I know we both tried this once before and it didn't work out, and you know that the stats on cops staying married for the second time aren't great. I wonder what the odds are for affairs between two officers."

"Probably lousy," she breathed, her gaze steady on his face.

"I don't really care what the statistics say."

"Me, either." She rubbed her thumbs across his knuckles.

He slipped his hand into his trouser pocket and held

up a diamond engagement ring. Simple and classic, the emerald-cut diamond sparkled in the living room light.

"Will you be my wife, Lanie?"

No hesitation, no thought. "Yes. A thousand times— yes."

He fit the ring on her finger and she threw her arms around him. "I love you...I love you." She kissed his cheek, his ear, the side of his neck where he smelled so incredibly good. Then his mouth.

Paul felt as if his body had been touched by lightning. He was hot and hard at the same time, an intensity that sizzled beneath his skin. How he loved this woman, this perfect mate for life.

She pushed her hips into his groin and he groaned, wanting her now, needing her now.

"We've got thirty minutes, darlin'," he whispered on her damp lips and traced them softly with the tip of his tongue.

"I got a new pair of handcuffs today," she said, gliding her tongue deeper into his mouth, sleek and sexy.

He clamped her head between his hands. "Don't say something like that to me unless you intend to do something with them."

"I intend to all right. They're under my sofa cushions."

The restrictive evening clothing between them made the moment feel urgent and hot. "God, you're amazing."

She kissed him thoroughly, then bent down to unbuckle her high heeled shoes and kick them off. They landed in front of the brocade sofa on the tapestry rug; then she came back into his arms.

"You know," she purred, "some departments frown on this sort of thing. Two of the officers fraternizing."

She lowered her voice and playfully murmured, "Sleeping together. Using handcuffs on the chief."

Keeping her close with one arm, he unzipped the back of her dress. A river of cranberry fabric fell to Lanie's feet and she stood in front of him, in a bra and panty set that about made him lose control on the spot. Velvet. Red velvet underwear with black lace.

"That only counts when we're in uniform." His fingertip traced the edge of her collarbone, trailed across the beat of her pulse in her neck. "When we're undressed," he said in a bourbon-fine voice, "we're just a man and a woman."

Then he took her into his arms and kissed her, loving her with the promise of a husband loving his wife.

Is he a stranger...or the man she once married?

New York Times **bestselling author**

LINDA HOWARD

Nothing could have prepared Jay Granger for the arrival of two FBI agents at her door—or for the news that her ex-husband, Steve, had been in a terrible accident. The FBI needed Jay to confirm his identity.

But the man whom Jay identifies as Steven is not at all as she remembers her husband. And he remembers nothing of their life together. Suddenly nothing is familiar. Not his appearance, not the intensity of his nature, not the desire that flashes between them. Who is this man? And will the discovery of his identity shatter the passion they share?

WHITE LIES

"Ms. Howard is an extraordinary talent whose mastery allows her to deliver unforgettable novels richly flavored with scintillating sensuality..."
—*Romantic Times*

Available the first week of October 2003, wherever paperbacks are sold!

One part laughter, two parts love.
Mix together and enjoy.

Curtiss Ann Matlock

Recipes for Easy Living

Thirteen-year-old Corrine is happy
with her life in Valentine, Oklahoma.
She has her aunt Marilee and Papa
Tate, her beloved horses, and an
almost boyfriend. She's happy, that is,
until her long-lost mother, Anita,
returns and upsets the delicate
balance everyone has achieved.

But Anita is determined to return
home for Christmas and fix the
mistakes she's made. And if only one
tiny miracle can find its way to
Valentine this year, everyone might
just get the most perfect gift of all....

"If home is where the heart is,
then the town of Valentine is the
perfect place to settle in."
—Joan Medlicott, author of the
"Covington Ladies" series

*Available the first week of October
2003, wherever books are sold!*

MIRA®

MCAM753

STEF ANN HOLM

66949   GIRLS NIGHT   ___ $6.50 U.S. ___ $7.99 CAN.

(limited quantities available)

TOTAL AMOUNT $_____
POSTAGE & HANDLING $_____
($1.00 for one book; 50¢ for each additional)
APPLICABLE TAXES* $_____
<u>TOTAL PAYABLE</u> $_____
(check or money order—please do not send cash)

To order, complete this form and send it, along with a check
or money order for the total above, payable to MIRA Books,
to: **In the U.S.:** 3010 Walden Avenue, P.O. Box 9077, Buffalo,
NY 14269-9077; **In Canada:** P.O. Box 636, Fort Erie, Ontario
L2A 5X3.

Name:_____
Address:_____ City:_____
State/Prov.:_____ Zip/Postal Code:_____
Account Number (if applicable):_____
075 CSAS

  *New York residents remit applicable sales taxes.
   Canadian residents remit applicable GST and provincial taxes.

MIRA®

Visit us at www.mirabooks.com

MSAH1003BL